THE

FITZOSBORNES

AT

WAR

The Montmaray Journals

Book I: *A Brief History of Montmaray*
Book II: *The FitzOsbornes in Exile*

THE

FITZOSBORNES

AT

WAR

Michelle Cooper

Alfred A. Knopf
New York

THIS IS A BORZOI BOOK PUBLISHED BY ALFRED A. KNOPF

All rights reserved. Published in the United States by Alfred A. Knopf, an imprint of Random House Children's Books, a division of Random House, Inc., New York. Originally published in Australia by Random House Australia Pty Ltd., North Sydney, NSW, in 2012.

Knopf, Borzoi Books, and the colophon are registered trademarks of Random House, Inc.

Visit us on the Web! randomhouse.com/teens

Educators and librarians, for a variety of teaching tools, visit us at randomhouse.com/teachers

Library of Congress Cataloging-in-Publication Data
Cooper, Michelle.
The FitzOsbornes at war / Michelle Cooper. — 1st American ed.
p.   cm. — (Montmaray journals ; bk. 3)
Summary: In this third installment to the Montmaray Journals, Sophie and her family come together to support the war effort during World War I, meanwhile fighting to protect their beloved Montmaray.
ISBN 978-0-375-87050-7 (trade) — ISBN 978-0-375-97050-4 (lib. bdg.) — ISBN 978-0-307-97404-4 (ebook)
[1. Exiles—Fiction. 2. World War, 1914–1918—England—Fiction. 3. Family life—England—Fiction. 4. War—Fiction. 5. Diaries—Fiction. 6. Great Britain—History—George VI, 1936–1952—Fiction.] I. Title.
PZ7.C78748Fhm 2012
[Fic]—dc23
2012009094

The text of this book is set in 11-point Goudy.

Printed in the United States of America
October 2012
10 9 8 7 6 5 4 3 2 1

First American Edition

Random House Children's Books supports the First Amendment and celebrates the right to read.

Selected excerpts from the journals of

Her Royal Highness Princess Sophia of Montmaray,

1939–1944

I'm quite sure that, in twenty or thirty years' time, people will say about this morning, "I'll never forget where I was when I heard the news." They'll say, "I was sitting in church and the vicar was halfway through his sermon," or, "We were washing up after breakfast and my sister decided to turn on the wireless," or, "I'd just come back from a long ride through the woods and I handed my horse over to the groom and *he* told me."

But the thing is, we could all be dead in twenty years' time, or even twenty *days'* time, the way the world is going, and so, for the record: when the British Prime Minister announced that the country was at war with Germany, *I* was in the breakfast room at Milford Park. My cousin Veronica was perched on the edge of the window seat, and my brother, Toby, was sprawled across the rest of it. Veronica was rigid with barely suppressed fury; Toby appeared to be asleep, although the tiny, unfamiliar dent between his eyebrows suggested he was listening as hard as anyone. My little sister, Henry, was kneeling at their feet, spreading anchovy paste on bread crusts and silently handing them, one by one, to our dog, Carlos, who'd been allowed upstairs due to the significance of the occasion. And Simon, my other cousin, was hunched over the wireless (which tended to lapse into static unless someone stood beside it, twiddling the knobs). Simon's face was utterly blank—impossible to read, despite all the years I'd spent studying him.

"Now, may God bless you all," the Prime Minister quavered.

(Veronica gave a derisive snort.)

"It is the evil things we shall be fighting against," went on Mr. Chamberlain. "Brute force, bad faith, injustice, oppression and persecution. And, against them, I am certain that the right will prevail."

There was a moment of crackling quiet, then "God Save the King" began wheezing out of the wireless. Simon switched it off.

"What a *hypocrite* that man is!" Veronica burst out, jumping to her feet. "He didn't consider them 'evil things' last year, when he was hobnobbing with Hitler in Munich and handing over entire *countries* to the Nazis!"

"Toby," said Henry urgently, twisting round to look at him, "Toby, do you have to go back to your squadron now, this very minute?"

"I don't have a squadron, Hen, not yet," said Toby, easing himself up on his elbows. "The air force won't assign me to one till I've finished advanced training."

"If Chamberlain had any decency, he'd resign!" said Veronica, still glaring at the wireless.

"But Toby, when *do* you have to go back?" Henry persisted.

"Tomorrow," said Toby.

"Oh," Henry said, blinking. *Her* face was easy to read. I saw, in rapid succession: dismay that he'd be leaving so soon, patriotic pride at having a brother already in the services, and burgeoning curiosity about what might happen to her now. "I suppose," she added, almost wistfully, "that the war will be over by the time *I'm* old enough to fight."

"Let's hope so," I said shortly. I was having trouble making my lips work, because a cold numbness had settled upon me the moment Mr. Chamberlain had begun to speak. As inevitable as this announcement was to everyone else, I realized I'd been praying all along for a last-minute miracle. For Stalin to change his mind, for the Americans to intervene, for Hitler to fall under a train . . . *anything*, anything at all. Now I understood how stupid I'd been.

"Don't worry, Soph, it'll be over by Christmas," said Toby, flashing me a smile. "Isn't that what they said last time?"

"And *that* went on four whole years," I said bleakly.

"Besides, Henry, you couldn't fight, even if you were old enough," Veronica said, frowning down at her. "You're a *girl*."

"So what?" retorted Henry. "Girls can join the air force. Julia told me! *And* the army, and the navy, too! It's just that the women's services have silly names, like 'Wrens' for the navy. *Wrens*, how idiotic. It ought to be 'Albatrosses' or 'Razorbills' or something like that. But that's the one *I* want to join, 'cause I can sail and row and—"

Carlos placed a paw on her arm and gave her a meaning-ful look.

"Oh, sorry, Carlos," she said, handing him the piece of bread she'd been waving around.

Toby sighed and slumped back against the window frame. "It's so odd, isn't it?" he remarked to no one in particular. "I mean, all those times when it seemed about to start, and then everything went back to normal. And now . . . Oh Lord, to think of old *Ribbentrop* being responsible for this! I met him, you know, I actually had *dinner* with the man who got the So-viets to join up with the Nazis. The Molotov-Ribbentrop Pact, isn't that what it's being called?"

Everyone's a political expert, these days. Even *I* knew that if that pact hadn't been signed, Germany wouldn't have in-vaded Poland and we wouldn't be at war now.

"And he seemed such a *joke* back then!" Toby continued. "Simon, don't you remember, that party at the Bosworths'? When he was still the German Ambassador and all the girls were calling him 'von Ribbensnob' and you spent ages chatting to him about—"

Simon shot Toby a withering look.

"Oh, right," said Toby. "Sorry." That dinner party had been the beginning of the end, for Montmaray. If Ribbentrop hadn't passed Simon's information on to those Nazi Grail hunters, then perhaps our home would never have been invaded . . . But what did it matter, now that the whole of Europe was at war? Which reminded me of something else.

"Do we have to declare war on Germany ourselves?" I asked. "On behalf of Montmaray, I mean?"

"Oh," said Veronica, her frown digging further into her forehead. "Yes, we'd better send a letter to the German Embassy straightaway. And another one to the Foreign Office, reminding the British that we're their allies. Otherwise, we might get interned as enemy aliens. They've already started rounding up Germans in London, Daniel was saying yesterday. Anyone who isn't a British subject—"

Carlos suddenly tilted his head towards the window and crinkled his brow.

"What's that noise?" asked Henry.

Veronica turned to stare in the direction of the village. "Surely it couldn't be—"

"Air-raid siren," said Toby, scrambling to his feet as Carlos added his howl to the rising cacophony. "Grab your gas masks and let's go!"

"Mine's upstairs," said Henry. "Or hang on—did I leave it in the stables?"

"Henry!" snapped Veronica. "I told you to keep it with you!"

There were thumps and shouts from the corridor, and a couple of maids rushed past the open door, trailing mops and dusters. I stood where I was, frozen with horror.

"You see, I took Lightning out for a ride before breakfast," said Henry. "Or maybe it's—"

"What's that under the table? Isn't that yours?"

"Oh, right. But, you know, it really isn't fair, *Carlos* doesn't have a gas mask. Nobody ever thinks about the poor animals—"

Harkness, our intimidating butler, loomed in the doorway, accompanied by several white-faced footmen. "Your Majesty, Your Highnesses, may I suggest you join us in the cellars immed—"

"Just a moment," said Toby, raising a hand. We listened in the abrupt stillness. The rise and fall of the siren had changed to a steady blare.

"That's the all-clear signal," said Veronica.

"Must have been a false alarm," said Toby.

We looked out the window at the serene countryside, then up at the vast expanse of pale autumn sky utterly devoid of aeroplanes. I sank into a chair, limp with relief.

"We really ought to have a drill," said Veronica crossly. "Practice what to do in a real emergency. That was just *hopeless*."

"I shall make arrangements for it at once, Your Highness," said Harkness, bowing. At no stage had he looked anything other than his usual imperturbable self. He swept the maids back down the corridor with a wave of his hand, gathered up the footmen, and disappeared.

"Well, that's it, then," Toby said, rubbing his forehead. "Come on, Hen, you can help me pack up my room . . . Yes, all right, Carlos can come, too." The three of them went off, followed by Veronica, who announced that if anyone needed her, she'd be in the library, drafting a letter to the German Embassy.

They left a ringing silence in their wake. I took an unsteady breath and looked down at my hands. They were quivering—as though a bomb really *had* exploded and the shock waves were still reverberating around the room.

"Although it's pretty unlikely the Germans *would* drop a bomb in the middle of Dorset," I said to Simon, who was unplugging the wireless. "I mean, it'd be a complete waste of time and effort for them, wouldn't it?"

"Would it?" he said. "There's an airfield not far from here."

"Simon, you could at least *pretend* to be reassuring."

He turned and gave me a look that spoke volumes.

"Sorry," I said. "Everything's horrible, I know. And it's so much worse for you and Toby."

"I didn't *have* to go into the air force," he said. "We all have some choices, even in these circumstances. Anyway, what are you going to do now? Have you decided?"

I sighed. I'd had a long chat about this very issue with our friend Colonel Stanley-Ross on our way back from Switzerland last week. (I think he'd wanted to distract me from what he termed "a spot of turbulence, quite routine," but was actually our aeroplane being battered by gale-force winds, eight thousand feet above the jagged tops of the Alps.) The Colonel had suggested that Veronica and I do a secretarial course—he thought typing and shorthand would come in handy, regardless of what we ended up doing. He asked what skills I had, and I explained I didn't have any.

"Now, Sophie," he said. "What about your writing?"

"Nearly everyone over the age of seven can *write*," I pointed out.

"You know what I mean. Governments always seem to require enormous quantities of pamphlets and reports and manuals during a war, and someone has to write and edit them. What languages can you speak?"

"English."

"And French?"

"Not really. I can read it, a bit, but I can't speak it. Veronica knows lots of languages, though."

"Latin and Cornish," she said. "And won't *they* be a huge help if there's a war? Assuming it's a war involving Ancient Romans and Bretons."

"She's fluent in Spanish, too," I told the Colonel. "Her mother used to speak it with her."

"Is that so?" he said, looking at Veronica thoughtfully. "Well, and the other thing to do is a first aid course. That's always useful."

"I couldn't," I said. "Honestly, I faint at the sight of blood."

"Can you drive?"

"No," I said, feeling more and more useless. "But Veronica can."

"Oh, look!" interrupted Veronica, pointing at the window with great excitement. "We must be over France now! It's as though we're floating across a giant map. Is that the Seine?"

I knew that if I looked out the window and saw how high we were, I'd be sick, so I concentrated even harder on my conversation with the Colonel. "Besides, Aunt Charlotte is never going to let us train for anything, let alone apply for jobs," I told him. "She doesn't even approve of girls attending school. She thinks it hinders their marriage prospects."

"Would you really want to marry the sort of man who's intimidated by educated women?" said the Colonel (reminding me of why we like him so much). "Although I do think your aunt's attitude will change if war is declared. Everyone doing his or her bit for the war effort, you know. You might find you have more freedom than you expected."

"We'll have to get jobs, anyway," said Veronica, "because she's cut off our allowances. And *that* was simply after Toby refused to marry that Helena girl—nothing at all to do with our League of Nations trip. She's going to throw a fit when we get back to England."

That was putting it mildly. Aunt Charlotte was completely *incensed* that we'd disobeyed her orders and sneaked off to Geneva. And that was before she even got around to reading the day's newspaper headlines:

Princess Rebukes "Brutal" Germany
League Condemns German Invasion of Montmaray
My Life in Exile: The Tragic Tale of a Beautiful Princess
(exclusive interview on page five)

And so on.

Most of our aunt's fury was vented on Veronica. "I've never

heard of anything so vulgar in all my life!" Aunt Charlotte raged. "Making a public spectacle of yourself! Giving political speeches! Allowing yourself to be photographed! And this *exclusive interview*—unchaperoned, no doubt!"

"It wasn't an exclusive interview," Veronica attempted to explain. "There were dozens of newspapermen there—"

"Dozens! *Newspapermen!*" Aunt Charlotte was actually rendered speechless for a moment. When she recovered, she turned upon Simon. "And where were *you* while all this was going on, may I ask?"

"I was *trying* to extract Toby from the depths of a Swiss police station!" he retorted, returning her glare. She looked rather taken aback—until that moment, Simon had always been the epitome of deferential diplomacy around her. But now he had chosen a side—ours, not hers—and he was sticking to it. Besides, the prospect of having to fly off to battle the Luftwaffe must have made Aunt Charlotte's wrath seem relatively inconsequential.

"No, I haven't yet decided what I'll do," I told Simon in response to his question. "But I do know I could never be as brave as you. Just getting into an aeroplane again . . . let alone being a fighter pilot!"

"I may not end up a fighter pilot," he said, "or any kind of pilot at all. It depends on how my basic training goes. But I don't think women in the air force do any flying—it's mostly administration. You could do that."

"There's no point in me aiming for any of the services," I

said. "Aunt Charlotte would never agree, she'd think the uniforms *too unladylike*. Anyway, there's so much to do here right now, I've barely had time to think about it."

For one thing, there's the blackout to organize. Every single window and skylight and glass door at Milford Park needs to be covered up at night so that not a sliver of light can escape (apparently, anything more than a pinpoint could act as a beacon for German bombers). I went round with Barnes, Aunt Charlotte's maid, to measure all the windows, and there were three hundred and seventeen of them, not including the gatehouse and the stables and the hothouses. There wasn't enough black material in the whole of Salisbury to cover them, but we bought what we could find and have started making curtains. Meanwhile, the groundsmen are busy constructing wooden shutters for those upstairs rooms that are hardly ever used, and Parker, the chauffeur, has made little masks to fit over the headlights of the motorcars and has painted all the running boards and mudguards white, according to the regulations.

Then there are our evacuees, the poor little things. They're all from the East End and have never been out of London before. One small boy had a screaming fit when he stepped off the bus and came face to face with a cow. (She'd been painted with white stripes to prevent her getting knocked over by motorists in the dark, so I suppose she looked a *bit* odd.) I went down to the village on Friday afternoon to help with the billeting arrangements, but fortunately, there wasn't much to do, nearly all the children being scooped up at once by villagers who remembered our Basque refugees and were eager to help. The only ones left were four brothers who refused to be separated— the eldest said he'd promised their mum that they'd stay together, no matter what. They looked so pitiful, cardboard labels strung around their necks, gas masks dangling from their bony shoulders, all their clothes stuffed inside a single pillowcase that the eldest was hugging fiercely to his chest. In the end, they went off to the rectory with the Reverend Webster Herbert. Aunt Charlotte decided against billeting any of the children at Milford Park, of course—in fact, I suspect she agreed to be the district head of the Women's Voluntary Service precisely so that *she* would be the one to get to make those sorts of decisions. She did put eight of the youngest children, accompanied by their expectant mothers, in the Old Mill House, which was recently vacated by its tenants . . . Oh, and here comes Aunt Charlotte now, back from church, and in a rotten mood by the sound of it. Will finish this later.

After luncheon, which was not very pleasant (the conversation, that is, not the food—although even *that* was not up to its usual standard, the cook having had her pastry-making interrupted by the air-raid alert). It appears that at least half the evacuee children are infested with lice, and quite a few are bed wetters. They are all desperately homesick, and crowded round Aunt Charlotte this morning, begging to be sent back to London. Also, two little girls turned out to be Jewish, and were horrified to be offered bacon and eggs for breakfast.

"Quite right," said Henry. "Eating pigs is cruel and disgusting. It ought to be illegal."

"*And* they refused to attend church this morning," Aunt Charlotte went on over the top of Henry (our aunt considers vegetarians to be almost as objectionable as Communists). "Poor Mrs. Heggarty is at her wits' end. She asked the girls to run up to the shop yesterday for some more sugar so she could make a pudding, and they said they couldn't run errands because it was the Sabbath! It really is *astounding,* that children could be so ungrateful when they've been rescued from certain death. I suppose you heard the air-raid siren this morning? Well, *that* may have been a false alarm, but one can be certain the Germans will start bombarding our cities any moment now." Aunt Charlotte sighed. "One would think the children could show a *little* more appreciation, being taken from those horrid slums and given a holiday in the fresh country air. But one can't expect much else from the lower classes."

"Because the upper classes have maltreated them for so long that they've lost any hope of improving their condition?" offered Veronica.

Luckily, Aunt Charlotte, down the other end of the table, misheard her. "Yes, you're quite right, it's a thankless task, but one must do what one can for the good of the nation. I only wish Pamela Bosworth could comprehend the enormous weight of *responsibility* that has fallen upon WVS leaders such as myself. *She* was complaining yesterday about running a couple of first aid classes for the Red Cross! That's nothing at all, a few hours a week, compared to laboring *night and day* to help these wretched evacuees! And all of this, of course, on top of one's usual duties, right at the moment when half of one's staff decides to run off . . ."

Here she fixed Simon with a gimlet eye, which was most unfair. After all, *she* was the one who ordered Simon to enlist in the RAF to keep watch over Toby (not that I think the air force works quite that way, especially when the two of them are at different levels of training and could end up at opposite ends of the country). But it wasn't *Simon's* fault that he'd have to give up typing Aunt Charlotte's correspondence, keeping track of her committee meetings, and doing a thousand and one other administrative tasks for her. I just hoped she wasn't expecting Veronica or me to take over from him.

"My secretary, three of the footmen, five gardeners, a scullery maid and the stableboy, all gone!" declared Aunt Charlotte. Then she turned to Henry. "And, as if that weren't bad enough, your *governess* has just resigned."

"Really?" said Henry with interest. "Miss Bullock's leaving?"

"Enlisted in the Auxiliary Territorial Service, if you please!"

"I'd have thought she'd be a bit *old* to join the women's army," said Henry.

"Old?" said Aunt Charlotte, frowning. "The woman is barely thirty."

"Exactly," said Henry. "Ancient."

Aunt Charlotte (at least fifteen years older than that) started to puff up with indignation. I quickly passed her the butter dish, even though she hadn't asked for it, and it seemed to work as a diversion at first. But then Toby said, "Well, poor old Miss Bullock should find army life pretty easy after two years of *you*, Hen. Perhaps the ATS could use you as a sort of one-girl training scheme, a means of toughening up new recruits and weeding out the—ow! See what I mean?"

"Henrietta, don't hit your brother!" snapped Aunt Charlotte. "You ought to know better, but apparently none of your governesses has managed to teach you any ladylike behaviors whatsoever!" Our aunt tore her bread roll apart and began stabbing at the butter. "And there's not a prayer of finding anyone else *remotely* suitable for the position, with things the way they are."

"Will I be going to the village school, then?" asked Henry. "That would be quite good, because my friend Jocko—"

"Don't be absurd," said Aunt Charlotte sharply. "Your manners are bad enough as they are. I will not have you consorting with a lot of village children, not to mention all those evacuees—and how *they* are all to fit into that little schoolhouse, I haven't the faintest idea. No, Henrietta, I will have to locate a suitable educational establishment for you."

"Boarding school," I translated for Henry, because she was looking puzzled.

"Oh," she said. "Oh, no, I don't think I want to go away to school, thank you. Carlos would miss me too much, and Mr. Wilkin needs me to help with the chickens and cows and things, now that his son's been called up."

"I do not recall asking for your opinion, Henrietta," said Aunt Charlotte. "My mind is made up."

"Also, there's Estella," said Henry. "Some people think pigs don't have feelings, but she gets very upset if I don't have a chat with her every single day and take her for walks and—"

"Henrietta! You may leave the table!"

Henry obeyed, in the slowest possible manner, and could be heard muttering mutinously as she stomped down the hall.

Meanwhile, Toby had poured himself more wine, and I saw Aunt Charlotte narrow her eyes as she tried to recall whether it was his second or third glass. On any other day, Simon would have jumped in at that point and steered the conversation into safer waters, but he was gloomily chasing a solitary pea around the edge of his plate. And then I remembered.

It was his *birthday*.

He was twenty-five years old today, and he'd just learned he was expected to go off and put himself in terrible danger and try to kill people, simply because a lot of politicians couldn't get along with one another. Poor, poor Simon! How unlucky for him to have been born a boy! And poor Toby, too.

I thought a bit more. Poor Henry, as well. And poor Aunt Charlotte. Poor *all* of us.

As I said, it was a pretty depressing meal.

I didn't have time to finish writing down all that happened on Sunday—in fact, I can see that keeping an accurate record of every significant event of the war is going to be impossible. That's supposing one can actually figure out what's significant and what's not, when one's in the middle of "living through history," as the newspaper put it this morning. I think I will just do as I've always done and write about whatever interests me, and if anyone rescues my journal from the ruins of civilization after the war is over, they will just have to pick out the significant bits for themselves. That's assuming they're able to decipher my abbreviated Kernetin, which is unlikely, given that Veronica and Toby are the only other people who can read our family's secret code—and even *they* don't understand my abbreviations.

Anyway, after luncheon on Sunday, Aunt Charlotte went back to the village to do more arguing with and about the evacuees, and the rest of us held a Council of War in my bedroom.

There was quite a bit of Montmaray business to sort out before the boys left. Firstly, there was our letter declaring war upon Germany, the draft of which Veronica read aloud. Toby and I nodded our approval; Henry didn't think it was threatening enough; Simon pointed out that we needed to include how Germany had ignored our League of Nations letter of protest.

"That'll remind everyone that we really *did* try every diplomatic means possible to resolve this," he said. "It might help get the Americans on our side."

"I don't think the Americans are even on *Britain's* side," I said as Veronica amended the letter. "They don't seem to want to get involved in a European war at all, according to Mr. Kennedy."

"Sooner or later," said Simon grimly, "everyone will *have* to choose a side."

"All right, how does this sound?" And Veronica read the revised letter to us:

The Kingdom of Montmaray was illegally invaded by Germany on the twelfth of January, 1937. Germany has neither apologized, nor restored the island of Montmaray to the Montmaravian people, nor responded to a request from the League of Nations to join mediated talks to resolve this issue. Therefore, on this day, the third of September, 1939, the Kingdom of Montmaray formally declares war upon Germany.

"That's fine," said Simon.

"No, it's not!" Henry exclaimed. "You forgot to say that we vow ETERNAL VENGEANCE on Gebhardt, because he was the one responsible for bombing Montmaray *and* he tried to assassinate you lot in Paris! Also, put in that the brave people of Montmaray will NEVER REST until justice is—"

"Henry," said Veronica, "it's a diplomatic missive, not one of your twopenny adventure comics!"

"I'm only trying to *help*," Henry huffed. "I just think it sounds a bit *soft*, that's all."

"I'll type it up now, if you like," I said. "Does Toby need to sign it?"

"That reminds me," said Toby, "I ought to give the Royal Seal to you, Veronica, for official correspondence. You and Soph can take care of all of that, can't you, while I'm away? Um, what else? Oh—money."

"That's simple," said Simon. "We haven't got any."

"I wonder what RAF officers get paid?" Toby said. "Not much, I'd imagine. But what about you girls—what are you going to do?"

"Well, Julia was telling us about this secretarial school in London that offers intensive courses," said Veronica. "Her friend Daphne's cousin did one of them. It's in Bayswater Road, so all we have to do is get Aunt Charlotte to agree to us living at Montmaray House by ourselves." Veronica gave a wry smile. "I thought I'd leave the getting permission bit to Sophie—she's our best strategist. After that, we'll just have to see what sort of jobs we can find. The Colonel said he'd help with that."

Simon had turned a searching look upon me. "But Sophie," he said, "do you *really* want to be in London if there are bombing raids?"

"No," I said frankly. "But then, I don't want to spend the war sitting in the countryside knitting socks for the troops, either. Especially the way *my* socks turn out, all lumps and no heel—although perhaps I could send them to the German troops, rather than our own side. No, the thing is, I want to do something really useful, and I think I'd have to be in London to do that."

Veronica nodded. "And we have to get out of here. Well, *I* do. Aunt Charlotte is already driving me round the bend, and the war's only been going for six hours. Imagine how I'll be in six months."

"You just want to go to London to be with your *boyfriend*," said Henry, still annoyed that Veronica had disregarded all her helpful letter-writing suggestions.

"I don't have a boyfriend," said Veronica.

"Right," said Henry. "So that's why you spent all that time on the telephone to Daniel yesterday. I heard the pips go twice. That's more than *six minutes*."

"Oh, and why were you eavesdropping on my private conversation?"

"Daniel won't get called up, will he?" I asked, suddenly confronted with yet another worry. "How old is he?"

"He's about to turn thirty—"

"Ancient!" shouted Toby and Henry.

"—*and* he can barely see a thing without his spectacles, so he'd never pass the medical," continued Veronica. "He speaks German, though, so I expect the War Office will want him as a translator or something."

"But what about his newspaper job?" I asked.

"Oh, he's going to close the newspaper down. He had a letter from the Ministry of Information on Friday, warning him not to print anything against 'the national interest.' And, of course, practically everything he *publishes* could fit into that category now. Interviews with pacifists, articles protesting against the world armaments trade, letters in favor of the Soviet Union—and his editorials often attack the Prime Minister. But there are new regulations against all that now, and he really doesn't want to spend the entire war in prison."

I suspected Daniel was being *slightly* paranoid there, but that's probably because he's a Socialist. I've noticed that even the nicest Socialists (and they're all lovely, the ones I've met) tend to be just a *tiny* bit unbalanced. The warning letter must have been a mistake, because why would the government care about a little weekly like *The Evolutionary Socialist*? We *do* live in a democracy, after all; journalists don't have to fear "oppression and persecution" here. Still, I didn't argue with Veronica about it. Daniel may not be her *boyfriend*, but she does seem to defend his point of view rather vigorously nowadays.

The rest of our meeting was taken up by Simon going

through a lot of tedious details with Veronica regarding bank accounts and master keys and so on. By the time he'd finished, it was time to dress for dinner. But as the others were leaving, Simon pulled me aside.

"There is one other thing," he said. "Sophie, could I ask you a favor?"

He'd reached out and curled his hand around my bare arm, which caused a familiar fluttering to start up somewhere in the region of my stomach. One would really think I'd have got used to his casual touch by now—after all, he *is* my cousin (probably). He's certainly not my *boyfriend*. I cleared my throat.

"Of course I'll help, Simon," I said, in my most businesslike voice. "What is it?"

"It's Mother," he said, and the delicious fluttering in my stomach turned into a much less enjoyable sensation. "Her clinic in Poole will probably have to be evacuated, because it's right on the sea. Apparently the army's already stringing barbed wire along the beaches, in case there's an invasion. The clinic staff are still looking for a suitable building, somewhere safer, but—"

"But she can't stay with us!" I burst out. "Don't you remember, she tried to kill Veronica!"

"Well, Mother wasn't exactly in her right mind then . . . but yes, I quite understand that she can't stay here. I just meant, could I give the matron your contact details, in case of any emergencies? I'm not exactly sure where I'll be from now on, and I might not always have access to a telephone.

I'll keep writing to Mother, of course, and visit her whenever I can get leave."

"Does she know you've joined the RAF?"

"Er . . . not yet," he admitted. "I didn't want to worry her. You know how she gets."

I certainly did. An agitated Rebecca was something to avoid at all costs.

"Well, she'll definitely realize once you turn up in uniform," I pointed out.

"Yes, I'd better do it soon," he said, with a sigh. "So, I'll let the matron know? And if there are any difficulties, and if you happen to be here at Milford when they telephone . . ."

I frowned. "I suppose I *could* go down there to sort things out. If it were absolutely necessary."

"Don't take Veronica with you," Simon advised, with a sudden, dazzling grin. "Thanks, Sophie, I knew I could count on you." He bent down and kissed me on the cheek, then strode out of the room.

And now simply *writing* that sentence makes the heat rush to my face. Sometimes I wonder whether he actually *suspects* something of my feelings for him (my past feelings, that is, as naturally, I am too sensible and mature to continue to be infatuated with him). Simon knowing about all that would be too mortifying for words, although it's not completely outside the realm of possibility. He is fairly perceptive, and must be something of an expert on women by now, given the vast number who keep throwing themselves at him . . .

So much for this journal being an accurate record of significant wartime happenings.

But it's not entirely my fault that this has gone off on a ridiculous tangent. This morning, I had another embarrassing encounter with Barnes, who persists in believing (despite all evidence to the contrary) that Rupert Stanley-Ross is not merely my brother's best friend, but also *my secret suitor*.

"The post, Your Highness," she said at breakfast, handing Veronica a dozen envelopes (letters of congratulation from Members of Parliament; requests for magazine interviews; tirades of abuse from Fascists, Germans, and men who disapprove of women getting involved in politics). Then Barnes came round to my side of the table. "And a letter for *you*, Your Highness." Only she said this in such an arch, knowing manner that I couldn't help blushing when I caught sight of Rupert's handwriting. Then Barnes hovered nearby, waiting for me to open it, as though she were expecting rose petals or a diamond ring to fall out. I gritted my teeth and attacked the envelope with my butter knife.

"Oh, look," I said loudly. "Henry, it's from Rupert. He's sent you a pamphlet on how to care for animals during air raids." I passed it over. "Do you want to read his letter as well?"

I knew Henry wouldn't—she was too busy poring over the pamphlet—but I hoped this would demonstrate once and for all that there was nothing amorous about Rupert or his letters. Barnes simply sent me a conspiratorial smile as Aunt Charlotte entered the room, then hurried over to ensure Aunt

Charlotte's favorite cup and saucer were in their correct position and that the teapot was full. (The departure of so many of our servants means that our household does not always run as smoothly as Aunt Charlotte expects, so poor Barnes is busier than ever.)

"What's 'bromide'?" asked Henry, frowning at her pamphlet. "It says to give dogs a dose of it when the siren starts."

"It's a sedative," Veronica explained. "Medicine to calm them down."

"Oh. And it says to put cotton wool in their ears," Henry went on. "That's a good idea, because Carlos hated that air-raid siren, and I don't think he'd like the sound of bombs. But it also says to put a muzzle on him, in case he gets . . . What's this word, Sophie?"

"Hysterical," I said.

"Yet another reason you will be better off at boarding school, Henrietta," said Aunt Charlotte, seating herself at the head of the table. "So that you can learn to *read*."

"I can read *English*," retorted Henry. "Just not foreign words like that. I know what it means, though, obviously. It means *frantic and biting*. Well, Carlos never gets like that, and he'd hate wearing a muzzle. In fact, I think muzzles are cruel and wrong, just like boarding schools, which I would *not* be better off at. So that's why I'm not going to one."

"Yes, you are," said Aunt Charlotte, perusing yet another letter sent by a prospective headmistress.

"No, I'm not," said Henry.

They have this exchange every couple of hours.

Meanwhile, I read Rupert's letter. It was quite long, but I will copy out some of it now. He is staying at Julia's house in London, because he had a job interview at Whitehall yesterday:

> Except they told me the job was mine before I'd answered a single question—they already knew I'd been at the "right" school and the "right" college at Oxford, you see. They didn't even bother to ask about my exam results. But the most important thing, in their opinion, was that I had a personal recommendation from the Colonel.

I think it's hilarious that all the Stanley-Rosses call him that, even though he's their uncle—apparently, he's too important and mysterious to possess a first name. Rupert went on:

> Sorry to be so unforthcoming about what the job actually is, but I'm supposed to keep it confidential. I expect you'll figure out what I'm doing anyway, as it involves one of the few areas in which I have any expertise at all. I start tomorrow with some meetings in London, but will have to do a lot of traveling after that, so they have given me a car.

Rupert was reading English Literature at Oxford, but I can't imagine *that* would be helpful to the War Office—unless he's saving *books* from bombs? Perhaps he's moving collections of rare books to the country?

It's a relief to have something constructive to do, because I felt so guilty watching all the men marching along the streets in uniform. Do you think women will go about handing white feathers to "shirkers," the way they did in the last war? It makes me want to wear a badge saying, "Heart Murmur—Failed the Medical." But the thing is, I know I would be absolutely useless at killing people, whereas this job could end up helping us win battles.

So—probably *not* moving books to the country. Unless the books are military manuals.

I never thought I'd be grateful for having had rheumatic fever, but now I am—although I'm also ashamed about feeling so grateful. Sorry, this is probably making no sense whatsoever.

Did Toby tell you he telephoned here? It was good to speak with him, and he sounded cheerful enough. I hope it was not too awful seeing him off on Monday. I expect your aunt was upset . . .

Aunt Charlotte was absolutely *heartbroken*. Thank heavens for Barnes.

. . . but he'll only be in the Cotswolds and will get leave quite often, and he isn't doing any actual fighting yet, thank God. Anthony is with an AAF squadron somewhere in Scotland.

Julia gets all weepy whenever she catches sight of the framed photograph of him in uniform, and has already written him three letters. Why, when all she ever seemed to do when he was home was argue with him? I think she feels guilty about that, now he's off defending the nation. By the way, she says you and Veronica are very welcome to stay with her when you come up to London. There are lots of spare bedrooms and she would love the company, especially as I will not be here very often. I keep telling her she ought to adopt some needy animals, because there are so many of them out there, desperately wanting homes. A lot of people are leaving the city and can't take their pets with them, and animals are not allowed in public air-raid shelters. It is so horrible—a friend of mine who works at the RSPCA said that literally thousands of cats are being put down every single day. Killing animals to save them from bombs! We don't do that to people, and I can think of some boys at my school who were far less intelligent, caring, and interesting than the average cat.

One can see why Rupert and Henry get along so well. But he's right, of course—it *is* terrible about the poor animals, and especially distressing for someone as compassionate as Rupert.

Hmm, I think his job must be something to do with animals . . . although how would that help us win the war?

However, I will have to ponder it at a later date. I need to get on with hemming five dozen blackout curtains right now.

15th September 1939

Written in London, where Aunt Charlotte, Barnes, Veronica, Henry, and I are staying at Claridge's. We don't have enough servants anymore to open up enormous old Montmaray House, so we couldn't stay there. Besides, it doesn't have any proper blackout curtains and the Air Raid Precautions people up here are ferocious. A few nights ago, Veronica and I were walking past a house that had a tiny window with the curtains not *entirely* meeting in the middle, showing the glow of a very, very dim bulb, and two wardens almost battered down the door, yelling, "Put that light out!" It was the first time we'd been out after dark since the blackout started, and London seemed a completely different place. We were only walking back to the hotel from the American Embassy, a mere block away, but we got lost twice, and were almost run over when we tried to cross the road. No streetlamps, all the illuminated shop signs switched off, car lights barely visible, and although we had a torch, it was masked by two layers of tissue paper and we weren't allowed to point it anywhere except at the ground. We might as well have been blindfolded. The newspapers keep publishing hilariously useless hints for coping with the blackout—for example, "pin a luminous flower to your lapel" and "carry a small white dog, such as a Pekinese." Honestly! I think more people are going to get killed tumbling down stairs or being knocked over by unlit trams than by falling bombs, especially as there hasn't been a single German aeroplane sighted so far.

If we'd realized how impossible it was to walk anywhere in the blackout, we might have accepted that offer of a lift back to our hotel from the party—except it was Joe Kennedy Junior who'd offered, and Julia had warned about him being Not Safe in Taxis (or in motorcars, presumably). Not that we really needed any warning, because he'd spent most of the evening trying to look down the top of Veronica's dress. He also kept barging into our conversations to boast about his experiences during the siege of Madrid. He'd only been an observer for the American Embassy—it wasn't as though he'd spent the entire Spanish Civil War single-handedly fighting off Fascists. Although he probably would have been fighting *for* the Fascists, not against them, because he always does whatever his father says. I am getting quite fed up with the Ambassador's pronouncements. During the toasts, Mr. Kennedy said that England was going to get "badly thrashed" in this war. Even if this were true—which I don't for a moment believe—it isn't a very diplomatic thing to say, especially at a party. The party, I should have explained, was being held to farewell Mrs. Kennedy and the children, who are all sailing back to New York (except for Rosemary, whom they don't want to move from her special school in the country, as she is making such good progress there).

Kick begged and begged her father to let her remain here, but Mr. Kennedy thinks it will be too dangerous (when England gets invaded, vanquished, demolished, and so forth). However, I would think that simply sailing back across the Atlantic would be perilous, and Mr. Kennedy ought to know all about that. He was the one who sent Jack up to Scotland to help the American survivors of the SS *Athenia*, which was sunk by a German torpedo on the very first day of the war. Jack told us about it—it sounded so dreadful. The SS *Athenia* was an unarmed passenger ship, crowded with civilians trying to get home to Canada, and more than a hundred people drowned. The Germans didn't even give the captain of the ship any warning—not that *that* surprises me one little bit.

Kick made me promise to write to her, and says she will miss all her English friends terribly much, but I suspect the one she will miss the most is Billy Hartington. I think that if Kick could ever get around her parents' violent objections to Protestants, he would be the one, out of her enormous crowd of admirers, whom she'd like to marry. He *is* a very sweet boy—I find it difficult to picture him as an officer in the army, but that's what he is now. I suppose it's no more bizarre than Toby becoming an officer in the air force (which I haven't *quite* taken in yet—perhaps it will seem more real once I've seen him in uniform).

The reason we have come up to London is *not* that Aunt Charlotte is allowing us to go to secretarial school (I still haven't found the right moment to ask permission), but to buy Henry's school things. Aunt Charlotte has finally located a suitably ladylike and rural establishment that is prepared to accept a new pupil halfway through first term—provided, of course, that said pupil arrives with the correct quantity of socks, vests, bloomers, tunics, blouses, plimsolls, and pajamas, as well as a lacrosse stick, a tennis racket, and dozens of other items. Not surprisingly, Henry is being less than cooperative about the whole thing. Aunt Charlotte rapidly lost patience with her, so Veronica and I have taken over the task of shepherding Henry around London's shops.

I can't say this has been an unalloyed pleasure, but it did have the benefit yesterday of allowing us to have luncheon with Daniel. Veronica thought she'd dash off to have a quick cup of tea with him while I took Henry to get fitted for her school blazer, but Henry overheard and said she hadn't seen him in *years*, not since she was a *child*, and wouldn't it be better if we all sat down and had a proper meal, because she was absolutely starving? And of *course* she wouldn't mention it to Aunt Charlotte; did we think she was a complete *idiot*? Veronica extracted a promise from Henry not to utter the word *boyfriend* in his presence, and we all ended up at Lyons Corner House. Daniel, wisely, treated Henry with the sort of solemn respect that she hardly ever gets from grown-ups, so she quickly decided she was On His Side.

"You should come and visit us at Milford," she said, over

her second helping of trifle. "Carlos will be glad to see you again. Do you remember him?"

"Of course I do," said Daniel. "He ate my hat."

"Oh, I remember that," said Veronica. "You'd just arrived at Montmaray and put it down on top of your suitcase, and he took off with it."

"Was it made of fish?" asked Henry.

I stared at her. I honestly don't understand how her brain works, most of the time.

"What?" she said to me. "It could have been made of sharkskin or something. Carlos loves fish."

"It was just ordinary gray felt, as far as I can recall," said Daniel. "I think he was upset that no one was paying attention to him. But when I went out into the courtyard to ask if he'd give it back, I got attacked by that giant rooster of yours. And then Rebecca appeared out of nowhere and started screaming at me for making too much noise and disturbing His Majesty's afternoon rest."

"And you thought, *What sort of crazy place is this?*" I suggested. "And wondered whether it was too late to run back to the boat and sail home."

"Not at all," he said, smiling at Veronica. "I could tell at once that I wasn't ever going to be bored there. It seemed a very *interesting* place."

"It was," said Henry. "It is. And Daniel, did you know that we're going back there, as soon as we win the war and get rid of the revolting Nazis? But in the meantime, our aunt is making me go to some horrible boarding school. Daniel, *you* didn't have to go to boarding school, did you?"

"I'm afraid I did," he said.

"*Afraid?*" repeated Henry, her eyes widening. "Why? What happened there?"

"Oh, that's just a figure of speech," he said. "Nothing happened, except for the usual sort of school . . . happenings." He was trying to read the nonverbal signals Veronica was sending him behind Henry's back. "And . . . there was a lot of sport. Yes. Outdoor sports."

"Hmph," said Henry. "But you went to a *boys'* school. You probably did exciting things like archery and hiking and cadets. Do you know what girls have to do at this school? Dancing lessons!"

"Now, Henry," I said. "There's also tennis and lacrosse and all sorts of outdoor activities. You'll love that."

"I won't love it, I'll loathe it," she said. "I'm not allowed to take my fishing rod or any pets, not even a tortoise, and anyone who rides the school horses has to ride sidesaddle, which is the stupidest thing ever invented."

"But remember how much fun you had with the Girl Guides?" I said. "And at school, you'll be sharing a dormitory with four other girls."

"Four other *awful* girls," said Henry. "Like Lady Bosworth's awful niece."

"I don't think she's in your year," I said. "And you haven't even met her, so how do you know she's awful?"

"Well, Lady Bosworth is, and that sort of thing usually runs in families," said Henry.

"I imagine you'll have a lot of fascinating *new* experiences at school," said Daniel diplomatically.

"Which reminds me," I said, glancing at my watch. "Henry, we really need to get going if we want to buy the rest of your uniform today." I was hoping to give Daniel and Veronica at least a couple of minutes alone together.

"*I* don't want to buy any of it," Henry said. "But I suppose Aunt Charlotte will yell at us if we don't turn up at the hotel with lots of packages." She rose and shook hands with Daniel. "Goodbye. It was extremely nice seeing you again, and I hope you'll come and stay with us when we go back to Montmaray. Veronica, aren't you coming?"

"She'll catch up," I said. "Come on."

"Oh," Henry said. "Well, after we've gone, Daniel, you can kiss her. If you really want."

"Thank you," said Daniel. "I'll keep that in mind."

I dragged Henry out of the restaurant.

"What?" said Henry. "I didn't even mention the word *boyfriend*. Oh, look, they're holding hands now."

"Leave them *alone*," I said. "Don't you have any tact at all?"

"I don't know. I might. What is it?"

"Thinking about how *they* might feel!"

"But I *was* thinking!" Henry said. "I was thinking he wanted to kiss her, because he kept giving her soppy looks—although I can't understand why anyone as nice as Daniel would want to kiss *Veronica*, when she's so grumpy. Did you see that look she gave me when we were saying goodbye?"

I steered Henry out of the way of some ARP wardens, who were stacking sandbags against a building.

"If anyone has no tact, it's Veronica!" Henry went on indignantly. "What about *my* feelings when she's giving me mean looks? Sophie, have *you* ever kissed a boy?"

"That's none of your business," I said.

"That means you haven't," she said. "Where are we going, anyway? I don't even *want* a blazer. It's such a waste of money, I'd much rather have new roller skates. You know, if Aunt Charlotte makes me go to this school, I'm going to run away as soon as I get there. Or *roll* away, if I can fix that broken wheel on my skates."

Veronica finally caught up with us in Debenhams, where Henry was busy despising pink pajamas.

"Oh, you're a marvel, Sophie," Veronica said, looking at the items crossed off our list. "That's *all* of the clothes done, and I thought it would take days! Well, I'll take her to Lillywhites now to get that lacrosse stick, if you want to do your own shopping."

"Did Daniel kiss you?" Henry asked Veronica.

"That's none of your business," said Veronica.

"That means he did," said Henry smugly.

I made a hasty escape before I could get drawn into their argument. Apart from outfitting Henry, Aunt Charlotte also wanted us to stock up on clothes and other supplies for ourselves. "I remember how it was during the last war," she'd said. "Running out of hairpins and buttons, and hardly any good-quality silk to be found by the end of it." So, my plan was to buy a really warm coat and hat, lots of stockings and underthings, and some smart blouses and skirts, suitable for working in an office.

But I quickly discovered that shopping for clothes during wartime wasn't much fun. All the department stores along Regent Street were crowded, and all the shoppers wore the same grimly determined expression as they gathered up armfuls of serviceable garments and dumped them in front of the weary-looking cashiers. There were still lots of pretty things on display, but I felt as though I'd be arrested for unpatriotic behavior if I tried on the pink picture hat laden with silk roses or the polka-dotted organdie blouse with cascades of frills down the front—not that I'd have occasion to wear anything so frivolous now. At one counter, they had a display of cases made out of velvet and suede, specially designed to keep one's gas mask in—because carrying protection against deadly gas attacks is now as normal as wearing a hat. It was all rather depressing. By the time I'd tried on several suits (none of which looked right on me) and bought a couple of plain shirts, I was more than ready to go back to the hotel.

Veronica arrived not long after me, with what looked like the beginnings of a headache etched across her forehead.

"This whole boarding school thing is going to be a complete disaster," she announced, unpinning her hat and flinging it at my bed. "Henry's simply refusing to go, and you know what she's like."

"I'll have a serious talk with her," I promised. "I know boarding school's not ideal, but I don't think there's any other option. She can't live with us in London if we're going to be at work all day."

"And she really needs a proper education," agreed Veronica. "She didn't have the slightest idea how much change was due when I was paying for things today. And her spelling's abysmal, and she never reads anything except comics and those Biggles books."

"She'll come round in the end," I said. "We're all having to deal with things we don't much like."

"I know," said Veronica, with a sigh.

"Sorry about luncheon," I said. "I mean, that you didn't have Daniel to yourself."

"That's all right," she said. She kicked off her shoes and collapsed onto her own bed.

"Has he found a new job?" I asked tentatively, just in case she wanted to talk about him.

"Well, he had an interview at the War Office last week, but he hasn't heard back yet. He thinks they're doing background checks on him—you know, to see if he's a member of the Communist Party."

"Is he?"

"No, but only because he's not the sort to join official organizations. He agrees with a lot of what the Communists *think*, of course. Anyway, Britain's not at war with the Soviet Union, so it shouldn't matter if he *were* a Communist."

"Well, the Soviets are friends with the Nazis now, so you can see why the government might want to check."

"Hmm." She was frowning at the ceiling. "Actually, he's more worried about his relatives than finding a job, just at the moment. Do you remember his two cousins from Vienna, the ones who escaped to Paris last year? Well, they applied for official papers to come to England, and they arrived here a week ago. The two of them were staying with Daniel's parents, but the police came round a few nights ago and took them away."

"Why? Was there a problem with their papers?"

"No, the government's rounding up anyone who's arrived recently and interrogating them, in case they're Nazi spies. His cousins spent a few days at the local police station, but now they've been sent off to some internment camp and Daniel's trying to find out where they are."

"But that's ridiculous," I said. "They're *Jewish*. They're trying to *escape* the Nazis! How could they possibly be Nazi spies?"

"I know, and Daniel said that when they were at the police station, they were locked up in the same room as *actual* Nazis. Or at least, Germans who seemed very keen on Nazi ideology and weren't at all fond of Jews."

"Someone must have made a mistake," I said.

"Well, yes, obviously," said Veronica. "The policeman Daniel spoke to did say that they're going to set up tribunals to examine each individual case, but who knows how long that will take? In the meantime, two innocent people who could be helping the war effort are locked up, and Daniel's mother is frantic, and Daniel's rushing around trying to figure out what's going on."

Veronica sat up abruptly and began taking down her hair, which had been twisted into a very large chignon at the back of her head. "These hairpins feel as though they're digging directly into my *brain*," she said.

"Shall I get you an aspirin?" I asked.

"No, thanks. It's just all this hair. I'm getting it cut off tomorrow."

I stared at her. "You're *what?*"

"Short hair's far more practical, and it's not as though I'm going to have a maid around now to pin it up for me each morning." She glanced over at me. "What? Phoebe won't want to come with us to London, will she?"

"No, she wants to go back to her village and work on a farm. But oh, Veronica, cutting off all your beautiful hair!"

"*You* have short hair," she pointed out. "So does Aunt Charlotte, and Julia, and practically every other woman in England."

"I know," I said sadly. And I knew Veronica would look lovely, regardless of what she did to her hair. It was just that I'd had enough of all these drastic changes in our lives, so many in such a short time. I forced a smile. "Well! Make sure you keep all the hair they cut off. Perhaps you could sell it, like Jo in *Little Women*, and become immensely rich."

"Perhaps I could braid it into a very long rope, and tie it to the window frame in case we need to escape during an air raid."

"Or you could weave it into blackout curtains."

"Or knit it into parachutes."

And we went on, getting sillier and sillier, turning the war—for a brief moment—into something we could laugh at.

Yesterday morning, I sat Henry down for a Serious Talk about boarding school. This mostly involved me admiring her bravery for agreeing to go (even though she still hadn't agreed to anything of the sort).

"I mean, *I'd* be terrified," I said. "Traveling all the way to Hertfordshire on a train by myself!"

"Well . . . ," she said slowly. "I quite *like* trains, actually. I never normally get to go in them."

"And then, getting off at a railway station I'd never seen before! Of course, a teacher will be waiting to take you up to the school, so it's not as though you'll get lost."

"I wouldn't get lost, anyway," said Henry. "I could take my compass and I know all about reading maps, from being a Girl Guide."

"And they did say that all the prefects know you're coming," I continued, "and one of them specially volunteered to show you round after she heard that you liked horses, because apparently she's won lots of ribbons for show jumping. But still, imagine meeting such a lot of new people! It would be like when all the Basque refugee children arrived. I felt a bit nervous beforehand, didn't you?"

"No, of course not," she said. "Why were you nervous? I couldn't *wait* to meet them, and they were all so much fun, especially Carmelita. Remember when she and I had that archery competition, and I *almost* got the bull's-eye, and she said, 'Oh, there's no way I can get closer than that!' except her next arrow landed right on top of mine and *broke* it—" And Henry continued reminiscing, getting further and further away from the point of the conversation. I eventually interrupted.

"Oh, and that reminds me," I said. "You must write to Carmelita and tell her all about your new school. You know how much she loves *her* school."

"Yes," said Henry. "I know. But hers is different. It isn't a boarding school, is it? *She* didn't have to move away from home."

"That's true," I said. "I really do admire how brave you're being about that."

"I am a *fairly* brave person," conceded Henry. "Usually. But it's not that I mind for *myself*. It's about leaving poor Carlos and Estella all alone."

"Oh, Henry!" I said. "Estella loves living at the Home Farm with the other pigs, and you know how well Mr. Wilkin treats them. They're the most spoiled pigs in the county."

"But . . . but what about *Carlos*?" Henry said, and her eyes suddenly filled with tears. "It would be different if you and

Veronica and Toby were there—but there'll be no one to look after him!"

I put my arm around her and, for once, she allowed me to console her. "I know he'll miss you," I said, as she sniffled a bit. "Of course he will—he's such a faithful dog. But the kitchen maids all adore him, and they're usually the ones who feed him, aren't they? And he always keeps himself busy, chasing rabbits, and swimming in the lake, and visiting his friends in the village."

"I suppose Jocko will still be there," she said. "And Mrs. Jones at the vicarage—I mean, she ended up keeping two of the puppies, so she must really like dogs. And I've seen Barnes talking to Carlos, sometimes."

"Even Aunt Charlotte has a soft spot for him," I said, "except when he tracks mud inside the house. But Henry, you're talking as though you're going away forever! There are holidays halfway through each term *and* in between terms, and then for the entire summer. Carlos will barely have time to miss you before you're back at Milford."

"I suppose so," she said. "But Sophie—" Then she stopped and chewed her lip.

"What?" I said.

"Well . . . what about the *school* part of it? In books, school-boys are always getting into trouble for not doing their prep or getting answers wrong in class. Sometimes they get *caned* for it."

By "books," I assumed Henry meant those awful twopenny boys' weeklies that she and Jocko buy at the village shop. "Girls are never caned," I said firmly.

"But what if I can't do the work?" Henry persisted. "What if Miss Bullock didn't teach me the right things? Or anything, really."

I was tempted to point out that Henry's failure to learn had not been entirely Miss Bullock's fault. However, Henry's fundamental honesty came to the fore.

"Of course, I could have tried harder," she admitted. "But even if I *had*—I bet all those girls at school will still know loads more than me about arithmetic and French and those sorts of things."

"I don't think they will," I said. In fact, I had a strong suspicion the school had been chosen precisely for its unacademic reputation (Aunt Charlotte detests bluestockings). "The headmistress said there are lots of new pupils who hadn't been to school at all before this term, so you won't be the only one."

I pulled away to look my little sister in the eye, uncomfortably aware that she was now an inch taller than me. "Henry, listen to me. If it's really unbearable—if someone's being horrible to you or you get terribly homesick—I *promise* that Veronica or I will try to sort things out. You just have to write and tell us. We'll telephone the headmistress, or visit you, or do whatever we can to make it better. But I'm counting on you to be really grown-up about this, to try your best to get along with everyone, to do your work and be sensible. There's a war on now, and we all have to do our bit."

"I will," she said, nodding solemnly.

"And you have to promise that you won't run away from

this place," I said. "Because if you suddenly go missing, we'll worry about where you are."

She considered this for a moment. "But what if the Germans invade and I *have* to run away because they've taken over the school?"

"They aren't going to invade an enormous country like this. Remember, Britain's got an army and navy and air force to stop them. But *if* it looks as though the Germans might invade, I want you to do whatever your teachers tell you, until we can come and collect you—which we *will*."

"All right, then," Henry said, after further thought. "I promise. Do you want me to swear a blood oath? Because I brought my penknife with me, it's in my suitcase—"

"That won't be necessary," I said hastily.

"All right," she said. "Oh—and Sophie!"

"What?"

"As I'm practically a grown-up now, can I come with you and Veronica to visit Julia this afternoon? Please? Because I haven't seen her for absolute ages, and I've never been to her house."

I didn't have enough energy left to argue about it, so we took her with us.

"Henry!" cried Julia. "Each time I set eyes upon you, you look more and more like your gorgeous brother!"

Henry glowed. "Did you know I'm *thirteen* now?" she said as Julia took our coats.

"No, I didn't," Julia said. "Darling, you *are* getting old. But

I do wish you'd stop growing, you make Sophie and me feel awfully short. Now, come into my sitting room—I was just doing some sewing. This wretched blackout! I had to pack away all my lovely sheer silk curtains, but look, I found this very heavy, dark blue velvet and I'm sewing silver stars onto it. See? When I draw the curtains after dusk, it will be as though we're outside on a clear night. Well, I say 'we,' even though I've been completely abandoned by everyone, including most of the servants. Rupert's just left, actually, off doing his super-secret job in Cornwall this week. He *will* be sorry to have missed you—"

"How's Anthony?" I asked quickly, before Julia could start teasing me about Rupert (she's worse than Barnes sometimes).

Julia sighed and shook her head. "Oh, the poor *darling*. He still hasn't got over the Soviets signing that treaty with the Nazis. He feels awfully conflicted, going off to war, knowing he's on the opposite side to the Communists. Thank heavens we aren't actually *fighting* the Communists yet . . . or fighting anyone, really. That's what I don't understand. I mean, didn't we declare war because Germany invaded Poland? But what have we done to help the poor old Poles? We just seem to be sitting back, watching them get annihilated in this awful blitzkrieg."

"I suppose the Allies are conserving their resources for when the Germans march into France," said Veronica. "Or whichever country they're planning to invade next."

"Oh, Veronica, don't say that! I don't even want to *think* about poor Ant going into battle. Can you imagine it? He wouldn't hurt a fly. Although I must say, he's loving the actual aeroplanes in the air force. All his letters are about how marvelously fast they are, and how well they turn, and something about g-forces, whatever *they* are. I'm just hoping he'll get a job training pilots and spend the rest of the war doing that, but of course, he'll want to do his brave bit if the time comes. How's Toby?"

Henry explained about Toby having finished his fortnight of marching drills and lectures, and how he'd been specially selected to train as a fighter pilot. "And Julia, he wears a *uniform* now!"

"He must look divine in that," said Julia. "What *is* it about men and uniforms? Even Ant looks debonair in one. And what's Simon up to?"

"He's in Leicestershire doing basic training," I said. "He's preparing for his flying test and the written exam."

"Your aunt must miss *him*, as well," said Julia. "Wasn't he practically running her household? And that reminds me—I saw her in Bond Street yesterday and she was *very* cutting. What on earth have I done now?"

"She's probably still furious that Toby's in love with you," Veronica said dryly.

"He's *what*?"

"He's not really," Henry said. "He only pretended to be, because Aunt Charlotte wanted him to marry that horrible Lady Helena. He told Aunt Charlotte that he was pining away because you were already married, and if he couldn't marry you, he wouldn't marry anyone. He's not *actually* in love with you."

Henry peered at Julia, who was almost crying with laughter by this stage. "He's quite *fond* of you, though," Henry hastened to assure her.

"Oh dear," said Julia, dabbing at her eyes. "He really might have warned me. Your poor old aunt! She probably thinks I led him on with come-hither stares and slinky, low-cut evening gowns . . . Well, I suppose it's no use asking you girls to come and live here in my Den of Debauchery now."

"No, she'd never give us permission," I said sadly. I adore Julia's house.

"And it's such a waste, all these rooms empty!" she said. "Of course, Mummy wants me to close up the house and move back to Astley, but I couldn't bear it. She'd have me rolling bandages all day, or knitting balaclavas, or whatever it is the Women's Institute ladies do down there . . . Henry, darling, would you run downstairs and see if Mrs. Timms has made us that pot of tea yet? And there might be some biscuits, too. You could help her carry it all up."

Once Henry had bounded off, Julia added, "Besides, if I went back to Astley, I'd have to put up with endless lectures from Mummy about how I ought to have a baby to keep me occupied while Ant's away. She doesn't seem to realize that might be a bit difficult when he's off in Scotland—I sometimes wonder whether my poor mother understands the Facts of Life. And as if anyone would *want* to have a child when we're at *war* and no one knows what's going to happen! So, I really do have to find some sort of job here in London. What do you think I ought to do? I did consider the Wrens or the WAAF, but then, I could get posted *anywhere*, couldn't I? And I might not get leave at the same time as Ant, and we'd never see each other. Oh, and that reminds me—you know Lady Bosworth's daughter, the horsey one? She's just joined the Mechanised Transport Corps! I ran into her as she was marching out of the recruiting office this morning. I expect she'll end up a captain or something. Can't you just see her, ordering people about?"

"Lady Bosworth will be unbearably smug about it," said Veronica. "Well—more so than usual."

"Yes, but Veronica, it's excellent news for *us*," I said, sitting up straighter. "Don't you see? The first thing Lady Bosworth will do now is go round to Aunt Charlotte and brag about how Cynthia is rushing to the aid of her country, carrying on a noble tradition of patriotic service, and so forth. It's the perfect time for us to tell Aunt Charlotte what *we* want to do. We'll just say we can't bear to allow others to take on all the responsibility for winning the war, and we absolutely *must* be in London to do our bit. Anyway, typing letters at the War Office is far more ladylike than driving lorries or whatever it is Cynthia's going to do—it'll make a secretarial course seem all the more acceptable to Aunt Charlotte."

"Good *thinking*, Sophie," said Veronica admiringly as Henry and the housekeeper entered the room with laden trays. "I knew you'd come up with something. Still, where are we going to live?"

"Can't you stay at Montmaray House?" asked Julia. "Oh,

thank you, darlings. Scones! And strawberry jam! Mrs. Timms, you *are* a wonder!"

"We did think about that," I said, "but Montmaray House is far too big for two people. Aunt Charlotte used to call it 'camping' whenever she took fewer than a dozen servants with her to stay there. It needs mountains of coal to keep the place above freezing point, and the bedrooms are up four flights of stairs, and the kitchen's an enormous dark cave."

"You could stay in the garage flat," remarked Henry, licking jam off her thumb.

"What garage flat?" said Veronica.

"The one at the end of the garden, behind the tennis court. When they turned the old stables into a garage, they built a flat on top for the chauffeur, except Parker never uses it. I saw it once, when I was exploring."

So this morning, Veronica and I went to visit the flat, having wheedled the keys out of Barnes. It consisted of two tiny bedrooms painted a bilious shade of green; a sitting room that overlooked the dingy alley behind the house; a kitchen furnished with a sink, a stove, and not much else; and (after we finally managed to shove open its warped door) a small bathroom. The bath was positioned in such a way that one would hit one's head on the handbasin whenever one leaned over to turn on the bath taps, several tiles had fallen off the walls, and the lavatory chain was broken. The whole flat was icy, and this was on a mild September day—I could only imagine how cold it would be in the middle of winter. No wonder Parker had declined to live there.

"But look, there's a gas fire in the sitting room," said Veronica. We were taking it in turns to point out the advantages of what was, after all, our only option. Even if I convinced Aunt Charlotte to let us stay in London, I couldn't imagine her shelling out rent money for a proper flat, and we wouldn't have any money of our own till we had jobs—and probably not much money then, either. "Once the stove's going," added Veronica, leading me back into the kitchen, "it will be lovely and warm in *here*."

"And we could paint the bedrooms white," I said. "Then they won't seem so small. We could borrow some curtains from the house. There are those thick ones in the drawing rooms— they'd be all right for the blackout if we doubled them up."

"It'll look much better once we've brought over some furniture."

"Two beds," I said, "a table and chairs, a sofa—"

A mouse poked its head around the stove at us, made indignant tutting noises, then disappeared.

"And a cat," finished Veronica.

"You don't think there are *rats* here, do you?" I asked, staring about fearfully.

"We'll stop up all the holes," she said. "It won't take long, it's such a little place."

"Cozy," I said.

"Compact," agreed Veronica. "Makes housekeeping so much easier."

"Perhaps we ought to clean it up a bit now," I said. "So that if Aunt Charlotte comes to look at it, she won't die of horror."

But when I tried the kitchen tap, we realized the water had been turned off, as well as the gas and the electricity.

"That doesn't matter," said Veronica. "If Aunt Charlotte thought it was good enough for Parker, I don't see how she could object to *us* living here."

I just looked at her.

"All right, she probably *will* object, but that just demonstrates what a hypocritical reactionary she is! I think it's *fine*. And look, Sophie, there's even a telephone . . . Oh." The cord had been chewed right through. "Never mind, we can easily get the telephone company to put in a new one."

We took a last look around, dismissing the paint peeling off the sitting room ceiling as a mere bagatelle, then went downstairs to examine the garage. It was empty except for a pile of very old tires decomposing in a corner, but at the back were some steps leading down to a disused cellar, which Veronica said we could use as a shelter if there were air raids. There were herbs in the kitchen garden, I noticed as we walked back towards the house, and we could plant vegetables in the flower beds. Possibly even keep some chickens . . . I was starting to feel quite excited.

"It'll be our very own home," I said to Veronica. "We'll be able to have things exactly the way *we* want them. No adults bossing us around."

"Right," said Veronica. "All you have to do is convince Aunt Charlotte."

"No problem," I said.

Of course, it was a *slight* problem, talking Aunt Charlotte round, but not an insurmountable one, not once I got Barnes on our side. It certainly helped that the anticipated air raids on London have failed to materialize. However, it's mostly that Aunt Charlotte thinks we won't stick at it, that it will all be too difficult and exhausting for us, and we'll go skulking back to Milford within a fortnight. Then she'll indulge in a good old gloat and, having regained the moral high ground, force us to do all sorts of awful things: help with mucking out the stables; take the minutes at her interminable WVS meetings; marry the vile nephews of her richest, snobbiest friends. All right, maybe not that last one, but Aunt Charlotte is definitely *wrong* about us not sticking at it.

For here I am, sitting in my very own kitchen, basking in the glow of the oven and waiting to see how the pudding I've made turns out. And oh, so *much* has happened since I last had time to write in my journal! Where shall I start?

Well, first, there's our lovely flat. Julia was a tremendous help, advising us what color to paint the bedrooms (a warm dusty pink, to go with the raspberry-striped velvet curtains we appropriated from the Montmaray House library), and showing us how to make our pale blue wallpaper stick to the sitting room walls, and lending us a Turkish carpet, and *giving* us an old armchair she found in the Caledonian Market, which she'd re-covered herself in dark blue drill. Daniel came over to help us move some furniture from the house, after Aunt Charlotte finally agreed we could take what we needed. None of the four-posters from upstairs would fit in our rooms, so we borrowed two narrow iron-framed beds from the housemaids' quarters. We also took a sofa that Henry can sleep on when she visits, a pine table for our kitchen, four ladder-backed chairs, a book-shelf, a wireless, an old wooden trunk to keep our spare bed linen and towels in, and a collection of silver cutlery embossed with the FitzOsborne crest (I did *look* for ordinary cutlery, but there wasn't any to be found in the house). I didn't want to take any of the good china—we would be on tenterhooks every time we washed up—so I bought a set of plain white bowls, plates, and cups from Woolworths, using most of my allowance for this month. (Aunt Charlotte has grudgingly restored this privilege to us, probably because it would be a bit embarrassing for her if we were seen getting around London dressed in rags and begging passersby for scraps of food.) We keep a list of things we still need and it never seems to get any shorter, despite our frequent trips up to the house or to Kensington High Street. This morning, I added *batteries for torch, soup ladle, hot-water bottles,* and *shoe polish.* I honestly don't know how working-class people can ever afford to get married and set up house together. We borrowed most of our stuff *and* we don't even have to pay any rent, in return for keeping an eye on Montmaray House. We just have to buy food and pay the gas, electricity, and water bills, which won't arrive for a couple of months, and hopefully we'll have jobs by then.

We have quickly settled into our new routine. My alarm clock goes off at a quarter past seven. I put the kettle on, have a wash, make a pot of tea, and take a cup back to my room while I get dressed. Then I check to make sure Veronica is up, which she often isn't, and we have breakfast. After that, we tidy up the kitchen, make our beds, peer out the front door to figure out whether we need umbrellas or heavier coats, gather up our books and papers and special Pitman pens, and walk across Kensington Gardens to our secretarial school. It's a fairly long walk, but much more enjoyable than being squashed in a bus, except when it's pouring (in which case, the bus tends to be even more crowded and unpleasant than usual, but still better than getting drenched). Walking also helps save on bus fares— although Veronica has pointed out that we're probably wearing out our shoe leather at a faster rate, so it may not be much of an economy in the long run.

Our first class, shorthand, starts at nine o'clock and goes for an hour and a half. It's very difficult, as though one's learning a new language. After three weeks, I can only write very phrases like "hit a cat" and "hug a dog" (which are probably not the sort of things most secretaries need to write, anyway), and it takes me so long to remember the symbol for each sound that I'd be better off writing it out in English longhand. However, Veronica thinks shorthand is absolutely fascinating—in fact, by the end of the second lesson, she'd worked out a way of doing it more efficiently, but then she made the mistake of telling the teacher about it. Apparently Mr. Pitman had already figured out that particular shortcut, but *we* aren't supposed to learn about it till Lesson Thirty-Seven. So now the teacher makes sarcastic remarks whenever it's Veronica's turn to read out something, and she refers to Veronica very sneeringly as "Your Ladyship" (she doesn't know we're actually princesses, of course, because we both enrolled as plain "Miss FitzOsborne").

I much prefer our typing classes. We pound out drills to the rhythm of a gramophone record in the morning, and after luncheon, we learn how to correct carbon copies, and set out a business letter, and that sort of thing. I'm getting very fast with the drills, although sometimes I get into trouble for not using the correct fingers. The teacher for this class is quite nice, except she loathes long fingernails and will occasionally swoop down on a girl and shriek, "Talons! Trim them at once!" She did this to one girl, Suzanne, who happens to have been a debutante with us and was once very rude about Veronica at a fork luncheon (we overheard her calling Veronica "badly groomed" and "unsophisticated," which Veronica thought was funny, although I didn't). Suzanne is always boasting about her frocks having been made in Paris and her stockings in America, and she takes out a gold compact and examines her perfectly made-up face about once every ten minutes. Anyway, the teacher made Suzanne file her nails down to a quarter of an inch, right there in class, and Suzanne was *still* wailing about it five hours later, when we were walking down the steps to go home. Veronica and I looked at each other and snickered and said, *"Schadenfreude!"* at exactly the same time, and the horrible shorthand teacher, who happened to be passing, gave us a deeply suspicious look, as though we were German spies. Veronica says that the next time Daniel comes to meet us after class, she's going to make him talk to us in German if that teacher's anywhere nearby.

The other students are far friendlier and more interesting than Suzanne. There's a vicar's daughter who wants to be a journalist, although her parents think she's training to be a secretary for a bishop; two sisters who bring in apples to share at luncheon, because their father's a greengrocer; a girl who was born in India and once toured the Great Pyramids of Egypt on a camel; and a girl who used to dance in the Folies-Bergère and tells the most incredible stories (Aunt Charlotte would *die* if she heard).

Our classes finish at four, and we either walk home or take a bus, usually going via the shops with our never-ending shopping list. The newspapers keep talking about food rationing, but that hasn't started yet, thank heavens. Deciding what to make for meals is challenging enough as it is. I must admit, we've become rather spoiled over the past few years, having someone else to cook for us. But there simply isn't time to make complicated dinners on days when we have classes, and we don't have a refrigerator to stop things going bad. Also, we keep realizing at the last minute that we're lacking vital utensils (no colander, for instance, after Veronica has taken the pot of macaroni off the stove) or ingredients (no nutmeg or currants in the cupboard, when I'm halfway through mixing up an apple pudding). So we quite often resort to baked beans or sardines on toast when we get home. We listen to the BBC news as we're washing up, then we practice our shorthand or write letters to Henry, Toby, and—oh, the telephone's ringing! Back in a moment.

Well! It was the Colonel, saying he was in the area and asking if he could drop in for a quick chat. So we threw ourselves into a cleaning frenzy, snatching up the damp stockings dangling in front of the stove and the newspapers carpeting the sitting room, slamming the bedroom doors shut on our unmade beds and piles of ironing, and making sure the bathroom was fit for company. It's a good thing the flat's so tiny, because we barely managed all this before we heard his knock on the door.

"Oh, this is absolutely *charming*," the Colonel said, gazing around after we'd ushered him into our only armchair and I'd offered him a cup of tea. "No, thank you, Sophie, very kind of you, but I'm afraid I can only stay a moment."

This was a relief, as I'd just remembered I'd used the last

of the milk in my bread-and-butter pudding. Veronica and I seated ourselves on the sofa and gave him expectant looks.

"The thing is," the Colonel said, "I've just been speaking to a chap I know in the Foreign Office, Veronica, and he's looking for someone who can speak Spanish. All his best translators have been called up, so he's very keen to find someone to replace them—especially someone with diplomatic experience."

"Diplomatic experience?" said Veronica, one eyebrow arching.

"Well, you certainly have *that*. I doubt if anyone else in his department has addressed the Council of the League of Nations, and you definitely know your way around the Foreign Office by now."

"But I thought the Foreign Office barred women from all jobs except typing and cleaning?"

"Well, yes," the Colonel conceded, "they do. But there's some pretty fierce lobbying going on behind the scenes to allow women to apply for higher-grade temporary posts, at least while the war's in progress. Anyway, here's my friend's card. He's expecting you to telephone him on Monday. I'm sure he'll be able to work something out—he's very resourceful. And Sophie, my dear, I haven't forgotten you. You can cook, can't you?"

"No!" I said quickly. I was imagining being asked to run a factory canteen, or cook meals at an army training camp, or something equally alarming and impossible.

"Oh, but Julia said you had lots of experience at it," he said, glancing at a smear of egg I'd neglected to wipe off my jersey. "And what's that delicious smell coming from the kitchen? Besides, it's not so much being able to cook as knowing about food. And being able to write, apparently. So, of course, I thought of you straightaway."

"What job is it?" I asked warily.

"I'm afraid I don't have *all* the details, but I do know it's at the Ministry of Food. I hope you don't mind, but I've put your name down for an interview on Thursday morning at eleven. Here's the name of the person in charge."

"An interview?" I said, staring at the piece of paper. "But . . . but I haven't even finished my secretarial course yet! My shorthand's terrible and I—"

"Oh, I'm sure that won't matter. They must have plenty of other girls to do that sort of thing. Well, I must be on my way—there's an aeroplane waiting for me at Croydon. Give my best to Toby and Simon, won't you, and to Henry?" And off he went.

!

The symbol above is my own personal shorthand for "I'm completely terrified about this interview, because I know I have ZERO qualifications for the job, whatever it might turn out to be, but how can I possibly get out of this without annoying the Ministry of Food people, and besides, the Colonel has the insane idea that I'm a competent and intelligent person and I'd hate to disillusion him."

See how my shorthand system is far more efficient than Pitman's?

24th October 1939

I had the loveliest surprise for my birthday tea on Sunday—
Toby had a forty-eight-hour leave pass and drove down
to London. He brought with him a bottle of champagne, a
chocolate-and-hazelnut log, and Julia. Veronica had already
bought a Victoria sponge, so there was an abundance of cake,
which is always a good thing. We took the remains of the
sponge to school yesterday and had a second party in our luncheon break, so my nineteenth birthday has now been thoroughly celebrated.

Toby looks amazingly grown-up in his RAF uniform, but
is otherwise unchanged. He says life in the air force is just like
boarding school—stodgy food, a complete lack of privacy, and
tyrants barking out illogical orders all the time.

"The flying makes up for it, though," he said. "We're in the
air all the time. Formation flying, spins, forced landings, night
flying, everything. It's brilliant! Well, except for the night flying, which is a bit of a strain. One can't see a thing apart from

one's instruments, of course, so it takes a lot of concentration. But I just need more practice at it. And oh—daytime flying! There's nothing like it. Taking off on a dull afternoon and popping up through the clouds into a whole new world. Endless blue sky stretched out above, fluffy white carpet beneath, the sun beating down till it's too hot to bear, then sliding open the canopy and getting a blast of freezing air. Absolute *heaven*."

"You're worse than Ant," said Julia, giving him a fond, exasperated look.

"I heard *he's* had a go at flying a Spitfire, the lucky devil," said Toby. "Was that his squadron that shot down those Junkers over the Firth of Forth this week?"

"No, and he's furious about it," said Julia. "Did you see the *Daily Express*? 'Saturday Afternoon Airmen Shoot Nazi Bombers Down.' The first enemy planes are brought down by auxiliaries, and *he* wasn't part of it. One would think he'd been cheated out of his turn in some sort of *game*."

"But it *is*, darling, the biggest game in the world," said Toby, tipping the rest of the champagne into her teacup (as we don't own any wineglasses). "Oh, and I forgot to tell you the funniest thing! I was talking to the commanding officer who recommended me for fighter pilot training, and do you know why he chose *me* out of dozens of others? He said he came into the mess one evening and saw me playing the piano! Apparently, he's always on the lookout for good pianists and horsemen and yachtsmen, because they've got the right touch to handle a fighter plane. It's all about good eye-hand coordination and rapid reflexes, he reckons—although he must have watched me fly as well."

"What are the other pilots like?" Veronica asked.

"They're great. A real mix. The usual lot from Eton and Harrow, but also some who've worked their way up from the volunteer reserves. We've got a former aircraft apprentice from Manchester, two Australians—they're completely mad, but loads of fun—a Canadian, even a Czech. He's the eldest, he's twenty-five. The youngest is barely eighteen, but he's a bloody good flyer—totally fearless."

"I hope *you* remember to be afraid," said Julia. "You do realize how dangerous it is, flying an aeroplane?"

"Not half as dangerous as being one of your patients," said Toby. Julia had been telling us about the first aid course she's doing, and how she'd tied the bandages on the poor volunteer so tightly that she couldn't get them off and his leg turned blue. This reminded her that she had to get up very early the next morning, so she said she'd better go. Toby decided to stay the night at her house, after giving our sofa a dubious look.

"But Toby," Julia said, widening her eyes, "aren't you *madly* in love with me? Won't it drive you *insane* with frustrated passion to be sleeping under my roof, knowing I'm all alone in the next room, wearing nothing but a flimsy negligee?"

Toby said he'd try to restrain himself. Then he hugged Veronica and me goodbye, and we went out to watch him drive off extremely slowly in his Lagonda, cursing the blackout all the while, as Julia waved out the passenger window at us.

Apart from large quantities of delicious cake, my birthday also brought lovely presents from Julia (the most beautiful silk scarf and a little opal brooch), Rupert (a carved pencil box, perfect for keeping all my school supplies together), and Veronica (a morocco-bound *Complete Poetical Works of John Keats*, which was extremely selfless of her, because she loathes the Romantics and thinks Keats the most morbid and sentimental of them all). Aunt Charlotte sent a check and a long letter about how frantically busy she is with her WVS work, and how much things have changed in Dorset since the war began. She disapproves of most change on principle, of course, although she's very pleased they're going to cover up the naked Cerne Abbas Giant that's cut into the chalk hillside near Dorchester, because she thinks he's unbearably rude. Apparently, there's a danger the Luftwaffe might use him (and his enormous phallus) as a landmark to navigate. I read this out to Toby and Julia, and they just about fell off their chairs laughing.

I also had a letter from Henry, written on the back of some lined paper torn from an exercise book (the other side was covered with blotchy sums and a great many red-inked corrections). She said she'd almost finished cross-stitching a bookmark for me in sewing class, but she kept pricking her fingers, and when she tried to wipe the dots of blood off the linen, they went all smeary and brown, so she wasn't sure I'd still want it. She seems to have made a lot of friends, but has already set a school record for the number of demerits collected in a single term. Pupils acquire these for such grave sins as failing to fold their counterpanes neatly at the ends of their beds, wearing hair ribbons of the wrong shade of blue, whistling, chewing gum, and talking in the corridors. If a girl has collected five demerits, she's sent to the headmistress for a lecture, which reduces most pupils to tears and elicits fervent vows to mend their ways. Henry has had twenty-two demerits, and shows no sign of even noticing what she's done wrong. Still, she seems happy enough, which is a relief.

Simon sent a letter, too. I'd like to say *he* sounded happy, but he didn't. He said he was "making progress with the aeroplanes" and that the rest of his time was "usefully occupied." Simon, unlike Toby, doesn't seem to be a natural at flying. Simon's feet are too firmly planted on the ground, I think. I can't imagine him actually being *incompetent* at anything, but I *can* see him working away doggedly at something he disliked, simply because he saw it as his duty—or as a stepping-stone to some higher position. I bet he hates being ordered about by the commanding officers. Anyway, he sent birthday wishes and thanked me for talking to the matron of Rebecca's clinic, following Rebecca's latest drama. The staff and patients recently moved north, to a place further inland. Rebecca wasn't very pleased about it, but then, she's not very pleased about anything right now. She went berserk when the matron told her that Simon had joined the RAF, and now she's not speaking to any of the staff. Apparently, she spends most of her time on her knees, muttering furiously at a little wooden crucifix on her bedside table. Poor Rebecca, she was born in the wrong era. A thousand years ago, people would have venerated her as a saint. Instead, she's locked up in a mental asylum, with doctors prescribing her sedatives and therapists trying to get her to take an interest in the clinic's sock-knitting circle.

And now thinking of Rebecca and her grim life has shattered all my lovely, shiny birthday feelings. Oh, how fleeting is Pleasure! "And Joy, whose hand is ever at his lips, bidding adieu . . ."

I am going to lie on the sofa, sunk in melancholy over Keats dying of consumption in a foreign land when he was only twenty-five and never getting to marry the love of his life. And also, fret about my looming job interview.

23rd November 1939

Another long and tedious day at the Ministry of Food, made bearable only by the thought that it's Thursday, rather than Monday. Sometimes I can't understand why Veronica and I argued so fervently to be allowed to work in London . . . No, I do. It was to help the war effort. Which *is* important, even if nothing very war-like seems to be happening. I'm just in a grumpy mood because I spent the entire day removing apostrophes where Mr. Bowker had erroneously added them, then retyping all the pages, then putting them in his tray, then having him summon me to his office so he could deliver yet another lecture about punctuation. This from a man who can't tell the difference between possessive *its* and contracted *it's*, who gets *affect* and *effect* confused, who spells *necessary* without a *c*! Why on earth is *he* in charge of editing the food information sheets, anyway?

Well, I suppose it's the same reason *I'm* working at the

Ministry—because we both have friends in high places. Apparently, Mr. Bowker is the son of a Very Important Parliamentarian, and *something* needed to be found for him to do. He used to work as an advertising copywriter, and he hasn't been called up because he has flat feet. He tells everyone how *unusually flat* his feet are (I once got in a lift with him, and he told a complete stranger standing next to us). I'm not even sure what flat feet *are*. Not that I'm planning to ask him about it—I'd have to suffer through hours of explanation if I did.

The others in my department are nicer, or at least more competent. There's a brisk lady called Miss Halliday, who does most of the work that Mr. Bowker is supposed to do, as well as her actual job, which is liaising with the people in the Ministry of Food kitchens and the scientific staff. Miss Halliday owns a dozen near-identical navy-blue suits and crisp white blouses, and her hair never moves at all—it looks as though a sheet of corrugated iron has been curved over her head and nailed into position with hairpins. There's also Mr. Bowker's secretary, Miss Thynne, who is rather fat, and two other editorial assistants, Felicity and Anne. They are all what Aunt Charlotte might call "our sort of people" if she were in a generous mood—that is, Mr. Bowker went to Marlborough, and the others to finishing schools. Felicity and Anne keep crêpe de Chine evening dresses and silver dancing shoes in their lockers downstairs so that they can race off to Claridge's straight after work to meet their boyfriends for dinner, and then spend the rest of the evening careening from nightclub to nightclub. They've invited me along, but so far, I've always said no. They're a few years older and far more glamorous than I am, and it's a bit worrying when they say they'll get their boyfriends to bring along a "spare man" for me. I usually go home to cook dinner and do some laundry and labor away at my shorthand, but Felicity and Anne are convinced I'm sneaking off to meet a secret lover, and they take great delight in teasing me about him.

I suppose I ought to describe my work in more detail. Well, the day I started was the day that Mr. Morrison, the Minister of Food, announced what *Picture Post* called "the most unpopular Government decision since the war began"—that is, that food rationing will start in a few months. Britain imports a lot of its food, you see, and the German U-boats are doing their best to sink all our supply ships, so we'll soon run out of things to eat unless the government takes action. Most of the people working at the Ministry are engaged in sending out ration books to householders, or having meetings with shopkeepers and farmers about the new regulations, or setting up Local Food Offices all over the country. However, my department is in charge of Food Education. It's our job to inform housewives how to cook a week's worth of meals with only four ounces of butter and twelve ounces of sugar, and to convince the British public that turnips and carrots and brown bread are far more delicious (and patriotic) than steak and bananas and chocolate cake. There is still debate about how we are to achieve these seemingly impossible goals, but the plan is that there will be official "Food

Facts" articles printed in the newspapers, and recipe booklets, and a poster campaign. Today I spent the morning proofreading a pamphlet extolling the virtues of oatmeal, while Felicity and Anne worked on a booklet about the vitamin content of various root vegetables. Mr. Bowker sits in his office, supervising us editorial assistants and (more enthusiastically) unleashing his creative energies on potential publicity campaigns. Yesterday, he showed me a sketch of his "Potato People," who had little legs and round, cheery faces and were singing a song about how "delicious and nutritious" boiled potatoes are. I'm not sure that making vegetables more human-like would motivate *me* to eat them in greater quantities, but at least it's keeping Mr. Bowker occupied. The more time he spends drawing spats and top hats on dancing potatoes, the less time he has to mess up my pamphlets with random apostrophes.

Veronica's job at the Foreign Office sounds more interesting than mine, but also more challenging. At her interview, they asked her actual questions (that is, questions other than "When can you start?"), and she had to do a written and oral examination in Spanish. The gentleman in charge told her she had an "aristocratic accent"—apparently that is a good thing, now that the Fascists have taken over in Spain. Officially she's a "clerical assistant," because it's against regulations for women to do anything but typing, but she actually translates letters and documents. Her boss, an old friend of the Colonel's, has lots of long luncheon meetings at expensive restaurants, and sometimes he'll say, "Miss FitzOsborne, I'll need you to accompany me as an interpreter," even though he speaks perfectly good Spanish. Then it always turns out that the Spanish businessman or government official whom they're meeting either knew Veronica's grandfather (who was a Spanish duke), or her mother, Isabella (who seems to have been the Spanish equivalent of Debutante of the Year, with a dash of Tallulah Bankhead). The lunchtime conversations never appear to have anything to do with the war or the government, but her boss says that maintaining amicable relations with influential Spaniards is helping keep Spain away from the Germans and out of the war. I asked Veronica if the Spaniards were all ardent Fascists, because I couldn't imagine her being polite to them if they were, but she said they don't seem to be. Although perhaps they're simply toning down their Fascism while they're here, so the British will agree to help them rebuild their country? Things must be in a dreadful mess over there, after three years of civil war. One wouldn't think Spain would be in any position to join another war, just yet. Anyway, Veronica says that she enjoys her work because there's always some fascinating political argument raging about the office, as well as interesting archives to read in her spare moments.

The other advantage of her job is that her office at Whitehall is just down the road from Daniel's. One of the first jobs his department did was to translate some propaganda into German, informing the German people that their Nazi leadership was corrupt, insane, bankrupt, and doomed to lose the war. Then the RAF dropped millions of these leaflets all over Germany.

I'm not sure what this was meant to achieve. Dampen general morale? Inspire the population to rise up and overthrow Hitler? I expect the Germans are using the leaflets as loo paper. Still, Daniel's colleagues must have done good work, because when Göring gave a speech about the "laughable flyleaves" that Britain keeps dumping on his country, he had to admit they were written in excellent German. Göring said they must have been produced by Jews and "other scoundrels," which made Daniel laugh. Daniel also found it amusing that when the newspaper reporters here asked what the pamphlets said, the British government refused to tell them. The government spokesman claimed it was classified information, and that to tell the British press about it would be to risk valuable knowledge reaching the enemy—even though about six million of the pamphlets had just been dropped on Germany.

Apparently, it would also benefit the enemy if the government told British citizens where their recently arrived relatives were being imprisoned, because Daniel still doesn't know where his cousins are, or when they will be released. Daniel keeps saying truth is the first casualty of war, which I *think* is a quote from someone important, but could simply be his own Socialist cynicism coming to the fore. I *am* beginning to see his point, though.

5th December 1939

The Colonel came to see me at work today. I think he's the only person in the world, with the possible exception of the Minister of Food himself, who could have persuaded Miss Halliday to let me start my luncheon break fifteen minutes early. Felicity and Anne pricked up their ears and craned their heads towards the door when they heard, subsiding (only slightly) when they saw the Colonel was old enough to be my father. Perhaps I ought to have explained to them that he very nearly *was* my father. Although I suppose if he'd married my mother, I'd be an entirely different person—not a FitzOsborne, perhaps not even a Sophie.

I waited till he and I had signed ourselves out at the Ministry desk and stepped into Portman Square before I said, "Well?"

"Well, what?" he said. "I just happened to be passing by and thought we might go for a stroll in Hyde Park. As it's such a lovely day."

I glanced around. It wasn't actually raining, but the sky was the color of tarnished silver, and the gentleman in front of us had just had his hat snatched off his head by a cruel wind. The hat was rolling along the footpath and the gentleman, trying to preserve his dignity, was walking very fast rather than running, bending down at intervals with outstretched hand only to watch his hat get tugged out of reach yet again. Then an especially strong gust made us all stagger, and when I'd re-fastened my coat, I saw the hat had blown onto the road and been squashed flat by a motorcar.

"Yes, lovely weather," I said, shaking my head at the Colonel.

He smiled, took my arm, and led me across the road. "Tell me, how's your job going?"

I explained I'd spent the morning toiling away at the Carrot Campaign. "Here's the slogan my boss has produced, after working on it for an entire fortnight. Are you ready? 'Carrots keep you healthy and help you to see in the blackout.' Brilliant, isn't it? And he keeps putting an apostrophe in 'carrots'."

"*Do* they help one see in the dark?" asked the Colonel, looking as though he were trying not to laugh.

"I don't know. They've got vitamin A in them, and I think a deficiency of that causes night blindness. But that doesn't mean nibbling on a carrot makes one instantly able to see in the blackout. If that were true, I'd be devouring them by the bucketful."

"Well, I'm sure it'll be very worthwhile, this campaign."

"Yes, absolutely *vital* to the war effort," I said. "Hitler will be shaking in his boots when he realizes our secret weapons are *carrots*, no apostrophe. I wouldn't be at all surprised if my work is the one thing holding him back from invading the rest of Europe."

"So," the Colonel said, "you feel you ought to be doing more?"

I stopped, directly under Marble Arch, and stared at him. "I knew it. I knew you had some scheme in mind."

"Oh, Sophia, what a suspicious look!" he said, steering me towards the park. "You act as though I were about to ask you to parachute into Berlin! No, no, I was simply going to inquire how your friend Kick was doing."

"Kick Kennedy?" I said. "She's all right, I think. She's studying art and design now, at a college in New York. Why?"

"Ah, you *do* write to her, then. I don't suppose you ever drop in at the Embassy these days?"

"No, why would I? I only ever went there to meet Kick."

"Hmm," he said. We'd wandered quite a way into the park, off the main pathway. "Well, perhaps—and this is mere speculation on my part, of course—perhaps you've bought her a Christmas gift. But the postal services are awfully slow these days, and you're not entirely sure it will get there in time, so you're planning to deliver it to her father and ask *him* to send it off in the next diplomatic bag."

"If you need to send a package to New York," I said slowly, "you surely have dozens of methods that are more reliable than that."

"Oh, *I* don't want to send anything," he said. "I just want you to have an excuse to visit the Embassy."

"Why?"

He glanced over his shoulder. The few people in sight were scurrying along with their heads bent into the wind, concerned only with getting under shelter before it started to rain. No one was within earshot. "Because I'd like to know what's going on there," the Colonel said. "A copy of a certain document has turned up where it ought not to be, and I suspect someone at the American Embassy is responsible."

"Not . . . *Mr. Kennedy?*" I breathed.

"Oh, no. He's certainly doing his best to cozy up to the Germans, but he's quite open about that. No, it must be one of his staff."

"Well, why don't you go there yourself and find out?" I asked.

"Because the Ambassador knows who I am and what I do, and he doesn't much like it. He wouldn't allow me to set so much as a toe inside the Embassy unless I had a pile of evidence and an arrest warrant. And I can't say I blame him. At the moment, all I'm going by is intuition, and I don't have the resources to keep every member of his staff under surveillance."

"But . . . I mean . . . what would I have to do?" I had a ludicrous image of myself creeping about the Embassy, picking the locks of filing cabinets with a hatpin.

"Oh, nothing at all out of the ordinary," he assured me. "Simply get yourself invited to a couple of Embassy cocktail parties, chat to as many of the staff as possible, ask them how they think the war's going, find out if any of them have visited Germany or Italy in recent months—"

"I don't know," I said uneasily. "I really don't think I'd be any good at that. Perhaps you should ask Veronica instead."

"*You're* the one Mr. Kennedy knows," he said. "You're his daughter's friend. Anyway, Veronica's too conspicuous."

"You mean, I'm forgettable."

"I *mean*, you're far more discreet and observant than she is, and she'd only get into an argument about Fascism and give the game away. No, you're perfect for the job, Sophie. You've the sort of innocent, trustworthy face that makes people confide in you. Just be your usual, interested self and I'm certain you'll discover all kinds of useful things." Raindrops began to darken the ground and the Colonel shook open his enormous black umbrella. "Come on, I'll walk you back. It's terribly kind of you to help me out this way."

"But . . . but I haven't said I'll do it!" I said, even though of course I knew I *would*. How could I refuse the Colonel anything, when he's done so much for us? The problem was that I didn't share any of his faith in my abilities. "I mean, even if I hear something suspicious, what am I expected to do about it? I don't even know where you work."

"I'll give you a telephone number. Tell whoever answers it that Colonel Stanley-Ross needs to contact 'Elizabeth,' then hang up. Can you remember this?" And he repeated the number till I had it. "Now—pay attention to names and faces, but don't write anything down, except in Kernetin. You're looking for someone with Fascist connections, probably a member of the British Union, the Right Club, the Nordic League, or the Anglo-German Fellowship. They might also mention something called The Link. Show an interest, but don't sound *too* enthusiastic. If anyone invites you to a meeting, get all the details, then telephone me at once, but don't, under any circumstances, agree to meet anyone outside the Embassy."

I must have looked completely overwhelmed.

"Oh, my dear!" he said. "Sophie, I *promise* it's perfectly safe. The worst that could happen is that you don't discover anything."

"No, the worst would be that they realize your lot are onto them and they get scared off."

"Then they'll stop what they're doing, which is what we want. But why would they harbor any suspicions about you? A well-born young lady, a close friend of the Kennedy children, dropping in to the Embassy to say hello? And I really think Mr. Kennedy will be pleased to see you. He hardly gets invited anywhere these days, he's so unpopular."

"He thinks we're going to lose the war."

"Yes, although there *are* a lot of Americans, including his President, who disagree with him—"

But I was too busy wondering how I was going to manage this whole thing to care much about American politics. "I'll have to tell Veronica, you realize," I said. "Otherwise, she'll think I've gone completely mad, hanging about the Embassy all the time."

"Yes, I expected that," he said. "I trust her. Just make sure she doesn't tell anyone else, not even that Communist boyfriend of hers."

"He's not a Communist . . . and how do you know about him, anyway?"

"Who do you think recommended him for that job?"

I sent the Colonel a look of mingled respect and exasperation. "Do you know *everything* about *everybody*?"

He pretended to consider this as we crossed the road. "Hmm. Not *absolutely* everything. For instance, while I *do* know my favorite nephew is returning to London on Friday, I've no idea whether you'd have dinner with him, if he were to ask you."

"I'm sure I would," I said. "If he asked." I always enjoy chatting with Rupert, and eating my own cooking is starting to get very boring.

"Then I must remind him to ask," said the Colonel. "He's turned out quite handsome, hasn't he? People say he bears a remarkable resemblance to me . . . although he has a nicer personality, of course."

"Much nicer," I said, smiling. "He's not as devious, for one thing."

"Yes, he completely missed out on the Stanley-Ross sneakiness. I think Julia got the lot. Well, here's where I must leave you. Give my regards to that charming Miss Halliday. Goodbye, Sophie—and good luck with that thing."

!!!

No need to translate *that* bit of shorthand.

15th December 1939

Back from a cocktail party at the American Embassy, which was a complete waste of time. This is especially galling, given how much nerve it took me to walk through the doors in the first place. I'd been to Embassy parties before, of course, but always trailing in the wake of Toby and Veronica, knowing that Kick or Jack would be around to chat with me. Still, I suppose it was some consolation that I didn't have to fight off Joe Junior tonight. Not even Joe Senior was present, despite the Ambassador being the one who'd actually invited me to the party, when I'd delivered Kick's gift earlier this week. Poor man, he *did* seem lonely. Whatever faults he may have, he absolutely dotes on his children and must miss them terribly. He's now on his way back to the States for meetings with the President and to spend Christmas with his family. Of course, this meant that there wasn't a single familiar face in the room when I entered, and I had to approach a *complete stranger* and *start a conversation*. It probably won't go down in history as one of those great acts of wartime courage, but for the record, I just want to say here that I think I was *quite brave*.

"So, how do you think the war's going?" I said casually, after the young man I'd accosted had fetched us both a drink.

"It doesn't seem to be going anywhere at all," he said, which was pretty much what I'd thought, and therefore not very enlightening. Then I made the mistake of asking him which part of the United States he was from.

"Vancouver," he snapped. It turned out he worked at the Canadian High Commission. Well, how was I meant to be able to tell the difference between an American and a Canadian accent? Anyway, he *could* have been sneaking off to photograph files whenever he came over to the Embassy for drinks, so I made a mental note of his name (and added it to my new dossier when I arrived home). Then I spent most of the rest of the evening with a group of glamorous Embassy secretaries. The conversation largely consisted of the same sort of office gossip that I heard at the Ministry of Food—who was in line for promotion, who ought to be sacked for incompetence, who was having an affair with whom—but was even less interesting because all the names were unfamiliar. Then the three of them moved on to a discussion of various American film stars and I tuned out for a while. I couldn't help thinking of last Friday, when I'd had dinner with Rupert and we'd talked about books and animals and our respective families. There was no question as to which experience had been more enjoyable—but I reminded myself firmly that I was doing important war work and tuned back in to the conversation, which had progressed to a debate about the superiority of nylon stockings over silk. They were awfully nice girls, though, I must say, and they did invite me to their Christmas drinks next week, so perhaps I'll hear something more useful then. And in the meantime, at least being invited to the American Embassy for drinks has raised my social standing in the eyes of Felicity and Anne.

24th December 1939

This is the coldest Christmas I can remember, although I'm not sure if it's the weather or simply the lack of heating here at Milford Park. My breath forms a white haze in the frigid air, the water in the vase on my dressing table has frozen solid, and I had to knock icicles out of my toothbrush this morning. But coal has become frightfully expensive, and I suppose there's no point keeping the central heating going when hardly any rooms are being used. There's a fire lit at the start of each day in the breakfast room, where we have all our meals now, and another in the kitchen. I suspect Aunt Charlotte has a fire in her bedroom at night, too, but I don't like to ask for one in my own room—the poor solitary housemaid is rushed off her feet as it is, without having extra grates to clean and coal scuttles to fill. So I've piled another three blankets and my dressing gown upon my bed, keep a thermos on my bedside table to top up my hot-water bottle, and wear a coat and mittens indoors as well as out. And I'm still *absolutely freezing*.

Some women from the village come in daily to do the laundry and help with the cleaning, and there's a kitchen maid for the cook, but otherwise, there are hardly any indoor staff left. Even Harkness the butler, who seemed as much a fixture of Milford Park as the marble flooring, has gone off to France—the brigadier for whom he was a batman during the last war asked for him especially. Barnes is still here, of course, acting as a combination of housekeeper, butler, lady's maid, and secretary. But many of the rooms have had to be shut up to save on cleaning—the furniture shrouded in dust sheets, the chandeliers enveloped in velvet bags, the carpets rolled up, the windows shuttered.

I was surprised that Aunt Charlotte, with her absolute mania for keeping up standards, had permitted all this. However, she's so busy with her WVS work that I'm not sure she's even noticed. The evacuees went back to London weeks ago (summoned home by parents who couldn't see the point of their families being separated when there's no sign of any bombs), but Aunt Charlotte is still in charge of the village sock-knitting campaign, the bandage-rolling roster, the paper salvage scheme and so on. She's also turned the Milford Park stables into a school to train racing horses and hunters to pull wagons and plows. Now that petrol rationing has started, horses will be needed more and more, to take the place of tractors, delivery vans, private motorcars, even the local bus. It's as though England has slipped backwards by about half a century, and Aunt Charlotte couldn't be more pleased. She much prefers horses to motor vehicles (indeed, to most human beings), and this way, she gets to keep her own favorite horses close at hand, out of reach of the war. Lady Bosworth is furious she didn't think of the idea herself, because a dozen of *her* best hunters have just been requisitioned by the army to be trained as officers' mounts. Aunt Charlotte's first pupil was Lightning, Henry's pony. He has settled into his new job quite happily and is now the household's main conveyance. He and Henry met Veronica and me at the railway station yesterday morning.

"It's a bit colder than the Daimler," Henry admitted. "But I threw in one of Aunt Charlotte's old furs for you to wrap around yourselves—there it is, on top of those sacks. Just pretend you're in a sleigh, Sophie, like in that Russian novel."

"You mean *Anna Karenina*?" I said as we jolted off, although the situation bore a much closer resemblance to *Cold Comfort Farm*. I was sharing my half of the cart with two empty milk canisters, some spare parts for the water pump, and a crate of unhappy chickens. But after three months of gray old London, it was a refreshing change to be jogging through this bright landscape, the trees and hedges frosted with new snow, the icy road glittering like diamonds; to be taking great gulps of bracing country air scented with horses and hay rather than breathing in coal dust and petrol fumes. Meanwhile, Henry shouted the news at us over her shoulder. Toby had a week's leave and was driving down that day; Simon only had forty-eight hours off, so was going to visit his mother instead; Carlos, who's taken to following Barnes around, insisted on "helping" her decorate the

Christmas tree, then got tangled in tinsel and nearly brought the whole thing down on her head; the cook was threatening to resign; and Estella the pig was pregnant.

"I've told her she can't have the piglets till Easter, when I'm home from school," yelled Henry. "But she's awfully stubborn, it'd be just like her to have them the week before. Do you think Aunt Charlotte would let me miss a few weeks of term, just in case? Because I really think—look! Isn't that *Toby's* car by the front door?"

She brought Lightning to a halt, then hurled herself off the cart and into the arms of her favorite person in the world.

"You must have driven a hundred miles an hour!" she exclaimed. "Or did you leave at four o'clock in the—Toby! You've got your *wings!*"

"Have I?" he said, glancing down at himself. "Oh, I wondered why they'd sewn that badge above my pocket . . ."

"Congratulations, Toby!" I said, hugging him, then handing him over to Veronica.

"Well done, Pilot Officer FitzOsborne." She held him at arm's length so she could admire his tunic. "When did this happen?"

"Wednesday," he said, breaking into an enormous grin. "You wouldn't believe how nervous I was before the test, but everything went like a dream. At one point, the instructor cut the throttle, to see how I'd manage a forced landing, and I'd practiced so much, I didn't even have to *think* about what to do. It just happened." He shook his head, looking slightly stunned but very, very pleased with himself. And I understood then how hard he had worked at this, and what a lovely, new experience it must be for him to have *earned* a prize rather than merely having it handed to him by right of birth.

"I can't wait to tell everyone at school!" Henry was saying. "There's this awful girl in my dorm called Loretta, who's always showing off about her brother being a captain in the boring old army, and now I can say *my* brother flies fighters in the RAF!"

"Steady on," said Toby, leaning around her to lift our suitcases off the cart. "I still have a bit more training to go before I get posted to a squadron."

Good, I almost said, before I bit my tongue. I didn't want to spoil a moment of this for him. And I consoled myself with the fact that there wasn't any fighting going on at all, not at the moment—none involving us or the Germans, at any rate. The Bore War, people have started calling it, the Phony War. Perhaps the whole thing would be over before Toby—or Simon, or Anthony, or anyone else—had to fly into battle.

But then, after I'd unpacked and run back downstairs, I discovered Toby in the hall, pulling on a heavy coat.

"Where are you off to?" I asked, staring at him. "And what on earth are you *wearing?*"

"Aren't I the very picture of a dashing young squire?" he said, swiveling to display his tweeds. "I'm going over to Lord Bosworth's to shoot pheasants."

"But you hate shooting!"

"Yes," he said, "but I need to learn how to do it." He took

down a cap from the hatstand. "I realized that this week, Soph. It's all very well being an expert at aerobatics, but the point of going up there is to shoot other planes down, and I'm not sure the instructors are teaching us anything useful about that. We've practiced aiming at a stationary target, but I can't believe the Luftwaffe pilots are simply going to sit there like lumps, waiting for us to take potshots at them. I think it has to be more like shooting birds, where one needs to aim ahead so they fly into the bullets . . . Anyway, that's what I'm going to learn about now. Lord B was awfully nice when I telephoned, said he'd take me out himself and give me some pointers." Then Toby caught sight of my expression. "Oh, don't worry, Soph. I promise not to shoot anyone in the foot."

It wasn't *that* I was worried about. But I plastered on a smile.

"Well, bring back lots to eat!" I said brightly. "Henry told us the cook's been complaining that the Christmas goose isn't big enough, and Aunt Charlotte really wants it to be a dinner to remember this year. I think the WVS rule book says it's unpatriotic to skimp on Christmas cheer."

"I'll do my best," Toby said as he tugged open the front door. "Ugh, it's *glacial* out here! The sacrifices a man must make . . . Oh, and don't tell Henry about this, will you? Or Rupert. They'll have the RSPCA onto me, for cruelty to pheasants."

Then I watched my gentle, sweet-tempered brother run down the steps, off to teach himself how to be an efficient killer.

So, even though I'm not entirely sure I'd call myself a Christian, I went to church this morning to pray for peace.

Kneeling there, I realized I didn't want *merely* peace, but also justice for the people of Czechoslovakia and Poland; Montmaray to be returned to us; the Germans to understand how evil Hitler is; and Stalin and Mussolini to stop invading places like Finland and Albania. Then (because we *do* seem stuck with war, for the time being), I thought I might as well pray that all the boys I knew in the services would be kept safe, that Rebecca would get used to Simon being in the RAF and become less miserable, and that I would stop feeling so awkward at Embassy cocktail parties and actually manage to uncover the spy who was causing such problems for the Colonel.

Poor God, dealing with humans and their impossible, endless demands! I know He's meant to be omnipotent, but even so, He must get a bit fed up sometimes, especially on Sunday mornings.

20th January 1940

The Colonel invited himself over to our flat for tea this afternoon. I'd planned to bake some biscuits, but all the recipes in Mrs. *Beeton* make a mockery of our minuscule food ration ("First, take a pound of butter and half a pound of sugar . . ."). Fortunately, the Colonel arrived with a large tin of shortbread, a jar of honey, and another of raspberry jam, all courtesy of Lady Astley.

"I know rationing is essential for the war effort and we ought to be embracing it and so forth," he said, "but thank heavens I have relatives with their own farm and a well-stocked larder. Are you very busy at work now, Sophie?"

"Frantic," I said. "But I feel like the Red Queen, running as fast as I can simply to stay in the same spot. And none of us *dares* tell anyone outside the office that we work for the Ministry of Food—otherwise, we get bombarded with complaints about how the shopkeeper cut too many coupons from their ration book, or that there weren't any eggs left after they'd queued for an hour. As though *we* can do anything about that! We're all dreading the start of meat rationing."

"Morale's that bad, is it?" said the Colonel. "Well, if it helps, I doubt Morrison will be Minister of Food much longer. And what's happening in your department, Veronica?"

"Nothing much, except a lot of rumors flying round about the Duke of Windsor," she said. "What's he doing visiting England, anyway? The Palace must be furious—didn't they create some harmless job with the Allied War Committee in Paris to keep him out of the way? Now everyone's saying he wants to open peace negotiations with the Germans."

"He's bored, poor chap, and terribly homesick," said the Colonel. "And he has a great need to feel important."

"Then he shouldn't have abdicated," said Veronica, "especially not in order to marry that dreadful American woman. Is it true, what they say about her links to the Nazis?"

The Colonel always knows the inside story, so he's marvelous to have around when one wants a good long gossip—although both he and Veronica insist it's not gossip, but serious political discussion. Another of today's conversational subjects was Unity Mitford, who's arrived here from Munich on a stretcher—too "ill" to be arrested or interrogated, even though she's an unequivocal Nazi.

"One of the girls at work is convinced that Unity is pregnant," I said. "And that it's Hitler's baby."

"Nonsense," said the Colonel. "She shot herself in the head because she couldn't bear to see England at war with Germany.

I read the doctor's report myself—it's a wonder she survived. It's her parents I feel sorry for."

"I know, how awful for them," I said. "I even feel a bit sorry for *her*. Imagine the desperate state of her mind, to do such a thing."

"Oh, honestly, Sophie!" said Veronica impatiently. "She knew full well what she was doing, just as she did when she was running about declaring all the Jews ought to be thrown out of England. What infuriates *me* is that she and her Fascist sister and that revolting Mosley person remain at perfect liberty, while anti-Nazis like Daniel's cousins are locked up on the Isle of Man!"

Daniel has just discovered that both his cousins were assessed by a tribunal last month and judged to be a security risk, because one of them had been a member of the Communist Party years ago, at university. They weren't allowed the services of a lawyer or an interpreter at the hearing and must have found it very difficult to protest their innocence in English, their third or fourth language. If only Daniel could have been there! And it's such a *waste*, when they speak German and one of them's a scientist—surely they could be helping with the war effort, if they were free.

"I know it's frustrating," said the Colonel. "But there's a committee being set up to review cases like theirs. They *will* be released—it's simply a matter of time. And I assure you, Unity Mitford is bedridden and in no state to answer any questions, let alone spy for the Nazis. I wouldn't worry too much about the Mosleys, either—someone's keeping a careful eye on them. And speaking of which . . ."

Veronica jumped up and began to clatter teacups onto the tray. "I think I'll do the washing up now," she announced. "In the kitchen, by myself. I shall do it VERY LOUDLY." She marched off with a great rattle of china, and the Colonel chuckled.

"I fear for your tea set," he said. "Perhaps I ought to arrange some remuneration for you, to cover breakages incurred as a consequence of security arrangements. So, what news?"

"Well," I said, "I don't know if this is worth much, but a girl at the American Embassy mentioned another clerk who's hoping to be posted to Berlin soon. I hardly know him, though."

"What's his name?"

"Mr. Kent. He has one of those first names that sound like a last name, Taylor or Tyler, something like that. Sorry, but you know how difficult it is to hear anything at cocktail parties—especially when everyone's talking American."

"Have you ever spoken with him?"

"Only briefly. He's about thirty, I suppose, well dressed, very loud. I've heard him complaining about the British trying to drag America into 'this hopeless war'—but really, half the Embassy staff feel that way. He *could* just have been trying to ingratiate himself with Mr. Kennedy. He's quite new, only arrived here a couple of months ago."

"That *is* interesting," said the Colonel slowly. "Was his last position in Moscow, by any chance?"

I shook my head. "I'm not sure. Do you know him?"

"Perhaps." The Colonel looked very thoughtful. "I don't suppose you've been invited to the next cocktail party at the Embassy?"

"Not yet, and I'm hoping I won't be," I said. "I'm not very good at cocktail parties, I've discovered—I'm never sure what I'm meant to be doing. It's too noisy to have proper conversations, and it's so difficult to eat those little bits of food they bring round, when one's holding a slippery glass and balancing on high heels and trying to talk. I honestly don't see how anyone could *enjoy* a cocktail party."

"Well, I don't usually attend them wearing high heels," he said, "but the general aim is to get drunk enough not to mind about the noise and the awkward eating arrangements. I don't want you to do *that*, though, so forget about the party. Hmm . . . but you'll want to deliver Kick's birthday present to the Embassy soon, won't you? As it's her birthday on the twentieth of next month?"

"How do you . . . Never mind. I'll telephone you if I find out anything, shall I?"

"I'd be very interested to find out if Mr. Kent has access to any confidential letters or telegrams, if he's had any visitors at the Embassy, and whom he meets outside work. But don't draw any attention to yourself, or to him. It's only if you happen to overhear something."

As if that's the sort of information one tends to *overhear*.

Still, at least *something* useful has finally resulted from all those uncomfortable hours at the Embassy—not that being forced to go to tedious parties is a true hardship, not compared to some of the things other people have to do now. Look at Simon, for example, slogging away at his pilot training so uncomplainingly. Reading between the lines of his letters, he seems to regard his situation as something to be endured, like a visit to the dentist. He doesn't even get much leave, poor thing. That was why I wrote to him, to see if he could make it to a party I want to hold for Veronica's birthday. She will be turning twenty-one, but Aunt Charlotte is completely ignoring this in favor of elaborate (and quite futile) plans for Toby's own coming-of-age. Toby would rather spend his birthday in London with us and Julia than in Milford, but *he* can't get any leave, either.

Really, this *war*! It hasn't even started in earnest yet, and it's already messing up everything for everyone.

How blissful Saturdays would be, if only one weren't forced to fill them with tedious chores. Scrubbing out the bath, sewing a button back on my coat, washing the sheets and draping them all over the kitchen to dry, queuing for half an hour at the greengrocer's and discovering there are no onions to be had for love or money . . .

But now I am settled by the stove with my journal, watching Veronica bat damp sheets out of her way as she searches for her muffler. She is going out to inspect the flower beds and determine whether the ground has thawed enough for us to start planting potatoes. She is being remarkably optimistic, in my opinion. I think spring has decided to give England a miss this year. Anyway, I'd prefer onions to potatoes. Actually, I'd *prefer* smoked salmon sandwiches and chocolate éclairs, but one can't grow those in the garden, unfortunately.

Apart from cleaning and shopping and mending, another of my regular Saturday chores is to write to Henry's headmistress, who does not seem to have grasped the concept of vegetarianism. Henry is supposed to be getting extra cheese and eggs to make up for the lack of meat in her diet, but the headmistress feels that serving Henry separate portions would simply reward her "obstreperous" behavior. Apparently, Henry had been talking very loudly at breakfast about how intelligent, funny, and charming Estella was—while her fellow pupils were trying to eat their bacon ration. After she made two girls cry and another rush off to be sick, Henry was moved to the end of her table and ordered to stay silent during meals. Then, last week, her archenemy Loretta complained that Henry had been "staring at her sausages" in an "accusing" way. Henry has now been banished to the prefects' table. This is meant to be a sign of deepest disgrace, but Henry says she much prefers this arrangement, because the prefects, being older, have far more interesting conversations than the girls in her year.

I fear this is all our fault. Henry has spent so much more time with Veronica and me than with children her own age, and we included her in almost everything we did at Montmaray. Toby, in particular, has always indulged her shamelessly. And Veronica must have been a greater influence than we ever suspected, because Henry has recently started up a vigorous campaign—stirring speeches in the common room, letters to the headmistress, even a petition addressed to the school's Board of Governors—for her portion of the school's meat ration to be packaged up each week and sent to Carlos. She claims it's a violation of her human rights to force her to eat animals or to prevent her giving her "fair, legal share" to anyone or anything that she chooses.

I'm amazed she hasn't been expelled yet, but I think the school likes saying that it counts a Royal Highness amongst its pupils. Also, the headmistress is still too intimidated by Aunt Charlotte to dare suggest to her that Henry might be better off elsewhere. That's why *I'm* the one to whom the headmistress addresses all her complaints.

Not that I mind, really—I did promise Henry I'd do whatever I could to make her school life easier. It's just that I'm beginning to feel a bit weary of dealing with all these adult responsibilities. I keep saying to myself, "But I'm only *nineteen*." (Of course, whenever Aunt Charlotte tries to stop me doing something because I'm too young, I think, very indignantly, "But I am *nineteen* now, you know!") When I was little, I longed and longed to be older, except now I can't recall what exactly it was that I most keenly anticipated. Being allowed to stay up as late as I wanted? To wear or eat or read whatever I pleased? Well, I *could* do all those things now, but mostly I don't—either because I have to get up early for work the next morning, or haven't enough money to buy the outfit I really love, or for some other boring, grown-up reason. Also, children don't realize what a huge proportion of adult life is used up *worrying* about things—from what to make for dinner and whether one's sheets will get dry in time to make the beds that night, to whether one will ever manage to meet the right man and marry him. Shouldn't being a grown-up be slightly more *exhilarating*? Is this the fault of the war? Or is it simply how life *is*?

What a depressing thought . . . but hooray, the telephone's ringing! With some exciting news, I hope!

Much later, nearly midnight.

I wonder if God (or Fate, or whoever) was reading over my shoulder this morning and thinking, *She's always moaning about how dreary her life is. Well, I'll show her. I'll give her* exciting.

I would vow to stop complaining forever if it meant I'd never again have to have a telephone conversation like the one this morning.

"Is that Miss Sophia FitzOsborne?" asked the voice, brisk and female. A nurse, I realized instantly, before I'd even grasped what that could mean. "You're the next of kin of Simon Chester?" she went on.

"Yes," I managed, feeling all the blood draining from my face. "Yes, what's happened?" A horrible rushing sound filled my ears, engulfing most of her words. The name of the hospital, I caught that. Something about surgery and a doctor. Simon couldn't be dead, then! They wouldn't operate on a dead person, would they? But I couldn't get my mouth to work, to ask the right questions. Thank heavens Veronica walked in at that moment—not soon enough to snatch the telephone receiver from me, but at least to stop me fainting on the floor.

"Keep your head on your knees," she ordered, tearing through the telephone directory for the hospital's number. "I don't suppose you caught the name of that nurse? Or the doctor? Never mind . . . Hello, do you have a patient called Simon

Chester? He may have been admitted just now . . . No, I don't know who telephoned. Yes, I'll wait . . . What? Why not? But I'm his *sister* . . . Oh, all right. Yes. *Fine*."

"Well, that was a waste of time," she said, turning to me. "He's there, possibly in surgery, but they wouldn't tell me anything else. Let's go." She bundled me into my coat and got us into a taxi. I don't remember much about the journey, except the driver was awfully kind and charged us far less than I would have expected for a trip across London. He said his son was in the army, so he could just imagine what we were going through. But *I* didn't even know what I was going through—I simply couldn't understand what had happened. What was Simon doing in London? Had he been in a motorcar accident? He couldn't have crashed his aeroplane, could he? I kept saying to myself, "But we aren't even at *war*, not properly! This just isn't *right*!"

As though it would have been much better if he'd been shot down in battle.

The hospital, when we reached it, was the sort of hulking Victorian edifice designed to frighten patients and visitors into complete submission. The reception desk was at the end of a gloomy corridor and was staffed by a gorgon, who sent us on a long journey to a ward that didn't exist. When we were finally directed to the correct ward, we were confronted with the terrifying sight of an empty bed.

"Oh, you're looking for that pilot who got himself smashed up?" rasped a nearby patient, raising himself on his elbows. He was horribly scarred, and his leg was suspended from something resembling a gallows. "I think they've moved him down the end, closer to the nurses' station."

So, when we finally arrived at the foot of Simon's bed, I almost burst into tears from sheer relief that he was alive and in one piece. Veronica, of course, showed her concern in quite a different way.

"What on earth have you done to yourself *now*?" she said, as if he did this on a regular basis. His chest was swathed in bandages, one arm was in a sling, and his shoulder was swollen and mottled blue and purple. But he managed to glare back at her with some of his usual spirit.

"I deliberately went and crashed my plane," he said, "just to annoy you."

"Well, you might have spared some consideration for poor Sophie," Veronica retorted. "That nurse who telephoned made her think you were *dead*."

"Sorry," he said to me. I sat down by his side and reached for his good hand, which was icy.

"How are you feeling?" I asked.

"Not too bad. The morphia seems to be working."

"What did the doctor say?"

"Broken arm, a couple of cracked ribs. I was pretty lucky, actually. The plane's a mess."

"What happened?" Veronica asked, frowning down at him.

"Engine stalled. Made a bad landing. Plowed into a stone wall. Satisfied?"

Veronica opened her mouth, closed it, then turned around. "I'm going to talk to the matron," she announced over her shoulder.

"You can talk to *me*," said the man in the next bed, in hopeful tones. She gave him a thin look, then stalked off.

"She's just worried," I told Simon, who'd closed his eyes. "You know how she is. Did they say how long you'll be in hospital?"

"A couple of days. I should be up walking tomorrow. I suppose I should be grateful it was my left arm, not my right."

I looked at his arm, which was encased in plaster from below his elbow to his wrist. "And you'll still be able to move your fingers. I expect you'll get a few weeks of leave now?"

"Well, I certainly won't be flying for a while," he said. There was a pause. "Perhaps never again," he added.

"You mean . . . But they wouldn't blame *you* for a mechanical failure, surely?"

"A better pilot would have brought that plane down safely."

"But you're still in training! You can't be expected to know everything yet!"

"Sophie," he said. He shifted his head on the pillow to look at me. "I'm not going to *get* any better than this. They only assigned me to pilot training because I work so hard and follow all the rules. They must have thought I'd turn out all right, if I kept putting in that much effort. But it's not enough. It's never enough . . ."

I stared back at him, into those dark eyes that were so like

Veronica's, yet so shadowed, so wretchedly unhappy . . . Well, of course, he was still in shock from the accident, and the morphia was clouding his mind. But, for a moment, I could almost have believed he'd done this on purpose, in some desperate attempt to escape his miserable situation. Perhaps Freud was right about the unconscious mind directing one's behavior—although I'm not sure an unconscious mind, even Simon's, could be powerful enough to disable the engine of an aeroplane.

"What would happen if you weren't a pilot?" I asked, choosing my words carefully.

"They'd transfer me somewhere else. Navigation, communications . . . there are plenty of other options in the air force."

"And you might like that better," I said. I gave him an encouraging smile, but he'd turned away.

"I don't think what I *like* has very much to do with it," he said heavily. He let his eyelids fall. Even his face looked bruised and tender. "Sorry, I'm a bit tired."

I gently pulled my hand away from his. "Yes, you get some rest. I'll telephone tomorrow morning. Do you need me to bring you anything?"

There was no answer. I thought he must have fallen asleep, but after I stood up, he suddenly said, "Sophie!"

"Yes?" I said.

"Could you let Mother know? Only don't tell her anything about . . . I mean, don't let her worry, will you?"

"I'll contact her clinic," I said. "And I'll write to Toby, as well. Don't *you* worry, either. I'll take care of it."

"Thanks," he said, and he did fall asleep then, almost at once. It was only as Veronica and I were walking back down the corridor that I realized he must have put *my* name down in his RAF records as his next of kin. I don't know why that surprised me. I could understand him not wanting to write Rebecca's name, or Veronica's—and Toby was in the RAF, too, so unlikely to be able to come to Simon's aid in an emergency. But it made me sad to think Simon had so few people to call family.

"Where's he going to go, when they discharge him from hospital?" I asked Veronica.

"Well, we don't have room in our flat." She was burrowing through her bag. "I think we'll have to take a bus home. Not enough money for a taxi."

"He could have my room," I said. "And I could have the sofa . . . except we'll be at work, so there'd be no one to look after him."

"He can go to Milford."

"Aunt Charlotte's still cross at him for abandoning her. I don't think she'd be very welcoming. Besides, who would look after him *there?*"

"Barnes?"

"She doesn't like him. I don't know why."

"*I* do," said Veronica. "It's his maddening character. He could go to his mother's."

"Oh, Veronica!"

"What? They have plenty of nurses there."

"It's a *mental asylum.*"

"Exactly," Veronica said. "It might lead to an improvement in his personality."

"I know you're only talking like this to distract me from worrying," I said, "and you're *almost* succeeding. I suppose the RAF has places where it sends injured servicemen to recuperate, but . . . Oh! What about *Julia*? She's got her first aid certificate now, and she has lots of room."

"Brilliant," said Veronica. "Inflict a grumpy convalescent relative on one of our dearest friends."

"She likes Simon," I said. "She thinks he's fascinating. And he'd probably be less grumpy with her than with other people, including us."

"Trust me, he'd be *more* grumpy," said Veronica. "He's one of those men who dislike the women they're attracted to—especially if the woman is unattainable."

The bus arrived while I was still spluttering. "Simon's not attracted to *Julia*!" I exclaimed, a bit too loudly. The conductor gave me an interested look. "Anyway," I continued, lowering my voice after Veronica handed over our fares, "what do you mean, 'one of those men'? Since when have you been an expert on this? How many men do you know?"

"The Foreign Office is full of them. And I've discovered that some of them—the ones who expect every woman to turn into a blushing, simpering idiot in their presence—don't take kindly to being ignored. Or to having their advances rejected."

"Gosh!" I said, sitting down with a bump. Veronica really *had* managed to distract me. "You've never mentioned this before."

"It wasn't worth mentioning. They don't deserve to take up the smallest part of any of my conversations."

"But isn't it difficult, dealing with that sort of thing at work?" I persisted.

"It's mildly annoying," she conceded, picking up the newspaper that someone had left on the seat. "Oh, look—it's about Finland's peace treaty! Not that they could have held out any longer against the Soviet invasion, but didn't they put up a valiant fight? I do so admire the Finns. Sophie? Don't you agree?"

Veronica is absolutely wrong. Not about Finland, or certain awful, arrogant men at the Foreign Office, or even men in general—just about Simon, who is definitely *not* attracted to Julia. Except in a sort of vague, admiring way, because she's so elegant and sophisticated.

But still, it *would* be ridiculous to ask her if he could stay with her. Quite inappropriate.

21st April 1940

Letter from Toby yesterday. Thankfully, it doesn't seem as if his squadron is going to be sent to Norway. This is reading between the lines, of course, as the commanding officers don't tell the pilots very much, and Toby wouldn't be allowed to say if he *did* know. However, as he spent an entire page complaining about not being able to use his lovely new Spitfire for anything more than a bit of aerial surveillance, I feel that I've been granted a reprieve—especially as Simon is now safely tucked away somewhere up north, being trained in some secret technology.

Rebecca, of course, is convinced that Simon's accident was the direct result of her own intervention. She prayed and prayed for Simon to be taken out of the firing line, and now he has been. She is so pleased about it that she's even started talking to the clinic staff again. I don't know what's more disturbing—that Rebecca believes God causes aeroplanes to fall out of the sky at her command or that we live in a world where a man smashing up his arm and half his ribs is a stroke of luck that may well save his life.

Actually, the really disturbing thing is that I (mostly) agree with Rebecca. I realize how inconsistent of me it is, to want the Nazis defeated without being prepared to have anyone I know killed in combat. (If I were really being honest, I would say "hypocritical" rather than "inconsistent," but there are limits to my ability to reproach myself.) The thing is, I only have one brother and one male cousin, and I don't want to sacrifice either of them, no matter how important the cause. Of course, I don't want Anthony, or even a complete stranger, to die in their place . . . Not that it matters, what I want. I haven't the slightest control over any of it.

I'm not sure who *is* in control, except it's definitely not useless old Chamberlain. He'd just given a speech about how Hitler had "missed the bus" and was never going to attack anyone, when the Nazis invaded Norway. Norway! It's just across the sea from Scotland! And the battles seem to be going very badly for the Norwegians right now. The King of Norway and his Parliament have fled Oslo, and Veronica says the Foreign Office is making plans to evacuate them to London. There *are* British troops over there, but they don't seem to be helping much. I expect it's pretty difficult, fighting in all that snow. But still, it doesn't make one feel very optimistic about the Allied forces, does it? What about when the Germans move on to wherever they're going to attack next? Perhaps it won't be Scotland, after all—there is quite a *lot* of sea they'd have to cross first. But

France is right beside Germany. Or there's Belgium. Or the Netherlands . . .

My sense of impending doom is not, I must point out, based on any political or military analysis of my own, but simply on observing Veronica and the Colonel. Veronica is currently downstairs, sweeping out the cellar so we can use it as an air-raid shelter. Our local ARP warden said the cellar was just as good as an official Anderson shelter, because "even if that flat of yours scores a direct hit, you've got that second cellar exit that comes out in the garden. That's far enough away that it won't get covered in *too* much debris—we'll probably be able to dig you out in a couple of hours if there aren't any gas leaks or unexploded bombs nearby." Oh, well, that's absolutely *fine*, then! Among other worrying signs, Veronica has become obsessed with listening to the BBC news and has lugged the enormous atlas down from the Montmaray House library so she can track the movements of troops in Norway. And she's bought a paraffin lamp in case the electricity goes out. *And* she asked Julia what we ought to keep in our first aid kit.

As for the Colonel, he's warned me to stay away from the American Embassy. *Something* is going on, but he says it's best I don't know about it just yet. He also asked me to write out a sample of Kernetin for him and asked if Veronica would be able to read it.

"Not the abbreviated form," I said. "She can read the regular code, though."

"Good," he said, in his annoyingly cryptic way, before departing.

So—as I am thoroughly in need of distraction, I decided I ought to make the effort to have a little fun, and therefore I agreed to go out on Friday evening with the girls from work. *Effort* is the right word, because it took a whole Sunday of searching through my wardrobes up in the house, plus a visit to Julia, before I had anything remotely suitable to wear. All my debutante dresses seemed so frilly and pastel, the skirts too full, the necklines all wrong. I'd worn my good suit and a silk blouse to those cocktail parties at the Embassy, but that wouldn't do for a *nightclub*. In the end, Julia helped me alter the skirt of an old blue satin evening gown to make it shorter and tighter. She also lent me some long, sparkly earrings.

"Don't worry if you lose them, they're only rhinestones," she said. "But darling, when did you last visit a hairdresser?"

"I never have *time* for that sort of thing now," I said, trying not to sound too resentful. Julia is only posted on at her ambulance station three nights a week, and they seem to spend the whole evening sitting around, playing cards and drinking mugs of tea.

"Well, just pin your hair up, then," she said. "Let's see if I can find a hair clip that matches those earrings . . . Where exactly are you going, anyway?"

"I'm not sure. Felicity and Anne both like the band at the Café de Paris."

"Do you have an evening bag?"

"Veronica's got a little black velvet clutch. Would that be all right, do you think?"

"Perfect. Well, darling, have a fabulous time, don't fall *too* madly in love with anyone in uniform, and tell me all about it next week. I'm so glad you're going out and having some fun!"

I didn't tell Julia that I'd only agreed to this outing because Felicity said her boyfriend had a cousin who was "just your type, Sophie." At last, I would find out what "my type" was! I decided not to invite Veronica to join us—partly because I'm trying to be more independent, but mostly because no matter what "my type" turned out to be, there was a fair chance he'd prefer Veronica to me. Anyway, nightclubs are not really her thing, and she's up to the second-last lesson in our shorthand workbook and was keen to finish it. She helped me fasten the back of my dress, pinned up my hair, and lent me some money for taxi fares. Then I skipped off to my date.

Well. "My type" proved to be a stout young man with beady eyes and a lot of sleek brown hair. He reminded me of a guinea pig. I do try not to judge people on their looks—after all, I'm hardly Helen of Troy. And guinea pigs can be quite endearing. But Nigel's appearance was the best thing about him. He didn't like to dance. He didn't like to laugh, smile, or make eye contact, either. When I tried to engage him in conversation, he answered in monosyllables or not at all, meanwhile staring over my shoulder at the dance floor—that is, at Felicity, with whom he was clearly besotted.

"*That's* why you brought me along, isn't it?" I hissed at Felicity in the powder room as she was repairing her lipstick. "To get him off your back!"

"Oh, sweetie! It's just that he's doing that training course and staying with Mark for a month, and we can't simply *abandon* the poor boy every time we go out, can we? Anyway, I thought you two would hit it off. He's from the country, too, you know—*and* he collects stamps."

"So?"

"Well, and you collect books."

"I don't *collect* them. I read them." (She seemed to think reading was some sort of *hobby*, as opposed to being as necessary as breathing, sleeping, and eating.)

"He is a bit dull," admitted Anne. "But his father's terrifically rich, Sophie . . . No? *Definitely* not?"

"We'll just have to find you someone else to dance with, then," said Felicity breezily. "There are hundreds of men here."

There were, but nearly all of them had arrived with their glamorous girlfriends. Anyway, once I decided to disregard Nigel's silently brooding presence, I found it quite enjoyable sitting there at our table, sipping my champagne, tapping my foot to the swing band, and watching the couples swirl past. Most of the men were in uniform (the navy officers looked the most impressive, with their glinting buttons and gold lace), while the women wore a gorgeous array of floating chiffons and clinging satins. I could see that an evening at a nightclub would be awfully romantic with the right person. There aren't many other social situations (actually, there aren't *any*) where a man can press himself against a woman for hours on end, in very dim lighting. One couple were so entranced with each other that they'd long given up any pretense of dancing. They simply stood there, her arms locked around his neck, his hands at her waist, staring into each other's eyes, until finally, he lowered his face to hers and their lips met. I looked away, half-wanting to fall in love with someone myself. But then I saw the miserable intensity of Nigel's gaze as he tracked Felicity around the dance floor and considered I was far more likely to end up a Nigel than a Felicity, loving and yearning and aching without the other person even noticing, or caring much if they *did* notice. I suddenly felt dispirited and very, very tired. So I was glad when Anne's boyfriend announced he was on duty at five the next morning and had to go.

"You'll see Sophie back to her flat, won't you?" said Felicity, batting her eyelashes at Nigel. Of course, *she* just wanted a taxi ride alone with her boyfriend.

"Actually," I said, glaring at her, "I can see *myself* home—"

"Of course I will, Felicity!" interrupted Nigel, although she was already turning away. "Well, er, good night! See you soon, I hope . . . Felicity."

She didn't reply. She was too busy giggling with her boyfriend, who was taking a very long time to wrap her in her cloak.

Nigel handed me awkwardly into a taxi, then proceeded to ignore me for most of the journey. It was only as we neared the end of what seemed to be Kensington Road (it was rather difficult to tell in the blackout) that he turned to me and drew in a breath. I thought he was going to make some sort of clumsy apology for his behavior. Instead, he *pounced*. There is no other word for it. I shoved him off fairly easily, and got the impression he was as relieved as I was. I wasn't even sure which part of my body he'd been aiming for. Did he imagine this was the *usual* manner in which one concluded an evening out with a young lady? (Perhaps it *was*. How would I know?) Fortunately, it had all happened too fast for me to feel frightened.

"Mostly, I was *baffled*," I told Veronica ten minutes later. She was still up, writing a list of provisions for our air-raid shelter. "He barely said a word to me the entire evening, and he's obviously in love with Felicity. Why on earth would he want to *kiss* me? Or whatever it was that he was trying to do."

She shook her head and got up to pour the cocoa she'd been warming for me on the stove.

"Perhaps he wanted to make Felicity *jealous*?" I mused aloud, wrapping my hands around the cup. "Or perhaps he wanted to get *over* his feelings for her by kissing me?"

"Perhaps he's an obnoxious little worm," said Veronica. "Who cares what he was thinking? It doesn't excuse his vile behavior."

"Oh, it wasn't *that* bad—not really. Nothing very terrible could have happened anyway, with the taxi driver sitting there."

"And he didn't even apologize? The boy, I mean, not the taxi driver."

"He did mumble something as I got out, but I think it was just 'Good night.' He might have been too embarrassed."

"So he ought to have been!"

"I don't think he's used to girls," I said. "He doesn't have any sisters, and he went to a boys' school, and he's only twenty. He probably thinks of girls the same way I think of . . . of llamas."

"Think of *what*?" Veronica stopped washing out the cocoa pan to stare at me.

"Well, I *like* llamas, from what I've seen of them, but I don't understand the way they think or how they're likely to act, so I might make a mess of things if I were to—"

"Catch a taxi with one," said Veronica, with a snort. "Firstly, llamas are a different species to you. Secondly, they're native to the Andes, not London, and you aren't a zoologist, so one wouldn't *expect* you to be familiar with their ways. Thirdly . . ."

She went on to make several more—very logical—points. I drank the rest of my cocoa, thinking that men might as *well* be a different species. Even Toby, whom I'd known all my life and most of his, could behave in strange and unpredictable ways. And as for Simon—he was a complete enigma.

13th May 1940

The trouble with keeping a record of the war is that either nothing whatsoever is happening in the world, which makes one's journal entries very boring, or else so *much* is going on that one doesn't have time to comprehend it, let alone write it down. It's the latter situation at the moment. However, I have the day off work today, and I think writing things down will help me make some sense of it all.

First, Norway. Well, what a *disaster*—not that Chamberlain would admit it. He gave a pathetic speech in Parliament in-forming us that we must not "exaggerate" the losses.

"There were no large forces involved," he claimed. "Not much more than a single division."

Such a comfort to all the British soldiers who were wounded or killed, I'm sure! And Simon, who came over for dinner last week, said things were even worse for the RAF squadron sent over there. The pilots were told to use an ice lake near Trondheim as their base, but the promised fuel supplies and communication equipment didn't arrive. Then they discovered that their planes' wheels had frozen to the ground overnight and all their controls were iced over, so when the Luftwaffe turned up, every single RAF plane was bombed to smithereens exactly where it sat, stuck to the lake. Simon said the only consolation was that the planes were ancient and probably wouldn't have lasted five minutes in battle anyway, and at least the navy managed to rescue the pilots. The awful part is that they are sending those same pilots back there, and probably others as well. (Not Toby, though, Simon assured us. Otherwise Toby would have been posted to Scotland instead of Sussex. But it's still worrying that Anthony is stationed up there. What if they send him?)

Anyway, as Chamberlain clearly didn't have any grasp of the situation at *all*, even his own Conservative Members of Parliament became fed up with him. During a ferocious debate in the House of Commons, one of them said, "You have sat too long for any good you have been doing. Depart, I say, and let us have done with you. In the name of God, go!"

Veronica especially enjoyed that bit, because it was what Cromwell said to the Long Parliament, and she likes politicians to have a sense of history. But then, while Chamberlain was dithering about whether to resign or not, the Nazis *invaded* Luxembourg, Belgium, and the Netherlands! The poor little Low Countries, who hadn't even declared war on Germany, or on anyone else! Queen Wilhelmina of the Netherlands and her family have already been rescued by a British ship, and the Grand Duchess of Luxembourg is meant to be coming to

London, too. (Very soon, one won't be able to walk five steps down Piccadilly without bumping into an exiled royal.) The French and British have sent troops and planes to help the Low Countries, but things aren't going very well for the Allies so far, which doesn't actually surprise me, given the Norway fiasco.

At long last, Chamberlain resigned, and now the British have a coalition government, which means they can choose the best people from each political party to be in the War Cabinet. That sounds very sensible to me. Winston Churchill is their Prime Minister, but I don't know what to think about that. We had tea with him a couple of years ago during our Montmaray campaign, and he was a very generous host, but didn't seem terribly good at listening to other people. I suppose if one *were* marvelous at oration, then one *would* want to talk a lot rather than listen. He gave a speech today about how he had "nothing to offer but blood, toil, tears and sweat," which was more uplifting than it might seem (written down, it actually sounds quite revolting). He reminds me of Lady Bosworth's fat, charming, but rather temperamental bulldog. Chamberlain is a droopy old basset hound, so we're probably better off with Mr. Churchill.

I asked the Colonel, who paid one of his whirlwind visits yesterday, for his opinion on all this, because he's Winston Churchill's cousin. He said Mr. Churchill was "mad as a March hare" and "drank like a fish," but that at least he'd wake up the Civil Service and keep the general population entertained while we lost the war.

"We're not going to lose the *war!*" I said.

"Perhaps just this battle, then," the Colonel said. He thinks the French army and air force are in a total shambles, and that it's only a matter of time before the Germans occupy the whole of France. Then he asked me if I'd ever met, at the American Embassy, a Member of Parliament called Captain Archibald Maule Ramsay.

"I don't think so," I said. "I'd remember a name like that."

"Or a Russian lady named Anna Wolkova? Or Anna de Wolkoff?"

"No."

"Anyone from the Italian Embassy?"

I shook my head ruefully.

"Never mind," he said.

I didn't even bother asking what *that* was all about.

"Oh, and by the way," he said as he was leaving, "do you recall that page of Kernetin you wrote down for me? Well, I gave it to a friend of mine, one of our best cryptographers, and he couldn't make head or tail of it."

"Really?" I said. Either I was cleverer than I'd imagined or the British Secret Service employed some very incompetent cryptographers.

"Mind you, he said it was only because the sample was so small, and I didn't mention it was boustrophedonic. Still, it's useful to know the code's so difficult to decipher. Just in case one ever needs to write a letter to someone. At some stage."

Well, that's nice and specific, isn't it? Typical of the Colonel . . . Oh, the telephone's ringing. Why does that *always* happen whenever I sit down to write? Good, Veronica's getting it . . .

It was Henry's headmistress.

"Henry's been expelled," Veronica reported, coming back into the kitchen.

"Oh, *no!*" I cried, dropping my pen (although it wasn't exactly a tremendous shock). "Why?"

"It's unspeakable," said Veronica.

I stared at her. "It's *what?*"

"No, I mean, that's all the headmistress would say when I asked. 'It's unspeakable.' Anyway, they're putting Henry on a train with her luggage. We have to meet her at King's Cross Station at three-twenty."

"Poor Henry, I hope she's not too upset," I said, although, of course, she looked absolutely delighted when we met her on the railway platform.

"I can't wait to see your flat!" she exclaimed after hugging us both. "How long can I stay with you? I know how to cook now—I made scones in Domestic Science—and I sort of know how to sew, if you have any mending to be done. Oh, are we getting a taxi? Do you think we could possibly stop at Madame Tussaud's on our way? I've never been, and I hear it's very educational and historical, especially the Chamber of Horrors—"

"We are going directly to the flat, and then you're returning to Milford tomorrow morning," said Veronica. "Aunt Charlotte's livid. What on earth did you do?"

It transpired that Henry's "unspeakable" act had been to explain the Facts of Life to one of the girls in her dormitory.

"But I had to!" Henry said earnestly. "She'd been bleeding for a whole day and was too scared to tell anyone. She didn't know anything about it at all! She thought she was *dying*."

"Couldn't you just have taken the poor girl to Matron?" I asked.

"*No*, because Matron's about two hundred years old and absolutely horrible! She would have yelled at me for leaving the dorm after bedtime, and then yelled at Cecilia and made Cecilia cry even more. And I bet Matron still wouldn't have explained anything, I doubt she even *knows*." Henry peered at Veronica with some anxiety. "But honestly, Veronica, it wasn't *my* fault the headmistress found out. It was that tattletale Loretta!"

Veronica had been shaking her head furiously, but it wasn't directed at Henry. "Can you *believe* this?" Veronica said to me. "Girls being sent off to boarding school in a state of complete ignorance! And then the school failing to teach them anything useful about human reproduction, and *punishing* them for discussing it!" She turned back to Henry. "You were quite right to put that poor child's mind at ease!"

Henry looked surprised but gratified, although I couldn't help wondering how comforting (or accurate) Henry's version of the Facts of Life had been. I also noticed the back of our taxi driver's neck growing redder and redder.

"Well, perhaps we can finish talking about this at home," I said, indicating him with meaningful looks.

"Why should we?" said Veronica, even louder and more indignantly. "Menstruation's a perfectly normal event! It's simply because women do it that the whole subject's treated with shame and disgust. If a *man* bleeds, he's awarded the Victoria Cross and gets an article in *The Times* explaining what a valiant hero he is!"

"Only if he were on a battlefield at the time," I protested weakly. "It's a bit different."

"Yes, one situation's about perpetuating the human race; the other's about annihilating it. It just demonstrates what our society really values, doesn't it?"

It was difficult enough to win an argument against Veronica before she joined the Foreign Office. Now it's impossible.

"Oh, and Sophie, I nearly forgot," said Henry, digging in her pocket and pulling out a crumpled envelope. "Here's a letter from the headmistress for you. I had to open it because I thought my train ticket might be in there. She says she couldn't allow me to stay till the end of term, because I'm such a bad influence on the other girls."

"*She's* the one who's a bad influence on girls," said Veronica, still fuming. "You're much better off out of that place, Henry."

"Although I expect Aunt Charlotte will find it pretty difficult to find another school for me after this," Henry said, trying to look mournful and failing utterly. "I'll just have to stay at Milford, I suppose, and help with the horses. And look after Carlos and Estella and all the dear little piglets."

Then she settled back in her seat with a sigh of satisfaction, looking, at that moment, *exactly* like Toby.

I have helped catch a spy! *Several* spies, in fact. What a good thing my abbreviated Kernetin is (probably) indecipherable, so I can record all the details here!

Well, it turns out I was right about Tyler Kent being a very suspicious character. Or, at least, the *Colonel* was right when he took note of my vague misgivings and investigated the man in more detail. Apparently Mr. Kent had already attracted the attentions of the police, because he'd been seen with someone they suspected was a German agent. He'd also become friends with a lady called Anna Wolkoff, whose parents run the Russian Tea Room, near the Natural History Museum. I'd walked past it several times with Henry; what I *didn't* know was that it was the meeting place for the Right Club, a secret Fascist organization set up by Archibald Maule Ramsay. He is a Member of Parliament, but a fairly deranged one, by the sound of things. He thinks all the Jews should be thrown out of Britain, and that Bolsheviks are plotting to bring down the government, and so on.

Anyway, it seems that Tyler Kent copied hundreds of confidential telegrams and letters at the American Embassy and showed them to Captain Ramsay and Miss Wolkoff. Then she sent the important ones off to her contacts at the Italian Embassy. I know we are not actually at war with the Italians, but they are Fascists and very much on Hitler's side, and it appears that they sent the information on to Berlin. I remember that Mr. Kent applied to be transferred to Berlin earlier this year, but had his request turned down. Perhaps that's why he had to send the information via Miss Wolkoff—who, by the way, used to make dresses for Wallis Simpson, now the Duchess of Windsor and also (according to Veronica) a good friend of several high-ranking Nazis.

I wonder how Mr. Kennedy reacted when he found out what had been going on at the Embassy, right under his nose! Obviously, I'm not allowed to know what was *in* any of the documents, but I think they must have been something to do with America joining the war. Officially, the United States is neutral and a lot of Americans want to keep out of the conflict, but President Roosevelt seems quite keen on helping the British. At any rate, the documents must have contained extremely important information, because all the people involved in the plot have been arrested. The Colonel says they'll be charged with betraying their country and helping the enemy. I don't see how they could charge Tyler Kent with that when he isn't British—although he *did* steal things that were the property of the American government, and that's certainly against the law.

But there is even *more* to this story! Oswald Mosley has been arrested, too! He didn't have anything to do with stealing the documents, though. He hasn't even been charged with a crime. I asked Veronica how Mosley could be imprisoned without any charge, and she explained that a new amendment to the Emergency Powers Act had been passed in Parliament the day before. This means the government can now detain not only anyone who is "hostile" to the "defence of the realm," but also any person who has associated with, or is "sympathetic with," any government that's at war with Britain. That definitely applies to Mosley, who thinks the war is a "quarrel of Jewish finance" and says Britain should sign a peace treaty with Hitler. Still, when I think of all the people I've heard deriding Jews and praising Hitler at debutante balls and dinner parties, it seems to me that half the English aristocracy could be locked up. Of course, quite a few of them changed their minds as the war approached—Lady Bosworth, for example, and poor old Lord Redesdale, who's Unity Mitford's father.

Anyway, I expect the government knows what it's doing (about arresting people who might be dangerous, that is). It's no wonder they're worried, with the war going so badly on the Continent. The Germans have advanced almost all the way to the English Channel. Yesterday, King Leopold of the Belgians surrendered to Germany (without the agreement of his government), leaving the Allied forces in an even bigger mess than they already were. The RAF planes have flown back home now, but I don't know about the British soldiers. I suppose they're still fighting there, alongside the French, who haven't surrendered. Not yet, anyway.

I wonder why the Germans are winning all the battles so far. Is it because they have those enormous tanks and thousands of aeroplanes, or is it just that they're better at military strategy? Not that they'd have to be *all* that clever to outmaneuver the French. Look at the Maginot Line, for example. A supposedly impregnable fort stretching along France's border with Germany—except the French forgot to build it all the way to the coast. So naturally, rather than trying to break through it, the Germans went around the end of it. And the French army was *surprised* by this! I suppose the Germans have also had far more battle experience, what with all the fighting they've done in Spain and Poland and Norway . . . and they do seem more passionate about winning. Is it because they all worship Hitler and are desperate to please him? I can't imagine any British soldier ever wanting to worship droopy old Chamberlain, or even King George (who's always struck me as rather feeble).

Well, perhaps Mr. Churchill will be a bit more inspirational for the troops. It seems to me they need all the encouragement they can get.

Written at Milford Park, to which Veronica and I were urgently summoned by Aunt Charlotte on Friday. The government has decided to requisition the house for use as a military rehabilitation hospital, and of course, our aunt is vehemently opposed to the idea. She claims she needs the whole house to accommodate her family (hence our presence), but the fact is, it's far too big for just her and Barnes and a couple of servants to manage, and most of the family is scattered now. Even Henry will be back at school after the summer holidays, assuming we can find a school willing to take her. In any case, there's nothing much Aunt Charlotte can do about it—one can't argue with the War Office. However, when Veronica said all of this, Aunt Charlotte drew herself up in a very familiar way.

"It is the *principle* of the matter," she declared in strident tones, as the poor gentleman appointed by the government to survey the house tiptoed past the doorway with his measuring tape. "At the same time that my only nephew is risking his *life* in service for this country, I am being *forced* out of my home!" She leaned towards the door to make certain the gentleman had heard. "A poor widow, being tossed out on the streets!"

Aunt Charlotte owns the entire village of Milford, as well as properties all over the country. I doubt she'd have any difficulties finding another place to live, although I quite understood that she'd want to remain close to her stables.

"Can't you just move into the gatehouse?" I asked.

"The *gatehouse*!" exclaimed Aunt Charlotte, as though I'd suggested a dirt-floored hovel in some remote fen instead of the large brick residence visible from where we sat. "No, no, that would be *quite* impossible. Where would Tobias stay when he comes home on leave?"

"It has five bedrooms," said Veronica.

"Three," said Aunt Charlotte, "and only *one* bathroom!"

"There are the two attic rooms as well, Your Highness," murmured Barnes as she handed round the scones. "And the Ministry might be willing to refurbish the house to make it habitable, if Your Highness were to explain the matter to them . . ."

Aunt Charlotte pursed her lips and glared out the window at the terrace, and beyond that, at the lawns that had been plowed up to plant potatoes. "This is entirely the fault of this new government," she said. "Attlee and those other Socialists who've wormed their way into the Cabinet. I know their game. They're determined to destroy the aristocracy, to snatch away our houses and dig up our rose beds and deny us petrol for our motorcars. We might as well be living in Russia. This sort of thing would never have happened when Neville Chamberlain was Prime Minister."

"We *are* at war," Veronica reminded her. "And you're not the only one being asked to turn over part of your property to the government." I knew that the clothing factory owned by Daniel's family had been requisitioned months ago and was now churning out barrage balloons and army tents. "Anyway, if you'd agreed to take in those schoolchildren from Stepney, the government wouldn't even have considered using Milford Park as a hospital."

"Evacuees!" said Aunt Charlotte with a shudder. "*Stepney!* Heaven forbid! I think I'd rather have wounded soldiers. So long as they were from the *officer* class . . ." She accepted a teacup from Barnes and heaved a sigh. "It's not that one minds doing one's bit for the war effort, you understand," she added, rather plaintively. "It's just that it's very disagreeable when certain *others* aren't being required to make similar sacrifices."

"Lady Bosworth is running a first aid center at her house," I pointed out to Aunt Charlotte. (One would think an international war might take priority over their personal rivalry, but clearly not.)

"And I thought you said Lord Bosworth had cleared out his study to make room for the Local Defence Volunteers headquarters?" added Veronica.

"Local Defence Volunteers!" sniffed Aunt Charlotte. "Another one of this government's ridiculous schemes, pandering to all those old men wanting to play at soldiers! They wouldn't last five minutes if the Germans *did* invade."

We lapsed into silence as we considered this frightening prospect. *Anything* seems possible now, following that desperate evacuation of British forces from northern France. More than two hundred thousand soldiers, starving, exhausted, some of them badly wounded, forced to abandon their tanks and cannons, sometimes even their rifles and boots, as they queued in the sea at Dunkirk. Then the navy ran out of ships to rescue them, and so ordinary people raced across the Channel in their fishing trawlers, their yachts and cabin cruisers and leaky rowing boats, hoping to save as many men as they could. Even the *Canterbury*, that luxury ferry we took to Calais last year, was pressed into service. And all the while, the Luftwaffe was bombing the boats and strafing the beach with machine guns. Tens of thousands of men died.

"Have you had any news of Harkness yet?" asked Veronica at last, referring to Aunt Charlotte's former butler. He'd been posted to France, the last we'd heard.

"Oh, yes, I meant to tell you," Aunt Charlotte said. "Barnes had a postcard from him, didn't you?"

"That's right, Your Highness," said Barnes. "He and his brigadier returned from France last week. Both are well, and he sends his regards to everyone."

"And I heard Billy Hartington and his battalion got back safely, too," said Aunt Charlotte.

"Oh, Kick *will* be relieved," I said. "She's been so worried about him."

"Yes," said Aunt Charlotte absently. (I could tell she hadn't been paying attention to me, because she hadn't responded to Kick's name by launching into a diatribe about "vulgar Americans" or "Catholic conspiracies.") "Of course," Aunt Charlotte mused aloud, "if one could be sure that gentlemen such as *Lord Hartington* were the sort of convalescents being sent to Milford, one would quite willingly offer up one's house. It would be one's patriotic duty to help men such as *them* . . ."

And they'd also provide Aunt Charlotte with some opportunities for matchmaking, I thought. She still seems to cherish a faint (and quite futile) hope that Billy Hartington will propose to Veronica. Oh, how Aunt Charlotte would *love* to be able to drop phrases like "my niece, the Duchess of Devonshire" into conversations with Lady Bosworth!

"Still, one would hope the *best* families would be spared having to hear that their sons had been wounded," Aunt Charlotte said. "Or even worse news. When I think of that poor Pemberton boy . . . So terribly brave and so tragic! Although I suppose there's always a chance he'll turn up as a prisoner of war."

"What?" said Veronica. "You mean, *Geoffrey* Pemberton?"

"Yes, his regiment was stationed at Calais," said Aunt Charlotte. "Ordered to fight to the death, apparently, to draw the Germans' attention away from the evacuation at Dunkirk."

Veronica and I exchanged horrified looks. Geoffrey Pemberton is—was—a rather awful boy who'd been at school with Toby, and had fallen briefly in love with Veronica. But just because neither of us had liked him didn't mean we'd wanted him . . . Well, he might not be *dead*. But oh, how his poor father must be feeling now!

"That's terrible," I said, blinking back tears. "Even if Geoffrey was taken prisoner . . . Imagine being a prisoner of the *Nazis*!"

"There are rules about how prisoners of war have to be treated," Veronica assured me, but her voice was far from steady. "The Geneva Convention and so on . . ."

"Oh, do you really think the *Nazis* care about those rules?" I said. "What about what Mr. Churchill said, about the Germans' treachery and brutality, about their 'originality of malice'?"

"Well, I prefer to concentrate on the other parts of his speech," said Veronica, raising her chin. "Where he says we'll defeat them. 'We shall defend our island,' that's what he declared, and I believe him. 'We shall fight on the beaches, we shall fight on the landing grounds, we shall fight in the fields and in the streets, we shall fight in the hills—'"

"'We shall never surrender,'" chorused all of us, even Barnes.

Mr. Churchill may be mad, but he certainly gives inspiring speeches.

15th June 1940

I am sitting in my kitchen, having just finished reading a very unhelpful booklet called *If the Invader Comes*. According to the government, if the Germans invade, my duty is to "stay put." I also have to follow any orders the authorities give, except "when you receive an order, make sure you know it's a true order and not a faked order." How on earth are we meant to tell? *The Times* says the Germans could drop English-speaking parachutists, dressed in civilian clothes, all over the countryside under cover of darkness. Apparently the German soldiers who parachuted into the Netherlands were dressed as *nuns* and *nurses*! Well, what if the Germans landing here disguise themselves as British policemen, or ARP wardens, or BBC announcers?

Then, if one *does* encounter an unambiguous German, the advice is "do not tell him anything" and "do not give him anything." Right. Presumably, once I've refused to say or do anything to help the Nazi storm troopers who've arrived on my doorstep, they'll just turn around and go meekly on their way.

Then they'll get completely lost, because all the signposts and railway station names have been taken down (I expect this will make them even *more* hostile, out of sheer frustration). But perhaps I'll be at work when they march into London—in which case my manager is supposed to have organized "some system by which a sudden attack can be resisted." Clearly, the writers of this booklet haven't met Mr. Bowker. Miss Halliday, on the other hand, would make a formidable opponent . . . except ladies aren't even allowed to be proper members of the Local Defence Volunteers, as Henry pointed out indignantly in her most recent letter.

Aunt Charlotte, not having found another school yet, has suggested Henry join the hundreds of British children being evacuated to Canada and the United States, but Henry refuses to be separated from the rest of us ("and anyway, I'm not a *child*!"). There are also rumors that the British princesses are being sent to Canada, and Henry says she's not getting on any ship if there's the slightest chance "that stupid Princess Margaret" is on it (the two of them are old adversaries). Henry also claims she's far too busy at Milford to be able to leave, what with grooming the horses, feeding the pigs, helping Barnes pack up the house, and running messages for the Milford unit of the Local Defence Volunteers. It's headed by her friend Jocko's father, who was a sergeant in the last war, and all the village men (those too old or too young to have been called up for the regular army) are currently occupied making bombs out of old jam jars filled with petrol, constructing roadblocks from logs nailed to bicycle wheels, and dragging hay wagons into the middle of fields so the Germans can't land their planes there.

Actually, the planes could just as well be Italian, because now Italy has declared war on the Allies, too. So Veronica hurriedly drafted a Montmaravian declaration of war on Italy and sent it off to Toby for his signature. She says Mussolini is a sneaky little coward, waiting till he was certain France would fall to Germany. Yesterday, the Nazis marched into Paris. How horrible to picture Hitler strutting down the Champs-Élysées, surrounded by a lot of fawning Nazis (Gebhardt probably amongst them). The French government has collapsed and the new President seems likely to sign an armistice with Germany within days . . .

Oh, it's all too depressing. I simply can't write any more.

20th July 1940

I arrived home from work yesterday to find Veronica cramming clothes into a suitcase.

"What's happened?" I cried, fearing the worst. The Germans had landed on the beaches! They were swarming across the fields and the hills, converging on our street!

"I just have to go away for a few days, that's all," Veronica said. "A work thing. Which dress do you think for evenings, the black silk or that red one with the gold ribbon?"

It was only then that I saw she'd been up to the house to collect some of her old evening gowns—definitely *not* the first items Veronica would snatch up during an emergency evacuation. "Oh," I said. "Well, it depends. Where are you going?"

"On second thought, that red dress would take up half the suitcase," she said. "It'll have to be the black."

"You'll need at least two evening gowns, if you're staying more than one night," I pointed out. "Take the blue chiffon. And our big trunk."

"I'm only allowed a small suitcase."

I frowned at her. "Veronica, you're not . . . You aren't going *abroad*, are you?"

Her gaze flicked up from the gown she was folding, but she remained silent.

"You're going to *Spain*, aren't you?" I said. "I don't believe it! There's a war on and you're flying straight into the middle of it!"

"Oh, Sophie," she said. "I'll be fine. It's only for a few days, and I won't be going by myself."

"Why would anyone from the Foreign Office need to go there at *all*?" I demanded, my hands now on my hips. "Isn't there a British Embassy in Madrid?"

"Yes," she said, with a sigh, "but only the British would appoint a new Ambassador who knows nothing of Spanish history or culture and doesn't speak a word of Spanish. Anyway, the Embassy staff are rushed off their feet trying to draw up a new trade agreement, whereas we'll be—"

"What?"

"Nothing." Veronica concentrated on tucking rolled-up stockings into the corners of her suitcase.

"Oh, I see," I said, "it's a *secret mission*! You do remember that Spain's right next to France, don't you? And France is crawling with Nazis now, and I can just imagine how they feel about *you* after that speech of yours at the League of Nations!"

"Spain is neutral in this war," Veronica said. "Or at least, nonbelligerent. Besides, I'm traveling on a British diplomatic passport, so I'll be perfectly safe . . . Oh, all my handkerchiefs seem to be in the wash. Can I borrow some of yours?"

"No," I said, but I went off to fetch some. "What's the difference between 'neutral' and 'nonbelligerent'?" I asked on my return.

"'Neutral' means they're not on anyone's side except their own. 'Nonbelligerent' means they aren't going to drop any bombs on Britain, but they're secretly doing everything they can to help Germany win."

"Oh, good, now my mind is completely at ease."

She gave me a fleeting smile as she snapped her suitcase closed. "Sophie, why don't you go and stay with Julia till I get back? It would stop me worrying."

"How come *you* get to worry when I'm not allowed to?"

"Because I'm older, and there's a far greater chance of air raids here than in Madrid—or wherever it is I'm going to be."

"You really can't say why you're going?"

She bit her lip. "Not at the moment. Anyway, I don't know all the details. But . . . well, I *can* tell you that it's important."

"Change-the-course-of-the-war important?"

She hesitated, then nodded. "I think so. I'm not sure it'll work, but the stakes are so high in this particular game that anything's worth trying." She heaved her suitcase off the bed, then added, "If it makes you feel any better, the Colonel knows all about it."

"The Colonel!" I stared at her with renewed dismay. "Why would *that* make me feel any better? I thought your trip was some sort of . . . of diplomatic peace mission! Now I find out it's one of his spy schemes!"

"Sophie, *please* go and telephone Julia."

"I'm going to have a word with *him*, the next time I see him," I muttered. "Dragging *you* into his ridiculous cloak-and-dagger business . . ."

I stomped off to telephone Julia, who said she'd be delighted to have me as a houseguest for as long as I cared to stay. So, after I'd waved Veronica off in a taxi this morning, I cleaned the entire flat, did a week's worth of ironing, packed my own suitcase, then took myself off to Julia's house.

I found her stretched out in the cool dimness of her sitting room with her friend Daphne, both of them drinking some strange green concoction.

"Darling!" Julia cried from the chaise longue. "*Too* kind of you to come and stay, just when I desperately needed cheering up!" She held out a hand to me.

"What's happened?" I asked, dropping my suitcase by the doorway and going over to work out whether she was genuinely distressed.

"Ant's been transferred to *Dover,*" she said, tugging me down beside her. "With German guns not twenty miles away in France, pointed straight at the town! *And* they've started bombing our ships in the Channel."

"You don't know that Ant will be involved with any of *that,*" said Daphne. "He'll probably just be doing patrols. And, Julia, think about how you'll be able to see so much *more* of him now. None of those awful treks up to Scotland, where you'd spend two days on a train, and then he'd get his leave canceled at the last minute, and you'd have to turn around and come straight back again."

"It sounds so much more *dangerous* for him in Dover, though," Julia said.

"Yes, but there's nothing you can do about it, and meanwhile, you're being a terrible hostess," said Daphne. "Sophie, what would you like to drink? I think there might be about half a glass of sherry left, or there's some gin somewhere, isn't there, Julia?"

"Just don't ask for one of *these*," said Julia, peering into her own frosted glass. "They're lethal."

"They're American," Daphne said proudly.

"Daphne's new boyfriend is from New York," Julia murmured to me, "or so he *claims*."

"All right, he may be Canadian," conceded Daphne. "But he's *been* to New York, and he dances like an angel."

"I didn't realize angels knew how to jitterbug," said Julia. "Does that mean there are swing bands in heaven?"

"Of course there are," said Daphne. "And he takes me to the most *romantic* restaurants—oh, and that reminds me! Julia, do you remember that darling little Italian place where we all went for my birthday? Well, it's boarded up now! The lady next door said the owner's been *interned*."

"Yes, I know," said Julia. "Someone tossed a petrol bomb through the window, the day Italy declared war. Of course, that poor man's been living in England for decades. He's about as much a Fascist as I am. Didn't you hear they've locked up the chef from Quaglino's, too, and the man who managed the restaurant at the Ritz? I just hope they weren't on that ship that got torpedoed—you know, the one taking our enemy aliens to Canada."

"Oh, yes," said Daphne. "But wait—the papers said it was only Nazis who drowned."

"No, there were Italians on board, too," said Julia.

"Well, honestly," sighed Daphne, flopping back into the cushions, "this government is the absolute limit! Don't they realize Italian restaurants are vital for the war effort—that they're essential for keeping up *morale*? As if it isn't bad enough that it's impossible to find silk stockings now or the right shade of lipstick! It's all very well *Vogue* telling us that beauty is our duty, that our job is to cheer up our soldiers on leave—but how exactly is one supposed to do that when the government keeps taking away all the *essentials* of *romance*?"

I smiled at her. She was dressed in her aircraft factory's standard-issue brown boiler suit and a cotton head scarf—an outfit that went not at all with the embroidered silk upholstery and gold tasseled cushions of Julia's sofa. But then I looked closer.

"Daphne," I said, "you're *glittering*."

She glanced down at herself. "Mmm. Those metal filings get absolutely everywhere."

"I don't know how you do that job," said Julia. "The hours you work."

"I don't know how I do it, either," said Daphne. "And I'm not sure I can stick it out much longer unless we get another foreman. He loathes women, makes our lives a complete misery—when he ought to be *grateful* to us. We work twice as hard as the men and get paid two-thirds of the wages."

"Well, darling, it's not as though you need the money."

"I'm not doing it for the *money*." Daphne sat up abruptly. "Can I have a bath?"

"Of course you can," said Julia. "Clean towels on my bed. I haven't had a chance to put them away yet." Then, after Daphne had gone upstairs, Julia added, rather sadly, "Daphne's brother's a pilot, too, you know. Flies *bombers*, poor thing— that's even worse than fighters. But she says that at least if he gets sent up in one of *her* planes, she'll know it's been perfectly put together."

Julia glanced at the photograph of Anthony on top of her desk, and he grinned back at us, his RAF cap tilted at a dashing angle. Julia frowned, and I saw she really *was* upset (and also, possibly, a tiny bit drunk).

"This bloody war," she said. "I *hate* what it's doing to us. Husbands and wives are meant to be *together*, but I haven't seen Ant for weeks and weeks—"

Some of my thoughts must have shown on my face.

"Oh, I know," she said quickly, "I *know* I wasn't always very nice to him, not at the start. But that was just the strain of . . . of trying to live up to his image of me. He put me up on a pedestal, Sophie, he really did, he worshipped me. He didn't have a clue how to go about living with the real me, let alone how to . . . Well, never mind about that, I don't want to put you off men, because they really are terribly sweet when one gets used to them. But that's what I mean, it was all *my* fault, for having my own ridiculous expectations about *him*."

She stared down at her drink.

"And it wasn't until the war started that I really understood that. Once I realized Ant would be in the middle of it, putting himself in danger . . . You see, that's why I'm determined to be the perfect wife now. Anything he wants, anything that makes him happy. I'd never, ever forgive myself if we had some silly tiff over the telephone one day and it turned out to be the last time we . . . Well. I'm not even going to think about that. But I *do* believe he's happy now. He so loves flying—I just wish they'd move him to a training unit. He's such a good teacher, so patient and persistent. He ought to think about doing something in that field, setting up a flying school or something—I mean, once the war's over."

She sighed, then shook her head. "But tell me *your* news, Sophie," she said. "Where's Veronica gone off to?"

"Who knows?" I said.

"Ah, something hush-hush, is it? There's a lot of that going around. Isn't there, Rupert?"

"What?" said Rupert, coming into the room. "Oh! Hello, Sophie." His hair was damp, and he was fiddling with his cuffs.

"You'd better not have used up all the hot water," Julia told him. "Now—take Sophie's suitcase up to her room, but before that, see if there's another bottle of sherry somewhere and pour her a drink, and then go and find a different shirt, one that doesn't clash quite so horribly with that jacket."

"Actually, I was going downstairs to make a pot of tea," said Rupert, giving me a sweet smile. "Would you like some, Sophie?"

"Yes, thank you, that'd be lovely," I said, because I secretly think sherry tastes like petrol. I followed him down to the kitchen, where Mrs. Timms was folding her apron.

"I've left cold chicken and potato salad for your dinner, and the peas are on the stove," she told him. "There's an apple charlotte for pudding, but no cream left to go with it, I'm afraid."

That reminded me. "I brought my ration book," I said, handing it over to her.

"Oh, bless you," she said, tucking it away in her bag. "I'll be queuing up at the shops first thing on Monday. Well, I'm off now. And I've fed that cat, Mr. Rupert, so don't you go giving it your share of the chicken."

I noticed a sleek tabby crouched on the windowsill, eyeing Rupert expectantly.

"I didn't know Julia had a cat," I said.

"She didn't, until a few weeks ago," said Rupert, putting the kettle on the stove. "I found him on the doorstep when I arrived here one morning. The poor thing was starving, and he'd got one of his paws tangled up in a piece of rope."

The cat, who appeared far from starving now, gave me a sly look. He'd probably wound the rope around his own paw, then arranged himself on the doorstep in a pitiful pose when he heard Rupert coming. Rupert's soft heart was the first thing—often the only thing—anyone noticed about him. But as I watched him move around the kitchen, handling cups and tea canister and milk jug with quiet efficiency, I perceived something different about him. He seemed taller, somehow, or simply more at ease in his own skin.

"Do you like your job?" I asked as he placed my cup in front of me.

"Yes," he said. "Very much."

"I suppose," I said, "that you enjoy it because you know you're doing something worthwhile."

"Mmm. Although I can't really talk about what I do." He sat down and offered me the sugar.

"I expect you're also very *good* at it. That would help."

"Oh, well . . ." The old, shy, self-effacing Rupert appeared, like a flickering film image, then vanished. "It's funny," he said, stirring his tea. "Right from the start, they assumed I was an expert in the field, that I'd manage everything perfectly without any help—and so I did. I wasn't given any opportunity to start doubting myself, so I didn't. I simply got on with it. I *do* still have moments when I feel as though I'm impersonating a responsible adult . . . but I think if one pretends something long enough, one eventually convinces even oneself." He leaned back to allow the cat, who'd been rubbing himself industriously against Rupert's ankles, to jump onto his lap. "But why do you ask? Don't you like your job?"

"It's all right," I said. "It just seems a bit pointless, that's all, compared to what most people are doing."

"Food is important," said Rupert. The cat popped his head up above the tabletop and seemed to nod, although he was probably just calculating the distance to the milk jug.

"I'm not actually *feeding* people, though," I said. "I'm just sitting in an office, editing pamphlets."

"Well, you're providing people with valuable information about . . . Oh, wait. Am I meant to be arguing with you? Or agreeing? Which would make you feel better?"

"Neither, probably," I said, although I already felt *slightly* better, merely from being the subject of Rupert's steady, sympathetic gaze.

"Is this about Veronica?" he asked. "About her going away for her work? Because I don't think you'd really want her job, would you?"

"No," I conceded. "I wouldn't be able to do it, anyway. But I can't help comparing myself to her—and of course, whenever I *do* compare, I always come off second best." Then, realizing that sounded as though I were fishing for compliments, I hurriedly added, "But you have older brothers. You know what it's like."

"No," he said. "Not really. David and Charlie were already at school when I was born, so no one ever bothered to compare us, least of all me."

"Oh. I suppose it's a bit like the gap between Henry and the rest of us," I said.

"Not at all," he said. "Henry adores you. I don't adore

David." Then Rupert grimaced. "Sorry, I know I shouldn't say anything bad about him when his regiment's abroad. Valiantly fighting for our nation, and all that."

I'd met David and knew he was an insufferable prig, so I just smiled. "What about Charlie? Did you get along with him when you were growing up?"

"He was all right. He used to take my side when David was being a bully, but that's only because he loved annoying David. Charlie's always been a bit . . . contrary."

"Have you heard from him yet?" I knew that when the war started, the Colonel had tried to track down Charlie, who'd been living abroad for years.

"Not directly. It seems he's joined the Canadian army, so he might get posted over here. Poor Mummy, I do wish he'd write to *her*, at least. She really worries about him." Rupert looked down at the cat, whom he'd now stroked into a stupor. "But speaking of brothers—I saw yours on Wednesday."

"Did you? In Sussex?"

"Mmm. I was driving back past his aerodrome, so we met for a drink. Well, we tried to, but he nearly started a riot when we walked into the pub."

"What? Why?"

"There were a couple of soldiers there on leave—hopelessly drunk—and they went berserk when they saw Toby's uniform. 'Where was the bloody RAF when we were getting shot up on that beach at Dunkirk?' and so on. Toby tried to explain there *were* planes there, they were just high up and hidden in all the smoke, but I could see he wasn't going to get anywhere with logical reasoning, not with that lot. So I dragged him out and we drove back to his base and had dinner. He's got everyone there, from the Wing Commander down to the cook—"

"—wrapped around his little finger," we both said, starting to laugh and waking up the cat. Then Julia came in to see about dinner, and I went upstairs to unpack.

Dinner ended up being very late, because Julia kept getting called to the telephone to argue about her shift at the ambulance station ("No, darling, I'm on tomorrow night, I swapped with Arthur"), then Daphne arrived unexpectedly with mascara smeared down her face ("That two-timing *bastard*!") and had to be consoled, then Julia burned the peas, the only item on the menu that required cooking.

"Thank heavens for Sophie," said Julia when we finally sat down in the dining room. "Daphne, she's an absolute *genius* in the kitchen—I think I'll kidnap her and make her live here always—and that reminds me, Sophie, don't forget to telephone your aunt, let her know you're staying here. Or perhaps write? And forget to post the letter until Monday? And oh, Daph, do you remember that strange metal thing we were puzzling over? The one Mrs. Timms left by the sink? Well, it's an *apple corer*. Sophie recognized it at once! Stop laughing, Rupert, you didn't know what it was, either. Now, let's all have a civilized meal with lovely, cheerful conversation. No talk of the war, please."

But no matter how hard we tried to get away from the topic, we kept wandering back towards it, like Alice in the Looking

Glass garden. Julia mentioned the difficulty she'd had finding tomatoes in the shops that morning, and Rupert pointed out that the tomato shortage would only get worse now that Germany has invaded the Channel Islands. I started to tell a funny story about my boss, then remembered he'd only fallen off that hatstand because he'd been trying to paste strips of gummed paper to the windows in case of bomb blasts. Then Daphne described the handsome Frenchman who'd kindly hailed her a taxi as she stood weeping outside the Ritz.

"A Free French officer, I suppose," she sighed. "The poor *dear*. I almost invited him back here for dinner, except I wasn't sure there'd be enough food."

"It's a wonder he was so nice to you, considering we've just destroyed their navy," said Julia.

"That wasn't the *Free* French navy," said Daphne. "It belonged to the other lot, those awful French who've joined up with the Nazis. And if we hadn't bombed those ships, Hitler would've used them against us."

"Well, it's very sad, anyway. All those hundreds of French sailors killed," said Julia.

"I thought we weren't meant to be talking about the war," said Rupert.

"No. We're not," said Julia firmly. There was a long silence as we ate apple charlotte and tried to think of something else to discuss.

"Can we talk about Diana Mosley being sent to prison?" asked Daphne.

"No," said Julia.

"'Saucepans for Spitfires' campaign?" offered Rupert.

"No, and you are *not* to give any of my saucepans to those collectors if they come calling," said Julia.

"Why? It isn't as though you know how to use them."

"I mean it, Rupert! Mrs. Timms would kill me. They can have all the fence railings and that old washtub in the laundry instead."

"I'm not sure saucepans are made out of the right sort of aluminium for aeroplanes, anyway," said Daphne. "This whole salvage campaign is probably just to make housewives feel more involved in the war. Far better to send a check to the Spitfire Fund, darling, if you want to help. And while you're at it, enclose a note telling Lord Beaverbrook to sack our foreman. That'd boost aircraft production in *our* factory, I guarantee. Otherwise, I might just have to organize a protest strike against the wretched little man."

"You can't," said Rupert. "All industrial strikes are banned now. It was on the news yesterday."

"Oh, well," said Daphne cheerfully. "It'll just have to be arsenic in his tea, then."

2nd August 1940

Letters from my family. First, Toby:

Dear Soph,

Still feels strange, writing to you in English, but I know the censors would tear my letter to shreds if I used Kernetin. I tried to explain that Kernetin is the native language of Montmaray, but they persist in believing it's some sort of secret code. Crazy, I know, but that's the air force for you.

This is written in the dispersal hut at 0700, waiting for the field telephone to ring and tell us if/when/where we're going up. Each morning, they drag us out of bed at some ungodly hour, drive us to the airfield in the half-light, then bring us greasy bacon sandwiches that none of us can eat because we're all sick with nerves. And then . . . nothing happens. All we do is go up, fly around, come back down again. Yesterday the squadron was scrambled south to meet a lot of German bombers that were supposedly attacking a shipping convoy, but by the time we got there, there was nothing but blue sky.

Still, anything's better than night patrol. I was sent up last week at midnight and nearly flew into a hill (I swear the stupid thing wanders about after dark, it was in a completely different position that morning). The whole operation was pointless, anyway—how the hell am I supposed to see any Germans in the pitch black, let alone shoot them down? Perhaps you could send me some of your special carrots . . .

Evening now. Two sorties today, the second involving a bit of action. That is—we ran into a German reconnaissance plane being escorted by a couple of fighters and we fired off a few rounds. Didn't hit a thing, as far as I could tell. The Germans turned tail and fled back across the Channel the moment they spotted us, so I guess we achieved that, at least. The whole thing lasted about ten seconds. Nice day for it, though—absolutely wonderful weather here.

Well, we're off to the pub now—the others are trying to teach me to like beer. Unfortunately, that's the only drink on offer, apart from a very inferior brand of Scotch. Have you seen Simon lately? Tell him to have a word with the RAF high-ups so that they ban all night patrols, would you?

Will post this now rather than waiting to add more to-morrow. Hope you're well.

Love to all,
Toby

P.S. Veronica not back yet? Will send this to Julia's, just in case.

Then from Henry:

Dear Sophie (and Veronica, if she is there),
How are you? I am ~~good~~ well. We have moved into the gatehouse now, but you can still send letters to the main house. The workmen are bilding ramps on the terrace so that people in weelchairs can get down to the lawn. The drawing rooms look HUGE now they are empty! They are perfect for roller-skating but soon they will be filled with beds, as that's where all the payshents will sleep. They will have fizical therapy (I don't know what that is) in the dining room and music room, and the nurses will live on the first floor. We've moved all Aunt C's furnicher and other stuff to the second and third floors. Only Barnes knows exactly where everything is, so we'll be up a gum tree if anything happens to her.

Estella bit one of the workmen on the leg, but he deserved it because he yelled at her and tried to kick her after she walked on some wet cement. So now I am not allowed to take her anywhere near the house when we go for swims in the lake. The workman was not hurt, he was wearing thick trowsers.

Sophie, could you please write and tell Aunt C that the school she has found is NO GOOD! I just read the school pamflet and it sounds worse than my last school! Anyway, I am too busy here to leave. There are still big boxes in our sitting room that we haven't unpacked (I think your stuff is in one of them). The first thing we did was get Toby's room ready, for when he has leave. He has the second-biggest room. I made a shelf for his books and put his gramofone by his bed, with all his records, so I think he will like it. I am in the attic, far away from Aunt C! You and V can have the other attic room when you visit.

I have to go now to help Jocko. We are sharpening hay-forks to use as weapons, because the Milford LDV (now called the Home Guard) only has two rifles to share be-tween fifteen men. Barnes says they should use Estella as an attack pig. Aunt C has given them her ~~opra~~ opera glasses, so that the lookout can see if the Nazis are coming. If he sees any, he will give the signal, and we will put up our roadblocks and throw petrol bombs at them.

Love,
Henry

P.S. If you haven't bought my birthday present yet, I would quite like a single-barreled shotgun and a box of cartridges.

I would share it with the Home Guard, of course. Otherwise, I would like a new fishing net with extendible handle.

P.P.S. Aunt C has just bought two Spitfires for the RAF! They cost £5,000 each! She heard Lady Bosworth had bought one, so she bought two! She is allowed to name them, so one is "Queen Clementine" and one is "Queen Matilda." Aunt C wanted to give the Spitfires to Toby, but I explained he already has one. But maybe he could have these as spares, or lend them to his friends.

And then there was Veronica's letter. If only *hers* had arrived through Julia's letter slot, too . . . but getting hold of it was a rather fraught business. I'd been growing more and more anxious, as Veronica's "few days" away became a week, then ten days, and still no word from her. I even went so far as to try to contact the Colonel, with no success. Then came the mysterious summons at work this morning. Two gentlemen arrived and claimed they had come to escort me to Whitehall.

"You aren't even in uniform," I said, looking them up and down suspiciously. "Why should I go anywhere with you?" For all I knew, they were Tyler Kent's henchmen, sent to wreak some awful revenge on me.

"We have written orders to collect Miss Sophia Fitz-Osborne," said one of them, and he handed a piece of paper to Miss Halliday.

"Is this Colonel Stanley-Ross's signature?" she asked me.

"Well," I said reluctantly, "it *does* look like his writing . . ."

And when we all trooped downstairs, the black motorcar parked by the front doors *did* seem very official. However, I made sure my car door opened from the inside, and I kept a careful watch on our route—which, it turned out, *did* lead directly to the Foreign Office. But this was almost as frightening as finding myself being dragged off to the East End and tossed into the Thames. What had happened to Veronica? What couldn't they tell me over the telephone? Was she hurt, kidnapped . . . even *dead*?

So I was in a complete state by the time I was ushered into a windowless room in the depths of the building. The sight of the Colonel did little to allay my fears. He was glaring at another middle-aged gentleman, this one in an army officer's uniform, who was glaring right back. They reminded me of two tomcats I'd once seen circling each other, keeping a precise, unchanging distance between themselves as they hissed and snarled and spat.

"Sophie!" said the Colonel, wrenching his stare from the army officer to give me a bright smile. "*Terribly* sorry to interrupt your work like this."

"What's going on?" I asked.

"Absolutely *nothing* to worry about," he said. "Have a seat. Oh, this is Major Beckett."

The Major jerked his head in my direction, and I tried to remember whether a colonel outranked a major. I *thought* so—but then, the Colonel wasn't in the army anymore, was he? He was with the Foreign Office now. I also noticed another man in khaki, much younger, hunched expectantly over a notebook.

"So!" the Major said to me in a belligerent way, as though we were already halfway through an argument. "Miss Veronica FitzOsborne has written a letter. In *code*." He brandished a piece of paper. "I have been informed that *you* will be able to read it."

I couldn't see why Veronica would write anything work-related in Kernetin, but at least if she was writing letters, she wasn't dead. I nodded.

"You will read it aloud," ordered the Major. "My secretary will transcribe it as you speak. Is that clear?"

I was beginning to understand why the Colonel disliked him.

"Yes," I said. "May I have the letter?" Then, as I read the first line, my indignation spilled over. "This is *my* letter!" I cried. "My own personal, private letter from my cousin, addressed to me, and you've opened it!"

"Any material sent by persons in the Foreign Service while carrying out duties abroad is subject to security," said the Major, puffing out his chest. "May I remind you that this nation is at *war*, Miss FitzOsborne?"

"That's 'Your Royal Highness' or 'Princess Sophia' to *you*," I snapped, and the Colonel gave a little cough of barely suppressed amusement.

"Please read the letter aloud, *Your Highness*," said the Major through gritted teeth.

Fortunately, Veronica was a step ahead of everyone else, as usual.

Dear Sophie, she wrote,

I expect they'll open this, even though it's private correspondence, and make you decode it—

I looked up to glare pointedly at the Major.

—but I thought I should write a quick note to let you know I'm all right.

> *Thank you for insisting on me packing a second evening gown, because much of my work involves interpreting conversations at dinner parties, which go on for hours, in rooms that are like saunas. I can't say much about that, of course, but I do wish I'd had a chance to visit this city before the war. It must once have been beautiful, but now nearly every building façade is scarred from machine-gun fire and bomb blasts, half the windows in our hotel are boarded up, and the nearest church is a burnt-out shell. As for the people: the few who are in power are fat, well dressed, and smug, and everyone else is starving, homeless, and terrified. The Americans ought to come over here so they can get an idea of how an entirely Fascist Europe would look. Perhaps then they'd stop dithering about entering the war.*

> *Anyway, I'm sorry this trip is taking so long, but I can see I'm needed here for another week, at least. None of the others speak much Spanish, you see, which can be*

a bit frustrating—for me as well as them. There was one particularly obtuse army officer who questioned absolutely everything I interpreted. Once I told him our waitress had said that a certain route out of the city was closed, but he insisted on sticking to his plan, and of course, it turned out a bridge had collapsed and we had to take a three-hour detour. Luckily he's gone back to England now.

I glanced up. The Major had turned a peculiar shade of blotchy purple.

I should be home very soon, and in the meantime, please don't worry about me. I do hope that you are well and Toby is all right. Regards to Julia and Rupert.

Love,
Veronica

"You see?" burst out the Major, whirling upon the Colonel. "Exactly as I suspected, clear evidence of Communist partisanship!"

"Really," drawled the Colonel, raising an eyebrow, "I fail to see anything of the *sort*. All I heard was a brief description of an unnamed city that's recovering from a terrible war."

"Only a Communist would use inflammatory words like 'starving' and 'homeless'!"

"Oh, is *that* what's upset you?" The Colonel tilted his head in an attitude of mock sympathy.

"It's the general tone of . . . of *disrespect*!" The Major's face was almost the color of a blackberry by now. "And what about calling the Falangists 'fat'? What if one of the Spanish authorities had got hold of this letter? It could have jeopardized the entire mission!"

"The letter was sent in the diplomatic bag, so how could they have got hold of it? And if they had, how would they have been able to read it? After all, *your* intelligence people couldn't."

The Colonel must have won the deciding point in whatever game they were playing, because he then reached for his hat.

"Come along, Sophie, I'll give you a lift back to your office."

"Yes . . . Well . . . I'll have that document *back*, thank you!" said the Major, waving his hand at me in a peremptory way. But I'd already tucked the paper inside my jacket.

"It's *my* letter," I declared, and I bolted out the door before he could stop me.

"Well done, Sophie," said the Colonel, looking very pleased with himself, once we were safely settled in his motorcar.

"What on earth was *that* about?" I burst out, in a rush of uninhibited relief.

"Oh, just a bit of healthy rivalry between the army's intelligence people and the Foreign Office," he said.

"There doesn't seem to be much 'intelligence' about it," I said. "You do realize you're supposed to be fighting the Nazis, not one another?"

"Yes," he said, pretending to look chastened. "Yes, you're absolutely right."

"I don't suppose *you've* seen Veronica?" I asked.

"No, I've been busy elsewhere," he said. "But she should be back soon, and she really is doing a marvelous job. Don't pay any attention to old Beckett; he's just jealous the Foreign Office is having more success than the army. Apparently Veronica got our man an audience with one of Franco's ministers—turns out he'd been a friend of her grandfather."

"I still think the whole thing sounds very dangerous."

"Well, when she gets back, you can tell her not to go on any more trips abroad," he said mildly—knowing perfectly well that diverting Veronica from a course she's set upon is like trying to turn back the ocean.

10th August 1940

I feel a bit uneasy, writing this in Kernetin—even in my abbreviated and newly modified form. I'm certain the army intelligence people made a copy of Veronica's letter, and now that they have its translation, they could easily work out most of the code, if they cared to make the effort. Still, the British government isn't very likely to be interested in my ramblings, and who else would bother to search for my journal, which I keep hidden away so carefully? I suppose it *could* be of some, very limited, value to the Nazis when they invade—but then, we'll all be dead or in prison camps, so it won't matter very much.

Does everyone do this, I wonder? Dwell upon the worst imaginable outcome in horrifying detail, in the superstitious belief that this will stop it happening in reality? Or that if it *does* happen, it won't come as too much of a shock? No, it's probably just me.

But it's no wonder I worry so much about everything when I have Veronica telling me all *sorts* of hair-raising tales. Her trip to Spain, for example, to stop the Duke and Duchess of Windsor being *kidnapped by Nazis!*

"What?" I gasped. "You were dealing with *Nazis?*"

"No, no," said Veronica, calmly unpacking her suitcase. "Well, not directly, although there were certainly a lot of them wandering about Madrid. No, we were just trying to dissuade the Spanish authorities from helping the Nazi agents."

Then she explained that after Paris had fallen to the Nazis, the former King Edward the Eighth and Mrs. Simpson—now the Duke and Duchess of Windsor—had fled to the south of France and then driven across the border to Barcelona. A ship was meant to be arriving there to evacuate some British diplomats, but there was confusion as to whether anyone actually wanted the Duke—and especially his wife—back here in England. Apparently the British royals were furious about the prospect. By the time they'd decided to allow the Duke to come here, he'd gone on to Madrid. And that's where he *really* started causing trouble—spending all his time with pro-Nazi Spanish aristocrats, talking loudly about how wonderfully the Nazis had transformed Germany and how Britain ought to sign a peace treaty with them.

"Well, you can just imagine what Churchill thought of *that,*" said Veronica. "Oh, and the Duke was making all sorts of personal demands, too—insisting on a job of 'first-class importance' if he returned to England and that his wife be titled 'Her Royal Highness,' and so forth. But he's still technically an officer of the British Army, so Churchill threatened a court-martial if the Duke didn't obey orders. And eventually, they packed up and went to Portugal as they'd been told."

Veronica shook out a very crumpled chiffon evening gown, bearing signs of repeated hand-washing. "I don't think this is fit to be worn ever again," she remarked.

"You have lots of other gowns," I said impatiently. "Go on, what happened in Portugal?"

"Well, the British Ambassador had organized for them to stay at a hotel, but they insisted on moving in with some local banker, who just *happened* to be a known Nazi agent. By then, Churchill had decided the Duke should be sent to the Bahamas as Governor. It was so far away, how could he possibly get into any trouble there? But it would take time to organize a ship, and meanwhile, that idiot Ribbentrop—you know he's Germany's Foreign Minister now—hatched this plot to get the Duke back to Spain. Once he was there, the Duke could be fed a lot of Nazi propaganda and 'hold himself in readiness.'"

"In readiness for what?"

"Why, to become King of England again, of course. And then he could appoint Oswald Mosley as Prime Minister, and Britain could surrender to Germany."

"But . . . that's insane!"

"Perhaps, but Hitler agreed with Ribbentrop's plans. And the Duke *did* send a telegram to the King, telling him to dismiss Churchill and the War Cabinet and set up peace negotiations with Germany."

"I'm surprised the Germans would *need* to kidnap the

Duke," I said. "It's a wonder he didn't just waltz off to Berlin of his own accord."

"Well, that's where the combined efforts of army intelligence and the Foreign Office came in, trying to persuade the Duke to stay in Lisbon till his ship arrived. And then another lot of us was in Spain, trying to convince the Spanish government to stay out of the whole thing."

"And you succeeded?"

"Or the Germans failed, one or the other. Anyway, the Windsors are on their way to the Bahamas now."

"Goodness!" I said, sitting back. "To think I was here in London, teaching Julia how to boil an egg, while you were doing all that!"

"I'd rather have been with you," she said. "The food would have been a lot better . . . Oh, but I don't mean to complain. Really, I was grateful we had anything at *all* to eat. It was so sad, Sophie, you've no idea. We'd drive past all these bombed villages, no crops planted, people huddled in makeshift shelters and eating weeds—and there isn't any effort whatsoever being made to rebuild industries in the cities. Franco seems determined to drag the entire country back into the Middle Ages."

"Did you go anywhere near the Basque country?"

"No, Madrid was the furthest north I went. We flew there from Lisbon." She closed the now-empty suitcase and set it on the floor. "Anyway, what's new here?"

"Not much. We had a letter from Alice in Fowey. Her brother-in-law took his fishing boat to Dunkirk and rescued five soldiers—it was awfully heroic—and now Jimmy's longing to be old enough to join up. Oh, and a parcel arrived for you from America. I think it's from Jack Kennedy."

"You could have opened it."

"I didn't like to." I didn't mention that the censor already had (and not done a very neat job of rewrapping it, either). I went to find it.

"*'Why England Slept,'* " said Veronica, reading the title of the book Jack had sent. "Oh, it's his thesis! He did mention his father was arranging for it to be published."

"What's it about?"

"Appeasement," she said, flicking through the book. "Why England was so unprepared for this war. How the pacifists and trade unions prevented effective rearmament in Britain. How feeble democracies are, compared to totalitarian states. You know, the usual Kennedy . . . Oh! I wonder where he got *those* figures."

And she sank onto the bed, her nose buried in the book. I thought this might be a good time to test out something I'd been wondering about for a while.

"Daniel telephoned twice, while you were away," I said casually.

"Hmm?" said Veronica.

"To see whether you were back."

"Right," she said. "Did you know that in March, Germany was producing forty-three percent more planes than Britain each month? But three months later, after Lord Beaverbrook took over, aircraft production here had increased to such an extent that it almost *matched* Germany's."

"Anyway, Daniel said he's being transferred somewhere else by the War Office."

"What?" she said, glancing up. "Where?"

Finally! A reaction.

"He didn't say. He thought he might have already moved before you got back, but he said he'd write as soon as he was settled, and meanwhile, you could get in contact via his parents."

"Oh. All right, then." She turned a page. This was *not* the behavior of someone who was head over heels in love, I thought, but I made one last effort.

"Do you have his parents' address?" I asked.

"Yes, I've been there for luncheon."

"What?" I goggled at her. "You didn't tell me this! When?"

"Um . . . a couple of weeks ago? Just before I went to Spain."

I reached over and tugged the book away from her. "*And?*"

"And we had some sort of chicken stew with dumplings, I think. Then apple strudel."

"What's his *family* like?"

"Oh. Well, his mother looks like him, only short and round instead of tall and thin. Plays the violin, speaks four languages, very charming and voluble. His father hardly said a word, just sat there glowering at his plate, but I think he was worried about some problem at the factory. What else? Oh, Daniel's eldest sister is religious and has about half a dozen children, and his other sister is a doctor."

"A doctor!"

"I know, it's impressive, isn't it? She did some of her training in Vienna. I didn't actually meet either of his sisters, though. There was a big family portrait hanging in the drawing room, and his mother explained who everyone was."

"And she invited you to luncheon?"

"No, I just turned up and demanded she feed me."

I hit her with the book. "Veronica! Honestly, you never tell me *anything*! For all I know, it could have been a party to celebrate your engagement!"

She started laughing. "Heaven forbid! No, they were just curious to meet me, after hearing Daniel mention my name."

"Mention your name about a hundred times a day! His parents wanted to see if you'd make a suitable wife for him."

"You think so? Surely they wouldn't have to meet me to realize how very unsuitable I'd be." She grabbed the book back and added it to the teetering pile beside her bed. "But I *would* have told you about that luncheon, Sophie," she added, more seriously. "It's just that it happened the day before I went to Spain, when everything turned so hectic."

"Hmm," I said, only partly mollified. "But *is* Daniel your boyfriend?"

"Well, we certainly aren't *engaged*. We haven't even talked about that. But then, neither one of us really approves of the institution of marriage—"

"Veronica," I interrupted, before she could launch into some Marxist-feminist critique of matrimony, "do you *love* him?"

"Yes," she said, without any hesitation. Then she sighed. "But the trouble with that word is that it has such a vast range of meanings. I may love him, but whatever I feel hasn't much to do with . . . with *romance*." She pulled a face. "I don't want him to bring me flowers or write me sentimental poems. I haven't any intention of changing my appearance to please him, not that he really cares about my hairstyle or whether I'm wearing lipstick. I don't need to spend every moment of every day with him. I did miss him while I was away—but then, I missed *you*, too."

She subsided into pensive silence. I was recalling her parents' short, disastrous marriage and thinking that that was bound to have shaped her views when she said, "I *do* feel a connection with Daniel. But I doubt it's the same as what he feels for me, even if we both call it love. Men and women are so different."

"You mean . . . he wants to go to bed with you?" I ventured, when she didn't say anything else.

"Well, yes," she said, "but it isn't as though he's *insisting* upon it."

"I should hope not!" I said, a little shocked, even though I was the one who'd brought up the subject. "You haven't . . ."

"No, I'm not curious enough yet. And even then, I'd have to be certain I wouldn't get pregnant." She frowned. "Oh, everything was so much easier when we were simply friends! Especially now you've informed me that even his *parents* have an opinion on our future."

"Sorry," I said.

"It's not your fault. But now it feels as though we've been shoved down a slippery slope that *has* to end in either marriage or estrangement, regardless of what we want."

"I thought *I* was supposed to be the melodramatic one," I said, making her laugh, as I'd intended.

"Oh, I'm just tired," she said, shaking her head, but she insisted on doing most of her laundry, while I cleaned out the kitchen cupboard, which, in my absence, had been assailed by mice. Meanwhile, I was wondering whether it was in fact *worse* to have parents as happily in love as mine had been. Perhaps it set up unrealistic expectations. And then, of course, my parents had *died* before they could pass on their secrets for wedded bliss to me. I tried to imagine what advice my sensible mother might have for me, or for Veronica, but it didn't really work. It did, however, distract me from my invasion fears for a few hours, so that was something.

Dear Soph and Veronica,

Don't worry, it wasn't our aerodrome that got bombed to bits. Not that the Germans haven't had a bloody good go at us, as well as practically every other airfield along the coast, but we're holding up all right. Sorry not to have written earlier, but it's been pretty busy. Three, even four sorties each day, and then they make us write reports. Well, they try to, but mostly I can't be bothered. I'm always getting into trouble for that.

Hard to believe we've only been at this for a few weeks. That first real battle seems years ago. I remember jabbing my thumb on the firing button and the whole plane shuddering, then sheer, overwhelming astonishment as I realized I'd hit something—that an actual Luftwaffe fighter was breaking up before my eyes, flipping over, hurtling towards the ground. I just stared at it, for whole seconds, watching the smoke spiral down, holding my breath, waiting for the crash. Then I happened to notice a line of little sparks winking their way towards me and thought, Oh, right, there's still another dozen Messerschmitts up here, and those pilots are probably a bit annoyed at me now. So I flung myself out of the way of that lot, dodged a few more, wheeled about, fired off a couple of rounds, dived through a bank of clouds—and suddenly there was no one there. Just endless sky. So unexpectedly peaceful, so strange, as though I were the last man left in the world. But I was out of ammunition, and nearly out of fuel, so I turned round and limped back home (those little sparks turned out to be bullets and tore a hole in my wing, but missed the engine, so no real harm done).

Since then, our squadron's shot down nine fighters and two bombers, or that's what we claim. Hard to tell for sure, when it's such a blur up there most of the time. One thing, though—and don't tell him this—I am so glad Simon's out of it. He thinks too much, and this sort of thing relies on sharp reflexes and pure instinct. He's better off where he is, at HQ, trying to get us all organized. Mind you, if he gets promoted above me, we'll never hear the end of it. I might have to pull rank and start making him call me "Your Majesty."

Sorry, I'm falling asleep. Will try to enclose a note for Henry before I send this off. Please pass on a bowdlerized version of this to Aunt C, as I haven't had a chance to write to her, and please do keep writing to me, even if I'm the world's worst correspondent! Don't know when I'll get any leave, not sure when I'll see you next.

All my love,
Toby

31st August 1940

The air-raid sirens have gone off, again, and we're down in the cellar, and I'm crouched on the end of our bunk, writing this by the swaying light of the single electric bulb. I already had a stabbing headache, and the dank, stale air down here is only making it worse. It's been an absolutely awful day, and all the signs are that it will be an awful night, too.

I suppose it's just that we're so exhausted. They've only dropped a few bombs on London so far, and none close to us. But each night, there's the interrupted sleep; the effort of dragging our bedding down two flights of stairs in the blackout every time the siren goes off; the uneasy feeling that this really isn't anything much to complain about, that it's all going to get much, much worse. Veronica and I debate each night whether we should just stay upstairs in our flat, but we did promise the ARP warden—and Aunt Charlotte.

She and Henry went back to Milford this afternoon, after our disastrous family luncheon at Claridge's. I'd been *so* looking forward to it—Toby had twenty-four hours' leave, and Simon managed to swap duties with someone else, so that, for once, he could come into town on a Saturday. But Aunt Charlotte had spent the whole morning, and most of the previous day, dragging Henry round the shops to buy school supplies, so was in a foul mood. And then Toby was nearly an hour late, providing her with ample time to harangue each of us in turn. Why did my hat look as though someone had sat upon it? Where were my gloves, and why didn't I have my hair pinned up neatly instead of letting it sprout all over the place? Surely a girl who sneaked off to stay with Julia Whittingham ought to have developed a better idea of how to dress, for wasn't that the one thing Julia was *good* at? Then Aunt Charlotte turned upon Veronica, who'd been seen brazenly holding hands with a known Bolshevik in the middle of Kensington Gardens.

"Spotted by Lady Bosworth, I presume," said Veronica. "Perhaps she could use her extraordinary surveillance skills for something helpful, like tracking German planes."

"Oh, I'm sure this is all very amusing for you *now*, Veronica, but wait a few years, until you're on the verge of turning into an old maid and are desperate to find a husband! *Then* you'll wish you'd taken more care of your reputation!" Aunt Charlotte was getting crosser by the second. "And as for that *job* of yours! Jaunting about the Continent, when there are so many worthwhile tasks you could be doing at Milford!"

"What, like bullying old ladies into handing over their only frying pan for salvage?" said Veronica. "Or lecturing villagers about how they're not allowed to toss an old chop bone to their dog anymore?"

Aunt Charlotte, who'd made a point of wearing her bottle-green WVS uniform (though with a nonregulation and very expensive suede hat), bristled at this. "Bones, as you well know, can be made into glycerin, which is needed for explosives," she snapped. "*And* they can be turned into glue, which holds together the very aeroplanes that are protecting this nation! It may be just an old chop bone to you, Veronica, but that's not how our brave young pilots see it . . . Oh, now, where *is* Tobias? I did tell him he ought to let Simon Chester make his own way here. And that's another thing—"

And she was off on a rant about how ridiculously expensive Rebecca's clinic was, and how the best therapy for all those so-called "patients" would be for them to do an honest day's work in a munitions factory. Meanwhile, Henry was bouncing up and down in her seat at the prospect of seeing Toby again.

"Have you been listening to the wireless? Have you, Sophie? Those dogfights over Kent, oh boy, are we *showing* those Nazis! Did you hear yesterday's score? Eighty-three of theirs shot down, and *we* only lost twenty-five!"

"So *many* people could be doing so much *more* for their country," said Aunt Charlotte, her furious gaze swiveling about the room like an anti-aircraft gun in search of a target. "I mean, just look at that young man over there, the one by the window. Why isn't *he* in uniform?"

So it was with great relief that I finally caught sight of Simon and Toby in the doorway. "Oh, here they are!" I cried, and everyone, even complete strangers, turned to smile at the two handsome young men in RAF blue making their way towards our table. But as they drew closer, my heart sank. Simon looked as though he hadn't slept for days, Toby had lost an alarming amount of weight, and it was clear the two of them had been arguing. They slumped into their seats with a few muttered words of greeting, and none at all of apology for their lateness.

"Did you go flying this morning, Toby?" said Henry. "Or did you have the whole morning off?"

Toby propped his elbow on the table and his chin in his hand, and stared blankly at the menu.

"Still, even if you left *very* early, I expect it would take ages to drive all the way from Sussex," said Henry, beaming her forgiveness at him. He didn't appear to notice.

"Yes, I do hope they give you pilots extra petrol coupons for your motorcars," said Aunt Charlotte, favoring Toby with her fondest, most indulgent look. "It's *so* important that those serving in the forces can get away for visits to their family."

"Well, it's not so much that they *give* us petrol," said Toby, glancing up at last. "More that there's so much of it lying about the airfield that no one notices when some goes missing."

Aunt Charlotte pretended she hadn't heard that. "Well!" she said brightly. "So, Tobias, what are you having for luncheon? Goodness, all these new food regulations make ordering so complicated, don't they? Only one main course permitted to be served at each meal . . . But Tobias, dear, you must order the lamb. A man *needs* red meat."

"I'll have the chicken," Toby told the waiter, although when it arrived, he did no more than prod at it with his fork.

"Don't you like it?" said Henry. "You can have my fish, if you want."

"I'm just not very hungry," Toby said. He did, however, drink most of a bottle of wine that some old gentleman sent over to our table in appreciation of "the courageous job you lads are doing up in the skies."

"*Everyone* thinks what you're doing is wonderful," said Henry. "Did you hear Mr. Churchill on the wireless? 'Never in the field of . . . something . . . was so much owed by so many to so few.'"

"Must have been talking about our drinks bills," said Toby.

"*No*, he was talking about how brave you are, and how you fighter pilots are the only ones who can stop the invasion! It's like knights in shining armor going into battle, isn't it?"

"Is it?" Toby said flatly.

"Yes! You're heroes facing the hordes of—"

"Henrietta," said Aunt Charlotte sharply. "Stop chattering, and finish your food before it goes cold."

"All *right*," she said, but she obediently applied herself to her plate.

Unfortunately, no one else was having any success at keeping a conversation going. Aunt Charlotte, after numerous attempts at drawing Toby out, turned to Simon to inquire about interest rates and war bonds, although his replies were so perfunctory that she soon gave up. Veronica started to talk about the newspaper reports of Oswald Mosley living a life of luxury in prison, but lost interest halfway through and trailed off. Meanwhile, I was darting anxious glances at Toby, trying not to feel hurt that he was ignoring me. But it was a bizarre situation; I acknowledged that. The men who'd fought in the Crusades, or the Napoleonic Wars, or even in the trenches of the last war, hadn't been able to take the day off to meet up with family and friends. But here we all were, having luncheon in a grand hotel. It made war seem so normal, so much a part of regular, everyday life. And yet, just *look* at what it had done to my brother. He was unshaven; there were dark circles, almost bruises, around his eyes; his whole body twitched when a waiter dropped a spoon on the table. And Simon looked almost as bad . . . But Henry had started in on *him* now.

"What is it you actually *do*, Simon? I mean, at Fighter Command HQ? Or aren't you allowed to say?"

"He bosses us pilots around," said Toby with a humorless smile. "Don't you, Simon?"

"That's right," said Simon. "Not that *you* ever pay much attention to orders."

"Oh," said Henry. "Well, I suppose it's an important job, whatever it is. Still, it must be annoying for you, Simon, being left out of the action. Gosh, it must be thrilling, getting to shoot down Nazis—"

At that, Toby let his fork fall with a clatter. "You want to know what it's like?" he said.

"No, actually, we *don't*," said Simon quickly. "Sophie! How's your job going?"

"Well, I'll tell you," said Toby, shoving his plate out of the way and leaning across the table. "It's exhausting and nerve-racking and bloody terrifying. The first time I landed after coming under fire, the ground crew had to prize me out of the cockpit because all my muscles had seized up. I couldn't stand, I couldn't talk, I was drenched in sweat. They had to drag me into the dispersal hut."

"Toby," said Simon, putting his hand on Toby's arm, but Toby shook him off.

"The first time I shot down a plane, I was amazed I'd managed to do it without panicking or throwing up or blacking out in the middle of it. The second time was right after I watched a friend go down in flames over the Channel. I shot the tail off a 109 and someone else did the rest, and yes, I was thrilled, I was exhilarated, I was *ecstatic* that I'd helped kill a man. What a hero!"

Henry was blinking rapidly at her plate. Aunt Charlotte cleared her throat, carefully repositioned her cutlery, and then glanced around, as though worried someone might overhear. Simon had closed his eyes. Only Veronica gazed steadily at Toby.

"It sounds like hell," she said. "But you're stopping the

bombers from getting through. You're putting your life at risk to save others. That *is* heroic."

"You don't understand," Toby said, his voice rising. "No one does! You think I give a *damn* about being heroic? I don't even know good from evil anymore . . . Oh, what's the point?" He'd lurched to his feet and was groping for his cap. "I have to go, I need to get back."

"You're not fit to drive anywhere," said Simon. "Sit down, for God's sake, I'll take you back after we've all—"

But Toby was already stalking towards the door.

"Oh, go after him," cried Aunt Charlotte. *"Please."* Simon shoved back his chair and followed without another word.

"I'm *sorry*," choked out Henry. "I'm really, really sorry, I didn't mean to upset him!" Aunt Charlotte, unexpectedly, reached over to pat her hand.

"Poor child," she said. "Poor, dear child." But she was looking towards the doorway, so she could just as well have meant Toby.

Dear Soph,

SORRY I was so utterly bloody on Saturday. I'd had a rotten week and then I had a row with Simon on the way over, but I had no right to take it out on you. I'll make it up to Henry, promise. Forgive me?

It's just that I was so tired, but I'm absolutely fine now. The doctor gave me a couple of sleeping pills when I got back, and I had ten hours' solid sleep, and that's made the world of difference.

Anyway, I feel terrible that I didn't even talk to you much. Hope your job is becoming more interesting and your boss slightly less stupid. Could you pass on my apologies to V? Although I am not so worried about her, as she already knows I'm a complete idiot.

Lots of love,
Toby

11th September 1940

We ought to be feeling more at home in our little cellar now. We've brought down books and writing paper and pencils, a tin of biscuits, water bottles, a rug, a folding tray that we use as a desk, and a box of candles in case the electricity goes out. Trust the Germans to wait till tea leaves were being rationed to two ounces a week before they started their bombardment—life underground would be far easier to bear with an unlimited supply of nice hot tea. It's also a nuisance having to lug our bedding up and down the stairs, but it's too damp to keep a set of blankets and pillows down here permanently. I dread to think what it will be like in the middle of winter—but surely these raids won't *still* be going on then. Will they?

Saturday was when it started in earnest. The weather had been glorious, and Veronica and I spent most of the afternoon working in the garden. When the siren went off around tea-time, we barely paused to look up into the sky.

"Oh, honestly," said Veronica, brushing the dirt off her

hands. "Can't they give it a rest on a Saturday? I'm going to have a bath."

"No, wait," I said. "Listen."

I thought I heard a very faint, dull rumbling. We peered up at the sky, but our patch of it was a brilliant blue, interrupted only by a few strands of cotton-wool cloud.

"Actually, I can hear something, too," said Veronica, after a moment. Then a fire engine started up nearby and rushed along our side road, bells ringing madly.

"Let's go up and have a look," I said.

We let ourselves into Montmaray House through a side door, groped our way through the dark, silent rooms to the servants' stairs, then climbed up and up, all the way to the roof, which provided a majestic view of Kensington Gardens and Hyde Park, and beyond that, Westminster and the City. But it wasn't lush greenery or historic architecture that caught our attention; it was the sky. It looked as though someone had flicked a giant brush, dripping with black paint, at London's clean blue ceiling. As we stared, each black speck grew bigger and bigger, then transformed itself into a tiny glinting aeroplane. There were hundreds of them, and they were all converging on the same spot.

"The East End," said Veronica. "They're aiming for the docks." And as she spoke, a cloud of white smoke appeared on the horizon. The aeroplanes had arranged themselves in neat lines above this and were taking it in turns to spiral down and drop their bombs and fly off. The cloud rose higher, and darkened, and then expanded to take over the entire sky. From halfway across the city, we could see the red-and-gold flames leaping from the ground to claw at the black air. It wasn't until the next day that we heard about the gasworks and the arsenal that received direct hits, the piles of freshly delivered timber that turned the docks into a towering inferno, the streets flowing with molten rubber and soap and paint from burning factories, the barges that caught alight and drifted off down the Thames like floating lanterns. At the time, we only knew it was the most monstrous fire we'd ever seen. It would have been more sensible to take cover, but we just stood there, gaping, awestruck at the scale of the destruction. I remember thinking, *Oh God, Julia's on ambulance duty tonight*, and, *Thank heavens that Daniel doesn't live in Whitechapel anymore*. It was as though I could only comprehend what was going on by focusing on a couple of people I knew who might be affected. Of course, I realized even then that hundreds of people must be dying as I watched, but that was just too much to take in.

Then the all clear sounded, jolting us out of our daze, and we whirled round and ran back down to the flat. I tried to telephone Milford, to let them know we were all right, but I couldn't get through.

"Those bombers will be back after dark," Veronica predicted. "The blackout's useless if there's an enormous fire lighting up the whole of London."

And, of course, she was right. They returned a couple of hours later, and it went on all night, and it wasn't just the East

End they were aiming at this time. Down in our cellar, I could hear the bombs whining closer and closer, feel the crump and the shudder as each one landed. The electric light flickered and died. The air filtering through the vents tasted of burning. I was amazed, when we staggered out of our shelter the next morning, to find the house and grounds still there. It had seemed as though the whole world was being pounded into oblivion, but our street was untouched, except for a fine layer of ash and powdered brick that had settled on everything.

The next night, they hit the City, and knocked out the southbound railway lines. On Monday night, another couple of hundred people died, including dozens of poor homeless East Enders who'd been evacuated to Canning Town. And on and on and *on* it goes. It isn't only after dark that we have to worry about, either. Every single day this week, we've had our work interrupted by raids. Once, after I'd dashed across to John Lewis in my luncheon break to buy some elastic, the warning siren went off and I had to spend an hour and a half in their basement. It *was* much nicer than our office shelter, though. They had a gramophone playing soothing music, and the shopgirls came round selling books and packets of biscuits, and handing out khaki wool so we could knit scarves for the army as we waited for the all clear.

And at least now, our own anti-aircraft guns seem to be firing back—I didn't hear them at *all* the first few nights. I don't know if they actually manage to hit any planes, but the noise of the guns makes me feel slightly less vulnerable. And I suppose things might be even worse if we didn't have those barrage balloons floating overhead. It's hard to believe that big silver balloons might be any deterrent to German bombers, but I think they force the planes to fly higher, so their bombs are aimed less accurately . . . not that *that* is particularly reassuring.

These are the sorts of things one thinks (and writes) about when stuck in a tiny cellar during a bombing raid.

23rd September 1940

Simon met me for luncheon at a little café near my office today—he had to drive some very important Air Marshal to Whitehall and had a couple of hours free. He tried to talk me into resigning from my job and going back to Milford, at least until the air raids stop, and I must admit I was tempted. I am so exhausted, and so sickened by the destruction. Each day on my way to work, I find more and more of the city has been reduced to cinders and crumbled brick and fragments of charred, twisted metal. Oxford Street got the worst of it last week—John Lewis is now a blackened skeleton. Even Buckingham Palace had its windows blown out when half a dozen bombs landed in its grounds.

But I would never leave Veronica here by herself, and she would never give up her job, and even *I* feel a tug of loyalty towards the Ministry of Food (office morale has improved markedly since Lord Woolton took over).

"I suppose you think it's going to get even worse," I said to Simon.

"If I did, I wouldn't say so in public," he said. "Isn't that illegal now, spreading gloom and despondency?"

"Oh, come on," I said, but very quietly (and I did glance about to see if anyone could possibly be listening, although no one was). "Just because the newspapers keep going on about how cheerful and defiant Londoners are doesn't mean anyone *believes* it. I know they're not telling us what's really happening. They don't even read out the number of casualties on the news anymore."

"Well, how would that help anyone? What does it matter whether they say it was a hundred killed last night, or a thousand? I doubt the authorities have the exact figures, anyway. They're usually still digging bodies out of the rubble days later."

"It's *barbaric*," I said fervently. "Don't those German pilots understand what they're doing? They aren't hitting military targets. They're destroying rows and rows of ordinary houses, shops, schools . . . even hospitals, and *they've* got big red crosses painted on their roofs."

"Pretty hard to know what one's going to hit when one lets a bomb drop from four thousand feet up. And we're doing the same back to them."

I wanted to say, "Good! They deserve it! They started it!" But I knew how childish that would sound, and I didn't actually feel that way (well, not *really*). Instead, I changed the subject.

"Have you spoken to Toby recently?" I asked. "I had another letter from him, after that big battle last week. It sounded as though every plane in Fighter Command was called in for that one. Not that he said very much about himself. He did mention he'd probably be getting some leave soon."

"He didn't tell you he's been promoted?"

"What?" I said. "No!"

"Flight Lieutenant." Simon hesitated, then added, "He's been awarded the Distinguished Flying Cross, too. But they certainly won't be presenting it to him at any official Buckingham Palace medal ceremony."

"Why not?"

"Why do you think? Because he's always in trouble! He never writes up his combat reports properly, he wore pajamas under his flying kit one morning because he slept in and couldn't be bothered getting dressed—he even invites the sergeants to play cards with him and the other officers." Simon saw my confusion. "That's a court-martial offense, officers socializing with other ranks on the base. Even when they're all pilots, it's against the rules."

"Well, that sounds like a *stupid* rule!" I said.

"Perhaps, but that's the way it is, and the air force is still a lot better than the other services. I doubt I'd have had any chance of becoming an officer if I'd joined the army, and I probably wouldn't even have been accepted into the navy. Anyway, Toby's had so many official warnings that if he weren't so good at shooting down planes and so bloody charming, they'd have got rid of him ages ago."

I took a moment to try to assimilate these various images of Toby: ruthless fighter pilot and convivial colleague and decorated serviceman and irreverent rule breaker (the last, at least, was familiar). But if it was difficult for me to merge all these Tobys into one whole, functioning person, how much harder must it be for *him*?

"Simon, what were you two arguing about?" I asked. "You know, that day we all had luncheon at Claridge's."

"What? Oh, I don't remember." He glanced about for the waitress. "Do you want tea? If one can *call* it tea these days, when it always looks and tastes more like dishwater—"

"*Simon,*" I insisted. "Toby was really upset. I was so worried about him! I still am, actually, even though he's trying to convince us all that he's absolutely fine now."

"It was nothing. We were both tired and on edge, that's all."

I kept gazing at Simon, and he kept avoiding my gaze.

"Anyway, it's not . . . it isn't a problem anymore," he said.

"Why not?"

"God!" he hissed. He looked about, then lowered his voice. "If you *must* know, it was about a new pilot posted to his squadron, some boy barely out of school. He was mooning about after Toby, completely besotted."

"Oh. But . . . that's not Toby's fault, is it?"

"Toby could have brought the whole thing to an abrupt halt right at the start with a couple of well-placed insults—God knows he's had plenty of practice fending off admirers—but no, he thought that would be 'cruel.' I told him it would be a damn sight more cruel if anyone found out. They'd both have been kicked out of the air force."

"Why? They weren't . . . doing anything, were they?"

"Sophie, they wouldn't *have* to do anything! The very *idea* of it is against regulations, against the law, against . . . against common decency!"

"I know you don't believe *that*," I said levelly.

"I just thought Toby should have done something to stop it, that's all. For the sake of that boy, if nothing else, to help him realize how futile it all was. But it doesn't matter now."

"What do you mean? Why . . . Oh."

"A third of Toby's squadron's gone now," said Simon quietly. "In just six weeks. The RAF's running out of men to replace them. They've cut training from six months to two weeks, and some of those new pilots don't even last a day in combat." Simon fiddled with his knife. "Toby was right. It would've been needlessly cruel to say anything to that boy."

The waitress came over to see if we wanted anything else. We didn't.

"I'm sorry," I whispered, after she'd gone. "About all those poor pilots. And . . . well, for making you talk about it when you didn't want to."

"You didn't *make* me," he said. "Anyway, you know what they say—a trouble shared is a trouble halved." He looked almost as exhausted as the last time I'd had luncheon with him—not at *all* as though his burden had been lessened by our conversation. I felt even worse.

"And I'm sorry that—I mean, your job must be pretty awful, if you have to keep track of how many men need to be replaced," I said. "And you're probably getting bombed just as much as the rest of us."

"It's not too bad where I am," he said. "It's not as though we're in the middle of the East End."

"The raids have changed everything, haven't they?" I said, looking through the window, crisscrossed with gummed paper, past the mound of leaking sandbags, across the cratered road to a shop that was missing its awnings and half its roof. "You know, when I'm saying goodbye to Veronica each morning, I sometimes wonder if . . . well, if we're both going to come home again that evening. It makes me feel I can't ever make plans, not even for the next day, because who knows what might have happened by then—"

"Stop it, Sophie," Simon said roughly. "You're being morbid! I mean it, you ought to go back to Milford."

"No," I said. "No, that's just what Hitler wants. He hopes we'll all flee to the countryside, and then he can invade London—so that's why I'm determined to stay." Simon opened his mouth to argue some more, so I rushed on. "Anyway, I can't resign from my job now. One of the girls in the office has just left to get married, and Miss Thynne's on sick leave. She burnt her arm putting out an incendiary on her roof. So, Mr. Bowker really needs me there in the office."

Simon sighed heavily. "Well, be careful, won't you? And tell Veronica . . . no, actually, don't tell her I said anything, because she'll just do the exact opposite."

"You be careful, too, Simon," I said when we were saying goodbye, and he said, rather gloomily, that he was always careful.

Which is quite true, he *is*. The problem is that being careful isn't enough anymore.

16th October 1940

Written at Julia's, because the firemen found an unexploded bomb in front of Montmaray House today and everyone in our street has been evacuated. I suspect the Germans do it deliberately—send down bombs with a delay mechanism—because they realize it causes even more anxiety and disruption to normal life than an immediate explosion.

I'm a bomb expert by now. I can tell the difference between a high explosive and an incendiary, just from the sound. I know that the Germans have started attaching cardboard pipes to the sides of their bomb cylinders, so that the last thing the victims hear is a terrifying whistle announcing their oncoming death. I know that incendiary bombs burst into flames on impact and shoot out shards of red-hot metal at anyone trying to put out the fire. I know there are bombs attached to parachutes, designed to drift down and explode in midair, flattening anything underneath.

Veronica threw out my *Evening Standard Guide to Air Raid*

Sounds last week, because she said I was becoming obsessed. But the more information one has, the more one feels in *control* of the situation. That's simply common sense. One would really think Veronica would understand that!

Anyway. She and I have Julia's house to ourselves at the moment, because Rupert's away, and Julia's at the ambulance station (or more likely, driving round in the pitch black over roads littered with rubble, on her way to yet another set of horribly injured Londoners). We're down in the kitchen now, as most of it's underground and the window is protected by sandbags. It's amazing how loud the Hyde Park anti-aircraft battery sounds from here. Julia says that sometimes she finds bits of shrapnel in her garden, depending on which direction they're firing. I certainly hope they shoot down a couple of bombers tonight. Except then, I suppose the planes would crash on someone's house, along with all their bombs, which would be even worse than bombs by themselves . . .

Oh, I don't know why I pretend I have any control over *any* of this!

To distract myself, I *was* going to copy Henry's latest letter into my journal, but I don't feel up to the task of trying to translate all the spelling errors into Kernetin. Her new school hasn't yet led to any significant improvements in her literacy skills. It's also far less "exclusive" than her previous school, which greatly distresses Aunt Charlotte (oh, the horror, her niece being educated alongside the daughters of shopkeepers). However, as there weren't many educational establishments willing to accept Henry as a pupil, we didn't have much choice—and she does seem to have settled in fairly easily. In fact, she's the most envied girl in the school at the moment, after Toby made a slight detour on his way back to his aerodrome last week and landed his Spitfire on her school's hockey field. Two hundred screaming schoolgirls rushed out of class to greet him, and there were several instances of swooning as he climbed out of the cockpit and peeled off his flying helmet. Even the head-mistress was observed to become slightly breathless and giggly when he asked her permission to take Henry to the village tea shop (they ended up having tea in her study). Henry devoted five sides of paper to an account of this momentous event—I think it's the longest letter she's written in her life. Most of the remaining page was about how it was a good thing she'd resisted when Aunt Charlotte wanted her to go to Canada, because one of the ships transporting the child evacuees has just been tor-pedoed by the Germans. I read in the newspaper that most of the children drowned. It was absolutely heartbreaking. Those poor, poor parents, believing their children would be better off if they left England—and then hearing that dreadful news.

It just goes to show that it makes absolutely no difference *what* one does. Mr. Bowker was telling me that his friend had a neighbor whose Anderson shelter in their back garden re-ceived a direct hit. Everyone inside the shelter was blown to bits, but the house was barely touched—they'd all have been fine if they'd stayed in their beds. And then, on Sunday, there was that bomb in Stoke Newington, where the upper floors of an apartment building collapsed into the basement—where everyone had gathered because they'd been told it was the safest place—and all the water and sewage and gas pipes broke, and the people who hadn't already been crushed to death were suffocated or *drowned*. Then, the very next day, a bomb drilled right through the road into the underground railway station at Balham, which hundreds of people use as a shelter, and a great gush of water flooded the dark tunnel and . . .

Now Veronica is threatening to confiscate my journal. She says she can tell exactly what I'm writing by the expression on my face, and that if I don't change the subject to something more optimistic, she's going to take away my book and put it on the highest shelf of the pantry, out of my reach.

Optimistic! Of course *Veronica* is feeling optimistic about life at the moment—*she* spent the whole afternoon with her *boyfriend*. Daniel has some hush-hush job in the north of London now, but he had the day off and she met him at the National Gallery at lunchtime. All the paintings have been taken down and stored somewhere away from the bombs, but there are concerts held in the octagonal room each day, and it only costs a shilling, and one can buy sandwiches to eat in the break. Today there was a string quartet playing Mozart, and the first violinist turned out to be a friend of Daniel's mother. After the concert, Veronica and Daniel wandered up Charing Cross Road, where all the secondhand bookshops are, and he bought her two books, one about prehistoric stone monuments in Cornwall and the other about European diplomacy in the

1920s, both written in the sort of dense, scholarly language that gives normal people a headache (Veronica is already half-way through the Cornish one and says it's absolutely riveting). Then they visited a professor friend of Daniel's at the University of London, and after that, it was time to meet up with me for dinner. I *had* told them not to bother, but I think Veronica felt guilty because it was supposed to be her turn to cook tonight. Or perhaps she didn't want me going back to the flat by myself, in case there was an early-evening air raid. Or else she felt sorry for me, having to type Mr. Bowker's badly punctuated letters all afternoon while she was enjoying herself. Whatever the reason, I almost wish I'd *insisted* on going home by myself because . . .

Oh, good, Veronica's safely engrossed in her book again, so I can fall back into despondency. The thing is, I *saw* them together. This evening. Walking beside each other, not touching but perfectly in step, their heads level, their gazes intertwined. Veronica was saying something, and Daniel was nodding in time, and it would have been obvious, even to a complete stranger, that here were two people who understood and trusted one another absolutely. They looked as though they'd been married for years, but still found each other fascinating. I stood there, watching them approach me, and felt a tremendous wave of . . . well, it was almost *grief* that washed over me. For I realized at that moment that I'd lost Veronica, that she belonged to someone else now.

Of course, I like Daniel very, very much, and I know perfectly well that he doesn't *own* Veronica. No one does; she wouldn't ever allow herself to *be* owned. And I was already vaguely aware that she and I had been slowly but steadily traveling in different directions ever since we left Montmaray—ever since we were first given the chance to explore life and *choose* our own directions. Really, *all* of us—Toby, Simon, even Henry—are drifting apart from one another, which is completely understandable and natural, and would be happening even if we weren't living through a war. But it's just that Veronica and I have always been so close . . .

Oh, I realize she still loves me. It's not as though I believe that she, or anyone else, has only a finite amount of love to offer, that she'll somehow use it all up on Daniel. And it's not as though she's going to abandon our flat to go and *live* with him (not in the immediate future, anyway). I knew all that, and yet I still felt absolutely bereft. It was then that I understood that part of my distress was probably plain old *jealousy*. Veronica had found her soul mate. And I hadn't, and probably never would.

I really felt *disgusted* with myself then. Why couldn't I be happy that *she* was happy, that she'd found someone who was perfect for her? How could I possibly be so selfish? I tend to think of myself as a reasonably good person at heart, but at that moment, I realized I was both deluded and despicable. Anyway, these were the thoughts and feelings rampaging about inside my head when Daniel glanced up and noticed me. The two of them broke into wide smiles, and quickened their pace, and seemed so pleased to see me that I felt even worse. Then

Veronica presented me with a book about Shelley that they'd both thought I'd like, which only heaped coals on the fire of my guilt. I developed a raging headache over dinner, from trying so hard to be delighted and sociable—a fitting punishment for my treacherous head. And then, after we'd seen Daniel off on his train, we arrived back at our flat to be informed about the unexploded bomb—more punishment, although it seems very unfair that Veronica and everyone else in my street should suffer for my sins . . .

Oh, Simon is right! I really *am* turning morbid. I must make more of an effort to concentrate on life's blessings. For example, that both Toby and Anthony have been moved away from the coast, to safer, quieter aerodromes, for a much-deserved break. And that the British government has finally agreed to stop interning enemy aliens. Admittedly, they haven't released the people who are already *in* the camps, but Daniel did sound hopeful that his cousins' case would be reviewed soon, and at least they haven't been shoved onto one of those horribly over-crowded ships being sent off on perilous journeys to Canada or Australia. And also . . .

No, can't think of anything else that's remotely positive. Not right now. I'm sure there *are* lots of good things happening in the world, though. Somewhere.

Anthony is dead.

I just can't believe it. Dear, sweet Anthony! He was so proud of being a pilot, so passionate about flying. He was so *good* at it. How *could* he have been shot down by some Nazi? It's unthinkable. Except I can't *stop* thinking about it.

He died a hero, his Squadron Leader insisted, as though *that* makes it all right. Oh, poor Julia, I can't even bear to imagine how she must have felt when she read the telegram. Thank goodness Rupert was there when it arrived. He was the one who telephoned us, just before he drove Julia up to Northampton, where Anthony's parents live. Anthony was their only son, and they can't even have a proper funeral, because the plane got burnt up and there's nothing left of him but ashes. Oh, please, *please* let it be true what the Squadron Leader said, that Anthony didn't feel a thing, that he really *was* knocked unconscious long before the plane crashed into the forest and burst into flames. But it *must* be true, mustn't it? Because otherwise, he would have bailed out with his parachute. Anthony knew his plane back to front, he would have understood exactly when and where he was hit, and whether he could bring the plane down safely or not, and he definitely knew how to use a parachute. All the pilots do, Toby told me—they're trained to abandon the plane in an emergency, because pilots are more valuable than machines. That's the way the RAF thinks. Quicker and cheaper to repair a smashed plane, or even build a new one, than to train a new recruit to the level of an experienced combat pilot. It's all about efficient use of time and money to *them*.

I know pilots are getting killed every single day, because I read the newspapers and listen to the BBC broadcasts. But I've always tried to regard the numbers as simply a score in a game. The smaller *our* number each day, the better. The higher the number for the Germans, the sooner this ghastly contest would be over. It was just too terrifying, with Toby in combat, to picture those numbers as actual human beings, as young men with wives and mothers and sisters. I still can't face that fact head-on—I glance at it sideways, then hurriedly squeeze my eyes shut.

That's why I can't really believe Anthony is dead. Despite the telegram and then the official RAF letter—despite hearing the news from Rupert, one of the most trustworthy people I know—I feel there must be some mistake. Perhaps some other pilot had taken Anthony's plane up that afternoon, perhaps Anthony had left the aerodrome, forgetting to sign out properly . . . Except no, that wouldn't work. If he'd had any leave, Julia would have gone up to visit him, or he'd have driven down to London. She'd been complaining that she hadn't seen him for months . . . No, he's probably in some hospital with a broken leg. He jumped out with his parachute and landed awkwardly, and there was a mix-up with his identity while he was unconscious. And he'll be all embarrassed when he wakes up and finds out what's happened, and Julia will rush off to collect him in her ambulance and bring him home, and she'll spend the rest of his sick leave fussing over him . . .

Veronica has just come in and said she's arranged for flowers to be sent to the chapel. For the memorial service tomorrow. It's just a small ceremony for his family—his mother couldn't bear to face a huge crowd.

Anthony really *is* dead. I'm never going to see him again. He won't ever again debate Marxist theory with Veronica, or have long, unintelligible discussions about aeroplane maintenance with Toby, or help Henry fix her roller skates. Anthony's gone, forever, and he was only twenty-six years old. That's much, much too young to die.

It was my twentieth birthday yesterday, but none of us were in any state to celebrate.

I know I was desperate for something to think about (*anything* other than poor Anthony), but I'd hoped for a *pleasant* distraction. That's too much to expect, though, these days. Veronica has just told me she might be going to Spain again. Apparently, Hitler's been making strenuous efforts to persuade Franco to join the war, and the British are equally determined to keep Spain out of it.

"But I thought Spain was in no position to fight another war," I said, trying to start up the sort of complex political discussion that would occupy all my concentration.

"No, they don't have many resources to spare," Veronica acknowledged. "But it wouldn't take much to attack Gibraltar, and Franco could make things very awkward for the Allies in North Africa."

"Right," I said, attempting to make a mental map of all that and failing. "But how does the Foreign Office know all this? About those secret meetings of Hitler's, I mean."

"Oh, they have plenty of intelligence sources in Spain," said Veronica. "Although that last meeting wasn't exactly *secret*. It was held in Hitler's railway coach, on the French side of the border, and that idiot Ribbentrop was in charge. He'd arranged for a German military band to be playing at the railway station when Hitler arrived, and the band wandered over the border into Spain wearing their uniforms and caused a diplomatic incident. Anyway, Franco seems noncommittal at the moment—he's still not sure who's going to win the war, and he doesn't want to support the wrong side. So it's vital that he understands Britain isn't anywhere *near* being defeated, and that's why the Foreign Office is sending more people over to Madrid to help convince him."

"And *you* need to be one of them," I said.

"Well, I *could* be very useful over there, I think, but my boss only got away with it last time because that was a crisis requiring urgent action. *His* boss was furious when he found out. Dreadful enough permitting a female to work in the London office, but to send one *abroad* . . . Oh, they've a dozen arguments against me going to Spain, even temporarily. The Spanish officials wouldn't take a female interpreter seriously—they'd be offended at the very idea. And the Embassy staff need to go out drinking at nightclubs and on overnight hunting trips in order to gather information, and I couldn't accompany them without causing a scandal. And being single, I'd be *bound* to distract the Embassy staff from their duties—or else I'd end up getting seduced by some local Don Juan. Of course, if I were married, they'd tell me I couldn't possibly leave my husband behind in England, or they'd worry about me getting pregnant and having to resign. And then there's the usual rubbish about women being too delicate to cope with the heat, or the cold, or the food, or the spartan accommodation. They ought to hear the Ambassador—*he* never stops complaining about all of that, and anyway, his wife is in Madrid, and she doesn't seem to have collapsed in a fit of the vapors just yet."

Veronica sighed.

"It *is* terrible timing, though," she said. "I'd hate to think of you alone here at night, with all the bombs. But if poor Julia's still at her parents' place and Rupert's away, you wouldn't be any better off staying at her house . . ."

We've had air raids almost every night for more than two months. I'm amazed Montmaray House is still standing. Even Kensington Palace took a direct hit last month. And it's not just London—it's going on *everywhere*, from Scotland to Cornwall. All the ports have been attacked, every airfield across the country, any town large enough to contain a factory or a power station or a gasworks (or that's simply unlucky enough to be located under a flight path). Coventry is a wasteland now, with so many hundreds of unidentifiable bodies that the authorities want to dig a communal grave and hold a mass funeral. The situation is so bleak that I can't see how the Foreign Office could *possibly* manage to convince Spain that we're going to win this war. I said this to Veronica, but she shook her head.

"I know it seems dire at the moment," she said, "but really, the situation is much better than it was even a few months ago. Then, there was a real fear we'd be invaded. But to do that, the Germans needed to knock out the RAF, and they've failed dismally at that."

"Thanks to our fighter pilots," I said. "Thanks to all those men who . . . who sacrificed themselves." I was suddenly close to tears.

"Anthony *didn't* die in vain," said Veronica fiercely. She reached over and grasped my hand. "Sophie, I *promise*, Germany is going to lose this war."

"That doesn't mean we'll *win*," I said, blinking hard. "How can we? We've already lost so much."

"We just have to stick it out a bit longer," she said. "Germany can keep bombing us and trying to cut off our supplies, but sooner or later, America will join in on our side."

"But what about what Mr. Kennedy said?" I protested. "'Democracy is finished in England.' That's what he said in that newspaper interview. He thinks we've already lost!"

"*Kennedy!*" said Veronica, with unmitigated scorn. "He won't be Ambassador much longer, I can tell you that. President Roosevelt doesn't pay any attention to *him*. Kennedy's career is finished now. The Americans *will* help us—it's just a matter of time. They've already introduced conscription over there, you know."

So depressing, to think of all those poor American boys being forced to register for military service. As though there aren't enough people dying already.

Now I feel even worse than I did before my distraction.

Today has been rather tumultuous. Not because of the air raids, but . . . Well, I ought to start at the beginning, I suppose. Veronica is still in Spain, so Toby managed to get a weekend pass and came down to London to visit me.

"I really don't think you should be here by yourself, Soph," he said, dumping his bag on Veronica's bed and frowning at the windowpanes, half of which have had to be replaced with plywood. "Aunt C would have a fit if she knew you were waiting out the raids alone in that cellar."

"Then don't tell her," I suggested. "Have you had luncheon? Do you want a cup of tea or something?"

"I mean it, Soph," he insisted. "Can't you go and stay with that girl from work? Or at least go to the public shelter?"

"Anne doesn't have any space—she shares a tiny bed-sitter with a friend—and that public shelter down the road smells absolutely disgusting. I'm not sleeping in *there*. Anyway, the ARP warden always comes round to check on me in the morning if there's been a raid. It's nowhere near as frightening as it used to be, and there haven't been any really big raids for ages."

"There *will* be," Toby said, with the grim conviction of one who'd spent the past three months studying the Luftwaffe at terrifyingly close range. "It's just that they're busy blitzing the north at the moment. You wait, they'll be back in deadly earnest any day now—"

The telephone rang to interrupt this cheerful conversation. It was Mrs. Timms.

"Sorry to bother you," she said, "but I'm going over to Bristol to stay with my daughter-in-law for a couple of days, and I can't get hold of Mr. Rupert, and I hate the thought of leaving poor Lady Whittingham here by herself."

"Julia?" I said, surprised. "But I thought she was with her mother at Astley?"

"No, no, she's here and won't barely leave her bedroom, either. Crying her eyes out most of the time, too."

"Let's go," said Toby, snatching up his car keys. So we drove straight around to Julia's Belgravia house, where Mrs. Timms met us at the front door in her coat and hat.

"She's in the sitting room," said Mrs. Timms, nodding over her shoulder. "Poor dear, I've left her dinner in the oven, not that she's eating anything much nowadays. She ought to be with her family at a time like this . . . But I do feel easier, now you're here to talk some sense into her. Well, I'm off."

We found Julia hunched over on the sofa nearest the fire, huddled inside a brocade housecoat that seemed far too large for her. I was horrified to see how ill she looked—her face greenish and drawn, with dark hollows under her eyes. She'd combed her hair and put on some lipstick, but this gave the impression of having been achieved with great effort.

"Darling, what are you *doing* here, all alone?" said Toby. "Why aren't you at Astley?"

"Oh," she said, making a feeble attempt at a smile, "you know how Mummy gets, fussing away. It all got a bit much for me . . . But what are *you* doing in London, Toby?"

I suddenly thought how dreadful it must be for her, to see Toby fit and well in his RAF uniform, when all that remained of Anthony was that photograph on her desk. But Julia barely seemed to notice what Toby was wearing—in fact, she seemed to be having difficulties concentrating on anything at all, possibly because she was so undernourished. There was a slice of dry toast with a few unenthusiastic bites taken out of it, sitting on the side table beside a glass of water. If *that* was all she'd been ingesting, no wonder she looked so thin and tired. I offered to go downstairs and make some sandwiches, but she shook her head violently.

"I couldn't face it," she said, then she clapped her hand to her mouth. "Oh, no. Back in a moment," she mumbled, and she hurried out of the room.

Toby and I exchanged looks. "Oh Lord," he said. "You don't think she's . . . *Could* she be?"

I was still busy calculating dates when Julia came back in, looking slightly less green.

"I always *think* I'm going to be sick, but I hardly ever am," she said, slumping back on the sofa. "I just feel queasy every single second of the day. I can't imagine why they ever decided to call it *morning* sickness."

"Have you seen a doctor?" said Toby.

She shook her head, frowning at her knees.

"But Julia, you really must," he urged. "You look dreadful and it can't be healthy, eating nothing but toast—"

"I can't!" she cried, startling us all. Then she said, more calmly, "I can't. He's Mummy's doctor, too, and he'd *tell* her. That's why I came back to London, as soon as I started feeling sick all the time. So she wouldn't work it out for herself."

"But what does it matter, whether she finds out now or later on?" said Toby, sounding bemused. He put a comforting arm around Julia. "I know the timing isn't . . . That is, it's all very sad that it's happened now, but your mother would be such a help for you. And Ant's family will be so pleased when they hear—" Toby looked over Julia's bent head and finally caught my frantic head-shaking. "Oh God," he said. "Sorry. I'm an idiot."

"Yes, you *are*," said Julia, but she sagged against him. I reached over and clasped her hand, and she gave a halfhearted squeeze back.

"You poor old *thing*," said Toby. "But are you absolutely *sure* that it can't be . . . ?"

"Certain," Julia said. "I hadn't seen Ant for two and a half months before . . . before he died. And I'd just written to his mother complaining about how he never seemed to get any leave anymore, and how I'd probably have to wait till *Christmas* to see him again." Her eyes filled with tears, but she swiped at them impatiently. "Anyway, I know exactly when it happened."

"Well, have you told . . . him?" asked Toby. "I suppose he's in one of the services?"

"I only saw him once," said Julia, "and I never want to see him again. The whole thing was completely *mad*, I do realize that now, but at the time I was just so . . . numb. So *dead*, really. I wanted to feel alive again. It was after the funeral, when I was traveling back to Astley and that wretched railway track got bombed. Our train just stopped, in what seemed like the middle of nowhere, in the pitch black. The railway station wasn't far away, but when we finally got there, I couldn't bear the thought of waiting about for hours on that freezing platform, so I went looking for a taxi and . . . and that's where I met him. Then the siren started up again and we could hear the planes coming back . . . Anyway, we went to a hotel, and he bought me a drink. Several drinks. And I felt so sorry for him. He was all alone, too . . ." She glanced up. "You think I'm dreadful, don't you?"

"Of course we don't," Toby said soothingly. "I go to bed with people I feel sorry for, all the *time*. I think of it as doing my bit for the war effort—you know, boosting the morale of Allied servicemen."

"Toby!" I said. "Be *serious*." But Julia had given an unwilling snort of laughter.

"If only everyone saw things your way, Toby," she said.

"But they don't, of course, which is why I'm in such terrible trouble now."

"I still don't see why," said Toby. "Really, how will anyone know that Ant isn't the father? Unless . . . this man wasn't from Jamaica or somewhere, was he?"

"No," said Julia dully. "No, he was Free French. Probably. I don't know, he could have been lying about that. He certainly lied when he promised me he'd be careful. Anyway, I've *told* you about not having seen Ant for months. His parents know all about that. They'd work it out straightaway."

"Well, never mind," Toby said. "You can marry me, and tell them it's my child. Actually, perhaps it *is* mine. I can't say I remember doing anything of that nature, but I suppose I could have been drunk at the time."

"Oh, stop it, Toby," said Julia. "I'm trying to figure some way out of this horrible mess, and you're just—"

"I'm being completely sincere," he said, tightening his grasp on her shoulders. "Julia. Listen. Aunt Charlotte's been trying to find me a wife for years, and I can't keep putting her off forever. And if *you* had a husband, you wouldn't have a problem, would you? I suppose there'd be a bit of gossip about how quickly you got married again, but Aunt Charlotte already thinks I'm madly in love with you, and everyone knows how irresistible I am. And we *do* love each other, don't we, darling? We've always had fun together. Lots of married couples have far less in common than we have."

Julia had been staring at him, open-mouthed, throughout this speech.

"What do you think?" he said. "Not that you have to decide this very second, but—"

"Oh, *Toby*," she said.

Then she burst into tears and flung her arms around his neck.

"Tea," he mouthed at me over the top of her head as he patted her back. I gazed at him in disbelief, shook my head slowly, then stalked off to the kitchen.

"This whole world has gone crazy," I told the cat, who was giving himself a vigorous bath on top of the draining board. I put the kettle on and sat down to have a think, but my mind was a whirl. Mostly I felt desperately sorry for Julia. I could only imagine her panic when she realized she was pregnant. And feeling so dreadfully sick all the time would make things seem even worse. Of course, I was shocked at the idea of her going off with some stranger like that—but then, she *was* a widow now. She hadn't been cheating on anyone. Anthony wouldn't have wanted her to spend the rest of her life in a nunnery— although I expect he'd have hoped she'd wait a bit longer than a *week* before replacing him. Still, it sounded as though she'd been rather drunk, and she'd *definitely* been under enormous emotional strain. Poor Julia! Being punished so severely for one bad decision—when that man, whoever he was, probably hadn't felt so much as a twinge of regret.

As for Toby's proposal . . . well, I suppose he and Julia *were* fond of each other . . . But no, the whole thing was absolutely ridiculous!

And so my thoughts seesawed back and forth as I waited for the kettle to whistle, and the cat scrubbed at his face with his paw. Then I made a pot of tea, found some jam biscuits in a tin, and took the tray upstairs. Toby still had his arm around Julia, and she was dabbing at her face with his handkerchief.

"So, should I be congratulating you on your engagement?" I asked as I set the tray down on the table. Oh dear, I hadn't meant to say that aloud . . .

Julia gave me a watery smile and shook her head. Then she turned to Toby. "No. It's awfully kind of you to offer, Toby darling, but I can't do that to you. Your aunt loathes me—she'd probably disinherit you. Besides, I can't go through with . . . with this. I can't bring a child into the world right now, not when everything's in such chaos. Especially *this* child . . . No, actually, I don't think that matters. I'd feel the same if it were Ant's."

She leaned forward and rested her face in her hands. "Oh God, and I don't even know how to go about being . . . not pregnant. Apart from hurling myself down the stairs. One would think all these bombs would have *frightened* it out, but all they do is make me even sicker. I just can't bear the thought of feeling like this, every waking moment, for months and months. If it goes on much longer, I really *will* end up throwing myself off the top landing—"

"Julia," I said worriedly, "you mustn't *say* things like that. Here, sit up and have some tea. Or . . . can you drink tea?"

"I can sometimes, if it doesn't have milk in it," she sighed.

"Or sugar. But coffee always tastes like mud now, no matter what."

She accepted the cup, took a cautious sip, and gave me a grateful nod. Toby took a biscuit, and Julia glanced at it, then shuddered.

"I know it's against the law," she said, after we'd sat in silence for a while, "but there must be doctors who'd . . . help. I wouldn't have a clue how to find one of them, though."

"Have you asked Daphne?" said Toby. "She'd know about this sort of thing, wouldn't she?"

Julia gave a croaky laugh. "I'm going to tell her you said that. No, she's away on a training course, learning how to be a welder."

"Well, ring her up," said Toby. "Or write, or go and see her. But you can't put it off too long, or the decision will be made for you. My offer still stands, by the way. Just so you know you *do* have options."

"You *are* a darling," she said, leaning over and kissing his cheek. She looked up at me as I poured her more tea. "You *both* are. I can't thank you enough for coming over here. I was in complete and utter despair before. Now, I'm just . . . very depressed."

"Actually, Soph, why don't you stay here for a while?" said Toby, which was just what I'd been thinking. He turned back to Julia. "Veronica's away, you see, and Soph's all alone at the flat."

"Oh, darling, yes, *do* come and stay," said Julia, at once. "If you can bear to, that is—I'm hardly cheerful company at the moment. You too, Toby, if you've got an overnight pass."

So after we finished our tea, we drove back to the flat, collected our things, and returned, arriving just in time for the warning siren. Which is why I'm writing this at Julia's kitchen table. The light is certainly better than in our cellar, but the clatter of the Hyde Park anti-aircraft guns on top of the screaming bombs is a bit annoying. Julia is asleep on the little bed in the corner, with the cat curled up in the bend of her knees, and Toby is hunkered over a bottle of brandy at the other end of the table, bracing himself at each whistle and wincing at each subsequent thud.

"God, this is awful," he says. "How do you *stand* it, night after night? Stuck underground, with no way of shooting back at them! When you can't even see what's going on outside!" The house trembles again, the brandy bottle clinking delicately against Toby's crystal tumbler. "And how on earth is Julia managing to *sleep* through this?"

"She's exhausted," I say.

"Poor old thing," he says, gazing at her. "This whole mess seems so unfair, doesn't it? It must be absolutely horrible, being a girl."

It is, sometimes. Still, being a boy during wartime must be fairly horrible, too.

24th December 1940

It's Christmas, and we're all together at Milford. Aunt Charlotte is thrilled about it—although she became slightly less
thrilled when she saw Simon climbing out of the passenger side
of Toby's car this afternoon.

"But I thought you were going to visit that *mother* of yours,
Simon," she said.

"She's on a retreat, ma'am," Simon said. "A prayer vigil for
peace."

"A *prayer* vigil?" said Aunt Charlotte. "At *this* time of
year? How extraordinary. But I do wish you'd told us you were
coming."

"I *did* tell you, darling Aunt Charlotte," said Toby, hugging
her, "when I rang on Sunday. But you must have been so delighted to hear my dulcet tones that you didn't pay any attention to the actual *words* I was saying."

"Well, I really don't know how we're supposed to fit another person inside this tiny little cottage," grumbled Aunt

Charlotte. "It's not like the old days, you know, when one lived in a proper *house*."

"Oh, Simon can sleep in my room," said Toby, turning back to the car for his bag.

"My dear boy, there isn't space in there for so much as a mattress on the floor!"

"He'll just have to share my bed, then," said Toby innocently.

"Don't be silly, Tobias," said Aunt Charlotte, leading the way back inside the gatehouse. "Now, let me think. Mr. Herbert still has all those evacuees at the vicarage, doesn't he, Barnes?"

"Yes, Your Highness," said Barnes. "And I'm afraid the village inn has soldiers billeted there this month."

"There is no room at the inn, Simon," said Henry. "You'll have to sleep in the stables."

"The stables!" said Aunt Charlotte, ignoring our collective giggling fit. "Yes, that's it, there's the flat over the stables. You can have the room that the stable girls use."

"Are the stable girls there?" inquired Simon.

"No, no, of course not, they've both gone home for Christmas."

"What a pity," he said. "It does get *very* cold at night in the country . . ."

"You can borrow Carlos to keep you warm in your manger," said Veronica. "As long as you don't mind the odd flea."

"And if you ask Estella very nicely, she might agree to join you," said Henry. "But you'll have to have all her piglets, too."

"You children are in a very silly mood," observed Aunt Charlotte. "The excitement of the holidays, I expect," she added indulgently.

But it wasn't that we were eagerly anticipating our presents or longing to gorge ourselves on festive treats. After all, not even Henry bothers to hang up a Christmas stocking anymore, and the combination of food rationing and a lack of kitchen staff means that this year's Christmas dinner is likely to be meager fare indeed, compared to past feasts. No, it was simply that we were all so happy to be here together, that we were all still *alive*. *That* was our Christmas miracle. And Aunt Charlotte felt the same, I could tell. Her usual fond regard of Toby was sharpened with a sort of anxious gratitude, and she seized upon his every remark with fervor. At one stage, as Barnes was serving tea, Toby happened to note that the angel was missing from its usual position at the top of the Christmas tree.

"Yes, you're quite right," said Aunt Charlotte at once. "Barnes, go and find it, will you? No point *having* a tree, if one doesn't do the thing properly! Where is it?"

"Well, Your Highness, it wasn't possible to bring *all* the decorations down here from the house, so I thought perhaps, just the tinsel and the glass baubles would—"

"Nonsense! Sophia, you've finished your tea, haven't you? You'll run up to the house for it, won't you? Barnes will tell you where she packed it away."

Which is how I found myself trudging up the long gravel driveway, shivering in the icy wind, all the way to "the house"

(Aunt Charlotte never refers to it as "the hospital," or even acknowledges that anyone else lives there now). The façade looked much the same, except for an ambulance parked near the front doors, and a pair of nurses in red capes chatting to the driver. I sidled past, hoping they were too absorbed in their conversation to notice me, and headed for the side entrance. Technically, I was trespassing on government property, although Barnes had assured me that the doctor in charge was fairly relaxed about rules. Not *entirely* relaxed, I realized, when I found two of the side doors locked. I continued round to the back of the house, where the terrace had undergone a transformation, and not a very attractive one. The marble steps had been replaced by a concrete ramp and aluminium handrails. One of the stone lions had lost an ear and part of his mane, and the terrace balustrade was mottled with ashy spots and the concertinaed stubs of cigarettes. The lacy wrought-iron table and chairs had vanished, too, probably sacrificed to Aunt Charlotte's WVS metal salvage scheme. Instead, there was a long wooden trestle table, a couple of benches, and a wickerwork bath chair—all unoccupied, which wasn't very surprising, given the weather.

I nudged open one of the doors, peered around the deserted hallway, then dashed up the servants' stairs to the third floor, where I found the golden angel inside a carefully labeled crate, exactly where Barnes had described it to be. Quietly closing the bedroom door behind me, I tiptoed off, managing to make it all the way back down to the ground floor without attracting any attention. I was just congratulating myself on this when I rounded the final corner, too fast, and almost ran into a hunched figure.

"Oh!" I gasped. "I'm so sorry!" The man was on crutches, one empty trouser leg pinned up high above where his knee should have been. Thank heavens I hadn't actually *collided* with him. "Are you all right?" I added stupidly.

He gave a hoarse laugh and shuffled sideways, closer to the window. "All right?" he repeated. I looked at him and swallowed hard. Half his face had melted away. There was a dent in place of an eye, a flattened cheekbone, a mouth wrenched down at one corner. His remaining eye, a shrewd blue, was taking in my reaction. "Now, what do *you* think?" he said. "You think I look all right?"

"I *meant*, I hoped I didn't startle you," I said, fighting a blush.

"Oh, no. Not at all. But I think *I* startled *you*," he said. He seemed to be taking a sadistic delight in my embarrassment, but why shouldn't he? In his position, I'd be tempted to go on the attack, too—better than constantly having to defend oneself against revulsion and pity.

"You didn't startle me," I lied. "But I have to be going—"

"Just a moment," he said. "What's that?" I whipped the angel behind my back, but he leaned closer and chuckled. "Well, well. You from the village?"

"No!" I said indignantly (although admittedly, I *was* wearing Henry's old duffel coat, which looked as though it'd been worn to muck out the stables).

"Right," he said disbelievingly. "Well, I'll tell you what. I won't mention you nicking stuff from upstairs, if you do me a favor."

"What?" I said warily, glancing over his shoulder. I really didn't want to have to explain the whole thing to some overworked nurse, but on the other hand, I distrusted the gleam in his eye.

"Get the door for me," he said, already moving towards it. "Then prop it open with something."

"It's freezing out there," I said, following his directions unwillingly. "And it'll be dark soon."

"Yes, but they won't let me smoke in the ward," he said, swinging himself over to a bench. He lowered himself onto it, arranged his crutches next to him, and tugged a crumpled cigarette packet from his top pocket. "I went out into the corridor, except that Sister came along and tore strips off me, said I was blocking the way. She's really got it in for me, she has."

"I can't imagine why," I muttered, "when you're so charming."

He looked up from his fumblings and grinned. "You think so?"

"Not really—" I began, and then I realized his hands were burnt, too. The stubs of fingers were fused into claws, thinly covered with something too taut, red, and shiny to be called skin. "Do you . . . need help with that?"

He finally got one of the cigarettes into his mouth, and

nudged his lighter closer to me with an elbow. "You could light it. Take one yourself, if you want."

"I don't smoke," I said, holding up a trembling flame. He inhaled, then started to cough. "And neither should you, by the sound of it."

"What, you reckon it'll damage my health?" he said. He gazed at me thoughtfully and blew a stream of smoke to one side. "You *aren't* from here, are you? Where are you from, then?"

"London," I said, rather than getting into some complicated explanation. "Right. Well, I'd better be off now. Good afternoon."

He waited till I was halfway down the ramp before calling out.

"Hey! You forgot your angel!"

I stopped, turned, and stomped back. "Thank you," I said through gritted teeth. He'd done it on purpose, I knew.

"You're welcome," he said, with his lopsided smile. "Oh. And merry Christmas!"

It felt as though he were dragging himself beside me on his crutches, all the way back to the gatehouse; peering over my shoulder as I helped Barnes prepare dinner; looming behind me as we ate. I couldn't get him out of my head. I'd recognized the remnants of the uniform he wore, of course. Air force blue. He was—had been—a pilot, I was sure of it. Who else could have suffered those sorts of injuries?

"Sophie!" said Henry impatiently. "I *said*, Toby wants the salt."

"Oh! Sorry," I said, passing it along. Simon was eyeing me curiously, so I quickly turned to listen to Aunt Charlotte—then wished I hadn't, because she was going on about Daniel again.

"I suppose *his* sort don't celebrate Christmas at all," she was saying.

"What sort?" said Veronica. "Socialists? Or atheists?"

"You know perfectly well what I mean. Not that one has anything against those of the Jewish persuasion, of course, but I do hope you realize, Veronica, that if you were to marry him, it would have to take place in some dreary little registry office. Just like poor Lady Londonderry's daughter, when she married the Jessel boy. No lovely white dress, no orange blossom, no bishop's blessing—that's what a mixed marriage means."

"Oh dear," said Veronica, "because that's my life's ambition, to walk out of a church looking like a giant meringue and have people throw bits of colored paper at me."

The conversation then went rapidly downhill.

"Aunt C's going about it completely the wrong way," said Toby, hours later, when everyone else was getting ready for bed and we were the only ones left by the sitting room fire. "The more violently she opposes them getting married, the more likely it is that they'll run off to Gretna Green. She ought to say she's delighted about the whole thing and pretend to give her wholehearted approval."

"Veronica doesn't need Aunt Charlotte's permission," I said. "She's twenty-one now. Besides, she doesn't even *want* to get married. She'd have to resign from her job, for a start. And Daniel hasn't even asked her."

"You think they'll end up Living in Sin, then?" said Toby, crouching down to push another chunk of wood into the fire. "That'd make Lady Bosworth's year, I expect. Well, good luck to the two of them, I say. Grab any chance of happiness you can."

His face, etched in firelight, looked old and weary. Then the wood slipped. Sparks shot out, and the fire blazed up with a short, savage burst of energy. I pictured that pilot I'd met, engulfed in flames now, his arms flailing helplessly at himself, his skeleton mouth stretched in a silent scream. I shuddered, and Toby happened to glance up at that moment. He couldn't have read my mind, but his thoughts must have been following a similar path.

"You know, I can't stop thinking about poor Ant," he said. "Such an awful way to go." He gazed into the flickering red-and-gold light for a moment, then said abruptly, "I'm not afraid of dying, you know. I mean, we're all aware, each time we take off, that we might not make it back. Most of the boys just hope it'll be quick. A bullet through the head, that's what most of them want, or a good hard midair collision, so they take a couple of Nazis down with them. But I don't care how long it takes. I wouldn't even mind coming down in the sea, floating about for a while before I went under. The only thing that terrifies me is fire. That's what gives me nightmares."

I didn't want to hear any of this, but I was willing to listen to Toby all night if it helped ease his mind a little. I didn't even dare say anything, for fear of discouraging him. I simply nodded.

"There was a friend of mine," Toby went on, "who went down with his plane, back in August. The thing is—he could have bailed out. He had enough time. He was over a village in Kent, though, when his plane got hit. I think he wanted to avoid crashing into the buildings. Didn't want anyone on the ground getting hurt. He just kept on flying, nursing his plane along until he could find an empty field, but by then, it was too late. The engine was on fire. Smoke everywhere. Then the petrol tank exploded. When they got to the wreckage a few minutes later, there was nothing left but some bits of blackened metal." Toby's voice was horrifyingly even. "He was a real hero. I could never be that brave."

I opened my mouth to say that what he'd already done was enough to make him a hero a hundred times over, but I couldn't get my voice to work.

"Anyway, that's what I think happened to Ant," Toby said. "That's the only explanation I can come up with. Otherwise, it doesn't really make sense . . . But Ant *would* do that sort of thing, wouldn't he? He'd sacrifice himself, if he thought it'd save lives on the ground."

I cleared my throat.

"Yes," I said. "Yes, that . . . sounds like Anthony."

Toby nodded slowly. "Right." But he seemed to be talking mostly to himself. "The letter they sent Julia said he was a hero.

That's what his Squadron Leader said. Yes, that *must* have been what happened."

The flames were dying down again, shrinking back into the glowing embers. Toby blinked, then smiled—a shadow of his usual beam. "Oh, but look at me," he said, "rambling on like this! Too tedious for words. Soph, you really are wonderful to listen to all that. An absolute *angel*, in fact."

We both glanced up at the Christmas tree, far too tall for the room. The green tip curled over at the ceiling, and the angel dangled from it precariously, clutching her filigree trumpet with pop-eyed alarm.

"Only *you* aren't annoyingly pious-looking," Toby added. "And your hair is less glittery."

I smiled back at Toby. I don't think he recognized the effort it took me—at least, I hope he didn't.

"Well, I'm off to bed," he sighed. He unfolded himself from the floor and rubbed the back of his neck. "You going up now?"

"In a minute," I said. "Good night. Sleep well."

"And you," he said, bending over to kiss the top of my head on his way past.

But I knew I wouldn't be able to sleep a wink. Not until I got all this written down.

25th December 1940

I suppose I ought to feel flattered that people keep unburdening themselves to me, but I wish their secrets weren't so weighty and oppressive. Today it was Simon's turn, while we were out collecting firewood after church.

"How's Lady Whittingham?" he asked with studied casualness as I dumped another armful of sticks in the wheelbarrow.

"Julia?" I said. "She's . . . all right. She's spending Christmas at Astley." I glanced over at him, wondering how much he knew. I was fairly sure Toby hadn't told—not about his marriage proposal, not about Julia's pregnancy, *definitely* not about her visit to that very expensive nursing home that Daphne had found. I'd spoken to Julia on the telephone the day before we'd left London, and she'd sounded subdued, but relieved.

"Mostly, I'm just glad not to feel sick all the time," she'd said. "I'm so tired, though. I went in to the ambulance station this morning, and my boss took one look at me and told me to go home, said the last thing she needed was me fainting in the middle of a call-out. They're short-staffed, too, so you can imagine how ghastly I must look. Anyway, I'm taking the train down to Astley this afternoon and I'm planning to sleep for a week."

"It's good that she's with her family," Simon said. "That she has their support, I mean. At a time like this."

"I didn't realize," I said, narrowing my eyes at him, "that you were so concerned about Julia's welfare."

"I just think what happened was very sad, that's all," he said rather defensively. "Anthony Whittingham was a fine pilot. It was a . . . a terrible thing."

Simon then busied himself dragging a log—far too large for our purposes—out from under a bush.

"Oh, come *on*, Simon," I said, not bothering to hide my exasperation. "What *is* it?"

I really didn't believe Julia's personal circumstances were any of his business, and he's been *very* judgmental about her in the past. But with Simon, it's often best to throw one's cards on the table, face up, right at the start. It disconcerts him, startles him into abandoning his game before it gets too complicated. Not that I understand which game he's playing, half the time, or what all the rules are. Anyway, my strategy worked. He abandoned the log.

"Give me your word that you won't tell anyone about this," he said, straightening up and peering round to ensure we were alone. "Not even Veronica. Not yet, anyway. I shouldn't even be telling *you*, except I need your advice—and your help. It's about Anthony."

"What is it?" I said again, starting to feel very worried. Simon's expression was frightening me. He took my arm and led me to a nearby rock, and we both sat down.

"I was on duty the day Anthony's plane came down," he said. "I knew about it before Lady . . . before Julia heard anything. It didn't surprise me that the official letter said that he was a hero, he hadn't suffered, all of that. They *always* say that sort of thing. But they specifically said he'd been knocked unconscious long before the plane crashed, that his body was burnt up with the plane, and that they found his remains in the wreckage. That's not true."

"How do you know that?"

"One of the WAAFs I work with heard Anthony over the radio that day. He knew his plane was hit and he said he was bailing out. He was high enough to parachute out safely. He had the cockpit hood open. It all sounded routine. She was so relieved, she mentioned it to the girl beside her as she was going off duty—well, that's natural. Those radio operators have to listen to so many things going badly, it must have been nice for her to know that at least one pilot had made it that morning. But two days later, one of the officers called her into his room and insisted she'd heard it all wrong. He's a bit of a bully and he tore into her. She was very upset. I saw her crying afterwards . . . Anyway, she told me some of it."

"But are you sure it was Anthony she heard?" I asked. "Perhaps she *did* make a mistake."

Simon shook his head. "I checked. As far as I could—and I

didn't get very far before I hit a brick wall. It was his squadron, his section, his number. He got out of that plane, I'm certain. The plane might have been on fire when it hit the ground, but he wasn't in it. They're covering up something, you see."

"Well, no," I said slowly. "I *don't* see." (I was actually thinking that the strain of his job, the long hours, the lack of sleep, had turned Simon a bit paranoid.) "Why would the air force cover anything up? If there'd been some sort of . . . mistake or accident or something, surely they'd want to investigate it at once, to stop it happening again? They wouldn't try to pretend it hadn't *happened*."

He gave a short laugh. "Remember the Battle of Barking Creek?"

"No," I said.

"No, of course you don't, because they covered that one up, too. Three days after war was declared, someone spotted what looked like an enemy plane crossing the Channel. So Fighter Command sent up a squadron to investigate. But there was something wrong with the system, and *that* squadron was identified as hostile aircraft as well. So some more fighters got ordered up and they opened fire—against regulations—and two RAF pilots were shot down. One of them died. You think they told his family the truth? There weren't any enemy planes at all in the sky that day. No one knows exactly what happened, even now, but I *do* know that one officer lied about giving the order to fire, and now he's got a nice shiny medal and he's one of those dashing Fighter Boys constantly being photographed and quoted in the newspapers. And it wasn't just that the *public* weren't told the truth about that incident—even within the air force, it wasn't admitted that anything had gone wrong until seven months later. Seven months! And that's not the only time they've hushed up things, either."

I sat there, struggling to comprehend all that. I was used to things going wrong in my department at the Ministry of Food—I'd even witnessed a couple of Mr. Bowker's futile attempts to conceal his own incompetence—but I'd truly believed that the armed forces were different. They *had* to be. They were the ones fighting this war.

"All right," I said at last. "I can accept that the air force might make up something to . . . to placate Anthony's family, if things had gone wrong. But there *wasn't* anything comforting about that letter, Simon! It said his body got burnt up. That's a horrible thing for his family to have to read. They couldn't even have a proper funeral. Why would the letter say that, if it weren't true?"

Simon looked troubled. "I don't think the air force wanted anyone to see his body. I think he bailed out, and they recovered his body, and they got rid of it. Or they burnt it and claimed they found it in the plane wreckage."

"But why? What do you think happened?"

"I don't know," he said. "But I think it must have been something to do with the parachute. I know sometimes they don't open—" He caught my wince. "Sorry, it's gruesome, but it *does* happen—everyone acknowledges that. This has to be much, much worse. Perhaps . . . a design fault in some new type of parachute, and they're protecting the manufacturer? Or perhaps the contract cost them a lot of money and was signed by an officer with connections in high places, someone worth shielding at any cost—"

"And you've been snooping around, asking *questions* about this?" I cried, suddenly furious at him. "What if they find out?"

"Shh!" he said, glancing about.

"Why are you even *telling* me this?" I hissed.

"I told you, I need your help!" he said. "I hoped that maybe . . . that you could ask the Colonel to investigate."

"But—"

"Sophie, this is important! Pilots' *lives* depend on those parachutes working! It can't wait seven months! What if it's Toby next time?"

I was silenced.

"I thought the Colonel would be the one person who could get to the bottom of it," Simon went on, more calmly. "But then I remembered he's Julia's uncle, and I thought that if he discovered anything unpleasant, it could be awkward for him. You know Julia better than I do, though. Do you think she'd *want* to know the truth? Or would it be kinder to . . . let sleeping dogs lie?"

I frowned. "I don't know," I said. "She's having a very hard time right now. I know what you think of her, Simon, but she really did love Anthony."

I recalled that conversation I'd had with her, months ago,

about her resolution to become the perfect wife. Perhaps she'd thought that if she devoted herself to making Anthony happy, she'd be rewarded. Anthony would *surely* be kept safe, when she was making such an effort to be good. If she'd believed that, even subconsciously, then how angry and bitter and betrayed she must have felt afterwards. No wonder she'd ended up . . . doing what she'd done.

"I can't say how Julia might react," I told Simon, "but I don't think it would help her at all to know that Anthony died because of the incompetence of someone on his own side. Especially if she found out that he'd . . . suffered."

"Yes," said Simon. "I see what you mean. Well, then, she mustn't find out."

"The Colonel's very good at keeping secrets," I said. "But, Simon, I haven't seen him for ages. I'm not even sure where he is."

I'd had only brief, irregular visits from the Colonel since the Tyler Kent affair had been uncovered, although I'd continued my cloak-and-dagger activities for a while. For example, I'd get a telephone call asking if I could go for a walk in Kensington Gardens at a specific time, and have a short rest upon a certain bench, whereupon a lady in a green hat would offer me her magazine when she'd finished with it—and could I then make some pretense of reading a few pages, place the magazine carefully in my bag, and stroll home? Then the Colonel would pop around a few evenings later to collect it. I never asked whether I was delivering vital photographs, or encoded letters, or microfilmed maps—I didn't *want* to know. But the Blitz had put an end to my secret assignments, anyway. People didn't take casual strolls or loiter in parks in the middle of an air raid, and there was no guarantee that any particular bench or statue or fountain selected as a rendezvous point would still be standing a few hours later. It must have been at least three months since I'd seen the Colonel.

"I *might* be able to track him down," I said, wondering if our telephone code still functioned, and suspecting it didn't. He was connected to the Foreign Office, though, so perhaps Veronica's boss might have some idea of how to find him . . .

"Please try," said Simon. "Just be careful."

"*You're* telling *me* to be careful?" I said incredulously.

He sent me a rueful, pleading look that melted all my reservations. Although I was careful to conceal this from him, with an enormous scowl. After all, I don't want him taking me for granted.

19th January 1941

Daphne telephoned yesterday to ask me to go out dancing with her and Julia.

"Come on, Sophie," she urged. "Julia says she'll go if *you* do, and she's only saying that because she thinks you'll say no. But she absolutely *needs* to get out, relax, enjoy herself a little. She hardly leaves the house now except to go to work, and that job's not exactly *fun*, is it?"

"Oh, Daphne," I said, "she just needs some time to herself."

"Nonsense!" said Daphne. "I've known her forever, and believe me, Sophie, she needs people around her, to help her get over things. Well, not get *over* it, exactly, but all this hiding away and moping, it simply isn't *her*. Now, be a darling and say you'll come out with us tonight."

"I'm too tired," I said, which was quite true. "I was on firewatching duty twice this week."

"You'll be home by midnight, I promise! Or one o'clock at the very, very latest! We'll have a nice early dinner at the Savoy and then go somewhere to dance for an hour or so, and you can toddle off after that. I've asked some friends to meet us—lovely Polish pilots, you'll adore them. Oh, and bring Veronica."

"She's not even here," I said. "She's terribly busy at work. I've scarcely seen her all week—oh, wait, here she comes now."

Veronica trudged into our sitting room, dumped her bag on the floor, and sagged onto the sofa.

"Do you want to go out tonight?" I asked her.

She flung an arm across her eyes.

"She doesn't want to," I told Daphne.

"Oh, what a pity! But never mind—we'll collect *you* at eight, darling, all right?" Then she rang off before I could protest.

I sighed, and wondered whether I had enough time to wash my hair. "How was work?" I asked Veronica.

"The usual," she said. "Translating hours of news broadcasts into Spanish, with a very unsubtle emphasis on how much economic aid we're giving to Spain, meanwhile inserting a lot of sycophantic commentary about how wonderful Franco is. I can't understand why we bother—everyone knows the Falangists are jamming the BBC's signal into Spain and confiscating any private wireless set they can find."

"Well—I suppose if any of it gets through, it'll help keep the Spaniards on our side."

"Yes, if *that's* worth compromising our integrity," she said. "I need a bath. I don't suppose the gas is back on yet?"

"No. But it's good the telephone's working again, isn't it?"

"Oh, the bliss of living in a modern, civilized city," said Veronica, subsiding further into the cushions.

I really wasn't looking forward to an evening out, but Daphne was determined we should have a good time, and she generally gets her way. She made me put on a brighter shade of lipstick, and she'd forced Julia into a clinging satin evening dress, which was slit up one side to the thigh. Julia was still protesting as we climbed out of the taxi.

"Really, Daphne, I'm supposed to be in *mourning*."

"Well, it's not *my* fault if that's the only black evening gown of yours that still fits. You shouldn't have lost so much weight. Anyway, that pearl choker lends a nice elegant touch, doesn't it, Sophie?"

"I'm not drinking, you know," said Julia. "And I have to be home early. I'm on duty tomorrow."

"Whatever you say, darling," said Daphne, herding us into the lobby of the Savoy. "Oh, look! There they are!"

In much the same way that other women collect shoes or china figurines, Daphne collects extremely handsome men. These came in a set, in matching RAF uniforms. There was a tall, slim, fair one; a strapping one with reddish-gold curls and a puckish grin; and a dark-haired one with the chiseled features of a matinee idol. They had lovely manners, too, rushing to pull out our chairs and light Daphne's cigarette and retrieve my wrap when it slipped off my shoulders. They were all from the same squadron—an entirely Polish squadron, the dark-haired one explained to me. He said to call him Peter, "although it is not my real name, you understand."

"Because no one here can pronounce your real name?"

"Yes, and because I have family in Poland. So if I get shot down over France and the Nazis catch me, they will not know my real name, and they cannot cause trouble for my family."

He told me he'd escaped from his homeland in 1939 after the Nazis invaded, and had eventually made his way to France, and then England. His two brothers, both Polish army officers, had disappeared, but his sister had written to him a year ago to say that she and their mother were safe at their country estate. He hadn't heard anything since. At this, his eyes darkened from blue to slate. So I told him a bit about Montmaray, and the two of us proceeded to spend a pleasant half hour roundly abusing the Nazis.

After dinner, we all piled into a taxi and drove off to the Four Hundred. The sirens started wailing as Peter was paying the taxi driver, and someone suggested taking shelter in the Leicester Square underground station. But the nightclub entrance was only a couple of yards away, so we dived down the stairs. It turned out to be not much of a raid, anyway—not compared to those awful ones after Christmas when the whole of the City caught fire and everyone thought St. Paul's Cathedral was gone (although, of course, it was saved).

I hadn't ever been to the Four Hundred and thought it very glamorous, once my eyes adjusted to the gloom. I sank into the burgundy velvet cushions of our banquette and gazed around at the silk-paneled walls, the heavy drapes, and the thick carpet, all in rich shades of red and very dimly illuminated by candlelight.

"Like going back to the womb," remarked one of the pilots, and Julia blanched, so Daphne quickly shouted across the table at me, "Oh, and Sophie darling, I forgot to tell you I ran into Simon *Chester* in here last week! Looking his usual gorgeous self, of course, girls fluttering about him." She turned to her companion, the gregarious redhead, and explained, "Simon's in the RAF, too, in Fighter Command. Anyway, he was dancing with someone, and guess who it was?"

"One of the Churchill girls," said Julia. "Sarah."

Daphne pouted at her. "Oh, she *told* you! I keep forgetting they're your cousins."

"You are related to Winston Churchill?" the blond pilot said to Julia, looking impressed.

"Second cousin, once removed or something. Believe me, we're the poor, insignificant relations. I've met him twice in my entire life."

"Still," said Daphne, "I bet someone's been gossiping about it to you."

"No, it's just simple deduction," said Julia. "Why would you bother telling us unless she was the daughter of someone important? And Diana's not Simon's type, too nervy—and Mary's too young."

"Well, she was draped all over him, not that I blame her. I'd do the same, if I ever got the chance, except he always pretends not to see me. I'm sure he thinks I'm a terrible influence on you, Sophie."

"Who *is* this man?" Peter asked me.

"Oh, a sort of . . . cousin of mine," I said. I was absolutely *fuming*. Simon had had an evening off and come into town and hadn't so much as bothered to telephone me! When I'd been turning myself inside out to track down the Colonel for him! As for the flirting, well, that was only to be expected—but really, the Prime Minister's daughter! Who also happened to be *married*. Did Simon's ambition know no bounds?

The band struck up again, and I raised my chin and turned to Peter. "Would you like to dance?" I asked him.

"I would be delighted to dance with you," he said, and he stood, bowed, and held out a long, elegant hand. They were playing a slow song, and after a couple of fumbling beats, Peter and I fell into a comfortable rhythm. He was a competent dancer, but not a showy one, so I felt no anxiety about having to keep up with any fancy steps. Not that there was *room* for anything complicated on that dance floor. The crush of bodies was curiously liberating, though—I began to feel as though I were quite alone with him, entirely unobserved. My irritation at Simon drained away, and the fatigue that had been assailing me all day settled into a pleasant drowsiness. By the second song, I had relaxed completely into Peter's arms, allowing him to tug me closer; by the time the band stopped for their break, it seemed inevitable that I would lift up my face to smile at him, and he would stoop to kiss me.

It was lovely. His mouth was smooth and warm and firm, and tasted of champagne. The kiss lasted exactly the right length of time, long enough for me to get over the tiny shock of his lips meeting mine, to feel the gentle pressure begin to slide into a delicious melting sensation . . . but not so long that I started to worry about how to breathe or where I ought to put my hands. Quite apart from how delightful it felt, I was relieved to discover that kissing was, in fact, just as nice as novels make it out to be (I'd had a vague fear that they might all be lying, or that I might turn out to be terrible at it).

The other good thing was that, as it happened on a crowded dance floor, I didn't have to concern myself with thoughts of how far I should go, or how to tell him to stop (he seemed an utter gentleman, but Aunt Charlotte's dire warnings about men's "uncontrollable urges" had sunk in). As it was, he broke it off himself, pulling away just far enough to give me a searching look. I must have assumed the right (or the wrong) expression, because he nodded, gave a tiny smile, then led me back to our table. And his behavior was entirely correct for the rest of the evening, if one doesn't count his leg brushing against mine several times under the table, which was probably accidental. We *were* rather squashed together on that seat, after all.

Julia announced at midnight that she had to leave, so I said I'd go with her. Her companion looked crestfallen, but he and Peter dutifully walked us up to the street and found us a taxi (Daphne was still dancing with the redhead, if one could call what they were doing "dancing"). Peter lifted my hand and pressed his lips to the back of it.

"Goodbye," he said, with his matinee-idol smile. "I had such a pleasant evening. Perhaps we shall see each other again, some other time."

But he said it in such a way that I knew it would only be by purest chance if we did. He no doubt went dancing with girls all the time, girls much prettier and more experienced than I, and he probably kissed most of them, and possibly did much more. And why shouldn't he? He was a fighter pilot. He might be dead tomorrow.

"Goodbye," I said, smiling back at him, "and good luck."

Those words never meant so much before the war. He handed me into the back of the taxi, closed the door, and raised a palm in farewell. Then we drove off.

"He was nice," said Julia sleepily. Then she blinked. "Oh! Should we stop and help?"

We'd turned the corner into what looked like a winter wonderland, except the glistening snow was actually crushed glass, and the red glow wasn't a brazier for roasting chestnuts and warming the hands of skaters, but a fire in the window of the nearest shop, which, according to the charred sign, specialized in ladies' undergarments. The taxi driver stuck his head out and made inquiries of the ARP warden, but it was all right. No one had been killed, the two gentlemen who'd been injured had gone off in the ambulance, and the firemen had the flaming corsets under control.

"Oh, I *am* glad to hear that," said Julia, settling back into her seat, and I was pleased, too. (Extinguishing fires is a messy business, in my limited experience—and I *was* wearing my favorite evening dress.) That this air raid had caused only minor damage added to my general feeling of satisfaction with the world. I had been kissed properly for the first time, and enjoyed it, and not embarrassed myself or hurt anyone's feelings. Overall, then, it had been a surprisingly successful evening.

And I feel just as positive about it this morning, which is even better. It's so nice when things go well for a change.

I'd tracked down the Colonel at the end of January and he'd agreed to investigate Simon's allegations. Then . . . nothing. Six whole weeks of nothing, which is a very long time to be constantly dashing out to the letter box to see if the post has arrived, and leaping for the telephone at the first peal of the bell. I'd decided not to burden Veronica with it until I knew more, so I had the additional anxiety of wondering what to say if she asked what was wrong. I didn't want to lie to Veronica. Perhaps I could imply I was brokenhearted over that Polish pilot and desperate to hear from him? But I would only resort to this story if it became absolutely necessary. This made me determined to stop it *becoming* necessary, so I renewed my attempts to contact the Colonel, leaving him half a dozen messages. At long last, he telephoned me at work, and we arranged to meet in Hyde Park during my luncheon break today.

"It's heartening, really, isn't it?" he said, as we walked past the muddy patches where the lawn had been ripped up to plant vegetables. "I mean, everyone, everywhere, digging for victory! And doesn't the park look better now they've taken away the iron railings? There's a flock of sheep grazing around here, too—I spotted them the other evening. We could almost be taking a stroll in the country."

That was only because we weren't in the section of Hyde Park that's been turned into a wreckage dump. All those depressing piles of broken brick and charred timber, those stacks of rusting girders and twisted sheets of iron roofing, those salvaged bathtubs propped up on their ends, looking like a row of gravestones. But the Colonel was intent on being cheerful, for some reason.

"Every cloud has a silver lining," he chirped, "and it's an ill wind that blows no good—"

Well, I could see how *that* had sprung to mind. A cruel sleet was stinging our faces.

"—because these days, nothing's absolutely bad or absolutely good, is it? But what do you think, Sophie?"

"I think," I said, "that you're prevaricating. Why won't you tell me what you've found out about Anthony?"

The Colonel stopped, took off his hat and smoothed back his hair. "Forgive me," he said, replacing his hat. The angle at which it was tilted hid his eyes. "Yes, you're quite right. The fact is, I haven't decided whether I *am* going to tell you."

"I've kept your secrets before," I pointed out.

"Yes," he said quietly. "Yes, you have. But this one isn't pretty."

"If you think that just because I'm a *girl*, I can't cope with—"

"No," he said. "No, Sophie. But I *do* think you're an idealist. And if you've managed to hold on to any ideals, after all you've been through, I'd hate myself if I tore them away from you." He pushed back his hat brim and stared off across the park. "'Beauty is truth, truth beauty.' Is that what you believe?"

He didn't *seem* to be mocking me, so I said, "Of course I think truth is important. That isn't to say I believe it's always *beautiful*. But given a choice, I'd rather know than not know. Ignorance isn't bliss." Then I added, "Anyway, why agree to meet me here if you had no intention of telling?"

He sighed. "Well, you asked me a question. I was worried that if I didn't respond soon, you might get impatient and go looking for your own answers. And I didn't want you getting tossed into Holloway for prejudicial acts against the defense of the realm and having to share a cell with Lady Mosley."

I suspected he was exaggerating, but nevertheless, I felt a thrill of fear. "This is bad, isn't it?" I said.

"Fairly bad, yes."

"I still want to know. I won't tell Julia."

"Or anyone else. *Anyone,* including Simon and Veronica. Promise me, Sophie."

"I promise," I said.

He scrutinized me for a moment. "All right," he said. "But let's walk. It's freezing out here."

I'd started to shiver, but I didn't think it was from the cold.

"Anthony *did* bail out of his plane before it crashed," the Colonel said, after we'd walked in silence for several minutes. "His parachute worked perfectly, so you needn't worry about any other pilots being in danger from that. He very nearly reached the ground safely, but he was shot at close range, just before he landed."

"By a German?" I asked, picturing a recently downed Luftwaffe pilot hiding in a nearby bush.

"No," said the Colonel. "By the local Home Guard."

"*What?*"

"Keep walking," he ordered, taking my arm as a couple appeared on the path ahead of us. They were young and utterly absorbed in one another, but the Colonel waited until they were far out of earshot. "The village Home Guard happened to be patrolling, and they watched the whole dogfight. One of the German fighter planes got hit, too, and crash-landed at about the same time as Anthony's plane. Apparently, it's fairly difficult to distinguish between an RAF uniform and a Luftwaffe one when the man is dangling from a parachute twenty yards above your head."

"And that's why they're not allowed to *shoot* anyone!" I said. "They can only take prisoners. That's what Henry told me, and she spent all summer trailing after the Milford Home Guard."

"Yes, that's what the regulations say."

My head was still reeling. "But how did they get hold of any ammunition when there's such a shortage? Even the army doesn't have enough! The Milford Home Guard has to make do with sharpened hayforks."

"Well, these men were very well-equipped, it turns out. They all worked and lived on the estate of a marquess, and he'd personally armed and trained them."

I shook my head. "And they . . . they shot Anthony? Before he hit the ground? Couldn't he see them? Wouldn't he have shouted out to them?"

"Yes, he did. But they were given a direct order to fire, so they did."

I closed my eyes. I'd wanted the truth. All right, there it was. At least Anthony hadn't suffered—apart from that moment of terror when he realized what was about to happen. But a bullet was what pilots prayed for, Toby had said. Better than getting stuck in a cockpit, choking on black smoke, as the flames roared in . . .

"Oh, poor Anthony," I said. "What a horrible mistake. But those Home Guard men disobeyed regulations and . . . wait. You said there was a direct order to fire. Who gave the order?"

"Their commander."

"The marquess? Well, has he been arrested?" The Colonel's face told me the answer. "What? He's not *going* to be arrested? Why not, for heaven's sake? It's not as though he's an army officer, battling the Nazis in North Africa! He's a civilian and he murdered a British pilot! All right, he might argue that it was a mistake . . . but why isn't he being sent to trial?"

"Oh, Sophie, why do you think?" said the Colonel wearily.

"Because he sits in the House of Lords. Because a marquess can't be tried in front of a jury, only in front of other peers of the realm, and the last time a peer was actually convicted of murder was in about 1760. Anyway, he didn't fire any shots. He merely gave the order. If it *did* go to trial in the House of Lords, he'd simply swear that he hadn't said anything of the sort— that if the men said otherwise, it must be because they were uneducated and easily confused. At most, the police would arrest some poor old villager who'd worked for the marquess all his life, someone whose wretched family are tenants on the estate and depend on the marquess's goodwill for their daily bread."

"Who is it?" I said. "Which marquess?"

"What does that matter?"

"Who? Tell me."

"No, this is pointless. You aren't going to get any-where by—"

"Lord Elchester," I said. I'd suddenly remembered where he lived—where Anthony's plane had been found. "It *is*, isn't it? It's that bloody Fascist!"

Elchester! That foul, loathsome, *evil* man who'd conducted a vicious campaign against the poor Basque refugee children we'd helped, who hated Veronica because her letter to the *Times* about him had made him look an utter fool . . . Well, after all those years of singing the praises of Hitler, he must have had a very nasty shock when war was declared. So, what better way to restore his reputation and demonstrate his patriotism than to sponsor his own private Home Guard platoon, and have them take potshots at anyone remotely resembling a German?

"What happened to the Luftwaffe pilot?" I said, my voice shaking. "Did they shoot him, too?"

"He landed half a mile away, in the middle of a field, and broke his ankle. The farmer rang the police, and they took him to a prisoner-of-war camp."

"A broken *ankle*?" I cried. "That's all? *He* gets to spend the rest of the war in a nice safe camp, while Anthony—"

"Sophie," said the Colonel, grabbing my arm. "Calm down! Now you know why I didn't want to tell you."

I shook off the Colonel's grasp and stepped back so I could glare at him more effectively. "And you're happy to watch that bloody . . . to watch *Elchester* get away with murder?"

"I'm not happy about any of this! I wish to God I'd never heard anything about it!" The Colonel sounded so angry that I took another couple of steps backwards. He put his hand to his forehead. "Sophie, I'm sorry. But there's nothing I can do. Revealing the facts wouldn't make things any better. Believe me, Elchester would escape punishment. I *know* he would. And then he'd use all his RAF contacts to track down whoever raised suspicions, and he'd make their lives a complete misery. That poor WAAF radio operator, for one, *and* Simon. As for Anthony's mother—well, she's out of her mind with grief right now, but at least she has the consolation of knowing he died battling the enemy. If she found out what really happened, I wouldn't be surprised if she went completely mad and tried to *kill* Elchester. And then there's poor Julia . . . Sophie, haven't the people who loved Anthony suffered enough?"

I clenched my hands into fists, whirled on one heel, and marched back down the path. I'd left my gloves in the office, but I scarcely noticed the cold, I was so filled with burning rage. I stomped along, my heels striking the ground so fiercely I imagined they must be giving off sparks. Gradually, though, the blaze began to die down, until all that remained were embers of frustration. I slowed my pace, allowing the Colonel to catch up with me as we neared Marble Arch.

"You'll find some way of reassuring Simon, without telling him the truth," the Colonel said.

It wasn't phrased as a question. I nodded sharply, averting my gaze from his.

"Sophie, I truly *am* sorry. Are you angry with me?"

"Not really," I said. Then, because we've all become adept at resolving quarrels without delay, for fear we might not have a later chance to do so, I added, "I hate what's happened, but I'm not angry at you. I know it's not your fault."

"Well, that's something," he said, with a sigh.

But as I stalked up the stairs at the Ministry of Food ten minutes later, my fury rekindled. It was all so wrong! So . . . *unfair*! I considered telling Simon about it. Or Veronica. *She'd* have some idea about how to force an official investigation . . .

But then, the RAF seemed so determined to hide the truth. Elchester must know someone *very* high up in Fighter Command. And the Colonel would deny telling me anything. He'd have to—he'd probably signed an oath, promising to lie for the good of his country. I slammed my bag on my desk, making poor Anne jump half a foot in the air.

"Oh, I'm so sorry!" I said. "It slipped out of my hand." (More lies.) But it was horribly thoughtless of me, because Anne had been in the Café de Paris on Saturday night, when that bomb went through the roof and killed the whole band and most of the people on the dance floor. She was up in the gallery with her boyfriend and saw the entire thing, including the men who ran in from the street and stole wallets from the dead bodies and—

Oh, bother, is that the siren?

Later, in the cellar. I spent half an hour trying to compose a letter to Simon that would manage to reassure him without giving away any facts or alerting the censor. After I'd crumpled up my third attempt, Veronica looked up from her book and said, with some concern, "Perhaps you ought to leave whatever you're writing till tomorrow, when you don't have bombs crashing round your ears."

"It's not the bombs," I said. I've learned to shut out the noise, and I don't get scared anymore unless the electricity goes out. "No, I'm just writing to Simon."

"Oh, is that all?" she said. "I thought perhaps you'd had a proposal of marriage from that pilot Julia was talking about, and you were trying to think of some kind way to turn him down."

I couldn't help laughing at that—and then it struck me. "A proposal!" I exclaimed. "What a good idea!"

"No, it's not," said Veronica. "It's a very *bad* idea."

"No, I meant . . . Never mind." And I snatched up another piece of paper and worked away a bit longer, and finally came up with this:

Dear Simon,

I hope that you are well.

 Regarding your proposal at Christmas: please understand that I have thought about it very *seriously. I even asked a wise and respected friend for his opinion. But my answer to your question is "No." I'm sure you feel you are right, but you were* quite mistaken *in your feelings. That is understandable, given the circumstances; however, you must trust me to know best about this.*

 I do hope that you will not persist with this matter, as that would be absolutely pointless. I feel sad about it, of course, but some things simply happen without any particular malevolent cause, and we must accept them and move on with our lives.

 Please take care of yourself, and try not to be dispirited by this. You know I have both our interests at heart, as well as those of our family, and I do hope we can remain friends.

With fondest regards,

Sophie

6th April 1941

We had a luncheon party today with two guests, Simon and Daniel. (We can't invite more than two guests for a meal because there's only room for four chairs around our table. Perhaps we should start having cocktail parties instead.) I made a Woolton pie—potatoes, carrots, swedes, cauliflower, parsley, and one precious spring onion, mixed with oatmeal and topped with a mashed potato crust. As Simon said, it was exactly like steak and kidney pie, only without the steak or kidney. Fortunately, he brought a bottle of wine and a jar of honey, and Daniel contributed a bag of apples. Jam and treacle went on the ration last month, so I'd thought we'd have to do without a pudding, but I baked the apples with some honey and cinnamon, and they were delicious.

Simon arrived first, just as I was putting my pie in the oven. Veronica was still up at the house, checking there weren't any smashed windows or ominous new cracks in the walls after last night's raid, so Simon helped me wash up and set the table.

"Thanks for your letter," he said.

"I was worried someone else might read it."

"I'm sure they did, but it was very cleverly done. So . . . you're *quite* sure there's nothing to worry about?"

"Yes," I said, looking him straight in the eye. "Absolutely certain."

He held my gaze for a moment longer, then picked up the saucepan to dry it. "Well, I was *heartbroken* to read that I'd been rejected, of course," he said. "But luckily, there were a lot of very pretty WAAFs around to console me."

"Not to mention the Prime Minister's most glamorous daughter," I said.

"How did you . . . Oh, Daphne Hamilton, I suppose."

"Is she a good dancer?"

"Lady Daphne? Wouldn't know. Haven't ever danced with her. Anyway, what's this I hear about you and some Polish pilot?"

Veronica arrived at that moment with Daniel, both of them looking rather flushed and breathless.

"You were a long time," I said. "Was there something wrong with the house?"

"No, I just happened to meet Daniel as I was going in," she said. "I was showing him some of the architectural features."

"Oh, is *that* what you young people call it these days?" said Simon, with a pointed look at Veronica's jacket, the buttons of which were done up incorrectly.

"Yes, Daniel's terribly interested in early Victorian cedar

paneling," said Veronica, calmly refastening her buttons. Daniel turned even redder, and handed me the bag of apples.

Simon likes Daniel, I think—or at least, respects his intelligence and integrity. However, they have such different perspectives on life that even their most casual conversations have a tendency to spark into heated political debate. Today it was over the ethics of buying up bombed houses cheaply, which Aunt Charlotte has asked Simon to arrange with Mr. Grenville, the family solicitor.

"And why not?" said Simon, with an edge of belligerence. "The property owners aren't covered by their insurance, and the government won't be paying any compensation till the war's over. In the meantime, these poor people are trying to maintain houses that are falling down round their ears—or round their tenants' ears, if they can actually find any tenants when half of London's escaped to the country. They want to sell, we want to buy. Where's the problem with that?"

"And you'll repair these houses, and let them to people who've been made homeless?" said Daniel, frowning.

"There aren't any building materials to be found, let alone tradesmen to do that sort of work," said Simon impatiently. "I expect a lot of the houses will have to be demolished. Then, after the war, we'll build nice blocks of flats with proper plumbing and all modern conveniences."

"And sell them at a nice profit," said Veronica.

"Yes, Veronica, that's the way capitalism works," said Simon, rolling his eyes.

"You know," said Daniel, "I can't approve of your motives, Simon. But if one good thing comes out of all this terrible destruction, it will be that, after the war, we'll have a new London. No more slums. Clean, affordable housing with lots of natural light, surrounded by parks and community halls and health clinics and well-designed schools . . ."

"All paid for by people like Aunt Charlotte, out of the pure goodness of their hearts," said Veronica.

"Oh, but Veronica, look at what most of them are doing *now*," Daniel protested. "If they're not in the services, they're in the ARP or running canteens or helping at first aid posts. They're working alongside ordinary people—even living with them, if they're looking after evacuee children. Their food is rationed just as everybody else's is, they've given up their motorcars, their servants have all joined up, so they're having to look after themselves for the first time in their lives. I tell you, this war will help people see that sharing is good and right—and that's all Socialism is, making sure that everyone gets a fair share."

Simon snorted. "You think a mere world war will have any effect on the British class system? You really *do* have your head in the clouds. Didn't you see that letter in *The Times* a few months ago? Some Lieutenant Colonel moaning about how useless working-class men are at being army officers. 'Never was the old school tie more justified than it is today.' They *all* think that way, the ones in charge!"

"Ah, Simon, we'll make a class warrior of you yet," said Daniel, with a smile.

My simmering rage over Elchester is already halfway to turning *me* into a Bolshevik, so it was probably a good thing the conversation then moved on to a happier subject, that of Daniel's cousins finally being released from their internment camp. Then Veronica mentioned women having to register for war work now. But women aren't actually being conscripted into the services yet, and they won't be sent into combat. (Of course, far more civilians than servicemen have died at the hands of the enemy since the war began. There *are* no civilians in this war, really, not since the Blitz started.) Besides, all the women we know are *already* doing war work.

After that, the others discussed the fighting in North Africa (the Allies seem to be winning some battles, for once), but nothing's more boring to me than military strategy. So I don't think I can be bothered to record it here.

11th May 1941

I've come to dread the approach of the full moon, and last night's was enormous, as round and white as a spotlight, with not a single cloud to shade it. *A real bomber's moon*, I thought as I stared up at it from our front step. Then the siren went off. We were still arranging ourselves and our belongings comfortably in the cellar when there was a tremendous thump and the electric light died. Veronica groped for our torch and we managed to get the candles lit, uneasily aware of a harsh creaking somewhere far above our heads. Then came a crack like a rifle shot, followed by a crumpling roar and an almighty crash. The walls of our shelter trembled. The candle flames shook, and the dark lightbulb shivered on the end of its cord. Then everything went still.

"Was . . . was that the house, do you think?" I asked, in a very small voice.

Veronica climbed the stairs to our reinforced trapdoor, but it wasn't hot, and she couldn't smell any smoke.

"Whatever that was, it was close," she said. "It doesn't seem to have blocked our exit, though."

Well, Montmaray House or our flat might be gone, but Veronica and my journal were safe down here; that was all that mattered. We settled back down on our bunk, nerves twanging but each of us determined to keep calm and carry on. Veronica retrieved her book, something heavy and Spanish, and I returned to Kick's latest letter. Billy Hartington's younger brother had just married Deborah Mitford—the latest in a "rash" of recent weddings involving Kick's friends, here and in America. *But I am still single, and sometimes feel I will stay that way forever!* she'd written. *Hmm,* I thought, picking up my pen and wondering whether I ought to tell her that Billy seemed to be spending all his leave with Sally Norton these days. I'd seen them together at the Four Hundred. But if Billy was keeping silent about his unofficial engagement, then it wasn't *my* business to tell Kick. And in any case, letter-writing by candlelight was proving to be rather a strain on the eyes. Unfortunately, we'd run out of paraffin for the lamp, and neither of us had had any spare time to queue up and buy more. I put down my pen with a sigh.

"Reminds me of all those nights at Montmaray when the supply ship was overdue," said Veronica, abandoning her book as well. "Struggling to read by the glow of the stove."

"Remember that time Carlos curled up so close to it that his fur started to smolder?" I said. "And after we dragged him away, he kept trying to sneak back, because it was so cold?"

"So we had to take him upstairs with us when we went to

bed," recalled Veronica, "and we all piled up in my bed, and Toby kept complaining about Carlos slobbering on his neck, but that was actually Henry."

All the while, the bombs were whistling down around us, punctuated by the stutter of the anti-aircraft guns, for what seemed like hours. Time tended to behave strangely underground, I'd noticed. It idled along for the first part of the night, stalling altogether at moments of high terror. It was only at two or three in the morning, after one had finally managed to fall asleep, that time began to sprint forward, in a belated attempt to catch up with itself. Veronica and I propped ourselves wearily against our pillows to wait out the raid, our conversation starting and stopping and going round in slow circles like the minute hand of the clock.

"I can't imagine why anyone would *choose* to smoke," said Veronica at one stage, as the air filtering through the vents began to take on a distinct smell of ash, "but look at all the people who *do*. And there'd be riots in the streets if the government ever decided to ration cigarettes."

"Tobacco probably tastes nicer than burning buildings, though. And perhaps they can't help wanting to smoke? I think cigarettes might be a bit addictive."

"Like opium," said Veronica, nodding. "Someone I know in the Foreign Office started on that when he was posted to Shanghai."

"How did it make him feel?"

"Drowsy, he said. And numb."

I pondered this for a moment. "That doesn't sound very enjoyable."

"No, I didn't think so, either. But it might be one of those things that appeals to men more than women. Like sex."

"I don't think *that's* just for men," I said. "Look at Daphne. And Julia told me it's very nice, once you find someone who knows what he's doing."

"Oh, well, *nice*," said Veronica. "Yes, I suppose it is. I'm just not sure how much time and effort ought to be devoted to something that ends up being fleetingly *nice*."

"You said you hadn't been to bed with Daniel!"

"I haven't." There was a pause. "Well, not really."

"More than kissing?"

"Quite a bit more," she said. "But not enough to worry about getting pregnant."

"Oh." Veronica didn't sound *madly* enthusiastic about it—but then, if she didn't like it, she certainly wouldn't still be doing it. It would be impossible for Daniel to coerce Veronica into that (or anything else), even if he were capable of behaving so despicably (which, of course, he isn't). But *I'd* found kissing to be wonderful, and I hadn't even been in love with the man. "Well, perhaps it'll become nicer when Daniel knows more about what to do," I said.

"He knows perfectly well what to do," she said. "He's had other lovers. No, I expect it's me. I prefer to think, rather than feel, which is probably a disadvantage in that area." She stopped to rearrange her pillow. "You know," she went on thoughtfully, "sometimes I'd be quite happy to be a disembodied brain, floating from place to place."

"Steered by willpower," I said, picturing it.

"Yes. Imagine how much easier that would be, not having a body that needed to be fed and rested and all those other boring things."

"Eating isn't boring," I protested. "Well, it is now, but think of all those delicious meals we used to have before the war. And you'd be missing out on long steamy bubble baths, and lying in the sun with the scent of fresh-cut grass wafting on the breeze, and slipping between clean linen sheets, and all *sorts* of lovely things. I suppose I'm more sensual than you, though. Or is it sensuous? I can never remember the difference . . . But wait, did you just say Daniel had been in love with someone *else*?"

"He's thirty-one years old," she pointed out. "It would be a bit odd if he hadn't. There was a girl at Oxford he was mad about, but her parents disapproved of him, and she finally married a much richer friend of his. That's why he took up the job at Montmaray, to get away for a while. Then, after he came back to London, there was some older woman, an Italian Communist. But that was years ago."

Well, *I* wouldn't have wanted to be someone's second love—or third love—but Veronica didn't seem the slightest bit jealous. That was where an aptitude for calm, rational thinking was an advantage, I supposed.

"And speaking of Italy," Veronica said, yawning, "I wonder how Mussolini's feeling, now the Italian Army in Abyssinia is about to surrender . . ."

At which point, I fell asleep. After what seemed only a few seconds later, I was shaken back into consciousness.

"Sophie, come and look!" said Veronica. She was fully dressed, and when I sat up and rubbed my eyes, I saw that the cellar was now filled with thick gray light. I tugged on my shoes and my coat and stumbled after Veronica. Outside, scraps of charred paper churned about in the smoky breeze, and the rising sun was a dull yellow ball. We walked up the path alongside Montmaray House—which was still standing, seemingly unscathed—and out into the middle of the road. Two unfamiliar men wearing ARP armbands and tin helmets were standing there, gazing at our neighbor's house. Except . . . it had vanished. It simply wasn't *there* anymore. I was struck by the realization of how much empty space makes up a building, for the house, a three-story Georgian mansion, had been reduced to an untidy pile of crushed stone and splintered timber that stood no taller than my shoulder. Thank heavens the owners had moved to the country a year ago. I gaped at the ruins for a while, then turned to peer at Montmaray House. There were some broken windows, but no other apparent damage.

"All the windows facing south on the third floor were blown out," said Veronica. "But the floors above and below are fine. It's so odd."

"That's nothing to what I've seen," one of the ARP men said. "I've seen a row of terrace houses razed to the ground, with the house at the end completely untouched."

"Is our flat all right?" I finally thought to ask Veronica.

"A big crack in the bathroom wall, but nothing that can't be patched up."

"I've seen a house in Notting Hill with the entire front peeled away," said the ARP man. "Like a doll's house, it was. The lights still worked and all."

"That was a bad raid, last night," the other ARP man told us. "Low tide, you see. The firemen couldn't pump enough water out of the Thames."

"Elephant and Castle went up like a tinderbox," said the first man, with a sort of gruesome relish.

"I heard they hit the Houses of Parliament, too," said the other.

"No!" chorused Veronica and I, horrified.

But he was right. The House of Commons, the War Office, the Law Courts in the Strand, Westminster Abbey, the Palace of St. James, St. Thomas's Hospital, King's Cross Station, the church where Julia and Anthony had been married, the cinema at Marble Arch where I'd seen *Wuthering Heights* . . . and worst of all, the one that made Veronica nearly cry when she heard about it, the British Museum. Hundreds of thousands of its books, burnt to cinders.

But of course, that wasn't *really* the worst. The *very* worst was all the people who lost their lives. I don't know how many died, because they don't tell us the numbers anymore. Hundreds, probably, and thousands badly hurt, and even more made homeless. That's why I disagree with Veronica, about fleeting pleasure being worthless. Everything is fleeting now. *Life* is fleeting. We have to savor any little bit of pleasure we come across, no matter how evanescent it may turn out to be.

It seems to me that there must come a time when our popula-tion will mostly consist of the dead, and the horribly injured, and those neither dead nor injured but so overwhelmed with grief that they are unable to function as normal human beings. At which point, I assume we will surrender. Unless the Germans get there before us, in which case *they* will surrender. There are mo-ments when I don't much care *who* reaches that point first, as long as the war ends. I experienced one of those moments today.

Of course, I do understand why we're fighting. I understand that the Nazis are wrong, that sacrifices must be made if we want to defeat them. I *know* all that, and yet this incessant suffering makes me so sick to my stomach that I simply want it to stop. The fact that I have avoided the worst of it so far—that all of my family is still alive—only adds anxiety and guilt to my despair.

But who *wouldn't* feel despair, on the day of a funeral? And *such* a depressing funeral, too. There is something badly wrong with a world in which so many parents are mourning their sons, and young wives their husbands . . . Oh, but what a *mess* this journal entry is turning out to be, much like my day. Let me start again.

David Stanley-Ross was killed in battle last week in the Middle East. He was buried where he fell, in the desert, some place with a biblical name, and afterwards, his brigadier sat down and wrote a letter to David's parents. He no doubt described David as a hero, cut down while valiantly leading his men to victory; official letters always say that sort of thing. I can't imagine it provided any consolation at all to Lord and Lady Astley, from what I observed of them at the funeral. Lady Astley seemed determined to maintain a dignified front and greeted everyone with a steely, straight-backed composure. It was only up close that one noticed the tremor. If Julia hadn't had a firm grasp of her mother's arm throughout, I really think poor Lady Astley might have fallen into a shaking heap. Meanwhile, Lord Astley slumped into the front pew, dropped his head into his hands, and wept. I'd never before seen a grown man cry—not in public, not in *England*. (I know Mr. Churchill does it sometimes at bomb sites, but he's half American and entirely eccentric, so he doesn't count.) Rupert—usually so compassionate—made no attempt to console his father, but perched at the very end of the pew, his face averted, his jaw clenched, his arms tightly crossed. There was no sign of Charlie, Rupert's elder brother. Most shocking of all was the sight of Penelope, David's widow. I hadn't realized she was having a baby (although the person most likely to mention it would have been Julia, who might have had her own reasons for not bringing up the subject). Poor Penelope! She looked so pale and bewildered as she was helped down the aisle to her seat. The sweltering heat, or clothes rationing, or advanced pregnancy, or perhaps sheer, unadulterated misery had led her to abandon her usual fashionable outfits in favor of a shapeless frock in an unflattering cotton print. I don't think I'd ever felt so sorry for someone I disliked. I hadn't liked David much, either, and I felt desperately sorry for *him*, too. So I was pretty much drowning in uncomfortable, mismatched emotions.

If only Veronica had been able to take time off work to come to Astley with me, or Toby had been granted leave. But all I had was Aunt Charlotte and Lady Bosworth, who'd collected me from Salisbury railway station in Lady Bosworth's official Red Cross motorcar. Aunt Charlotte had insisted on sitting in the front so she could give Lady Bosworth helpful driving hints (never mind that Aunt Charlotte has never held a driving license). As a result, the journey was less than peaceful. Sitting between them in church wasn't much better. In addition, the vicar was one of those excessively patriotic types who fancied himself a great orator—he even affected a Churchillian lisp. He held forth on "defending our great and mighty Empire" and "standing firm against the brutish Hun" and how "every drop of our boys' blood spilled in the sand brings us closer to victory." Poor Penelope looked as though she was going to be sick, and even I started to feel a bit queasy. It was a relief when the final hymn was announced, despite this being "The Son of God Goes Forth to War" (I refused to sing it; the lyrics are simply *too* gory and awful).

"So kind of you to come," Lady Astley said afterwards on the church steps. She pressed Aunt Charlotte's hand and gave us both a gracious smile. "Everyone has been so—"

She looked over my shoulder, and her mask slipped for a second, revealing naked anguish.

"Oh, Sophia," she cried, "won't *you* try to talk to him?"

I turned to see Rupert shoving past the vicar and stalking off round the corner of the church. I was still gaping when Aunt Charlotte, to my surprise, added urgently, "Yes, dear. Go on!"

So I ran after him. I was wearing my narrow black skirt and city shoes, though, and he was striding so quickly between the gravestones that I hadn't a hope of catching up.

"Rupert!" I called. "*Rupert!*"

He whirled about, scowling, his fists clenched. Then he blinked. "Sophie?" he said, his voice rough and strange.

I took a cautious step forward. "I . . . I only wanted to see if you were all right," I said, feeling as though I ought to be crouching down and holding out my fingers, the way one does with a wary, unfamiliar dog. "It's fine if you'd rather be alone, but I thought I'd ask."

I decided not to mention his mother's concern.

Rupert pushed his hair off his damp forehead. "I just wanted to get away from that lot, that's all," he said, jerking his head at the church. "I'm going back to the house. You can come, if you'd like." Then he walked off.

It wasn't the most cordial invitation I'd ever received, but I picked my way after him, past raw wooden crosses with wilting posies propped against them, and on into the old section of the graveyard, where the grass and the wildflowers brushed my knees and weathered fragments of gravestones were sinking back into the earth at odd angles. Then the grass flattened out, and we came to a low stone wall and a gate that was hanging off its hinges.

"I think we're meant to be responsible for that," said Rupert, nudging the gate with his shoe. "Fixing it, I mean." A path meandered out of the graveyard, past a cornfield, and up the hill towards Astley Manor. But Rupert turned his back on the house and sat down on the wall, in the shade of a broad chestnut. I went over to join him.

"Sorry," he said, after a while.

"What for?" I said. "I don't need an apology."

"But I was rude to you," he said, "and I ignored everyone else, when they were just trying to help. *And* I snapped at the vicar."

"Well, vicars ought to be accustomed to people getting upset at funerals," I said. "Besides, he didn't seem a very *sensitive* vicar. I wanted to throw a hymn book at him myself, when he started going on about boys bleeding to death in the sand."

"Wasn't it disgusting?" said Rupert. "I thought poor Penelope was going to pass out. 'Young David's blood was not spilled in vain'! I could hear my father muttering, 'Yes, it *was*!' *He* just wishes it'd been *my* blood."

"He didn't say that!"

"He might as well have. That's what he thinks. Much

better *I* were killed than his beloved David. His favorite, the *heir*." Rupert grimaced. "We had an almighty row last night, as you might have gathered. He said something stupid to Penelope at dinner, about how she'd better make sure the baby was a boy. It was one of those joking remarks that's not really a joke. So she burst into tears and rushed out, and Julia went after her, and I told him he was an unfeeling clod. You can imagine how it went from there. Oh, and my mother made it all ten times worse by taking my side. It reminded him *yet again* of what a pathetic mama's boy his youngest son is. He hates the idea of me as the new heir. The last five Lord Astleys were officers of the Royal Wiltshire Yeomanry, and here am *I*, so feeble I couldn't even pass the army medical!"

I wasn't even sure where to begin with this. I had to admit that Lord Astley was rather gruff at the best of times, and now, grief-stricken, might well have lashed out and said something insensitive. But it was also true that Rupert and his father had always been sadly at odds with each other. And then this baby of Penelope's . . . I understood that if the baby turned out to be a boy, he was destined to be the next Lord Astley, now that David was dead. Still, if the baby were a girl . . . well, wasn't *Charlie* the elder son now?

"Oh, but I haven't told you," said Rupert, following my thoughts. "Charlie's gone missing, you see. Not missing in action—we just don't know where he is."

"You mean . . . he's deserted?"

"No, apparently he's changed his name, which makes it

hard to track him down. He could even be with the British Army now. The Colonel thought he might have been recruited into a commando unit, which wouldn't surprise me in the least. If Charlie had been stuck with a lot of Canadian soldiers in billets up north, doing absolutely nothing for months on end, he'd have leapt at the chance for some excitement." Rupert dug the tip of his shoe into the dust, and added, without looking at me, "It *is* possible he was sent to Crete last month."

"That . . . didn't go very well for the Allies, did it?"

"Complete disaster, according to the Colonel. If Charlie *was* there, he's probably a prisoner of war now. If he wasn't killed in action."

"Oh, Rupert," I said helplessly. "I'm *so* sorry."

"Even if he's alive, he'll never want to settle down *here*. He used to say to me, 'The only good thing about David is that *he's* responsible for all this, not us. He'll be stuck here forever, and we'll be free.' It's true, you know. David got all the attention and all the privileges, we were just the spares. And David *loved* strutting about, lording it over us—"

Rupert broke off.

"Listen to me," he said, his voice uneven. "He's *dead*, and I still can't find anything nice to say about him."

I forgot Rupert wasn't my brother or my cousin, and I put my arm around him. "People don't magically become nicer after they die," I said. "You had good reason to dislike him, and it'd be hypocritical of you to pretend otherwise now. It's not as though you *wanted* him to die. Quite the opposite."

Rupert's shoulders rose and fell in a trembling sigh.

"Anyway, you're worrying about something that may not even happen," I went on, less certainly. I was suddenly conscious of the hard muscles flexing under my fingertips, of how I was so near to him that I could hear each breath he took. "I mean . . . Penelope might have a boy. Or Charlie might come back from the war completely changed. Besides, your father will probably live to a hundred."

"He *definitely* will, if it means keeping the estate from me," said Rupert, with something closer to a sob than a laugh.

"Well, it seems a pretty nice estate to inherit," I said, getting up to survey the view and using this as an excuse to drop my arm from Rupert's shoulders. I wanted to give him some privacy as he fumbled for his handkerchief, and I must admit, I needed some space myself. I could feel myself blushing. It was so strange to be thinking of Rupert as a . . . well, as a man. "Look at those fields!" I said. "Like a giant patchwork quilt! Does it *all* belong to your family?"

"As far down as the river," he said in a voice that now sounded almost normal. "You've seen the manor, though. Leaky roof, smoking fireplaces, chunks of plaster dropping off the dining room ceiling into the soup—and the whole thing's falling apart even faster now that there aren't any servants or tradesmen."

He came to stand beside me and we both gazed at the manor. From this angle, the ivy-speckled lump of gray stone bore an uncanny resemblance to an enormous toad squatting on top of the hill.

"Perhaps the Germans will drop a bomb on it," Rupert said. "That'd solve all our problems, one way or another."

"Don't even *think* that," I said, with a shudder. "Anyway, the raids seem to have stopped for the moment."

"I expect all the Luftwaffe's bombers have been diverted to Russia."

"Poor Russians," I said. "People are saying the Germans will crush them in a matter of weeks."

"The Colonel doesn't think so," said Rupert. "He says they'll hold out for years, that no one's able to endure suffering like the Russians. But they shouldn't have signed a deal with Hitler in the first place. They ought to have known he'd go back on his word. They could have been on our side, right from the start."

"Did you hear Mr. Churchill's speech?" I asked. "Pledging support for the Russian people?"

Rupert's mouth twitched into a wry smile. "All that sentimental twaddle about brave Russian soldiers guarding the fields, while the maidens laugh and the children play? After my dear old cousin's spent the past thirty years railing against the evils of Communism in general, and the Soviet Union in particular? What did Veronica think of it?"

"She almost threw a saucepan at the wireless when he said the bit about Russian mothers and wives praying for their loved ones. She yelled, 'The Soviets are *atheists*, you idiot!'"

Rupert huffed out a laugh.

"But she *is* a bit grumpy with Mr. Churchill at the moment," I conceded. "She doesn't agree with his policies about Spain."

Actually, she's *furious* at him, because she's just found out he's arranged for huge bribes to be paid to Franco's generals, to keep Spain out of the fighting in North Africa. Yet another example of this government's moral flexibility, I suppose—paying one lot of murderous Fascists, in order to help us defeat a slightly different lot of murderous Fascists.

"Still, it's good we have a European ally again, isn't it?" I said. "And the Communists were always *supposed* to be against Fascism. It's as though things are back to how they ought to be."

"If only Anthony were here to see it," said Rupert sadly.

I sighed. Poor dear Anthony, he'd been so idealistic about Communism.

"Perhaps Anthony *does* know," I ventured. "Perhaps he *is* watching what's going on."

"Sitting on a cloud, peering down at us over his harp?"

"You don't believe in heaven?" I asked. I wasn't sure *I* did, either, but it was a bit depressing to think that this dusty, over-grown graveyard was the best we could hope for.

Rupert was silent for a moment, thinking. I liked that about him, that he always took our conversations seriously.

"I *want* to believe in some sort of afterlife," he said at last, "but the logistics have always baffled me."

"Oh, I know!" I said. "So many questions, and the answers never make any sense. Do dead children ever get a chance to grow up? Do people who die of old age have to stay old forever, even if they were happier when they were young? And that bit in the Bible about the widow who marries again—you know, the idea of the woman and all her husbands living together for eternity. What if they didn't get along?"

"That would be hell," Rupert said, and we couldn't help sniggering.

"I know there aren't supposed to be bodies in heaven, only souls," I said, more seriously, "but what would one *do* for eternity, without a body? Would one simply feel abstract joy, forever and ever? It sounds a bit tedious, doesn't it?"

"The thing that got to me," said Rupert, "was when our Sunday school teacher announced that animals didn't have souls—that when they died, they were like plants, they just went back into the earth. How could anyone spend any time at *all* with a dog and not think dogs had souls? If dogs don't have souls, then we don't, either. Dogs feel the same things we do—happiness and loyalty and love and loneliness. I've seen birds get distressed when their mates died. Even lizards and insects must have thoughts and feelings—it's just that humans can't understand them. So I think life is a continuum, as Darwin said, and humans aren't anything special. Except, unlike other animals, we make up a lot of stories about eternal life, because we're so terrified of death."

"Being able to make up stories *is* special," I said. "A special, comforting skill." I glanced again at the gravestones. "Of course, that doesn't mean the stories are true."

"And we won't find out if they are," said Rupert, "not until it's too late to change anything about our lives."

"This is *such* an optimistic conversation," I said.

Rupert smiled. "I suppose we ought to be getting back to the house," he said, without any enthusiasm.

"Yes," I sighed. "I suppose so."

I straightened my hat and he pushed back the lock of hair that kept falling over his face, then we turned towards the gate.

"Thanks," said Rupert. "For the conversation, I mean." He caught my eye and seemed on the verge of saying something more, and I held my breath. But then he bent down to drag the gate out of our way and point out some wild orchids beside the path, and the rest of our walk was like that, mild and soothing and familiar. It was a brief period of tranquility before an awful, tense hour up at the house, followed by an equally uncomfortable drive back to Salisbury, during which it became clear that Aunt Charlotte and Lady Bosworth had known perfectly well who Lord Astley's new heir presumptive was. It prompted them into a series of arguments on everything from the value of the Astley estate to the look of my hair. I was amazed at how those women positively *thrived* on all the bickering. But perhaps that's more common than I'd thought. It would certainly explain why humans are always having wars. Then my train, when it finally arrived, was crammed with soldiers and took hours to drag itself back to London, especially past the last few miles of gray, bombed-out suburbia. When I eventually reached home, I was grimy and exhausted and, yet again, overwhelmed with dark and depressing thoughts—which I have now put down in writing.

24th August 1941

Toby had a forty-eight-hour leave pass, so the two of us drove down to Milford yesterday as a belated birthday surprise for Henry. She is fifteen now, and seems to consist of nothing but long, skinny limbs that are constantly getting tangled up in the curtains or tripping over chairs or knocking down vases. I asked if she'd like to come back to London with me, so I could buy her some new clothes before she goes back to school, but she said she couldn't imagine anything more boring. Pretty much everything except Toby is "boring," in her considered opinion. School is "boring," but so is being on holiday, especially when she's required to tidy her bedroom or help Barnes with the cooking. Even the village is "boring," with Jocko and all her other friends out in the fields, bringing in the harvest, and Henry not allowed to join them (Aunt Charlotte says there are more than enough chores to keep Henry occupied at home).

Henry is currently sprawled across the floor of the sitting room, wearing a pair of khaki shorts spattered with blackberry stains and an old shirt of Veronica's with the sleeves rolled up. Carlos is using one of her legs as a pillow, his eyelids drooping as she reads out a newspaper article about Bamse, the mascot of the Free Norwegians stationed in Scotland.

"Look, Carlos," she says, holding up a photograph of a sooty-eyed St. Bernard sporting a Royal Norwegian Navy cap and jaunty neckerchief. Carlos gives the paper a polite sniff, then lets his head slump back onto her leg. "Bamse displayed great courage in action last year, refusing to move from the gun platform of the ship *Thorodd* while she was under fire," Henry continues. "He now accompanies the sailors on their rounds, plays football with them on deck, and rides the bus into town by himself to gather up his fellow crew members if they are late returning to their ship. Bamse is essential to the morale of the Free Norwegian forces, who may be separated from their home-land, but valiantly continue the fight against the Nazis."

She lets the newspaper drop. "See what a brave, hardwork-ing dog Bamse is? And look at *you*, Carlos, lazing about, wait-ing for your dinner! What are *you* doing to help the war effort?"

Carlos heaves an enormous sigh.

"Yes, I know," she says, patting his head. "You're *far* too doddery to be able to do anything now. Look at these creaky old legs! Look at all these white hairs!" She reaches down to rub his stomach and he collapses onto his side, tail thumping the floor. "He'd be eighty-three years old if he were human," she informs Toby and me.

I can't remember the ratio of dog to human years, but this

figure doesn't seem quite right. I suspect Henry's arithmetic skills haven't progressed much over the past school year.

"Well, I hope *I'm* still chasing down rabbits and knocking over the postman when I'm that old," Toby says, glancing up from his book. He hasn't turned a page in twenty minutes, but he does seem calmer now. All through luncheon, I could feel his leg jittering under the table, and his glass trembled when he lifted it. I think it's all the pills they give the pilots. Pills to keep them alert while they're flying, pills to help them sleep when—if—they get back. I hope the doctors know what they're doing. But the RAF probably doesn't care if the pills *are* toxic or addictive in the long term. All that matters is that the job gets done now, and too bad if the job is stupid and dangerous.

Toby told me a little of what he's been doing, and it sounded absolutely terrifying. Last year was awful enough, but at least *then,* he and his fellow fighter pilots were flying over familiar, friendly territory, defending their homeland. Now they're protecting the RAF bombers being sent to destroy Nazi targets in northern France.

"Which means we have to plod alongside those big lumbering beasts, keeping in strict formation, with Luftwaffe fighters swooping down on us from above and those bloody flak guns firing up from the ground. I wouldn't mind if our bombs were wiping out Nazi ships or aerodromes or something, but the targets always seem so pitiful. A railway yard or some pathetic little workshop—when we're sending over hundreds of planes and losing so many men." He shook his head. "But ours is not to reason why; ours is but to do and die."

What's truly scary is not just that they might *die;* it's that if a plane gets hit, the pilot has to bail out over Nazi-occupied territory. That's what had the Colonel so agitated last week, when he came round to see me.

"What was Toby *thinking?*" he exclaimed, flapping a magazine at me. Cecil Beaton had visited Toby's aerodrome to take photographs of some dashing young pilots, and of course, Toby featured prominently. "I *told* Toby, right at the start!" went on the Colonel, thoroughly exasperated. "If he *must* go into combat, use a pseudonym, like all the Poles and Czechs do! What if he gets shot down over France? He isn't some ordinary British pilot. Just imagine how the Nazis will react if they discover they have the King of Montmaray in their grasp!"

But Toby waved our concerns aside. "*Naturally* that Beaton fellow wanted me in all the photographs," he said airily. "I'm the best-looking man on the base. It's not as though my *name* appears in any of the captions."

Not in *those* photographs, perhaps, but it's written in bold capital letters on that huge LEADERS OF THE ALLIED NATIONS WHOSE HEADQUARTERS ARE IN BRITAIN poster. Photographs of General de Gaulle of France, Queen Wilhelmina of the Netherlands, the Grand Duchess of Luxembourg, Dr. Beneš of Czechoslovakia, General Sikorski of Poland, all arranged in a V for Victory shape—and right at the top, King Tobias of Montmaray, in RAF uniform. Toby isn't worried about *that,* either.

He isn't worried about *anything*. Last year, he seemed grimly resigned to his own death. Now, having made it this far, having been promoted to Squadron Leader (because all his previous Squadron Leaders have been *killed*), he seems to believe he must be invincible. I'm not sure which state of mind I find more disquieting.

I should also note that the Colonel brought the news that Penelope Stanley-Ross had a healthy baby girl last week. Let's hope the poor little thing turns out to be pretty—that might provide some small consolation to her mother. I wanted to ask the Colonel how Rupert was—I haven't seen or heard from him since the funeral—but felt awkward about it. Besides, it was one of the Colonel's lightning visits. I expect he's keeping very busy liaising with the Russians, who are now desperately trying to keep the Nazi forces out of Leningrad . . .

21st December 1941

Veronica and I still haven't decided if we're going to Milford for Christmas. Neither Toby nor Simon has any leave, Veronica thinks she might be called in to work on Boxing Day, and I've come to loathe that long train journey south. The carriages are so often packed with soldiers (who spend the whole trip whistling at girls and making the most *indecent* comments), and then there's waiting about for hours at Salisbury for the bus, and those final horrible miles, jolting about in the pony cart in the freezing sleet . . . It makes one tired just thinking about it.

But then, I quite *often* feel tired now. Tired and glum. I suppose it's good news that the United States has finally entered the war on our side, but oh, all those hundreds of poor American sailors killed at Pearl Harbor! The Colonel happened to be dining at Chequers with the Prime Minister that night, and told us that when the news came over the wireless, Mr. Churchill jumped up in great excitement, crying out that we were "saved," that this was "a blessing" for the British Empire.

I do hope Mr. Churchill managed to calm down a bit before he spoke to President Roosevelt on the telephone, because I can't imagine the Americans feel the same way.

How *could* the Japanese be so cruel as to attack like that, without any warning or any declaration of war? No wonder Hitler loves them. He's even declared them "honorary Aryans." They may not be tall and blond and blue-eyed, but they're certainly just as skilled at terrorizing their neighbors as the regular Aryans are. One would think having control of large chunks of China would be enough for them, but no, they also want Burma and Malaya and Hong Kong and Singapore and the Dutch East Indies and the Philippines, and they've already sunk *two* British warships. Veronica, Simon, and I held an emergency Council of War (Toby was flying operations at the time, but he agreed with our decision afterwards) about whether we should declare war on Japan. Of course, we can't provide any practical aid to the troops, and I doubt Japan has even heard of Montmaray. But Britain has been kind enough to grant us asylum, and Japan *is* officially part of the Axis with Nazi Germany and Fascist Italy, so we felt we ought to join all of Britain's other allies and declare war, too.

The first consequence of the war spreading to the Far East has been the shops' running low on rice and tea. (Of course, I've now developed an absolute craving for rice pudding.) I also had to queue up for *three-quarters of an hour* yesterday to buy our fortnight's ration of sugar. It was a good thing I had *Barchester Towers* with me. (How would Mrs. Proudie react to rationing, I wonder? She'd probably have married Lord Woolton and seized control of the Ministry of Food by now.) On my way home, I saw another queue and automatically joined it, not even thinking to ask what it was for until I'd been standing there ten minutes. But luckily, the shop had just received a carton of tinned meat from America and as I had enough points, I bought some Spam. We'd tried it at Julia's the night before—studded with cloves and baked with a glaze of plum jam—and it was quite nice, as long as one didn't try to think of it as actual *meat*.

At Julia's, we somehow fell to talking about what we missed most from before the war. "Silk stockings," Daphne said, then corrected herself and said no, it was being able to buy new clothes whenever one wanted. "I can't stand having to *think* about every single little purchase! I was about to buy some handkerchiefs the other day, and then I remembered I need another sturdy pair of shoes for work and I ought to save up my coupons for that. And yet, all my handkerchiefs are oily rags and completely useless and oh, the *agony* of indecision!"

"What makes *my* heart sink is when Mrs. Timms tells me the Hoover's blown up or something like that," said Julia. "Because I know it'll be impossible to get spare parts for it or buy a new one. Also, I remember when I was looking for a teddy bear for Penelope's baby—absolutely *nothing* in the toy shops. Think of all the poor children, growing up with no toys!"

Veronica said she missed proper newspapers. What with limited supplies of paper, and censorship, and most of the newspaper reporters having been called up, even *The Times* is down to only eight pages.

"Oh, yes," sighed Julia. "And the weather reports, I miss those. I can never decide what to wear each morning."

Weather forecasting—or even mentioning the weather of the past week—is strictly forbidden, in case the Germans use the information to plan air raids.

"Which is *so* ridiculous," Veronica pointed out. "All the Nazis have to do is stand at Calais and look across the Channel if they want to know about the weather in England."

"What *I* miss," I said wistfully, "is orange juice. I used to drink a big glass of it every morning at Milford, before the war. But the price of fruit is ruinous nowadays, if one can *find* any in the shops. It's a wonder we aren't all riddled with scurvy."

"Yes, I desperately miss lemons," said Daphne. "Gin and tonics just aren't the same anymore. And I miss lemon icing on cakes."

"Stop it," said Julia. "No talking about food, especially after I've just given you such a pathetic dinner. How did we get onto this subject, anyway? Who started it?"

"You did, I think," said Daphne. "But better to have a good honest whinge every now and again than to go all Mrs. Miniver-ish, exclaiming over the lovely smell of sandbags, and how sweet the barrage balloons look, and how utterly thrilling the blackout is. Easy for *her* to gush about how wonderful the war is, when she buggered off to America long before the Blitz started."

"Well, the poor Americans know a bit about bombing now," I said.

"Hawaii," mused Julia. "I didn't even *realize* the Americans owned part of it, did you? And *I* thought the only islands in that part of the Pacific were the Sandwich Islands."

"Hawaii *is* the Sandwich Islands," said Veronica. "They're the same thing."

"Mmm, *white* bread," said Daphne, "with *real* butter and—"

"What?" said Veronica.

"Sandwiches," said Daphne. "I desperately miss smoked salmon sandwiches."

"Will you please stop talking about food!" said Julia.

So we talked about Daphne's latest boyfriend, who's one of those Americans being sent out here to tell us how to win the war. He couldn't believe the daughter of an earl worked six days a week as an aircraft welder. "A qualified semi-skilled mechanic," Daphne corrected him, with some pride. She told him how all single women here under the age of thirty are conscripted into the army if they aren't already doing war work, and he was absolutely horrified and said that back home, they'd never even *contemplate* asking that of their "womenfolk." Isn't that funny, when America seems so modern and progressive? But then, I suppose they haven't been fighting off invaders for the past two years.

Very excited letter from Henry, who was meant to go back to school last Monday after the Easter holidays, but broke her thumb while trying to fix the henhouse door. Her excitement was not merely due to having an extra week off school, but also to an incident in Milford on Friday. She was walking to the village shop with a list Barnes had given her when an army lorry pulled up outside the inn to ask directions. (I suppose it's quite confusing for them, navigating with no road signs and having to make constant detours around bomb craters and broken bridges, but it does make one wonder how they'd manage in a war zone.) While the captain was talking to the innkeeper, a few of the soldiers climbed out of the lorry to stretch their legs, and Henry caught sight of a familiar face. She dropped her basket, shrieked out his name, and rushed over to fling her arms around him.

And it was *Jimmy Smith*! Alice's son, from Montmaray! Fancy Henry recognizing him after all these years! But they *were* best friends for most of their childhood, and it turned out he'd sent her a card at Christmas, saying he was desperate to leave home because he hates his stepfather. Apparently the old man, never very amiable, has been in a permanent black mood since the navy requisitioned his fishing boat.

Still, Jimmy *couldn't* be eighteen—Henry doesn't turn sixteen till August, and he wasn't quite two years older than her. He doesn't have a birth certificate, though, and he's always been big for his age. It's probably easy enough to join the army, if one's determined enough. Boys are called up anyway, the moment they turn eighteen, so it's better he goes in as a willing recruit, even if it *is* a few months early.

Jimmy told Henry it was his first week with the company—which is a *bomb disposal* company, of all things! They were on their way to Exeter, to help defuse all the unexploded bombs after that dreadful air raid. *Raids*, I ought to say, as there was another one in Exeter that very night, and then several in Bath, and now the Luftwaffe has moved on to Norwich. The Baedeker Blitz, the Germans are calling it—apparently they're trying to destroy every historical building awarded three stars in Baedeker's guidebook to Great Britain, in retaliation for the RAF bombing German cities. And *those* RAF raids were probably retribution for the razing of Coventry, and the Coventry massacre was no doubt ordered by Hitler to avenge some earlier British insult to the Fatherland . . . No wonder wars go on for years and years, when the people in charge have that sort of attitude.

Henry said that she invited Jimmy's entire company to

the gatehouse for luncheon (I'm sure Barnes would have been thrilled by their arrival), but of course, they had to be on their way at once. She also wrote that Jimmy sent his love to all of us, including Carlos, so now I feel horribly guilty about not having written to Alice and Mary for ages. Poor Alice must be *so* anxious about Jimmy—her only child, away from home for the first time and doing such a dangerous job—and I must say, her husband doesn't sound very pleasant. It also reminds me that I must send Phoebe something nice for her birthday next month. She loves working on that farm in Somerset and seems to be unofficially engaged to the farmer's son, but her favorite brother is fighting in the Middle East, which is a constant worry for her.

Really, it seems everyone is fretting about *someone*. Veronica had luncheon with Daniel at his parents' house on Sunday, and came home terribly concerned about him. She thinks his work is making him ill. He's lost weight—as if he weren't thin enough already—and he looked as though he hadn't been sleeping. Of course, he's not allowed to breathe a word about his job.

"But what do you *think* he's doing?" I asked Veronica.

"Well," she said slowly, "I'm starting to wonder if he's interrogating prisoners of war."

"German prisoners of war? But we don't have any here, do we? Except a few Luftwaffe pilots who've been shot down, and they wouldn't know much."

"There's Rudolf Hess."

"*Hess?*" I stared at her. "That deputy of Hitler's who flew here, claiming he wanted to make peace with Britain? But he's *mad*, isn't he? Besides, that was a year ago—they'd have run out of questions by now."

"Perhaps," she said. "But there have been a lot of battles in North Africa and the Middle East lately. The Allies must have taken some Wehrmacht officers prisoner by now. *They'd* have valuable information."

"Well, I can't imagine they'd be willing to share it."

"No, not at *all* willing."

"You can't think . . . Veronica! The *British* wouldn't torture their prisoners!"

"Wouldn't they?"

"No, of course not! It's against the Geneva Convention! The British aren't like the *Nazis*—"

But then I stopped. I was thinking of Chamberlain's speech, that day he'd declared war on Germany, when he'd said the Nazis stood for "brute force, bad faith, injustice, oppression and persecution."

Brute force—well, we were bombing Germany just as hard as they were bombing us. Their women and children must be dying by the hundreds, too. And injustice—what about poor Anthony? What about all those innocent German refugees still locked up on the Isle of Man, and the ones shipped off to the Dominions? What about the Mosleys? Admittedly, *they* probably lived in much nicer conditions than the refugees, and Oswald Mosley was a truly detestable man. But if there was evidence that he and his wife were guilty of treason, then why hadn't the two of them been put on trial? If the British government could do *that*—keep its own citizens in prison indefinitely without charging them with a crime—then perhaps it *might* be as capable of evil as the Nazis . . .

"You know those houses up the road?" Veronica said. "The ones everyone says have been requisitioned by the War Office?"

"The ones with barbed wire round them?"

"Yes. Well, a few days ago, I saw some men outside there and I could have sworn one of them was wearing a Wehrmacht uniform. He didn't look very well, either. He was sort of hunched over and the other men shoved him into a car. I couldn't help thinking . . . well, you know. That they'd been interrogating him, inside that house."

An interrogation center, in Kensington Palace Gardens? It doesn't seem very likely—and yet, Veronica isn't usually given to flights of fancy. It was such an alarming idea that I hastened to reassure both of us.

"But *Daniel* could never be involved in anything like that," I said. "How could he possibly intimidate anyone into giving up their secrets? He's too . . . *nice*."

"Perhaps someone else does the interrogating, and he writes it down and translates it," she said. "*I* don't know. I just know he's unhappy. And I can't do anything to help him, because he's not allowed to talk about it."

Then she went out into the garden to vent her frustration on the dandelions that are threatening to annex our potato patch. I left her to it, because I had a week's worth of ironing to do. Unfortunately, ironing doesn't require much brain, so my thoughts were free to wander back to what Veronica had said—and then they drifted into areas that were even *more* uncomfortable.

For instance, so much of this war seems to be about us hiding the truth from one another. I know "careless talk costs lives," but sometimes all this enforced silence seems completely counterproductive. For instance, it was only a few months ago that the censors allowed the newspapers to report that Bank underground station had been bombed, even though that raid happened a *year* ago. The newspaper report couldn't even say how many people were killed, even though I know it was more than a hundred (Julia was on duty that night). The Luftwaffe pilots must have understood they'd hit something big—they only had to look out the windows of their planes to see the devastation. And all the survivors and the emergency workers (and the German spies who are supposedly hiding behind every second lamppost) saw exactly what happened. By suppressing the facts, the government simply encouraged people to speculate about what *else* they weren't being told. It caused "bad faith"—as Chamberlain said about the Nazis. As for "oppression and persecution"—well, what about last year, when the BBC announced they were banning any actors or musicians who supported the People's Convention, which had called for a negotiated peace? The Communist newspaper, *The Daily Worker,* is still outlawed, even though the Soviet Union is on our side now. And it's all very commendable for Mr. Churchill to sign that Atlantic Charter with Mr. Roosevelt, saying the Allies support the right of all peoples to choose their own government—but what about India? It's a bit hypocritical to attack the Nazis for occupying France and Belgium and all those other countries when Britain's been occupying India for *decades*, and whenever Indians say they want self-government, they get thrown into prison or shot dead.

Everyone says that now, with both Russia *and* America on our side, the Nazis cannot possibly win. But when the fighting eventually stops, will there be freedom and justice for all? I don't remember it being that way at any stage of history *before* the war.

14th May 1942

The telephone rang this morning as Veronica and I were getting ready for work, rushing about in our usual last-minute hunt for clean handkerchiefs and lost gloves. I was closer, so I picked up the telephone receiver.

"Hello, Sophie," said Simon's voice. "Is Veronica there? Could I speak with her, please?"

"Yes, here she is," I said, handing over the receiver. "Simon," I explained to her, and she gave an impatient huff.

And I didn't even stop to wonder why he'd be ringing us at that hour. Because I'd suddenly remembered Anne had asked to borrow my copy of *Ariel* and I was trying to recall where I'd left it. I'd just turned to peruse our bookshelf when I heard Veronica gasp—as though Simon had reached down the telephone line and slapped her. I whirled about. Veronica was now asking a lot of crisp, practical questions—"When?" and "Where, exactly?" and "To Milford?" But her voice had a crack running through it, and her face was starting to crumple.

And even *then*, I hadn't the slightest inkling. If I was imagining anything at all, it was that Aunt Charlotte had had an accident. She'd fallen off a horse, broken her leg, something like that.

Then Veronica said, "Thank you, Simon. It's very good of you to think of contacting us first. I can't tell you how much I appreciate it," and I realized the world had tilted on its axis. But I still didn't comprehend the cataclysm until Veronica put down the telephone and held out her hand.

"Sophie," she said, and I went to her, and she folded her arms round me.

"It's Toby," she said.

I had to put down my pen there. I couldn't—physically could not—write the next bit. And I'm not certain I can *now*, although at least I've stopped crying. Mostly.

So. What happened next was that Veronica told me what Simon had said. Then she tried to telephone Milford, except she couldn't get through.

"But Barnes will be the first to see the telegram," Veronica said. "She's the one who usually answers the door. She'll know how to tell Aunt Charlotte."

"What about . . . What about Henry?" I said, but I couldn't get any further with that thought. Neither could Veronica.

"Later," she said. "We'll think about that later." We perched on the sofa, gripping each other's hands, unable to move. We seemed to be waiting for someone to come and tell us what to do. At last, Veronica said, "I should go in to work." This idea invigorated her. She jumped up, grabbed her coat, and darted into her bedroom for her bag.

"I'll keep trying to get in touch with Milford from the office," she said. "Perhaps I could ring Henry's headmistress—no, a letter's best, don't you think? And someone ought to get in contact with Julia. Do you want me to do that? I could call the aerodrome, too, ask to speak with his Wing Commander."

I managed to stand, and to nod and shake my head in the appropriate places. All I knew was that I couldn't bear the thought of being alone in the flat, and that I wanted to keep busy. Going to work seemed the logical thing for me to do, too.

But when I reached the office, it was even worse. Miss Halliday snapped at me for being late, and I couldn't explain why I'd missed my bus. I simply couldn't find the *words*. I'd never before had any sort of conversation with her that wasn't about my work. I knew Anne would be sympathetic, but I didn't want sympathy. I hadn't earned it. I wasn't in pain, not at that stage. I was still numb with disbelief, almost paralyzed with it. My tongue had turned heavy; my limbs seemed to belong to someone else; my fingers fumbled with the easiest and most familiar of tasks. It took three attempts to thread a piece of paper into my typewriter. Then I stared at the brochure copy I'd proofread the previous afternoon, and it might as well have been written in Swahili, for all the sense it made.

Sometime later—after I'd remembered how to use a typewriter and finished a clean copy of the brochure and dropped it into Mr. Bowker's tray and sat back down at my desk—I decided the RAF had made a mistake. It *couldn't* be true, what Simon had said about Toby. Their error was quite understandable, of course. I forgave them at once. One couldn't expect the RAF to keep track of *every* plane, every single pilot—especially a pilot who made a habit of ignoring regulations. And it certainly wouldn't have been the first time the RAF had blundered . . .

But then I recalled Simon. He'd waited till this morning. He must have checked and double-checked before he'd picked up that telephone. He hadn't even been able to bring himself to tell me. He'd left that to Veronica. Which was exactly how he'd act, if he were convinced it were true . . .

The Colonel. The thought flashed across my mind, lighting it up with hope. *He* would be able to discover what had really happened! He was the one I needed! I snatched up my bag, informed an astonished Miss Halliday that I was taking an early luncheon break, then dashed out of the office and down the stairs before she could stop me. I knew where I was headed—that café up the road, the one with the pay telephone. But when I arrived, my heart hammering, my breath coming in painful puffs, I realized I didn't have any pennies in my purse, only a ten-shilling note. So I sat down at a table and ordered a cup of tea.

And as I waited for it, my hope flickered and died. For how could the Colonel help with *this*? He hadn't been able to do anything for poor Anthony. And if the Colonel *did* discover something hidden by the RAF—or something unknown even to them, something awful—then how likely was it that he'd tell me the truth?

No one ever told me *anything*. Simon hadn't even trusted me enough to talk to me! Did he think I was too young—too *feeble*—to be able to cope with the news? Perhaps he was right. At that moment, I was fighting the urge to lay my head on the greasy tabletop and weep. I must have looked as miserable as I felt, because when the waitress set my teacup in front of me, she asked what was wrong.

"My brother's a fighter pilot," I told her. "He was shot down over Belgium yesterday, and one of his squadron saw his plane crash into the ground and burst into flames, and no one knows if he was in it, or if he bailed out, or if he survived the landing, or if he's been taken prisoner. We don't know *anything*."

Yes, I blurted all that out to a complete stranger. But the poor woman probably gets that sort of thing constantly, in her job. It would have served me right if she'd said, "Is that all? I've had three in here just this morning, exact same thing. There *is* a war on, you know." She was awfully kind, though.

"It's the not knowing that's the worst, isn't it?" she tutted. "You drink up your tea, love, and try not to fret. I'll wager you'll have news soon enough, and he'll be all right if he's a prisoner. My neighbor's boy's been over there since Dunkirk, and he's allowed to send letters home and everything."

I wanted to explain that Toby wasn't like other missing servicemen. He was special. But I just nodded and tried to drink my tea. I suppose everyone thinks their missing boy is special.

We held a family council yesterday in Aunt Charlotte's suite at Claridge's, after Veronica and I had collected Henry from the railway station. I'd been sick with worry over Henry, but she looked almost cheerful. It turned out this was because she's convinced herself that Toby's disappearance is all part of some secret intelligence mission.

"I know you're not allowed to tell us anything," she said to the Colonel, who'd generously found time in his busy schedule to meet with us. "But it's so obvious, isn't it? Toby's plane wouldn't crash unless he *made* it crash. He's too good at flying. I expect he was chosen for the mission because he speaks French so well."

"Oh, yes, he *does*, doesn't he?" said Aunt Charlotte, a faint light dawning in her reddened eyes. Barnes took the opportunity to prize the sodden handkerchief out of Aunt Charlotte's fist and replace it with a fresh one. "Yes," went on Aunt Charlotte, nodding, "I remember, the French Master at Eton always spoke *very* highly of Tobias."

None of us had the heart to point out that Toby's plane had crashed in the Flemish-speaking part of Belgium. By then, we knew that one of the other pilots in his squadron had been confirmed as dead, his Spitfire seen plummeting into the Channel, trailing black smoke. The planes flown by Toby and his second-in-command hadn't even made it back as far as the sea. Both had smashed into farmland near the coast and exploded on impact. There was some vague talk of a parachute being spotted, but no one knew whose it was. Of course, Henry was certain it was Toby's.

"I bet he had a huge lot of supplies in his pack when he bailed out," she said. "Enough to last for ages, until he meets up with the Resistance agents. He'll be fine, once he makes contact with them."

Veronica shot her a look composed of equal parts concern and exasperation, then turned back to the Colonel. "Should we contact the Red Cross, do you think?" she asked him. "They visit all the prisoner-of-war camps, don't they? Do they keep a register of names?"

"Actually," the Colonel said, "I'm wondering if it might be a good idea to . . ." He cleared his throat. "That is, forgive me, but I think we ought to make an announcement that Toby is dead."

"What?" cried Aunt Charlotte, her eyes welling afresh. "Oh, no!"

"Just to deceive the Germans, that's all," the Colonel added hurriedly. "We don't want them realizing the head of state of one of the Allied nations might be wandering about Belgium. If we say he's dead, they won't be looking for him."

Henry gave a firm nod, as though this confirmed all her theories, but Aunt Charlotte kept shaking her head, distress written across her face. I could quite understand how she felt. There was no way Toby would read the announcement or hear of it—even if he *were* still alive—but to agree to this felt as though we were giving up on him. I glanced at Veronica, who was frowning hard.

"Yes, it *would* be a sensible move," she muttered, although I wasn't sure whether she was talking to herself or to us. "There *have* been cases of Allied servicemen avoiding capture in France and making it across the Spanish border. Except the Spanish government's being very difficult at the moment, and Belgium is so *far* from Spain. I don't suppose . . ." She looked up at the Colonel. "Could he cross the Channel, do you think? Would there be any fishermen willing to take him across?"

"I think that would be . . . very unlikely," the Colonel said. "I understand the Germans have destroyed or requisitioned all the boats along the Channel coast in the occupied territories. Which hasn't endeared them to the locals, of course, so there's a distinct possibility there'd be villagers around who'd be prepared to help Toby."

If he'd survived the crash. *If* he wasn't so badly wounded that he was beyond help.

"Look," said the Colonel bracingly, "if he *does* get picked up by the authorities and they don't realize who he is . . . well, so far, they've been pretty decent. Look at Douglas Bader—you know, that pilot with the two artificial legs? He got shot down last year, and had to leave one of his legs behind in his plane when he bailed out. But the Germans actually let the RAF drop off a replacement leg for him, at his prisoner-of-war camp! Jolly nice of them. Of course, they've threatened to confiscate *both* his legs now, because he keeps trying to escape . . ."

Henry was the only one who laughed.

I can't help admiring her steadfast loyalty to Toby. To her, Toby is a god—indomitable, immortal. She simply refuses to contemplate that he might be gone. Perhaps it would be kinder to start preparing her for the very worst . . . and yet, Henry's belief that Toby is alive and well is not only keeping *her* going, but it's just about the only thing sustaining our poor aunt. The only times she showed any signs of animation were when Henry was talking. I watched Aunt Charlotte begin to nod as Henry recalled Toby's excellent sense of direction and superb map-reading skills; she almost smiled as Henry described how the village girls would be fighting amongst themselves for the privilege of hiding Toby in their barn. It may even be some comfort to our aunt that Henry *looks* so much like Toby. That same tangle of golden curls, the same mischievous blue eyes, the same wide smile, quirking up at one corner . . .

Oh, God.

That waitress was wrong. I would readily endure years and *years* of the agony of not knowing if it means that, at the end of it, I will see my brother again.

Veronica and I visited Toby's aerodrome on Saturday. I think the RAF would have much preferred to bundle up Toby's belongings and post them to us, but we insisted on collecting them in person. We'd hoped to meet some of the men who'd flown with him—Veronica thought they might reveal some tiny, seemingly insignificant snippet of information that hadn't made it into the official report, something that might give us cause for optimism. But she was too eager, too anxious—too intense.

"Wait," she said, leaning over the table in the pub, where one of the pilots had brought us for a drink, "was this *before* or *after* the first Messerschmitt opened fire?"

I could see the poor boy was regretting having agreed to talk to us. He couldn't have been any older than I was, and his uniform hung on him awkwardly, as though it'd been thrown together for a much broader man. He was so shy (or perhaps so unused to women) that he could barely look Veronica in the eye.

"I . . . I really couldn't say," he stammered. "It was too quick. I don't even know if it *was* Toby or . . . or someone else."

"But you definitely saw a parachute," Veronica said.

"I *think* I did . . ."

I gave him an encouraging smile and he took a shaky breath.

"Yes, I did," he said. "Actually, it may have been two parachutes."

"*Two?* You're sure about that?"

"Um . . . yes?" He gazed helplessly about the pub, then plunged his face into his pint of beer.

Veronica persisted a little longer with her questioning, without success. It was only as we were gathering up our coats, preparing to leave, that he said, "Um . . . There *is* one other thing. One of the boys asked me to . . . to mention it to you."

"Yes?" said Veronica, and I held my breath.

"Well . . . it's about Toby's car, you see. The Lagonda. Toby sort of said that Wicksy—I mean, Pilot Officer Wickstead— that he could have the car, if Toby ever . . . um, if he didn't make it back from an op. Not that he wrote it down officially or anything, but—"

"Keep it," said Veronica shortly. "It's not as though civilians can get hold of any petrol these days."

"Oh, jolly good!" he said, brightening. "Thanks! It's what he would have wanted, you know, and we'll take good care of it. And, of course, if Toby *were* to make it back—"

"Yes, of course," she said.

We watched him tug on his cap and make a rapid escape out the side door, before turning to each other.

"What a *complete* waste of time," Veronica said.

I had to agree. But after she'd gone up to the bar to ask about the bus schedule, the girl wiping down the tables came over to where I sat.

"You're Toby's sister," she said, setting down her tower of glasses. "I could tell as soon as you walked in. You look just like him."

"You knew . . . know him?" I said.

"Oh, all the flyboys come in here," she said, "and you could always count on Toby being right in the middle of the rowdiest lot! But don't get me wrong—he was polite, you know? A real gentleman. Not like *some* of those boys, always trying to sneak a kiss! He was never like that."

"No," I said, smiling despite myself, "no, he's not like that at all."

"I *was* sorry to hear," she said. "You'd think I'd get used to it, wouldn't you, living next door to the aerodrome? But it's always sad."

"He's not dead," I said. "Just missing."

"Yes," she said gently. "Yes, of course." And the look she gave me was so kind that I had to turn away, blinking furiously.

And it *keeps* happening. I'll be doing something completely ordinary—typing a letter at work or queuing outside the grocery shop—when, all of a sudden, I'll be overwhelmed with anguish. Where is he now? Is he hungry? Is he cold? Does he have somewhere safe to sleep? Is he injured, is he in pain? It's such agony that I can hardly bear the sight of the people around me, going about their usual lives. How can they be so *unfeeling*? At my worst moments, I find myself wondering if it would be better if he'd never survived that crash—but then my mind goes blank. I *can't* think about how he might have died, I simply can't.

The person who best seems to understand how I feel is not Veronica, oddly enough, but Julia. She came round to our flat that first terrible night, and threw her arms around me, and didn't even attempt to offer any consoling words. She knew there was nothing to say. It's not that Veronica doesn't hurt as much as I do—I know she does, perhaps *more* than I do, if that's possible. She and Toby were "the twins" for most of their child-hood, after all. But right now, Veronica's and my methods of coping with Toby's disappearance are so different that we aren't much comfort to each other. *I* can hardly manage to get out of bed each morning, whereas she's throwing herself into learning everything she can about Allied pilots who've been shot down over Nazi territory. What percentage of them have been con-firmed dead, how many have been taken prisoner, which factors have led to successful escapes . . .

But no doubt her approach is more sensible than mine. As I write this, she sits across from me, pounding away at my typewriter. When I managed to stir myself out of my apathy to ask what she was doing, she said she was writing to someone she knew at the British Embassy in Madrid, a man who's been helping escaped Allied servicemen evade the hostile Spanish authorities. Presumably he's working unofficially; hence the need to correspond with him outside office hours. She also said she's campaigning to be allowed to take up another temporary post at the Embassy next month.

Where *does* she find the energy? It took all my strength just to get dressed this morning. What does it matter anymore, whether my stockings match? Who cares if I've lost a button from my coat? What's the point of combing my hair? I haven't even opened today's post, even though one of my letters is addressed in Rupert's handwriting. I'm sure his letter will be thoughtful and sensitive, but I cannot face any kindness right now. In fact, I cannot write another word. I'm going to bed.

We've had news, of sorts, from Belgium. The parents of the other missing pilot from Toby's squadron received a small parcel a few days ago, containing the silver four-leaf clover that had been their son's lucky charm. Not a terribly *potent* charm, it turns out. The accompanying letter was from the Belgian Red Cross, and stated that the pilot's body, still strapped to his open parachute, had been found near a small village not far from the coast. He appeared to have died of head wounds, probably sustained when his plane was hit. A farmer had reached the body before the Luftwaffe police and their search dogs, and he'd managed to retrieve the charm from the pilot's pocket, along with a recent letter from the pilot's mother that contained her address. These had been handed on to the local Red Cross, and they'd forwarded the items to England.

So, at least one family now have a definitive answer. Or have they? The items certainly belonged to the pilot, but had the Red Cross been deceived by the villagers about the manner of the pilot's death? If so, to what aim? Could the man still be alive? Could he be hiding, or aiding the local Resistance? Or is the whole thing, even the "Red Cross" letter, some sinister trick of the Nazis?

All these questions are courtesy of Veronica, who appears to have taken leave of her senses. The moment she heard the news, via the Colonel, she dashed off to interrogate the bereaved parents, who have a house just outside London. She even copied out their Red Cross letter, in case it contained some secret message in code. The poor couple must have thought she was *mad*.

"Oh, no," said Veronica. "When they heard I was from the Foreign Office, they just assumed I was an intelligence agent."

She admitted she had not corrected their mistaken assumption. She also conceded that her visit hadn't actually provided us with any additional information about Toby. Not that this seems to have deterred her in the slightest. She even wrote to Simon, demanding all the details he possessed and asking him to investigate further. Simon sent a terse, uninformative response—although that's quite normal for correspondence between the two of them.

Henry, of course, remains optimistic. To her, the parcel is conclusive proof that Toby is alive. She says that if he *had* been killed, his body would have been found near his fellow pilot's. She's also heartened by this evidence that the local population is keen to thwart the Nazis, even in small ways. *The villagers probably passed Toby on to the Resistance weeks ago*, she wrote to us—and presumably to Aunt Charlotte, as well. Heaven knows what our poor aunt makes of it all, but she pays more attention to Henry than to anyone else these days, so she's probably feeling more positive than *I* am.

19th June 1942

A few days ago, I began writing a frank account of what happened last week. But I was struck by the terrifying thought that
someone might read it, so I tore out the pages. I was on the
verge of ripping the paper up and setting fire to the scraps—and
then I stopped and considered. I don't regret what happened.
It's true that I'm unlikely to confide in Veronica about it when
she returns from Spain—but I'm not *ashamed*.

Besides, what is the point of keeping a journal if one lies to
oneself about significant events in one's life? Especially as there
really *is* very little chance that anyone will be able to decipher
this, apart from me.

So, I will start again—at the beginning this time, rather
than at the end, even though *that* is the bit occupying most of
my waking thoughts and quite a few of my dreams.

Right. Well, Saturday was Julia's birthday, and Daphne was
determined that we should celebrate it with as much lavishness
as the war would allow. I'd agreed to go out with them—not

because I was feeling at all celebratory, but because I was too listless to argue with her. On Saturday morning, then, I collected my blue evening gown from the cleaners on my way home from the shops. With Veronica away for a few weeks, my shopping list had been shorter than usual, but nevertheless, I was weighed down by a wicker basket, a bulging string bag, and a heavy silk gown. I plodded down the narrow path towards our flat, wondering if I'd be able to summon up enough energy to repaint the bathroom before Veronica returned, now that the plasterer had finally fixed all the cracks in the walls . . . Then I glanced up, and my heart seemed to stop.

For there, sitting on the steps leading to the front door of the flat, was a tall, slender young man in RAF uniform. His head was in his hands and his cap hid his face, but I hadn't any doubt as to his identity. Who else could it be, except Toby? I dropped my burdens and began to run.

As I drew closer, he heard my footsteps, and he sat up straighter and pushed back his cap. Now I saw his hair was not blond but black, that he was older than Toby, that he was family and yet . . . unfamiliar. Because it was Simon, but when he turned his face to me, I scarcely recognized him. It wasn't just that he was pale and unshaven and hollow-cheeked—he looked utterly defeated. I slowed to a walk to give myself time to prepare for what was obviously going to be horrible news.

"Hello, Simon," I said unsteadily when I stood at the foot of the steps.

He nodded at me and said nothing. His eyes were sunken and dull.

"You gave me quite a shock," I said, trying to smile at him. "I wasn't expecting you. I hope you haven't been waiting long. Veronica's not here, of course, she left three days ago for Spain—"

I think I had the notion that if I kept babbling, he wouldn't be able to tell me anything awful. Actually, an even *more* effective way of avoiding the news would be to remove myself from his presence altogether, and it was then that I recalled my scattered shopping.

"Here," I said, pushing past him to unlock the door. "You go in and put the kettle on, and I'll go back and collect my things, and then we can have a nice cup of tea and we can, can—"

I couldn't get any further. I rushed off, back down the path. "Get ahold of yourself, Sophia!" I scolded myself. "For heaven's *sake*! Yes, this might be easier to bear if Veronica were here, but really! You're a grown woman of twenty-one years, not a child! Stop being such a *coward*!"

And by the time I walked into the kitchen, I was reasonably composed.

I couldn't say the same of Simon, though. He'd managed to seat himself at the table, but I wasn't even sure if he knew where he was. I pulled my chair up close to his, and placed a tentative hand on his shoulder.

"Simon?" I said quietly. "What is it?"

In response, he laid his head down on his crossed arms.

Then he made a horrible rasping sound, and it took me whole seconds to understand what he was doing. But the poor man simply didn't know *how* to cry. He probably hadn't done it since he was an infant. I reached out to stroke his back, and when he didn't shrug me off, I moved closer and put my arms round him and rested my cheek on the top of his hair. I didn't cry myself. I was too frightened, I think. I felt as I had when I'd seen the bombed Houses of Parliament last year. That was when I'd understood that nothing was safe anymore—that everything, no matter how old or powerful or important, could be reduced to dust and ashes.

Simon's agonized gasping didn't last long—certainly not compared to some of my own crying fits. I handed him a tea towel to wipe his face, because I didn't think my tiny lace-trimmed handkerchief was up to the task, then I got up and bustled about the kitchen, putting together a pot of tea in the noisiest manner possible.

"Sorry," he said at last, in a voice that sounded as though it were being dragged over gravel.

I placed a mug of tea in front of him and stirred in most of our remaining sugar. Wasn't that meant to be good for shock? I could have done with a few tablespoons of it myself. My hands were trembling as I sat down opposite him.

"I think," I said, rather bravely, "that you should tell me all about it."

"I shouldn't have come here," he said, staring at the table-cloth. "Except . . . I didn't know where else to go. Sophie, I think I'm going mad."

This was not what I'd expected.

"You aren't going *mad*," I said, with more certainty than I felt. "You're just upset. We all are. It's perfectly understandable—"

"But I can't get it out of my head," he said. "I keep hearing it. Over and over again, all the time, even when I try to sleep! I think it's in my *blood*."

"In your . . . Simon, you aren't making any sense."

"No, because I'm going mad! Like my mother. Like my *father*."

"What?" I said, now seriously alarmed. "No, listen to me. Your parents weren't . . . that is, they *were*, but only because they'd had terrible things happen in their lives and—"

"And *I* haven't?" he asked, and I had to admit that he *had* had some fairly terrible things happen to him. I mean, we all have, really.

"But, what exactly do you mean?" I went on, speaking as calmly as possible, because he *did* look a tiny bit mad at that moment. "Tell me, what is it that you keep hearing?"

He swallowed. "I . . . I used to listen to the pilots getting shot down," he said. "If their radios were still working, I'd hear everything they said. Every last word. While the cockpit was filling with smoke, after the engine cut out. They'd always know what was coming, *always*. They'd say, 'That's it, lads,' or, 'It's over.' Or just . . . swearing. Cursing Hitler, cursing God. I even heard some of the Luftwaffe boys. They used to say exactly the same things, except in German."

"Did you . . ." I cleared my throat and started again. "Did you hear Toby, the day he was shot down?"

"Yes . . . No. I don't know." Simon raised his anguished eyes to mine. "No, *no*, I couldn't have, I don't even work in that section anymore! But I keep hearing him, anyway. All the time."

"What does he say?"

"What all the others said. But it's *his* voice, I know it is!"

"It isn't him," I said firmly. "Simon, you're just imagining it. I dream of him, too. But it's not *real*. It's only happening because we're so worried and we just don't know the truth—"

"Yes, we *do*! He's gone. I know it. And it's all my fault. I'm to blame—"

"Have you heard something?" I demanded. "Something official?" After all, that was what I'd assumed when I'd realized it was Simon sitting on the steps.

"No, the air force doesn't know anything else. But Sophie, you're not listening to me. I mean it—I'm to blame for everything. *I* was the one who passed on the order to his base that day. *I* sent his squadron out, knowing he was on duty. And I *knew* other planes had been shot down in that area a few weeks before. I knew that even if they hit the target they were aiming at, it wasn't worth the risk. But I still gave that order."

I stared at him.

"I shouldn't have come here," he said despairingly. "You hate me."

I shook my head, still searching for words.

"You *ought* to hate me! I hate myself!"

"Oh, Simon! Of course I don't hate you," I said, grabbing his hand. "But you sound as though you *want* me to hate you. As though you're waiting for me to punish you. Well, I'm not going to do that."

He looked down at our hands as I tightened my grip.

"Toby was the one who signed up first," I said. "He didn't have to, but he did, before the war even started, and if it weren't for him, you probably wouldn't have joined the air force. Toby was doing his job—a job he *chose*—the day he got shot down. And you were doing *your* job. I know the air force sometimes gets it wrong, but don't you believe in what you're doing, on the whole? I do. I think the air force saved this island from invasion. I don't exactly understand your job, but I *do* know that you're not the one in command. You couldn't have changed anything about that day. You're not *that* important."

He made a snuffling noise that might have been a laugh.

"If you insist on wallowing in guilt and self-pity, I can't stop you," I added, releasing his hand. "I think it's a waste of your time and energy, though, when you ought to be concentrating on your job."

I know that last was rather hypocritical of me, but I'm better at giving advice to others than to myself. And he did look slightly less anguished by the end of my speech.

"But Sophie, I don't think I *can* do that job anymore," he said. "I just keep sending men off to be killed. I dread the thought of going back, of having to—"

"Simon," I interrupted, struck by a horrible notion, "you

do have a leave pass, don't you? I mean, you haven't just . . . deserted?"

"What, you think I care about what they'd do to me?" he said. "A nice, quiet prison cell sounds a hell of a lot better than what I've got now."

But he was joking—mostly—and he sounded a little more like himself. I got him to finish his tea, and made us both a sandwich, and then he fell asleep on Veronica's bed. By the time he'd woken, I'd had a bath, mended a hole in my only pair of silk stockings, and located my missing pearl earring, which had slipped down behind my chest of drawers.

"Go and shave," I told Simon, when he appeared in my doorway with his hair standing on end. "Do you have a clean shirt in your bag? I'll iron it while you're having a bath."

"What?" he said.

"It's Julia's birthday," I explained. "We're going to the Mirabelle for dinner."

I didn't mention Daphne, because he can't stand her, but even so, he protested. I stood firm. I wasn't going to disappoint Julia, and I wasn't prepared to leave him alone in the flat. I had a suspicion *he* didn't really want to be alone just then, either— although, when he finally agreed to accompany me, he said it was only because he didn't like the idea of me taking taxis alone at night. He trudged off to the bathroom, and I ironed his uniform and laid it out on Veronica's bed. Then I rushed back to my room to get dressed—and froze.

Because I'd just remembered my evening gown fastened up

the back with fifty-two tiny buttons that were impossible to do up by myself. I'd always had Phoebe or Veronica to help me with them in the past. I stared at the rack that held my dresses, hoping some alternative outfit would suddenly appear. Perhaps I could wear my good suit? I'd seen girls in khaki uniforms at nightclubs; once, even a girl in a boiler suit and steel-capped boots. However, I could just imagine Daphne's reaction if I turned up in anything other than my nicest evening dress. The shabbier and gloomier London became, the more determined she was that we should always look bright and glamorous. I considered racing up to the house with a torch and rifling through my old debutante dresses, but even if I found something clean and free of moth holes, nothing would suit me as well as the blue gown Julia had helped me alter. It had become one of those rare, perfect dresses that was both comfortable and flattering. It clung in the right places and draped exactly where drapes were needed. It matched the blue of my eyes. The soft, heavy silk felt like some magical liquid splashed against my skin, transforming me into an elegant figure quite unlike my usual daytime self . . .

Well, I'd just have to ask Simon for a hand. Goodness knows he'd had enough experience doing up girls' dresses—or at least, undoing them.

I wriggled into the gown, managing to fasten about a dozen of the buttons after much contortion and peering over my shoulders, and I slipped on my shoes. I twisted my hair into a knot and secured it with a handful of pins, and I rubbed on some of my carefully hoarded lipstick. Then I raised my chin and walked into the next room, where Simon was peering in Veronica's tiny looking glass to check that his tie was straight.

"Could you do up the buttons on the back of my dress?" I said. "I can't quite reach all of them."

Simon stared, then blinked. No, I suppose he *hadn't* seen this dress before. Perhaps he thought it too grown-up for me? Well, too bad. About time he stopped treating me like a child.

"Hurry up, or we'll be late," I added imperiously, swiveling away from him. I heard him move behind me and felt his touch at the small of my back.

"You've done them up wrongly," he said, and he slid his hand around to my hip and tugged me closer. "Stand still."

So I stood still for what seemed like hours as his fingers slowly worked their way up my spine. I felt my face grow warmer. My pulse pounded in my ears. When he brushed against bare skin, I had to suppress a shiver. I hadn't acted so idiotically around him for *years*.

"That's it," he said at last, in a low voice. One of my shoulder straps slipped, and we both reached for it. I jerked my hand back when it came into contact with his.

"Thanks," I said, pulling away, my face aflame. But my awkwardness appeared to be contagious, and a strange tension persisted between us all the way to the restaurant. As we approached the table where the others were gathered, Daphne stood up and shrieked out a greeting, and I felt Simon's arm tighten under my hand, as though he were battling the urge to bolt.

"We don't have to stay long," I whispered. "It'll be all right.

We'll just wish Julia a happy birthday, and have a nice dinner, then go home."

He glanced down at me, his jaw clenched, then nodded.

Unfortunately, Daphne was in excessively high spirits that night, and she'd brought along her latest American, a Lieutenant Colonel with very strong opinions. As we sat down, he was holding forth on how unnecessary this war was.

"All you needed to do," he said, "was be firm with old Adolf, right from the start. But you Brits, you're too polite! You never come right out and say what you mean!"

The Brits at *our* table were certainly too polite to tell him to shut up, not that he would have listened.

"Between you and those damn useless French," he went on, "it's no wonder Adolf gave up on talking and figured it'd just be easier to invade Poland. Now, don't get me wrong—I love you guys—but you've never learned to talk tough. Talk tough *or* fight tough, neither one of 'em. You gotta be able to do both in this world!"

"Then why didn't you lot join the League of Nations?" snapped Simon, sounding remarkably like Veronica at her most acerbic. "You could have talked tough to Hitler and saved everyone a lot of trouble. Failing that, why didn't you join the war in 1939? If you'd thrashed the Germans with your tough fighting when they invaded France, it'd all be over now."

"*Now* you're talking!" cried the Lieutenant Colonel. "You're right on the money *there*, pal!" And off he went on a long rant about the incompetence of the British Army. Finally,

Daphne interrupted with a "Yes, darling, we know all that," and dragged him away, onto the dance floor.

"Are there any *quiet* Americans?" wondered the girl sitting opposite Julia.

"Yes, but Daphne only ever goes out with the loud ones," sighed Julia. "The loud, handsome ones."

"Do you *really* think he's handsome?" said the naval officer beside her, his face falling. I'd met him before, but I'd forgotten his name. I knew he was in love with Julia, and that she was too kind to banish him entirely from her presence, even though she wasn't interested in anything but friendship.

"I don't think I'll ever get married again," she'd told me sadly, late last year. "Well—perhaps when the war's over, to some nice man who'd make a good father. But I don't think the war will *ever* be over, not really. Do you?"

And, studying Simon's tight, shuttered face that evening, I realized the war *would* go on forever. Even if it ended tomorrow, we'd still have to live with its consequences until the day we died. I reached out and touched his hand.

"Dance with me?" I asked, and he rose at once and led me into the middle of the swaying couples. Things were better there. With his arm round my waist and his other hand clasping mine, I could feel him begin to unwind. The band segued into a slower song, and I rested my cheek against his shoulder. He drew me in closer, gazed down into my eyes, and smiled. *How odd*, I thought. *I probably know him better than anyone, right at this moment, and yet I haven't the faintest idea what he's thinking.*

Two songs later, our main courses arrived and he led me back to our table. Under cover of the clink of silver on china, Julia leaned over and whispered, "Is he all right?" But then Daphne and the Lieutenant Colonel started up a noisy debate about where we ought to go dancing after dinner.

"Julia, you absolutely *must* come with us. I *know* you're not on duty tomorrow," Daphne shouted across the table. "And you too, Sophie and Simon!"

"No, I don't think so," I said, with a glance at Simon. "Not tonight."

Later, as I was saying goodbye to Julia, I had the impression she wanted to say something further. But then Simon walked over with my wrap, and she simply smiled and thanked us both for coming. Then we left.

The night, when we stepped out into it, was cool and quiet after the bustle of the restaurant. I tilted my head back, and a roll of black velvet, sprinkled with diamonds, unfurled before my eyes. It went on forever. It was almost like being back at Montmaray. It was dizzying. Simon grabbed my hand to stop me falling backwards, and he kept hold of it after he'd helped me into the taxi, and he was still holding it as I searched for my key outside the flat, even though it would have been more sensible to use both hands. But I didn't want him to let go. And *he* didn't want to let go, either.

I think, now, that I knew what was about to happen. It was as inevitable as the sun setting at the end of a long, hot day.

Anyway, we got inside. He closed the door (one-handedly)

and we walked straight through the kitchen and the sitting room, down the narrow hallway into my tiny bedroom, and I turned on the light, and then he took me in his arms and kissed me. I'd been kissed before, of course, by Peter, that Polish pilot. That had been lovely. But it bore about as much resemblance to Simon's kiss as a flickering candle does to the blazing sun. I felt as though I'd burst into flame, using up all the oxygen in the room. I gasped for air and he did, too—it was *both* of us burning up.

Finally, he pulled away and said, "Stop. Sophie, we *can't*."

I took a deep breath and closed my eyes and said, "All right. Fine." It wasn't fine at all, I wanted it to go on and on. "Fine," I said. "Undo my buttons. Then go, if that's what you want."

He turned me round, and neither of us moved for a long, silent moment. Then his hands swept up my hair (which had all fallen down by that stage) and I felt his lips on the back of my neck, and I *melted*. I could barely stand up long enough for him to get the dress unfastened. He laid me down on the bed and I tugged him on top of me and . . .

And now I'm at a loss as to how to describe it. His hands, that's what I recall most vividly, his warm palms smoothing across my skin, his fingers lacing with mine when I stretched my arms over my head. But then there were his lips, and his tongue, and oh, just the *weight* of him. He kept breaking off and saying, "Is this all right?" and I'd say, "Yes!" or, occasionally, something like, "No, your shirt's scratching me. Take it off."

It did turn out to be a bit messier than I'd expected, but

on the whole, I was too caught up in breathtaking sensation to remember to feel shy or awkward. The other thing that struck me was how he was so much more knowledgeable about what I might like than *I* was. It wasn't that *everything* he did was blissful—some of it was merely nice. But at one point, he slid my fingers down my own body and stopped kissing me just long enough to say, "Here," and it was like flicking a switch, setting off a shiver that ended with a jolt of electricity flashing all the way up my spine. Why hadn't I already *known* that? (I didn't need to wonder how *he* knew it. Years of practice with girls other than me, of course.)

At last, we fell asleep, huddled together on my very narrow iron bed. Even then, he kept hold of me. When I woke a few hours later, his arm was curled round my waist, his face was pressed into my neck, and the rest of him was squashed against the wall. It couldn't have been at all comfortable, but when I twisted round to examine his face, he looked more peaceful than he had all day.

I considered that he must trust me a great deal, to allow me to see him at his most vulnerable. Then I started thinking deep thoughts about love and romance and intimacy and what we'd just done, and I pictured them all as interlocking circles, overlapping only in parts. But then I fell asleep again, and the next thing I knew, the blackout curtain had been pulled aside, sunlight was striping the blanket covering me, and Simon was burning toast in the kitchen.

We pretty much spent the rest of the day in bed, after

Simon delivered an entirely predictable "Oh, no, how could I have done this to you?" speech, and I told him to stop being such an idiot. I wasn't interested in being the subject of a new load of guilt on his part. (I hadn't been drunk. I was of age. I could have stopped it anytime I'd wanted. If anything, *I'd* taken advantage of *him*. And it wasn't as though we'd done anything that could have dire and irreversible consequences—technically, I was still a virgin.) It wasn't very difficult to convince him. I held out my arms and he hesitated for about half a second before crawling back into them. Not that I thought for a moment that this was due to my captivating beauty or alluring nature. It was simply that Simon was lonely and desperately unhappy and in need of comfort, and I was there, able to offer comfort.

Still, there was nothing noble or self-sacrificing about my own actions. I'd been feeling miserable, too, and it was wonderful to have his undivided and expert attention, especially after I'd been infatuated with him for all those years. I'd been curious, too. What was sex *like?* Now I realized it was both overwhelming *and* nowhere near as significant as people made out. I was the same person I'd been the day before. I hadn't fallen either into or out of love with Simon. I wasn't sure love had much to do with it at all. However, I was certainly feeling very *fond* of him as I lay there, stroking his chest and marveling at how different the bodies of men and women were, quite apart from the obvious bits. Wherever I had soft curves, he was all hard lines and planes. It seemed odd that some people—Simon, for instance—could be attracted to *both* sorts of bodies. Then the thought occurred that he was here with me because I was the closest he could find to *Toby*. I didn't like that thought at all, so I shoved it away and concentrated on other things. How pretty the pink glow of sunset looked when filtered through my dusty window, for one thing. How hungry I was, for another.

"I never know what you're thinking," Simon sighed. "Especially when you smile like that," he added.

"Actually, I was wondering whether there's anything interesting in the kitchen to cook for dinner," I said, quite truthfully. "Or we could go to that British Restaurant down the road. The food's not too bad and it's really cheap and we wouldn't need our ration books for it. What do you think?"

"I think," he said, propping himself up on one elbow, "that we should get married."

I started to laugh, then saw his face.

"Why not?" he said, hurt suffusing his voice. "People *do* get married, when they care about one another. Don't you think I'd look after you? You once said I was hardworking and clever. You thought I'd make a good husband *then*."

I couldn't believe he'd remembered that conversation. Or that we were having *this* conversation. Usually, conversations with Simon made some sort of *sense*.

"Is it because your family wouldn't approve?" he went on, pulling away from me.

"You *are* my family," I reminded him. "Besides, it's not even legal, is it?"

"Of course it is. Royalty are always marrying their cousins. Look at Queen Victoria and Prince Albert. Anyway, we aren't officially cousins." Then he grabbed my hand. "Oh, Sophie! Don't think about what everyone will say! Don't worry about any of that. We'll go away, *far* away. Scotland or, or . . . Ireland! Yes, Ireland's neutral! There's no war there."

"Is this about you leaving the air force? Because you can't just *desert*! Simon, this is ridiculous."

I sat up and retrieved my dressing gown from the floor. When I turned round, he was glowering at the wall behind me.

"You haven't even mentioned the word *love*," I said gently. "You just want to escape. So do I, sometimes. But this is real life."

"Just say *yes* or *no*," he said tightly.

I leaned over and kissed the top of his tousled dark hair. "No," I said. "But thank you for asking." He averted his face from mine, so I sighed and walked off to the bathroom. When I came back, he was in Veronica's room, getting dressed.

"You don't have to go," I said, but he only frowned and concentrated on knotting his tie. "Well—can you at least promise me that you're going back to your job?"

He buttoned his tunic and glanced around for his cap, his lips pressed together.

"Oh, *honestly*!" I said. He was probably already regretting his impulsive proposal. He'd probably only done it because he'd thought he *should*. He always did have such old-fashioned, hypocritical ideas about women. I stomped off to get dressed myself, and a few minutes later, he appeared in my doorway.

"Sorry," he said.

Asking what he was apologizing *for* might have led to another argument, so I simply said, "I'm sorry, too." He came over and kissed me, very quickly. "Are you *really* going?" I asked.

"Yes," he said. "I'm supposed to be on the early shift tomorrow."

I didn't like the uncertain sound of that verb phrase, but he refused to discuss it.

"I'm fine," he said, turning his cap around in his hands. "I'll be fine. I have to go now."

He didn't even want me to walk him up to the taxi rank. I bit back an entreaty for him to write to me, because I was starting to feel I'd forfeited my role as his confidante. He did look better than he had when he'd arrived—there was *that*, at least.

After he'd gone, and I was certain he wasn't going to return, I threw myself across my bed and pretended I was Anna Karenina, a fallen woman abandoned by her cruel lover. I needed an excuse to cry. My emotions had been so tossed about over the past two days that I felt some ardent sobbing would help, and, not surprisingly, it did.

I think men would have far fewer problems if they learned how to cry properly.

11th July 1942

Henry has arrived for a visit. She's also decided that she wants to leave school and join the Wrens. She announced this about two minutes after we collected her from the railway station this morning.

"But I thought you *liked* this school," I said. "You've made all those friends, and you're captain of the hockey team, and you even had a decent report at the end of term."

"For once," added Veronica.

"Yes, and that means I've learned all I *can* there," Henry said. "Now I should be doing my bit for the war effort. I want to join the women's navy."

"Don't be ridiculous," said Veronica. "You're fifteen years old."

"Sixteen, in a couple of weeks!"

"They don't let sixteen-year-olds join up."

"They do! Jimmy wrote and told me about his friend's

cousin, who lives in Plymouth. She joined the Boat's Crew Wrens, and *she* was underage! She just had to get her parents' permission!"

"Well, then!" said Veronica. "You know what Aunt Charlotte thinks of girls joining the services."

"That's how she *used* to think. She's different now. She'd agree if you two talked her into it."

Then Henry twisted round in the backseat of the taxi and directed her most winning smile at me.

"No," I said.

"All right," she said mildly. But we knew perfectly well that she wasn't going to let it rest there. When we got home, she "unpacked" (this involved upending her duffel bag over the sofa, scattering socks, fishing magazines, and gnawed pencil stubs across our sitting room floor), then snatched a piece of paper out of the clutter and followed me into the kitchen.

"Look," she said, thrusting a pamphlet under my nose. "They want girls who can sail, row, and swim, and I can do all of those. And Wrens only need to be five foot three, and I'm five foot *seven and a half*! Plus, I already know Morse code."

"Where did you get this?" I asked, taking the pamphlet from her.

"There was a recruiting van parked outside the tea shop where all us girls go on Saturday afternoons," Henry said. "Did you know that women can be *officers*?"

"Have you actually looked at this WRNS motto? It says, 'Never at sea.'"

"Some Wrens *do* go to sea! Like Jimmy's friend's cousin—she takes a motor launch out to the big ships to deliver supplies."

"It's very difficult to get into the Wrens, you know," said Veronica, pulling cutlery out of the drawer. "You don't even have your School Certificate yet. Anyway, I think you're temperamentally unsuited for any of the services."

"What do you mean?" Henry said indignantly.

"Well, you'd have to follow orders, for one thing."

"I can follow orders!"

"All right. I order you to clean up your mess in the sitting room."

Henry rolled her eyes. "Yes, fine, I'll do that later. Anyway, Wrens don't do *housework*. They do important, useful stuff like coding and mechanical repairs. I could do that!"

"Besides," Veronica went on, "they prefer girls who have relatives in the Royal Navy or the Merchant Navy, which you don't have. Even if you did, you'd still need references from someone important."

"Really?" said Henry.

Then she looked thoughtful, which is always an ominous sign.

Still, it *is* nice having her around. She's so irrepressibly cheerful that it's difficult to remain glum in her presence, and our clothes-shopping expedition this afternoon (no doubt, part of her Soften Up Sophie campaign) was a pleasant distraction from my worries, if only for a few hours. My anxiety over Toby is like a bad toothache that nags constantly, except for brief moments when I forget and bite down too hard, and it flares into agony. But there's nothing I can do about that pain, except endure it.

My concern for Simon is different. It's not as intense, and yet I feel more responsible for it, more *guilty*. I began wanting to check that he was all right almost as soon as he left the flat, but I didn't feel I could contact him. Would a letter make him feel worse? How would *I* feel if he didn't respond? So I was very relieved, a few days after Veronica returned from Spain, to find an envelope in our letter box addressed to her, in his handwriting. It was probably just some correspondence regarding Mr. Grenville, the family solicitor, who's arranging some London property purchases on Aunt Charlotte's behalf. But it was a good sign that Simon was thinking about those sorts of practical, sensible things, surely? I tried not to look too eager as Veronica opened his letter—I didn't want to prompt any awkward questions. All I'd told her was that Simon had visited while she was away.

"Oh, he's been sent off to do some new training," she said, scanning the letter. "Hmm. It doesn't sound as though he'll be going back to his old job after he's finished his course, either."

"Right," I said, as though I knew all about this. "Well, he wasn't very happy where he was."

"But I don't know why he expects *I'll* have time to meet with Mr. Grenville this week," Veronica went on, frowning. "Absolutely typical of Simon. He always believes that whatever *he's* doing has to be more important than any job of mine! When I'm so *busy* with all of this—"

But I didn't hear the rest, because I was thinking of how I'd felt after Simon left. Sometimes it seemed as though his visit had been a particularly vivid dream. Surely it hadn't actually *happened*? I could have dismissed it as a product of my fevered imagination, except for the fading finger-shaped bruises on my hip, where he'd grabbed me when I'd started to fall out of bed. And the scent of his hair cream, which lingered on my pillow for days. And the raw, tingling feeling of my skin whenever I ran my hands down myself, wondering if I could re-create the sensations he'd drawn out of my body . . .

So, perhaps I'd been wrong to regard the experience as insignificant, to assume I'd be unchanged by it. I wish there was someone I could *talk to* about it. Certainly not Veronica, not when it involves Simon. Anyway, I'm not sure someone who thinks pleasure is a waste of time and effort would understand what I was going on about. Perhaps Julia, if I didn't mention any names . . . but no, she'd know exactly whom I meant. It would be too awkward, too embarrassing. And I couldn't discuss it with Anne—she'd be shocked that I'd done anything at *all* with a boy without getting engaged to him first . . .

Anyway, I'm fine, really. If Simon is all right—if he's busy with some fascinating new training course, if he's managed to escape the job that had such awful memories attached to it— well, then, I'm all right, too.

Such *horrible* news. The Stanley-Ross family have just learned that Charlie was part of that disastrous Allied raid on Dieppe last month. He was captured by the Nazis almost as soon as he landed and it seems he's been sent to Germany, to some camp. That's all the family knows—that he's alive, that he's a prisoner of war. They're supposed to be grateful for that. More than a thousand Canadian and British soldiers were slaughtered in a couple of hours during that raid, with twice as many captured, and for what? For *nothing*. The rest of the Allied troops were forced to withdraw without achieving any of their objectives. They didn't destroy any of the German coastal defenses. France is still firmly under Nazi rule. If the raid was meant to divert German troops from the eastern front, to bring some relief to the poor besieged Russians, then it was an utter failure. How are we meant to win this war when the Allied armies are so *useless*?

I wrote to Rupert, via Julia, but haven't yet heard back. I

don't know where he is or what he's doing. He, at least, can't be sent into combat. Can he? No, *surely* not.

Henry returned to school last week, but continues to bombard us with letters, pleading to be allowed to join the Wrens.

Veronica is so busy with her work that I've scarcely spoken with her for days.

Simon continues to pretend that I don't exist.

There is no news whatsoever about Toby.

Also, I hate my job.

I hate my *life*.

Today, for the first time in months, I woke up feeling happy. Or no—not *happy*, exactly, but I didn't feel crushed flat by the leaden weight of my despondency. It was possible to sit up, to fling out an arm and throw back the heavy curtains and let in some sunlight. And there actually *was* sunlight—admittedly, rather weak and gray sunlight, but then, this *is* London. One can't expect miracles (and if any miracles *were* being offered round, I certainly wouldn't waste mine on brightening the weather).

I think it was the church bells that lifted my spirits. I hadn't realized how much I'd missed the sound of them. They'd been banned, of course, years ago—permitted to be rung only in an emergency, as a warning, in the event of the Germans invading. But an invasion seems far less likely now, after our definitive victory in North Africa. All the German and Italian troops there have surrendered, so Mr. Churchill ordered the bells of Britain to ring out in celebration yesterday morning. Veronica and I sat on our front step to listen, the chimes floating towards us on the breeze with the last of the autumn leaves. It made me think of Sunday mornings at Milford, the congregation spilling out of the church doors, set free by the peal of the bells. It made me picture beaming brides with their veils thrown back, and infants in long christening gowns being held up to an admiring crowd.

It was the sound of hope, and not even an extended lecture on punctuation from Mr. Bowker could dampen its resonance this morning. Then Rupert, back in London for a few days, telephoned to ask if I'd meet him for luncheon, and luckily, Miss Halliday wasn't in the office to scold me for taking personal calls at work or order me to finish all my typing before I took my break.

I skipped downstairs and out the front doors to find Rupert standing at the edge of the square, apparently having a conversation with a pair of starlings. I felt my face shift in an unaccustomed way then—into a *smile*. Not the sort of dogged, forcing-up-the-corners-of-one's-mouth that I'd been doing for so long, but a real, spontaneous smile that spread all the way to my eyes. I ran up to Rupert, not caring if the birds got frightened away, and was absurdly pleased to see that he, too, broke into a wide grin when he caught sight of me.

"I brought sandwiches," he said, holding up his satchel, "as it's such a nice day. We could go to the park."

I knew Anne and her giggly friend from the typing pool would be there, and the prospect of having to introduce Rupert to them and make polite, meaningless conversation (and then endure endless hours of teasing about him in future lunch breaks) made me say, "I know somewhere quieter. Come on."

I led him up the road and round the corner and along a side street to a block where half the houses were derelict, the roofs blown off and the sky showing pale blue through the empty windows. One of the houses had collapsed, and the remaining residents had raked the rubble into piles and planted vegetables in the cleared spaces. Summer's abundance had now come to an end, but there was a square of feathery carrot tops, three rows of cabbage, and a sturdy line of leeks that marched off towards what had once been a formal garden at the back of the house. The battered remains of a fountain were still there, along with a fragment of mosaic paving that I liked to pretend was Roman and an ancient, twisted fig tree. Rupert was suitably impressed.

"Why, this is *wonderful*," he said, gazing around.

"Thank you," I said, as though I were responsible for it. I pointed at one corner. "A few months ago, there were sunflowers over there—half a dozen of them, with faces like dinner plates. The birds went crazy over them. I don't suppose there was ever enough sunlight before, but everything's so opened up now."

We sat down on a broken slab of marble chimneypiece and unwrapped our sandwiches.

"It's like St. Paul's Cathedral," said Rupert. "It looks so much more impressive now, doesn't it, with all those surrounding buildings having been razed to the ground? Not that I want to give the Nazis credit for anything—least of all for creating something beautiful in the world."

I glanced over. "Have you heard anything from Charlie yet?"

"No, but the Red Cross says they've passed on our letters to him. They're very good, the Red Cross in Switzerland. They send packages to all the prisoner-of-war camps. Food, medicine, blankets, all sorts of things—even footballs."

"He must hate it so much, though. Being locked up."

"Yes," sighed Rupert. "Yes, I imagine he does. He's with the rest of his unit, though. He's not alone. And he's probably already started digging an escape tunnel with a teaspoon."

"At least you know where he is," I said. "Rupert, do you think—"

Then my courage failed. I took a big bite of my sandwich so that I had an excuse for not continuing. But I'd forgotten that Rupert's years of communing with animals had given him a preternatural ability to read unspoken thoughts.

"The thing about Toby," Rupert said, staring off into the garden, or perhaps into the past, "was that he always had the most extraordinary luck. Whenever he broke the rules at school—which was pretty much all the time—he'd manage to get away with it. Although perhaps it wasn't luck, but cleverness, or charm, or just sheer audacity. Once, for instance—"

And Rupert began to laugh.

"What?" I said.

"Well," he said, "there was this really awful bully, a couple of years ahead of us, and Toby came up with a mad scheme to get revenge. I *begged* him not to go ahead with it, I knew there wasn't the slightest chance it would work—except it did. And no one ever found out it was Toby! I couldn't believe it."

"But he got expelled."

"That was much later. And he made sure he was caught then. He *wanted* to be expelled."

"Rupert," I said, grasping the nettle, "do you think he's alive?"

Rupert's smile faded. "Oh, Sophie," he said. "It's been so long—"

"Twenty-six weeks and four days."

"I know." He cleared his throat. "And the rational part of me knows that he's probably dead—that they didn't find his body because it was burnt up with the plane. If he'd bailed out, he must have been captured by now, surely, and we'd have been told about it. And yet . . . I can't help thinking that if *anyone* could manage to escape, it would be Toby. If he'd got out of that plane, even if he'd been wounded, he'd be able to talk people into hiding him, giving him food. Even though they'd be putting their lives at risk by helping him. But then I think . . . Well, maybe I only think that because I so badly *want* him to come back. It's as though, if I *hope* enough, if I believe in him, it'll be all right—"

"Oh, Rupert!" I cried. "That's *exactly* how I feel!"

"There's always a chance, isn't there?" he said, trying to smile at me, and failing, and looking away.

Sorrow has made me so self-centered and stupid. I hadn't understood till that moment just how much Rupert grieved for Toby, too.

"Veronica thinks there's a chance," I told Rupert, taking his hand, "and she's the most rational person I know."

"Yes," he said.

And we sat there for ages, holding hands, not saying anything, until we were startled by a rustling noise behind us. I whirled about, and there, stalking towards us through the undergrowth, was a ravening tiger.

"Poor little thing," said Rupert. He peeled apart his sandwich, pulled out the slice of Spam, and tossed it over. The tabby froze, then narrowed its eyes. It stretched out its thin neck, sniffed at the offering, shot us another wary look, then crouched over the meat and devoured it in a couple of gulps. I could count every one of the ragged little creature's ribs. I was sorry I'd finished my own sandwich (but not *completely* sorry, as I'd been quite hungry myself). Rupert gave the cat his crusts, then searched through his satchel.

"Nothing else for you, I'm afraid," he told the cat. "Unless you like apples?"

The cat considered this, then retreated a few steps to a faded patch of sunlight.

"More for us, then," Rupert said to me. I poured two mugs of tea from his thermos, and he took out a penknife and sliced the apple into quarters. The cat followed all of this with an unnerving yellow stare.

"One can understand why cats used to be regarded as the devil in disguise," I remarked.

"Oh, no, they're on the other side, really," said Rupert. "Think of Christopher Smart's cat, Jeoffry: 'For he is the servant of the Living God, duly and daily serving him.'"

"What?"

"'For he keeps the Lord's watch in the night against the adversary.

For he counteracts the powers of darkness by his electrical skin and glaring eyes.

For he counteracts the Devil, who is death, by brisking about the life.'"

I thought that was a very comforting idea. Sometimes I feel so guilty about enjoying the smallest pleasures in my life, knowing that Toby—wherever he is—can't share them. But living life to the fullest *is* a way of counteracting death.

"Although," I couldn't help pointing out to Rupert, "cats are quite often the *bringers* of death, if one happens to be a mouse."

"Ah, but even then, cats are kindly:

'For when he takes his prey he plays with it to give it a chance.

For one mouse in seven escapes by his dallying.'"

I smiled, then caught a glimpse of Rupert's watch.

"Oh, no!" he said, jumping up at once. "Will you get into trouble for being late?" He started snatching up sandwich wrappers and bits of apple core.

"Probably," I said, following his movements at a more leisurely pace. A lecture from Miss Halliday for being ten minutes late would be no worse than one for being two minutes late, so I wasn't terribly concerned. "I mean, it's not as though there's anything important to be late *for*," I told Rupert. "Do you know what we're working on at the moment? The Christmas Potato Fair. It's going to be held in Oxford Street, in the bombed-out John Lewis site, and I'm working on the wording of the Potato Pledge. Each person who visits the fair is going to be asked to promise to eat homegrown potatoes instead of bread made from imported wheat."

"I'd sign," said Rupert. "I like potatoes."

"You wouldn't if you worked in my department," I said. "You'd detest the sight of them by now." Then, as we walked back up the road, I asked, "What *is* it, anyway, that you do?"

But he just said something vague about working in "communications."

"You won't be sent abroad, will you?" I said. "I mean, when the Second Front starts in earnest and we do invade France?"

"Oh, no," he said. "No, I shouldn't think so."

We'd reached the Ministry of Food by then and we said goodbye in our usual awkward manner. If he were family (or a friend who was a girl), I'd hug him, or kiss his cheek, but he's not, so I can't. Yet shaking hands seems ridiculously formal after our conversations, which are nearly always heartfelt ones these days. So we just sort of waved at each other and then I ran inside.

It was only after I reached my desk that I thought about what he'd said. He *shouldn't think* he'd be sent abroad! What does that mean? I'd imagined there'd be no chance at *all* he'd be in danger. There—something *new* to worry about! I should have realized my cheerful mood couldn't last.

12th December 1942

I've been feeling absolutely *furious* at Simon, but had to suppress it because I didn't want Veronica asking too many questions. I was so angry, I might just have *told* her everything, which would have been a disaster—I could just imagine her storming off to berate him for taking advantage of me. Which made me even angrier—after all, I'm not a *child*. I don't need her to protect me, least of all from my own decisions! Fortunately, I realized how idiotic I was being—condemning Veronica for something she hadn't even done—and I took myself off to bed before I could do or say anything too stupid.

But now she has gone off to her meeting at Whitehall and I can scribble down all my rage, although I must admit it has subsided a bit. After all, it wasn't *totally* unexpected news. I was aware Simon wanted to leave his job, and I ought to be glad he's had the opportunity to get away. I'd just thought he'd tell me first—and I'd never dreamed he'd go so *far* away.

"You saw him *where?*" I asked, staring at Veronica as she unpacked her suitcase.

"The aerodrome at Gibraltar," she said. "I couldn't believe it, either. You know how it is when one sees a familiar person in an unfamiliar place—and anyway, men all look the same in uniform. But as I got nearer, I saw it really *was* him. I called out, 'Simon! What are you doing here?' And he looked as startled as I felt, but the Air Commodore next to him said, 'Ah, a friend of yours, Chester? Do introduce us.' So he did, and then I had to run off to my plane, but before I did, I told him, 'Write to Sophie!'"

"And he didn't say where he was going?"

"Well, he couldn't, could he? Not in front of his commanding officer. I expect he's on his way to Cairo, or somewhere else in the Middle East. That's where most of them were headed."

The Middle East! Where all the fighting is going on! I must have looked absolutely horrified, because Veronica stopped unpacking long enough to pat me on the shoulder.

"Don't worry, it's not as though he's flying fighters," she said. "It's probably just some administrative job."

Then, this morning, she added kindly, "You know, I doubt Simon got much notice of his new posting. In the services, they move people about constantly, without telling them a thing. He probably didn't have *time* to tell you."

Right. More likely, he's a complete and utter *coward*. I bet he *requested* some dangerous overseas posting. What better way to punish himself over Toby, while avoiding any embarrassing future meetings with me? Why I *ever* felt—

Oh, someone's knocking at the door.

Much later. It was Daniel, who'd received the message that Veronica was back from Spain, but not the one about her having to go in to work today.

"Sorry," I said, even though it wasn't my fault. Actually, I wasn't sure if Veronica *had* told him about her meeting—she couldn't have expected he'd come straight round. Usually it takes ages for him to arrange a day off.

"I don't suppose she mentioned when she'd be back?" he asked, rather plaintively.

"Well, when she goes in on Saturdays for meetings, she generally doesn't get home till quite late." All the lines in his face sloped downwards at this, so I said, "Look, why don't you come shopping with me? We'll leave a note about where we've gone, just in case she comes home early, and then I'll make you luncheon. I've got a new Ministry of Food recipe to try out—it's mock goose and there's no meat in it at all. For pudding, we can have the rest of last night's mock-apricot flan. With mock cream!"

He assumed an expression of mock horror, but obediently picked up my basket and followed me off to the shops. As I'd hoped, he cheered up a bit when we got there, especially after a woman wearing a fur stole and silk turban joined the line behind us. Daniel thinks wartime queues are fascinating opportunities for sociological observation, and he adores seeing rich and poor joined by a common goal (in this case, trying to buy under-the-counter chicken). Not that there are any *really* poor people around here. Anyway, it's hardly a representative sample of the British population. I rarely see any *men* at the shops—even though nearly all women now have to do some form of war work, unless they're looking after small children or a male relative (female relatives don't count, in the government's opinion). Today the only man in evidence, other than Daniel, was an elderly gentleman with his head swaddled in woolen scarves. His daughter-in-law told us he had an earache, but she couldn't leave him home alone because he tended to wander off and get lost. Then she and Daniel had a long discussion about the inadequacy of the old-age pension.

"Yes, and what about pensions for people who've been injured in the raids?" said another woman, further ahead of us. "Twenty shillings a week! How far does that go, with food prices as high as they are?"

"Well, my sister lost her *leg* in a bombing raid," said another indignantly, "and they told her that housewives weren't entitled to a pension, only people who'd been working! They said if she'd had a husband, then *he* could have an allowance to pay a maid to replace her. But she's a spinster, isn't she, looking after our mother. So she's not entitled to anything at all! Hasn't *she* been wounded by the enemy, just as badly as any soldier?"

"If the recommendations of this new Beveridge Report are implemented, things will be much better for *everyone*," Daniel said firmly. "The unemployed, the elderly, the disabled—they'll *all* receive enough to reach a decent standard of living. There'll be a special allowance for bringing up children, too, and everybody will be entitled to free medical treatment."

"Yes, well, it all *sounds* wonderful," sighed the daughter-in-law. "But it won't really happen, will it? Churchill says we can't afford it."

"If the government can spend millions of pounds on bombers and warships," came the unexpected contribution of the fur-draped lady, "then it can surely afford to help the needy."

Then someone else said that the priority ought to be helping ordinary, decent people to rebuild their bombed-out houses, not handing out money to people who didn't want to work, and the woman with the crippled sister snapped that if there wasn't going to be a kinder, more compassionate world after the war, then what on earth were we fighting *for*?

I do love Daniel, but honestly, something like this happens every time I go out in public with him. It's so embarrassing. At one stage, it looked as though the fur-draped lady and the rebuilding-houses lady were about to come to blows, but luckily, the queue had moved closer to the shop window by then, so I pointed at it and said, "Look! An onion!" and everyone was distracted.

After we finally arrived back at the flat with our shopping, Daniel sat down at the table and polished all our silver while I made "mock goose." We both wondered how potato, apple, and sage, cooked in vegetable stock and sprinkled with grated cheese, could possibly taste anything like goose—and what a surprise, it doesn't. Daniel diligently praised every aspect of the meal, but grew quieter and more downcast as it progressed and Veronica failed to appear.

I tried to divert him by asking whether he thought one had to be religious (or mad) to appreciate Christopher Smart's poetry. Rupert had sent me a copy of *Rejoice in the Lamb: A Song from Bedlam*, but apart from the bits about Jeoffry the cat, I'd found it quite incomprehensible—even allowing for Keats's idea of negative capability and being content with "half knowledge" of poetry. Daniel said that Christopher Smart had been confined to a madhouse due to his habit of praying loudly in public, and that a sincere and personal devotion to a divine being could well seem insane to others—perhaps even to the man himself.

Then, as if this followed on quite logically, he asked if I thought Veronica was in love with "that Michael person."

"Who?" I said. "You mean Michael from the Embassy in Madrid? Oh, *Daniel*! He's her colleague, that's all."

"But she's always talking about him," said Daniel miserably.

"Because she *works* with him! He's the one helping to get Allied servicemen out of France."

This task has become even more urgent in the last month, because the Nazis have taken over the southern bit of France that they'd previously allowed the Vichy government to administer.

"Why not ask *her* about all this?" I said. "She'd tell you the truth."

"Yes, that's what I'm afraid of," he said.

I could only assume that all this foolishness was the result of his stressful work, combined with his long separations from Veronica. Daniel's the most important person in the world to Veronica, outside our family—anyone can see that.

"Oh, I *know*," he said, catching my exasperated look but misinterpreting it. "I know I'm being ridiculous. I haven't any right to ask for reassurances from her! She's entitled to fall in love with whomever she wants. It's not as though we're . . ."

"Engaged?"

"Well, I'd *ask* her to marry me, if I thought there was the slightest possibility she'd say yes."

"I thought you didn't believe in marriage."

"I don't, really. It all seems so bureaucratic and repressive. Personal relationships oughtn't to have anything to do with the government. But then, I've always thought of myself as quite uninterested in owning things—or people—and look at the way I'm behaving now! Perhaps marriage is actually a very sensible way of managing jealousy and possessiveness. Perhaps people *aren't* very good at sharing, after all."

"That doesn't bode well for the Beveridge plan," I said.

"No," he said gloomily. "Oh, I don't know—about marriage, I mean. It's still a very inequitable institution for women. I wouldn't blame Veronica in the least for not wanting to consider it. All that business of having to give up one's job, even change one's *name*—"

I smiled. It might as well have been Veronica talking.

"Perhaps you could offer to become a FitzOsborne instead?" I suggested. "Although then you'd have to stop being a Bloom."

"I wouldn't care. It isn't even our real family name. My grandparents changed it from Rosenblum when they arrived in England. They knew that having a name that was obviously Jewish would be a terrible disadvantage here."

"How awful!" I said. "I mean, that they felt they had to do that. But at least attitudes are better now."

"Are they?"

"Well, since the war started," I said. "I mean, you never see any of those disgusting slogans painted on walls now. And the British Union of Fascists is banned."

"What does that matter, when so many in the government are blatantly anti-Semitic? When the only Jewish member of the War Cabinet is forced to resign because the Prime Minister says there might be 'prejudice against him'?"

"Who?"

"Leslie Hore-Belisha."

"Oh, but that was when *Chamberlain* was Prime Minister. Chamberlain was an idiot. Everyone knows that."

"Chamberlain was acting on the advice of the King and the military. And Churchill's not much better. Most of the upper classes are the same. Look at your aunt. Imagine what she'd say if Veronica announced she was going to marry a Jew."

"I don't think Aunt Charlotte would care much, right now," I said. "She's too upset about Toby. Besides, you aren't *actually* very Jewish, are you?" The last time I'd been to a National Gallery concert with Daniel, he'd bought us both Spam sandwiches for luncheon. He didn't even believe in God.

"Well, perhaps I ought to be far *more* Jewish," he said, with uncharacteristic ferocity. "Given what's happening to all the Jews in Europe—"

He broke off and looked away.

"What do you mean?" I said. "What's happening to the Jews?"

He just shook his head. I remembered what Veronica had said, about Daniel interrogating German officers. What *could* he have heard? I know that the Nazis are often arresting Jews, and putting them in camps, but once the war's over, they'll all be let out, won't they?

"Churchill is determined to defeat Hitler," I reassured Daniel, "and so are the Americans. The Allies just need a bit more time to plan a Second Front so that it all works properly. We *will* win the war, you know."

"Yes," he said, after a moment. "I'm sure you're right. Sorry. I'm just in a horrible mood, that's all. No wonder Veronica's avoiding me."

"She's *not* avoiding you," I said, determined he should understand that, at least. "She'll be home soon, and then you can—"

"No, I really ought to be going," he said, without looking at his watch. "I don't want to miss my train."

He thanked me for luncheon and for listening to his "wretched ramblings," then trudged off.

Well, that certainly puts my own unhappiness into perspective, doesn't it?

I'd hoped Christmas might cheer us all up a bit, but when we arrived at Milford, everything was so topsy-turvy that I felt more unsettled than ever. Aunt Charlotte was rushing about making cups of tea and fetching aspirins for Barnes, who'd slipped over on the icy front path that morning and sprained her ankle. Barnes was ensconced in one of the two armchairs pulled up to the sitting room fire, her leg propped on a footstool. The other armchair was occupied by Carlos, his snores providing a not-very-harmonious accompaniment to the concert playing on the wireless. Most of the sofa cushions had been arranged on the floor in a series of steps to make it easier for him to climb up there.

"Carlos mustn't sleep on the ground," Henry explained. "The drafts are bad for his arthritis."

Henry herself is being conspicuously helpful, hauling in armfuls of firewood, driving the pony cart to the village for groceries, tramping through the snow to feed the hens, even making a big pot of vegetable soup for luncheon today. Of course, all of this is to demonstrate how grown-up and responsible she is, so that she'll be allowed to leave school. Aunt Charlotte is being annoyingly indecisive about this issue, while Veronica and I maintain that sixteen-and-a-half is still far too young to join up. The two of us discussed it as we gave the attic bedrooms an unseasonal, but much-needed, spring clean.

"Imagine being given the opportunity to go to school," said Veronica, "then wanting to *leave*."

"Not everyone's an intellectual like you," I said, "and I bet if you'd gone to Henry's school, you'd have been bored stiff."

"It's true the academic standards there don't seem *terribly* high," Veronica admitted, "and I expect they'll fall even lower now that half the teaching staff's been called up."

"I don't actually mind if Henry leaves at the end of this school year," I said. "I just don't want her joining the services. It's been bad enough worrying about Toby and Simon—I don't want *her* in any danger. I wish she'd simply stay here at Milford and work on the farm, but she's so desperate to have her revenge on the Nazis."

"Yes, she must be the most bloodthirsty vegetarian in England," Veronica agreed. "You know, these floorboards really need a good scrub."

"Better not, they'll freeze over in this weather before they have a chance to dry. Besides, there's only about half a bar of soap left in the laundry."

"We should have brought our soap coupons," she said.

"I used them all up last week," I said. I suddenly felt flat and tired. It didn't feel like Christmas at all. No Christmas tree. No Christmas goose, no oranges, no plum pudding. No wrapping paper for the presents. Worst of all, no Toby or Simon. This was the fourth Christmas of the war. How many *more* of them would there be? What if this ended up being another Hundred Years War? (Which, come to think of it, had gone on even *longer* than a hundred years.) I sank down onto one of the beds, feeling very depressed.

"Should we go downstairs now and clean Aunt Charlotte's room?" Veronica was wondering aloud.

"Not just yet," I said. "She went in there after she accidentally called Henry 'Tobias.' I think she wants to be alone for a bit."

"Oh," said Veronica, frowning. "Right."

"Thank heavens for Barnes," I said. "I really don't know how Aunt Charlotte would manage without her support." I was glad I'd found Barnes a really nice present. There'd been nothing much in the department stores, so I was giving everyone secondhand books, but I'd come across a set of leather-bound Agatha Christies in near-perfect condition in a shop in Charing Cross Road. Barnes loves detective novels, but hardly ever gets to the library in Salisbury these days. "How old do you think she is?" I asked Veronica.

"Barnes? Not sure. She's the sort of person who looks forty for most of her life, isn't she? She must be older than Aunt Charlotte, though."

"Fifty-five or so, then. It's a wonder she never married."

"She and Aunt Charlotte are turning into the Ladies of Llangollen," Veronica said.

Then Henry yelled that Daniel was on the telephone, and Veronica dropped her broom and rushed downstairs. She'd been terribly concerned when I'd explained about Daniel's visit (I hadn't mentioned the marriage bit, just that he'd seemed very downhearted and needed to talk with her). She'd arranged to meet him the following day, and then they'd had a long, serious conversation, partly about themselves, but mostly about his work.

And this is where it all gets very vague, because his job is so secret. However, from what I *gather*, he'd been working at a place where very high-ranking German officers were being kept prisoner. It wasn't that they were being tortured. In fact, it seems the very opposite—that they were treated almost as guests at a grand country house, presumably to encourage them to relax and talk amongst themselves. I wonder if it was set up so that fluent German speakers like Daniel could pretend to be officers, too, and mingle with the prisoners? Or perhaps he had to act as their servant? Or just secretly record their conversations and translate them? Imagine poor Daniel having to listen to fanatical Nazis vilifying Jews and Communists for hours on end! But Veronica thinks it was even *worse* than that, that he heard the details of some horrifying new Nazi scheme.

"Of course, he couldn't say anything about his work to me," Veronica said. "This is all just conjecture on my part. But there *have* been rumors at the Foreign Office about a change in Nazi policy."

"Hitler's not going to try to invade Britain, is he?"

"No, no, it's to do with the Jews. They're being arrested at an even faster rate now—not just in Poland and Germany, but in France, the Netherlands, even Italy. *Something's* going on, but no one's sure exactly what."

"Perhaps they're being forced to work in Nazi factories, doing really dangerous jobs," I said, with a shudder. "Making ammunition. Or bombs."

"Perhaps," said Veronica, her grim tone suggesting something much worse. But what could be worse? Death, of course, but the Nazis couldn't be planning to kill all the Jewish people living in the occupied territories. There must be millions of them. Apart from being insanely evil, it wouldn't even be *possible*, surely?

But regardless of whatever vileness Hitler is planning, it seemed obvious to Veronica that Daniel was on the verge of becoming really ill from the stress, and that a change of job would be a very good idea. He agreed, but felt there wasn't much he could do about it. However, when Veronica and I approached the Colonel for advice, *he* turned out to be looking for more German speakers for some secret project of his, one that has suddenly become vital to the war effort. So, after a few interviews and tests, Daniel was transferred to a place in Buckinghamshire. It *is* a bit further away from London, but presumably does not involve having to interact with Nazis, and

Daniel sounds much happier already. Veronica reported after his telephone call that he'd found lodgings with some other people who work at the same place.

"He says his colleagues are really nice and the job is very interesting," she announced cheerfully. After Veronica had gone into the kitchen to help Henry with dinner, Aunt Charlotte turned to me and said, with a sort of glum resignation, "She's going to *marry* that man, isn't she?"

I thought it far more likely they'd end up living together, but that would be even less appealing to Aunt Charlotte than a registry wedding, so I just made noncommittal noises.

"Oh, well," she sighed, "at least his father has money." Then she went off to see if Barnes needed another hot-water bottle.

4th March 1943

It's Toby's birthday today. Veronica was red-eyed and silent at breakfast, and the postman brought careful, kind notes from Rupert, Daniel, and Julia. I telephoned Milford when I came home from work, but Aunt Charlotte was too upset to talk, although Barnes reported our aunt had been "bearing up remarkably well" until then.

Nearly everyone is acting as though Toby's dead. It's been more than nine months, and I think I've just about given up hope. There are times when I actually wish I knew for certain he was dead. Then I could mourn properly. As it is, we're like people flung up into the air after a bomb blast. At some undisclosed moment in the future, we'll come crashing down and smash into pieces, but for now, we flail about, suspended in a choking gray cloud.

If there was some indication of an end to the war—if all this suffering seemed to have a *purpose*—then it might be easier to bear. But the terrible slaughter in Russia and elsewhere continues, and London is more battered and dreary than ever. There is still the occasional air raid—not long ago, a school was hit in broad daylight, killing dozens of children and their teachers. At the start of the year, Mr. Churchill and Mr. Roosevelt announced they would only accept "unconditional surrender" from Germany—in other words, if the Germans *do* come to their senses and decide they want an end to the fighting, even if they get rid of Hitler, we won't negotiate with them. All they can do is throw themselves upon our mercy, which, of course, they'd be far too proud (or scared) to do. I suppose this means the war will drag on for years and years. I cannot even remember "normal life." It seems incredible that there was ever a time when children played in Kensington Gardens, when shops displayed pyramids of oranges and lemons, when streetlights blazed out at night. The past has vanished—and yet I find it impossible to imagine any kind of future. All that exists is this endless, bleak present.

29th April 1943

Poor Veronica nodded off into her dinner last night. She didn't get home till eleven o'clock, for the third time this week. It's one crisis after another at the Foreign Office. First, Spain announced it was going to send any escaping Allied prisoners of war that it caught straight back to the Nazis, and threatened to close its border with France. Then it ordered its officials in the border zone to track down anyone who might be helping people flee the Nazis.

"So much for Spain claiming to be neutral," said Veronica bitterly. "Obviously, Hitler's putting pressure on Franco, but it also gives the Spanish Fascists an excuse to harass some of their old adversaries. It's mostly Basques guiding people across the mountains from France, you see. They know the land and they're expert at evading the Guardia Civil patrols. But all the guides are having to lie low for the moment, and Michael's really worried about some Allied airmen stuck on the French side of the border."

The situation is so critical that the British Ambassador to

Spain has actually lodged an official protest. Sir Samuel Hoare is one of Chamberlain's old friends and an arch-appeaser, and Veronica's always regarded him as completely useless. She says Mr. Churchill sent him to Spain to get rid of him. However, Sir Samuel has, on this occasion, pointed out rather forcefully that Spain is in violation of the Hague Convention if it treats escaped prisoners of war in this manner, so the Spanish government has backed down a bit. Franco's afraid of losing British and American trade, but he also wants to keep Hitler happy, so matters are far from settled.

Apart from the Spanish crisis, there's also been the horrifying discovery of thousands of dead Polish officers, prisoners of war who'd been executed and dumped in mass graves in Katyn Forest. My first thought was of Peter, that Polish pilot I'd met a couple of years ago—I remembered he'd told me his brothers, both army officers, had vanished in 1939, during the invasion of his homeland. What if *they* are among the dead? Not that I know if Peter himself is still alive. Anyway, the discovery of the graves was announced by the Nazis, who are blaming the Soviets for the massacre. The Soviets deny it. They claim the Polish prisoners were working in the forest when they were captured and executed by the Nazis. However, it *seems* the men were killed in early 1940, when the area was still under Soviet control, so the Nazis may, for once, be telling the truth.

"The whole thing's so terrible," said Veronica. "I mean, apart from the horrible loss of life—and killing prisoners of war, which is illegal—the Nazis are using this to drive a wedge between the Allied nations. The Polish government-in-exile is absolutely furious, of course, and wants an independent investigation by the Red Cross, so the Soviet Union's broken off diplomatic relations with the Poles. And *now* it seems the British and the Americans are going to support the Soviets."

"Does Mr. Churchill think it was really the Nazis who killed all those men?" I asked.

"Oh, no, he understands it's far more likely the Soviets were responsible. But as the Soviets are doing most of the fighting against the Nazis, the Soviets' demands trump those of the Poles. This isn't about discovering the truth. It's about winning the war."

And then, in the midst of all this, I discovered that Henry has been pestering the Colonel! It's quite possible *he's* the one trying to calm down General Sikorski, the Polish Prime Minister, and set up new meetings with the Soviets. The last thing the poor Colonel needs right now is to have to deal with Henry's nonsense about joining the Wrens, but I received this note in the post today:

My *dear Sophie*,
Enclosed is a letter your sister sent to me. I trust your judgment entirely, so if you approve of her plans, let me know and I'll do what I can to assist.

Yours fondly,
[illegible but very familiar Colonel signature]

How did Henry even get his address? I suppose she must have sent the letter via Rupert, and he was too kindhearted to put her off. Of course, if *anyone* could wangle her a posting with the Wrens, it would be the Colonel . . . but I refuse to consider the matter until the school year is over. I'm certainly not going to bother Veronica with it now.

Still . . . the Colonel "trusts my judgment entirely"? That's a rather nice thing to say, isn't it?

10th July 1943

I was walking out of Harrods this afternoon, feeling mildly tri-
umphant about having procured a packet of sewing needles and
some elastic, when I heard someone calling, "Sophie! Sophie!"
The next thing I knew, a girl had flung her arms round me and
my face was full of honey-blond curls. She loosened her grasp,
I blinked . . . and it was *Kick*! Kick Kennedy, back in London!

"But when did you arrive?" I cried, after we'd each babbled
about how wonderful it was to see the other. "And what are you
doing here—oh, American Red Cross, yes, I can see that now,
but why didn't you *tell* us what you were planning?"

She grinned at me. "Well, I didn't know for sure where I'd
be stationed—I mean, I could have ended up *anywhere*, even
Iceland! But can you believe it, I'm right around the corner
from our old house. I've just started as program assistant at the
Hans Crescent Club and guess what, I'm a second lieutenant in
the US Army, too! They figured they ought to make all us Red
Cross girls into officers, just in case we get captured."

"You look so impressive," I said, admiring her smart blue-gray uniform. "What is it you do, exactly?"

"Oh, I keep our officers entertained," she said. "Play gin rummy and Ping-Pong, jitterbug with them, write letters to their mothers, organize their leave passes. Often it's just sitting and listening—sometimes those poor boys get so homesick, all they want is to talk to an American girl. But it's exhausting, I'll tell you that. I can't *wait* for my next day off. Lady Astor invited me to Cliveden last weekend, and I've had dinner with Lord Beaverbrook, and next weekend, I'm going down to Compton Place with Billy—"

"Oh, Billy Hartington?" I said, and she blushed.

"Well, I always knew he wasn't really *serious* about Sally Norton. She's a nice girl and they've known each other since they were kids, but . . . Anyway, when he broke off their engagement a few months ago, I thought, 'I can't sit around here in Washington, waiting till the war is over! This is crazy!' And I always *did* want to do something useful for the war effort—so here I am. He's stationed at Alton now, did you know? That's only an hour from London. And oh, Sophie, have you *seen* him in his uniform? He was telling me all about Dunkirk and boy, was he ever *brave*—"

And she went on about Billy's many wonderful qualities for some time. When she stopped for breath, I asked after her two elder brothers, who I knew had joined the US Navy. She said that Joe was flying a patrol plane near Puerto Rico, searching for German U-boats, and Jack was commanding a motor torpedo boat in the South Pacific, attacking Japanese destroyers. I told Kick about how we'd finally given in to Henry's pleadings and allowed her to join the Wrens and there still being no news of Toby, and she listened politely for about a minute before shifting the conversation back to Billy. If sorrow makes one self-centered, then so does being in love. I couldn't begrudge her that, though. I'm glad she and Billy are enjoying whatever time they have together before their disapproving parents—or the war—tear them apart.

Kick suddenly remembered that she was on duty and was supposed to have been back at the club a quarter of an hour ago, so she had to dash off, although she shouted something over her shoulder about Friday evening and the Four Hundred as she ran. I waved goodbye, then went to catch my bus, marveling at how *rich* Kick had looked, with her glossy, luxuriant hair and plump cheeks and immaculate stockings. Goodness knows how haggard and threadbare I must have seemed to her.

When I got home, Veronica had finished the week's grocery shopping and was weeding our overgrown vegetable patch. She was covered in dirt, but looked far more relaxed than she had for a long while. It's been another horrible month at the Foreign Office. The leader of the French Resistance was tortured to death by the Gestapo, who also arrested many others in the Resistance, so life has become even more difficult and dangerous for Allied servicemen trying to escape into Spain. In addition, some Spanish workers managed to smuggle a bomb into Gibraltar last month and the resulting explosion set fire to the docks, so now the British are frantically trying to prevent further attacks. Worst of all, poor General Sikorski, the Polish Prime Minister, was killed when his plane crashed into the sea, just seconds after taking off from the aerodrome at Gibraltar. His death is so very convenient for the Soviets (and indeed, for the British and Americans) that there is much speculation over whether his plane was sabotaged—and if so, by whom? It is all very worrying, but Veronica said that her afternoon of ripping up weeds had been quite therapeutic.

"I pretended each one was a Fascist," she said. She pointed to an especially thick specimen sprawled at her feet. "Look, that's Göring. And that tall, limp one over there is Ribbentrop."

After I'd helped cart Hitler, Mussolini, Franco, and all the others to the compost heap, I came inside to write letters to various family members. Henry has finished her initial training—three weeks of marching about in blue overalls—which she absolutely loved. Now she's in Plymouth, learning how to navigate a motor launch so that she can ferry people and stores out to naval ships. As she spent most of her childhood messing about on boats, I can't imagine any of this is particularly challenging for her—except for having to obey all the rules and regulations, of course. She wrote to say that her new uniform kit included knee-length knitted knickers, which were far too thick and scratchy to wear. As she had plenty of her own underclothes—and the sea breezes can get quite cold—

she cut out the gusset of the knickers and wore them as a pull-over, putting her head through the new opening, and her arms where the legs were supposed to go. Then all the other Wrens started doing the same, and when their commanding officer finally noticed, Henry pointed out it *was* a part of their uniform and the regulations didn't specify *how* the knickers were to be worn. Lucky for her that the officer couldn't help laughing. (Or perhaps it wasn't luck; perhaps it was that famous Fitz-Osborne charm.) Henry does seem very happy where she is, but I can't help feeling anxious about her. She's so *young*. Still, it's a comfort to know Alice lives fairly close by, just in case there are any problems.

I also sent a page to Simon with our news. We've had half a dozen letters from him now, but they are carefully addressed to both Veronica and me, and are utterly devoid of any real information or emotion. Of course, all his correspondence is censored, which must be a bit off-putting for him. As it is, his letters sometimes arrive with pieces cut out of them, where he's slipped up and accidentally mentioned the name of a place or a colleague. I can only imagine the letters of other, less careful servicemen—their poor families must receive something resembling paper doilies.

After that, I wrote to Aunt Charlotte and Barnes. I think they both miss Henry quite a lot—she has become a sort of substitute for Toby in their eyes—so it really *was* unselfish and generous of Aunt Charlotte to sign the permission forms. I feel doubly obliged now to send them cheerful missives as often as possible.

I wrote another note to Toby, too—just saying that I was thinking of him and hoped he was all right. I don't ever *send* the notes, of course. I don't even keep them. But I find the act of writing them strangely comforting.

Jack Kennedy is a hero! His boat was sunk by a Japanese destroyer somewhere in the South Pacific, but he rescued most of his men from the burning wreckage. Then he swam for hours, clutching one injured mate and encouraging the others, until they all managed to reach a tiny island. They were stranded there for days without any supplies, but finally some natives turned up and agreed to fetch help, and the men were rescued.

What an ordeal! Especially as Jack is really not very strong—he has a bad back and is constantly falling ill. Actually, I'm surprised he passed the medical to get *into* the navy, but I expect his father pulled strings. Poor Kick was worried half to death by the newspaper headlines until she had a letter from Jack himself, who sounded the same as ever. He has refused to take any leave, and has gone straight back on patrol.

At least all of this has (temporarily) distracted Kick from the drama of her love life. Billy has turned very serious now that the Allied invasion of France appears imminent, and the two of them are discussing marriage. Of course, it is utterly impossible. His father loathes Roman Catholics and besides, Billy will be the next Duke of Devonshire. How could Billy, the future head of one of the leading Protestant families in England, possibly wed an Irish American Catholic girl—particularly one who insists on bringing up their children as Catholic? Veronica tried to explain some of the historical and political context to Kick, but I don't think she took much in. She was too busy worrying about eternal hellfire. She consulted some priest and he assured her that she'd be "living in sin" if she married a Protestant, and that she and all her Protestant children would proceed directly to hell when they died.

After Kick left, Veronica shook her head. "If that's what going to school and college does to one's brain," she said, "then I'm glad I'm uneducated. How *can* such an intelligent girl take those superstitions seriously?"

"It isn't only Kick," I said. "Millions of people believe it."

"Millions of people used to believe the earth was flat. That doesn't make it true. And even if something *did* create the universe, I very much doubt that that Creator would care, millions of years later, about one particular human being deciding to mate with another, let alone about who gets to splash some water on their infant offspring."

I cannot argue with this logic, but the fact is, people often behave illogically. Personally, I think Kick's more concerned about her family's reaction than God's, especially as Joe's planning to go into politics after the war, and she doesn't want to do anything that might damage her brother's appeal to Catholic voters. But honestly, what did her parents *imagine* they were doing, bringing a girl as lively and charming as Kick over here for the Season, buying her lots of beautiful ball gowns, and introducing her to dozens of eligible British lords? What other result could they have expected?

Oh, well, it will all get sorted out in the end, one way or another, but what a mess, and *poor* Billy and Kick, being made to feel miserable about falling in love! Aren't there enough *other* things in the world right now to make us feel miserable?

It really is a relief to turn to the uncomplicated good cheer of Henry's latest letter.

Our boat's crew got inspected this week, she wrote, *by a very old Lord Someone. I led the parade, because I'm the tallest and loudest and the best at drills. I gave such a good salute that he stopped in front of me, so I smiled at him, and he said, "Young lady, I hope you won't smile like that if you encounter the enemy, ha ha," and I said, "No, sir! If I see any foul Nazis, I will glare at them like THIS," and he said, "Good God!" and stepped back and his monocle fell out. Afterwards, our Petty Officer Wren said could I please be a little less egzuberant and I said yes, of course, I would try my best to do that, even tho I'm not completely sure what it is, so how can I be less of it?*

Oh! Rita just reminded me! Thank you so much for the biskits you sent, they arrived a bit crushed but everyone loved them! Also, Aunt C and Barnes just sent me an ENORMOUS bag of toffees that must have used up all their sweets ration for about two months! I am hardly ever hungry here as the helpings at meals are huge, even if the food is a bit boring for vegetarians. But when we have days off, we go into town and have fish and chips, which is my favrite food in the world!

Really, everything is perfect here—the weather, the other girls, the work. Best of all is when a ship comes into the harbor after being at sea for ages, and we take out their letters and parcels, and all the men line the decks and cheer like mad when they see us coming! On the way back yesterday, the sun was making the waves all silver and sparkling, and the breeze was blowing in our faces, and I said to Rita, "Aren't we LUCKY to be doing this job?" and she agreed. Then she said the only other thing to make it perfect would be if Douglas Fairbanks Jr. was visiting the ship and we got to bring him ashore. It might happen, too, because he's in the US Navy. For me, the thing to make it perfect would be if Carlos could come out on the motor launch with us one day. It is very warm now and hardly ever rough—he could easily stand on the prow, or lie down if his legs got tired. I bet he misses the sea. I didn't realize how much I missed it till I got here. Everything smells so lovely, of salt and tar and wet rope, and at night, I can hear the sloshing sound of the sea and the docks creaking. It's almost like being at home at Montmaray. Of course, the most important thing *about being here is helping defeat the Nazis, but I'm so for-chunate I get to do vital war work AND have a really brilliant time sailing about the harbor!*

Better go, it's nearly lights-out. Just like boarding school, except here it's far more useful and fun AND I get to wear trousers every day!!!

Lots of love,
Henry

25th September 1943

The leaves are turning bronze and copper, the afternoons are shorter, I've put another blanket on my bed—and yet, somehow, it feels like spring. It's the news from Italy that is making me more hopeful, I think. Mussolini has been overthrown, and the Allies are now fighting their way up through Italy—against the Germans, because the Italians have surrendered. Could the end of the war actually be in sight?

Veronica says the battles are not going nearly as smoothly as the newspapers suggest, but surely it can only be a matter of time before the Germans are forced into retreat? Why would they keep on fighting to defend Italy when the new Italian Prime Minister has just signed an armistice with us and . . . Oh, the telephone's ringing.

Good, Veronica's getting it. Sounds as though it's Aunt Charlotte. But why would she be telephoning at this hour of the—

27th September 1943

Post Office Telegram

To: HRH PRINCESS CHARLOTTE MILFORD PARK
MILFORD DORSET

DEEPLY REGRET TO REPORT DEATH OF YOUR
NIECE HENRIETTA C FITZOSBORNE BOATS CREW
WREN ON WAR SERVICE LETTER FOLLOWS.

2nd October 1943

If funerals are supposed to comfort the living, why do I feel so much worse now it's over? Is it because it wasn't a proper funeral, only a memorial service? That there was no coffin, no procession through the churchyard, no grave? But this, to me, has been the only consolation—that they *didn't* manage to re-cover her body. That Henry slipped free, as unconstrained in death as she ever was in life, that she drifted to the bottom of the ocean and is even now making her slow way home, to Montmaray. I picture George and Isabella and all those other Montmaravians buried at sea, waiting to welcome her . . .

But no, it's impossible to believe she's gone, especially here at Milford. Everything shouts of her presence. Her bedroom in the attic, which she never *did* tidy up properly before she left to join the Wrens. The tangle of un-ironed shirts shoved into a drawer, the fishing rod propped against the wall, the row of tattered Biggles books slanting along the window ledge. In the kitchen, there's a vegetarian cookbook on the shelf beside the stove, and a black ring on the scrubbed pine table where she once set down a sizzling frying pan. Her wellingtons are lined up beside the back door. The henhouse gate is tied shut with one of her hair ribbons.

Then there's Carlos, curled up in his armchair upon the remnants of her old tartan dressing gown. He insisted on coming to the funeral with us—he always accompanied Henry to church services, and he knew where we were going because Barnes had put on her Sunday hat. The church was packed, but the woman standing in Carlos's usual spot by the side door obligingly shifted further along the wall to make room for him. Just about everyone from the village and the surrounding farms was present—even the evacuee children staying at the vicarage, who told me that Henry used to take them for pony rides. There were Wrens in navy blue, Jimmy Smith in sapper's khaki, three prefects from Henry's last school in their maroon blazers, Aunt Charlotte's stable girls in Land Army breeches, and the entire Milford Home Guard in full uniform, standing to attention in two lines at the back of the church. Mrs. Jones from the vicarage and Jocko's mother had brought in armfuls of beautiful autumn foliage to fill the vases, and the Reverend Webster Herbert delivered a lovely eulogy. But I couldn't help imagining Henry fidgeting beside me, growing bored with all the talk, staring out the window in the direction of the river and wondering whether the fish were biting, rooting through her pockets to see if she'd brought any fishing line, and wishing there was some Communion bread about that she could pinch for bait. I could almost hear Aunt Charlotte hissing admonishments at her along the pew . . . but there my imaginings died, because in reality, Aunt Charlotte was hunched and silent, aged twenty years in a week. She had managed, with considerable effort, to transform Henry into her beloved Tobias, and now *both* of them had been taken from her. It was an indication of how shattered our aunt was that she hadn't even noticed Daniel, who sat with his arm round Veronica's shoulders. Veronica herself had been a pillar of strength for days—making all of the arrangements, even telephoning my office to arrange my leave—but midway through the service, I watched her start to crumble. There was nothing I could do to help her, though. There was nothing I could do about *any* of it.

I think that was why I felt so angry afterwards—I was consumed with impotent fury. Mrs. Jones had set out scones and potted meat sandwiches in the vicarage, and people crowded about me in the front parlor, saying the same useless things. "Such a dreadful waste . . . so young . . . but so brave . . . at least it was sudden . . . wouldn't have known a thing . . . and killed in action, the way she'd have wanted to go . . . ."

"She wouldn't have wanted *any* of this!" I snapped at the unfortunate village woman who'd contributed that last remark. "Henry didn't want to *die*! She wanted to *live*, she wanted to see the Nazis beaten!"

Then I slammed down my teacup and stormed out. I couldn't stand to be in the same building as any of those stupid people for another second. One of them had had the utter *gall* to tell me she understood how I felt—just because her uncle had died at Dunkirk! That wasn't the same at *all*! It had nothing to do with my situation!

Not one of them seemed to comprehend that I was now completely and utterly alone. My parents were dead. My brother was gone. And now my sister had been killed—murdered by Nazis—and I'd been abandoned. I stomped along the road, grinding my teeth and clenching and unclenching my fists. Daniel had driven Veronica back to the gatehouse in the car he'd borrowed, and Barnes had taken Aunt Charlotte, who'd fallen apart entirely during the final hymn, to lie down in Mrs. Jones's room. No one cared about me. Well . . . except for Carlos, who'd stopped begging people for sandwiches when he'd noticed me leaving, and had faithfully followed me outside. He moved so slowly these days, though, that when I glanced over my shoulder, I saw he'd only just reached the vicarage gate.

So I sat down on the front step of the village shop to wait for him. The sign on the shop door said CLOSED FOR FUNEARAL, possibly in some sort of tribute to Henry's creative spelling. I was still shaking with anger, although I was already feeling pangs of guilt over my behavior in the vicarage. It wasn't *their* fault that this had happened.

No, I blamed the Germans—*all* of them, every single one of them, but especially Hitler, for starting the war, and the Nazi general who'd ordered the attack on the south coast of England that day, and those Luftwaffe pilots who'd machine-gunned the harbor and dropped their bombs on the anchored ships.

I blamed the Wrens commanding officer, too, for sending off Henry in the motor launch that morning, and the navy for not sending its *own* launch out to collect those maintenance men from the ship, and the RAF for not giving enough warning that bombers were approaching. I blamed the Colonel for writing Henry a reference, Aunt Charlotte for signing the permission papers, Henry herself for wanting to join the Wrens in the first place . . . but most of all, I blamed myself. The Colonel and Aunt Charlotte had only given in to Henry because I'd *asked* them to do so. *I* was responsible for Henry joining up—when I knew she was just a *child*, far too young to be away from home, let alone to do a difficult, dangerous job like that . . .

At some stage, I became aware that Carlos was licking my face. I put my arms round his comforting woolly bulk and went on weeping until finally a car pulled up beside me, and it was Lady Bosworth, and she drove us home.

19th October 1943

The letters of condolence continue to arrive. Rupert's was so touching—his recollections of Henry so fond and true—that I can hardly bear to mention it here, because it will only make me start crying again. The Basque refugees in Manchester sent a beautiful card, and Carmelita wrote from Mexico. Phoebe posted us a box of wildflowers from Somerset. Kick delivered a kind note from her mother, with a postscript scrawled by her little brother Teddy. I hadn't even realized he'd known Henry, but apparently he'd met her in Kensington Gardens one day and been "mighty impressed" with both her and Carlos. It isn't just letters, either—everyone here is being so supportive. Julia, in particular, has helped in all sorts of little practical ways. I don't know how we would have managed without her these last couple of weeks.

Veronica and I have both gone back to work, of course, but I've been making so many mistakes that I wouldn't be surprised if I received an official reprimand. The thing is, I can't be *bothered* about it anymore. What does it matter if I'm five minutes late to work? Why *should* I respectfully defer to Mr. Bowker's directives when he's so often wrong? Who cares if the updated potato fact sheet lists the wrong vitamins?

Veronica has gone to the other extreme—rushing off to her office at seven each morning, eating her sandwich at her desk, and staying late into the evening. It isn't just that she believes her work is important, although she does—it's that she can't bear to be idle for a single, waking moment, because she's as racked with guilt and grief as I am and would rather not contemplate any of it at all. Before this, there had been some talk of her taking up a three-month posting at the Embassy in Madrid. Now she says she couldn't possibly leave me here in London by myself. But I could move in with Julia. Or I could resign from my pointless job and go back to Milford. Aunt Charlotte isn't at all well—she came down with a bad cold after the funeral, and now it's turned to bronchitis. It isn't fair to expect Barnes to nurse Aunt Charlotte, in addition to looking after the house and taking over all Aunt Charlotte's WVS jobs. I'm sure I could be of help there . . .

Except I'm so weary that the mere *thought* of having to make a decision about this makes me want to take to my bed and not get up again for days.

Oh, I forgot to mention—Rebecca also sent a note, saying she'd pray for Henry's soul and for us. Apparently she's become even more wildly religious, and is a constant visitor to a nearby abbey, where the nuns all love her. (Of course, it's the *job* of nuns to love disagreeable people; the more disagreeable the person, the holier the nuns probably feel.)

Not a word from Rebecca's son, though. Perhaps he hasn't received Veronica's letter. Or perhaps he just doesn't give a damn.

I handed in my resignation letter to Miss Halliday the week before last, and I think she was almost as relieved as I was. Now she
can replace me with someone genial and obliging. I dithered over
the decision for a while, but the matter was settled for me when
I heard that Lord Woolton was being transferred to another position. He'd been such an enthusiastic and capable Minister of
Food, and he always made our jobs seem so important and useful.
It was difficult for me to imagine working under the leadership of
anybody else—so I'm not even going to attempt it.

Lord Woolton's now been appointed Minister of Recon-
struction, which I suppose means the government thinks the
war is almost over and they ought to be planning for what happens next. But as they have been wrong about so many other
things, I am not making any effort to feel hopeful (and it *would*
be an effort, believe me). I don't even read the newspapers anymore, because Veronica is the one who bought them and she's

in Spain now. So I have no idea what's going on with the war, and I don't much care.

Julia and the others have been making valiant attempts to raise my spirits, but I wish they'd stop it. It only makes me feel guilty when their efforts inevitably fail. Last week, Kick invited me to a party for her brother Joe, whose squadron has been posted to England to work alongside RAF Coastal Command. There are thousands of American servicemen in London now, and nearly all of them turned up at the party. It wasn't at all enjoyable. Someone kept playing the piano far too loudly, and a drunken soldier accidentally set fire to Billy's sister's dress. Joe looked very smart in his uniform, but otherwise seemed much the same—I overheard some girl complaining he'd proposi-tioned her in the taxi on the way there.

I suppose I ought to make allowances for him, because he's very brave to be doing such a dangerous job, but frankly, I am fed up with men right now. A girl can't walk anywhere after dark in the West End without being accosted by some GI trying to be "friendly." As if I can be purchased with a pair of nylon stockings and a bar of chocolate! And it isn't just men I *don't* know who are making me fume. Simon hasn't bothered to write us one single word of condolence. And as for Mr. *Bowker* . . . Well! I am still absolutely flabbergasted.

Today was my last day at work, and I went into his office to deliver my final set of corrected brochures and to say goodbye. I was mildly interested in how he'd react to my departure—after all, I'd been in his department four years, and I'd been a fairly diligent and efficient worker for all but the past few weeks.

"So, I hear you're leaving us, Miss FitzOsborne," he said, after I'd handed him all the paperwork and explained (in words of one syllable) what still needed to be done. "Moving to the country, I believe."

"Yes, Mr. Bowker," I said. As usual, he hadn't asked me to sit down, so I was standing at attention on one side of his desk, and he was leaning back in his chair on the other side, gazing up my nostrils.

"Leaving the Civil Service," he went on, shaking his head slowly. "I'm not sure I approve of that." Just as I was thinking he might actually be about to deliver a *compliment*, he added, "I mean, a lady of your age, getting on a bit—you need security, don't you? The Civil Service provides that."

I gaped at him. A lady of my age! Getting on a bit! But he hadn't finished.

"And you'll be called up now, won't you? The services. Not very nice for ladies, being in the army."

"I won't get called up," I snapped, "because I'm not a British citizen!"

He blinked. "Aren't you?"

"*No*. I'm Montmaravian!"

He ignored this, the way he always ignored anything he didn't immediately understand. "Of course," he said, leaning forward and raising his ginger eyebrows, "*married* ladies aren't forced to join the services. And now that you've resigned from the Civil Service, you *are* permitted to *marry*." He shifted his gaze and peered over my shoulder at the ceiling, apparently deep in thought. "Yes . . . *marriage* might be a very good idea for you."

A horrible notion began to form in my brain.

"I myself," Mr. Bowker continued relentlessly, "have been considering marriage. When a man reaches a certain point in his life—when he has a good position in the Civil Service and a house of his own—he begins to think about such things."

Then he gave a very artificial jolt.

"Oh!" he said, as though he'd just had a brilliant idea. "I wonder if . . . Well, perhaps you and *I* might . . . Knowing each other as we do . . . That is, it's something to consider, isn't it?"

He shot me a look to gauge my reaction, then pressed on, seemingly heartened by the fact I hadn't said anything. (I *couldn't* speak. I simply couldn't find the *words*.)

"That is to say, having worked together all these years . . . it would make *sense*, I think you'd agree? And then you wouldn't need to leave London. Very convenient for all concerned—"

"Mr. Bowker," I interrupted, "are you asking me to *marry* you?"

"Oh, well . . ." He gave a little cough. "That is, perhaps in *time*, to come to a mutual arrangement, to consider an engagement . . ."

"Mr. Bowker," I said, drawing myself up, "'I had not known you a month before I felt that you were the last man in the world whom I could ever be prevailed on to marry.'"

Then I marched out of his office.

Veronica is quite wrong when she claims there is no value in reading novels such as *Pride and Prejudice*. Of course there is. They provide one with the exact words one needs when one is *speechless* in the face of *extreme provocation*.

Anyway, after collecting my things and saying goodbye to Anne, I stomped out of the building and up the road towards Oxford Street. It was hours before the end of the official working day, but I'd completed all my allotted tasks and besides, what was Miss Halliday going to do about it? Sack me? If she'd tried to object, I would simply have pointed out that it was *unconscionable* to expect any girl to remain in that office a minute longer, after her boss had behaved in such a disgusting manner. All those times he'd called me in to lecture me about apostrophes, and he'd secretly been looking at me and thinking . . . Ugh! It was *humiliating* to have been proposed to by such a man! It was absolutely *mortifying* to realize that *he* was the sort of man I attracted!

I was so busy feeling insulted that I nearly ran into a woman holding a clipboard.

"Excuse me!" she shouted. "Sign the petition?"

"Er . . . sorry," I said. "What?"

"Petition to put Oswald Mosley back in prison!"

"He's been let *out* of prison?" I said. "When?"

She gave me a scornful look. "Don't you read the papers? Let out last weekend, he was. He and his wife living in luxury in some great big house in the country now, while ordinary working men and women are slaving away in factories and sacrificing themselves in the services! Sign here."

I took the proffered pen.

"There's a protest march to Trafalgar Square being held on Sunday," the woman went on. "A Fascist like him, being let loose when we're fighting a war! It's a stab in the back for working people, isn't it? It's a slap in the face of freedom and democracy!"

I bent to add my name to the long list—and then I paused. *Was* his release a blow against democracy? He'd never been charged with any crime. He'd never been convicted of treason. The British Union of Fascists had long been disbanded, and Mosley had lost whatever political influence he'd ever had, which hadn't been much—after all, his own political party had never even come *close* to winning a seat in Parliament. Mosley would never be Hitler's puppet Prime Minister now, with the threat of a Nazi invasion having vanished long ago. And I was certain the Colonel's men would be keeping a very close eye on Mosley's current activities to make sure he posed no future threat to national security.

I handed back the pen. "No, I don't think I will sign, thank you," I told the woman. "Mosley's one of the most loathsome men I've ever had the misfortune to meet—but I don't think a democracy ought to lock people up indefinitely without a trial. If we put people in prison simply because we don't like their opinions, we might as well be living under the Nazis."

Then I walked away quickly, because she looked very cross. But I did feel that I'd been right. I think even Veronica would have agreed with me.

13th December 1943

I've been in Milford a fortnight, but it feels as though it's been a year. Everything is horrible here. It's freezing, and it never stops raining. I spend half my day squelching through the mud to the henhouse, the stables, the village, and the Home Farm, then the other half scrubbing floors and doing the laundry and cooking meals that nobody feels like eating. Aunt Charlotte has still not recovered from her bout of bronchitis, and alternates between irritable demands and long, pitiful silences. Barnes is a saint, but the only conversations I have with her are about household chores or WVS jobs. I do talk to Carlos, but I think he's going a bit deaf. I miss Veronica. I miss Julia, and Kick, and Anne from work, and the ARP warden who lived down the road from us in Kensington, and that nice lady conductor on the 73 bus. I miss my talks with Rupert (it's true he was hardly ever in London, but he's even *less* likely to visit Milford). I am lonely and tired and miserable.

This morning was the worst yet, because I had an awful row with Aunt Charlotte. She announced that she was arranging for a plaque to be put up in the church, as a memorial to Henry. That was distressing enough—the idea of someone as vibrant and alive as Henry being reduced to a few words inscribed on a cold, flat piece of brass—but then I saw what it was going to *say*. *Henrietta* rather than *Henry*! Barnes stepped in and negotiated a compromise of *Henrietta (Henry) Charlotte FitzOsborne*, although not before quite a lot of tears and shouting, mostly on my part. But *then* Aunt Charlotte revealed that she was also commissioning a memorial for *Toby*!

"How *can* you?" I cried. "You wouldn't even know what date to put on it! He's not dead, you've got no proof of that!"

Actually, I *do* secretly think he's dead, but it would be a horrible betrayal of Henry's beliefs ever to admit this out loud. So I yelled a bit more, then stormed out and went for a very long walk in the pouring rain, and now I have a sniffly nose and scratchy throat. I'm meant to be down at the church hall doing a stint of camouflage net weaving, but instead I am hiding out in the stables with my journal. I've told myself that all the dust and lint from the strips of fabric will only make my throat worse, but really it's that I hate having anything to do with the war now, and besides, I still haven't managed to get all that nasty brown dye off my hands from last night's weaving session—

Ow! Lightning the pony just hit me *very hard* on the top of my head with his chin because I'm sitting outside his stall and haven't brought any carrots for him! Even the *horses* hate me!

I don't know why I bother continuing with this journal when there's never anything nice to write.

28th December 1943

We pretty much ignored Christmas, on account of our lack of seasonal cheer, and yesterday began like any other day for me. Up at half-past six, let Carlos out, feed the hens and check for eggs (only two), bring in the milk canister left by Mr. Wilkin on the doorstep, go out again to find Carlos and herd him back inside, make porridge. Check with Barnes about the division of the day's chores over breakfast. Write out a shopping list for Aunt Charlotte, who was taking the pony and cart to the village. Wash some blouses and stockings, and drape over clotheshorse in front of the sitting room fire. Tidy bedroom and attempt to plug the drafty gap in the window frame with bits of Henry's modeling clay. Go back downstairs to retrieve damp clothes from sitting room floor, Carlos having knocked over the clotheshorse while clambering down from his armchair. Do lots of boring ironing. Make half a dozen cheese, carrot, and chutney sandwiches, and take them and a thermos of soup over to the stable girls at lunchtime. Get stuck there for an hour helping them muck out stalls. Return to gatehouse and do washing up. Bring in more firewood from woodshed, stack logs next to fire in sitting room, then go out to collect more kindling.

I was trudging through the wood, basket dangling from the crook of my arm, when it struck me how like the awful bits of a fairy tale my life had become. Here was the impoverished princess, banished from her kingdom, deprived of family and home, bidden to wander the forest in search of twigs and pinecones. What enormous shaggy wolves might lurk ahead, or be stalking in her wake? (Well, none actually, because I'd sent Carlos back to the house with Barnes when I'd met her at the gate.)

What I *really* needed was a prince on a white horse to gallop to my rescue, I thought as I set down my basket and knelt to gather handfuls of twigs scattered around a stout oak. It had stopped raining, but each gust of wind shook a hail of icy droplets from the branches onto my bare neck. I'd just scrambled to my feet, clutching an armful of kindling, when I happened to glance through the trees to the driveway—and my heart seemed to stop. I thought I was going *mad*. I was surely seeing things.

For cantering across the grass came a beautiful white horse, and astride it was a man, fair and lean and graceful. He held the reins lightly in one hand, as though they were simply for show—as though he had only to murmur a word and the animal would obey. He caught sight of me, and I dropped my burden and started to run, and by the time I'd reached the drive, he'd swung down from the saddle and taken a few steps in my direction, and I threw myself into his arms.

It felt as though I'd come home. *This* was where I belonged—with Rupert. We clung to each other, words tumbling out about how much we'd missed the other and how glad we were to be together again. *Soppy,* Henry would have said, rolling her eyes—but she always did like Rupert, so I think she'd have secretly approved. Rupert finally drew back and smoothed my hair behind my ear, his fingers trailing down to trace my cheek. It *might* have progressed to kissing then—except the horse had grown very bored by that stage, so it stuck its nose in my ear and gave a loud snort.

"She's just jealous," said Rupert, laughing as he reached past me to take hold of the reins. "She knows I love you *far* more than her."

Which was pretty much the most romantic thing anyone has ever said to me, even though I'm aware that being placed ahead of a horse in someone's affections is not exactly the same as, say, being serenaded on a moonlit balcony.

Rupert took my hand in his free one, and we walked up the drive, towards the stables. The emotions bubbling up inside me were making me quite light-headed, so although I knew there was much to discuss regarding the two of us, I was content, for the moment, simply to *be* with him. I sensed he also needed some time to become used to the idea that there *was* an "us"—he'd turned a bit pink and seemed to be having a sudden attack of shyness—so to put us both at ease, I asked about the horse. He explained she was Lady Bosworth's, sent over to be trained at Aunt Charlotte's school.

"There's hardly any petrol to spare, so I said I'd ride her over. We came through the fields and back lanes, and it only took a couple of hours. I tried to ring first, but your telephone seems to be out of order. Of course, I was hoping like mad that you'd be here."

And then he squeezed my hand and I squeezed back, and we beamed at each other. Perhaps some things *didn't* need a lot of talking, after all. I couldn't remember the last time I'd felt so bathed in warmth.

He'd had a few unexpected days off work over Christmas, he went on to say, which he'd spent at Astley. Then that morning, he and his mother had driven over to visit Penelope and her daughter, who both live with the Bosworths now. The little girl is nearly two and a half.

"She's very sweet," said Rupert. "She talks nonstop, although I can't say I actually understood any of it. Penelope dotes on her."

"Does she look like David?"

"Well, my mother thinks she does, but Lady Bosworth insists the child takes after *her* side of the family. Poor old Lady Bosworth, she was in a fearful temper when we got there. The War Office has just requisitioned their big farm in Devon, you see, the one near the coast—along with about thirty thousand acres of the surrounding lands. All the villagers have had to be evacuated. I passed streams of US Army lorries driving south this morning, so I suppose that's where they were headed."

Getting ready for the big invasion of France, no doubt,

but we'd arrived at the stables by then, so we didn't have to talk about the horrible war any further. Rupert handed over the mare to the stable girls, the youngest of whom *definitely* tried to flirt with him. I suppose they're a bit starved of male company, and he's so nice and so good-looking (those beautiful hazel eyes, that firm jaw, his hair burnished gold where the light hit it) that I couldn't really blame her. I was surprised at how irritated I felt, though—in a sort of "Hands off, he's mine!" way. I didn't *say* anything, of course, but I realized I'd experienced a muted version of that feeling several times in the past. What an idiot I'd been, to fail to understand the reason behind it!

Barnes had been right all along, it turned out—and I must say, she positively *radiated* smugness when Rupert and I arrived back at the gatehouse, still holding hands. She ushered us into the sitting room (fortunately, she'd already whisked away the clotheshorse dripping with underclothes) and brought us cups of tea, then took herself off to the kitchen to start dinner, even though it was my turn to cook. Aunt Charlotte had been unable to resist going over to the stables to inspect the new horse, so Carlos was our only chaperone (and a sleepy one, at that). Rupert and I had a lovely long chat, in which he said a lot of admiring things about me, and I said similar things about him. He said he'd fallen in love with me ages ago, so I asked why he hadn't *said* anything, and he admitted that, for a long time, he'd felt it was hopeless.

"I mean, the first time we met, I made you *cry*," he pointed out.

"Oh, so you did!" I said, remembering the scene in his pigeon loft. "Except that wasn't really your fault. And I needed a good cry at the time. I felt much better afterwards."

"And then your aunt was determined to find you some rich, titled husband, and didn't seem to approve of me at all. And also . . ." He trailed off and looked down at our clasped hands.

"What?"

He glanced up at me. "Well, sometimes I got the impression that, um, you and Simon . . ."

"Heavens, if you think Aunt Charlotte disapproved of *you*, you ought to hear her on the subject of Simon!" I said. "Anyway, whatever I felt about him, it's over now."

"Good," said Rupert, his gaze clearing.

"I'll tell you about it someday, if you like," I added.

"I don't *need* to know. But you can always tell me anything you like." And he gave me one of his sweet, serious smiles.

"And *you* can tell *me* anything," I said, because regardless of how muddled the notion of truth seems to be in the wider world, I feel Rupert and I ought to be completely honest with each other. But just as he was saying that he didn't have anything very interesting to tell, Aunt Charlotte walked in with Mr. Herbert, who said he was driving to Salisbury the next morning and could give Rupert a lift back to the Bosworths'. Mr. Herbert also kindly offered to ring Lady Astley from the vicarage to tell her, as our telephone hasn't been working all week (I suspect the wires have succumbed to the perpetual damp).

So Rupert stayed for dinner, and was absolutely charming, and showed admirable composure when Aunt Charlotte started interrogating him about his "prospects." (There's a *war* on, for heaven's sake—no one knows *anything* about his prospects! We could all get wiped out tomorrow by that secret weapon the Nazis are rumored to have invented!) Still, it was nice to see a return of the old Aunt Charlotte, because she's been so very sad and weary and diminished of late. She *did* object to Rupert staying overnight in Toby's room, though. She regards it as a sort of shrine, and we're only supposed to go in there to clean. Henry's room is also a shrine, albeit to a slightly lesser deity, but Barnes and Aunt Charlotte weren't comfortable with Rupert staying in there anyway, as it's separated from my room by a mere plywood partition and curtained doorway, so he could easily sneak in and ravish me. (Mercifully, this ridiculous conversation occurred in the kitchen, out of earshot of Rupert.) But I couldn't see why poor Rupert should have to sleep on the sofa and put up with Carlos's snoring all night when *Toby* wouldn't have minded his best friend borrowing his pajamas or sleeping in his room. I had my way in the end.

After Aunt Charlotte and Barnes had gone upstairs to get ready for bed, Rupert and I remained in the sitting room a while longer, and there *was* kissing this time, and it was blissful. Rupert is *so* sweet and gentle and considerate. The only problem was that Carlos kept trying to climb onto our laps, so we finally gave up on the kissing (probably a sensible move, as Barnes and Aunt Charlotte kept thumping downstairs to do completely unnecessary tasks like fetching glasses of water and checking that the back door was latched) and we let Carlos drape himself over us. I asked Rupert about dogs and arthritis, because Carlos seems so much slower than he was even a few months ago. But Rupert thought we were already doing as much as we could.

"He's not overweight, which helps, and you say he's still going for walks. He's got a warm, comfortable bed, but I suppose you could give him a hot-water bottle as well. Does he have a good appetite? Carlos? Do you enjoy your dinner?"

Carlos grinned and said, "Ha ha ha!" the way he always does when anyone mentions food. He hadn't had two people's undivided attention for quite a while, and he was enjoying every second of it.

"Yes, he loves his food, and everyone else's food, too," I said. "But I've noticed him limping, and some mornings, it takes forever for him to get going. I hate the thought of him in any pain, but it's even worse to imagine him being . . . you know, put down. I realize he's very old and that it's silly to be fussing over a dog when we're in the middle of a war, but . . . well, he was *Henry's* dog."

And my eyes unexpectedly filled with tears and I found I couldn't say anything else. But Rupert was very understanding, and after I'd wiped my face, he talked a bit about Henry and, more importantly, *asked* me about her. And I realized I hadn't talked about her death to *anyone*. I hadn't needed to tell people in the family, because they all knew about it, obviously, and Veronica was the one who'd let all our friends and acquaintances know. Then, at the funeral, I'd been so angry and spiky that no one had wanted to broach the subject with me afterwards.

So, when Rupert asked me how I was feeling, it all surged out: how I still had moments when I forgot Henry was dead and how awful it was when I remembered; how I hadn't ever appreciated her properly until it was too late; how guilty I felt because I hadn't kept her safe. Rupert was a very good listener. It wasn't that he *agreed* with me, just that he didn't dismiss what I said as irrational or stupid, even though some of it probably is. In fact, he said it sounded quite natural, in the circumstances. As I spoke, I began to feel lighter. Sad rather than anguished, not *quite* so filled with fury and bitterness when I thought of her . . .

Then Barnes came in for about the fifth time and suggested that Rupert should get some sleep, because Mr. Herbert was leaving *very early* the next morning. So we obediently went upstairs, to Carlos's great disappointment.

14th January 1944

I've come up to London for a week, because Veronica is back from Spain, and already it's been far more eventful than I could possibly have anticipated. I'd planned to arrive before her, so that I could make the flat a bit more welcoming—turn on the electricity and gas, go out to buy some food, that sort of thing— but my train was late. Well, to be honest, I *missed* the train. After Aunt Charlotte dropped me off outside Salisbury station, I sat down on a bench to read Rupert's latest letter again, and I sort of lost track of time. But then the next train *was* late, and when I arrived in London, I couldn't find a taxi for ages, and all the buses were packed.

Anyway, when I eventually climbed the steps to our flat, I saw that the front door was ajar, with Veronica's suitcase blocking the way. I could also hear what sounded like Daniel's voice. I nudged the door open and stepped over the suitcase, then noticed the filled kettle sitting on the stove and the gaping cutlery drawer. Veronica and Daniel seemed to be having a loud debate in the sitting room—although there was nothing unusual about that. *Probably politics*, I thought, as I set my own suitcase down. Then I heard Veronica say, "But what about Sophie? Should I tell her or not?"

I gasped and rushed into the next room.

"Tell me what?" I demanded. "What's going on?"

Veronica leapt to her feet and flung her arms around me. "Oh, Sophie!" she cried, in a muffled way, into my hair.

"Hello, Sophie!" Daniel said. "Um . . . I'll just finish making that tea, then, shall I?" And he hastened into the kitchen.

"What is it?" I asked, tugging away from Veronica so I could search her face for clues. "What aren't you telling me?"

"Oh, it's not *bad* news," she said. "Truly, it's not. Here, sit down. It's just . . . well, I didn't want you getting your hopes up and having it all come to nothing. I thought it would be better if I kept quiet until I knew for certain . . . but now I suppose I *have* to tell you."

Then she stopped and chewed her lip, gazing at me with anxious intensity. I was ready to strangle her from sheer frustration.

"Veronica! Just *say* it!"

"Well, it's a long story. It's about . . . That is, it *may* be about . . . about Toby."

I stared at her, all the words in my mouth drying up.

"You see, I've been in the northern bit of Spain—Basque country—for the past few weeks," she began. "Michael's up there most of the time now. It's pretty much his full-time job, liaising with the people who bring Allied pilots across the mountains from France, then getting the pilots out of prison once the Spanish authorities catch them, which they generally do. We were based at the consulate in Bilbao, but we went to San Sebastián quite a lot. Anyway, a British intelligence person arrived last week and he needed to talk to one of Michael's Basque contacts. The Basques aren't just bringing pilots across the border, but all sorts of information valuable to the Allies as well. Michael was busy with something else, so I went along to introduce them and to interpret."

Daniel came in and handed us mugs of tea, then tactfully disappeared back into the kitchen. Veronica continued.

"So, this intelligence officer—I'm not supposed to be telling you any of this, of course, but let's call him Tom—sits down next to me at the agreed place, and we wait and wait, and finally, the Basque man—José—turns up, except he has a young man with him, someone I've never seen before. But José says, 'No, no, it's fine, he's my wife's cousin.' And you know how clannish the Basques are, so I nod at Tom and he starts asking his questions and I'm interpreting away, when suddenly the young man leans over to me and says, 'Are you from Montmaray?'"

I gaped at Veronica. "But how would he know that?"

"Exactly," she said. "Everyone just calls me 'Miss Fitz-Osborne' at the Embassy. Older Spaniards sometimes know about my mother's family, but no one *ever* mentions Montmaray. So I looked about in a wild panic, expecting to see Gestapo agents running over to *kidnap* me or something. Tom didn't have a clue what was going on, of course, but José hit the young man on the shoulder and said, 'You idiot! You're scaring her! Tell her properly!'"

Veronica took a deep breath.

"Anyway, it turned out his name was Zuleta. He's the Basque captain's nephew. And, oh Sophie—captain Zuleta's *alive*! You know how we all thought he'd died at Guernica? But he was in the basement of a church with his youngest daughter when the bombing started, and they both survived. They were pulled out of the ruins the next morning. His wife died, though, and so did two of their children. Then, after the Fascists defeated the Basque Republic, he and his daughter escaped over the mountains into France. His wife had relatives there, and he wanted to start a new life."

I shook my head, sad and happy and amazed all at once. But Veronica hadn't even arrived at the *most* amazing bit.

She went on to explain that the captain's in-laws in France hated the Nazis so much that they decided to dedicate themselves to helping the Resistance. His wife's aunt runs a hotel near the Spanish border, at the foot of the Pyrenees, and she's an important part of an escape line for Allied servicemen—that is, escaping prisoners of war, as well as those who've managed to evade the Nazis entirely after getting stuck in occupied territory. They arrive from the north of France, and she finds them safe houses and organizes Basque guides to take them over the mountains into Spain. Last month, a new group of men arrived, delivered by the usual Resistance workers, and she had her son take the men to a friend's house to hide. They all seemed to be American aircrew, and they were exhausted after their long, stressful journey across France. They fell asleep at once, and had to be shaken awake when it was time to leave that night. But one of the men heard the woman's son and the guides talking, and, still half-asleep, said hello to them in Euskara.

Well, how many Americans recognize the language of the Basques—let alone know how to speak it? So they dragged the airman straight down to the basement and started interrogating him, worried that he was some sort of double agent. Most of the original leaders of that particular escape line had been captured by the Gestapo earlier that year, and it seems they were all betrayed by someone working within the movement. What if this man had been planted on them by the Spanish Fascists?

But the man said he spoke just a few words of Euskara, and only because he used to know some Basque people. The guides were still suspicious, because they could see now that he definitely *wasn't* American. All the airmen had been disguised in the same sort of rough farmer's clothes, but the Americans looked as though they'd spent the war eating steak and buttery mashed potatoes and chocolate layer cake, which they probably had. *This* man was rake-thin, like everyone else in France. The Americans swaggered along with their hands in their pockets; *he* walked like a European. He spoke French very well, which none of the Americans did, but he didn't sound like a native speaker. He said he was RAF, but he didn't seem familiar with any of the latest RAF operations over France. He said he'd already given all this information to the people further up the escape line. Eventually, after the guides threatened to take him outside and shoot him, he said, "Look, I'm not English. I'm from Montmaray."

"Toby?" I whispered, my heart pounding painfully. "Could it *really* be him? After all this time?"

"Now you understand why I didn't want to tell you," said Veronica. "Because I just don't know. It could be someone who knew Toby, or knew about him, and stole his identity. But after he said 'Montmaray,' one of the guides said, 'I know about Montmaray.' And it was because his little cousins had been sent to England during the Civil War, and they met Carmelita and her family at Stoneham Camp and kept in contact with her. So, after that, the Basques felt a bit more friendly towards him, and eventually, they sent off a message to Captain Zuleta, who lives further up the coast—"

"But what about *Toby*?" I cried. "Where is he? Is he in Spain now?"

"I'm getting to that. The man—if he *is* Toby—is still in France. By the time they'd finished questioning him, it was too late for him to cross the border with the Americans. He had to wait for the next lot, and then the river flooded, so nobody could get across the usual way, and after *that* there was an incident in which a guide and an American pilot died. Either they drowned, or they were shot by guards on the Spanish side. No one knows. So Allied escapes over the border have practically stopped for the moment, although local people are still traversing the mountains. The Basques in France thought Michael ought to know about all this, especially as this man, whoever he is, gave *my* name and said I was associated with the British Embassy in Madrid. So, they sent the captain's nephew over with a message."

She sighed.

"And that's as much as I know. I asked them to move this man, whoever he is, over the border as quickly as possible, and Michael's waiting for him in San Sebastián. If he's an impostor, or if it's all just some terrible misunderstanding, then we'll find out pretty soon. Michael wanted some questions he could ask the man, things that only Toby would know, so I said to ask what our sword was called. Do you think that's all right? I didn't want facts that anyone could find out easily, like our birth dates. Oh, and I said to ask about old George from the village, and what breed Carlos is, a few things like that. And that's it. Now you know as much as I do."

But I wanted to talk and talk about it, even though there wasn't much else to say. We both agreed we shouldn't mention it to Aunt Charlotte, or anyone else, until Veronica received confirmation of the man's identity from Michael. I felt like a balloon that had just been inflated—buoyant, bobbing about happily on the ceiling, but aware I could pop at any moment. By the time we'd talked ourselves hoarse, it was dark, and Daniel said he'd take us out for dinner, as there wasn't anything edible in the flat.

"Sorry," I said to Veronica as we were brushing our hair and putting on some lipstick. "I did mean to arrive here earlier and do some food shopping."

Then I told her about Rupert—not that I'd suddenly fallen in love with him, but that I'd realized I'd been gradually falling in love with him for years, and that, even more amazingly, *he* was in love with *me*. Veronica was delighted, although she didn't seem all that surprised.

"Well, of course he loves you," she said. "Why wouldn't he?"

I could think of lots of reasons why someone might not love me, but I certainly didn't want to win a debate about it. Mostly, I was pleased that she approved. It would be very uncomfortable to fall in love with someone she *didn't* like—well, I'd had some experience of that, even though I'd never called what I'd felt for Simon "love." For that matter, I don't think Veronica would have lasted long with someone *I* disliked or distrusted. Luckily, Daniel and Rupert are both perfect for us in their own unique ways, so it's all worked out brilliantly.

We ended up at a dimly lit Turkish restaurant, where we ate some sort of lamb casserole and then a delicious pudding that tasted of honey. Veronica and I fell to discussing Toby again, but Daniel firmly steered us both off the topic.

"You're going round in circles," he said, "and simply making yourselves more anxious, when there's nothing more you can do for the moment. Michael is working on it, and he'll let you know as soon as possible, won't he? He seems a very capable and trustworthy man."

Which was really quite generous of Daniel, given how

jealous he's been of Michael in the past, as well as being a very sensible thing to say. Veronica smiled at Daniel and agreed he was absolutely right, then asked what had been happening in politics since she'd been away. He started telling her about some by-election that a Socialist friend of his is contesting, and I was only half-listening when I heard a familiar name.

"Hang on, did you say West *Derbyshire?*" I said to Daniel. "Isn't that where Billy Hartington is running as the Conservative candidate? Kick's going up there to help him canvass for votes."

"Billy *Hartington?*" said Veronica, astonished. "Running for *Parliament?* I thought he was in the army."

"He was, but he's resigned his commission," I said. "His father must have pulled strings so he could leave the army. Apparently their family's held that seat in the House of Commons for centuries."

"Then it's about time it was won by a man of the people, someone who's actually had to *work* for a living," said Daniel. "What's Hartington like?"

"Gormless," said Veronica.

"Veronica!" I protested. "He's really very sweet."

"There you go, he's *sweet*," Veronica told Daniel. "That's all you need to become a Member of Parliament, if your father's the Duke of Devonshire. You don't need to be intelligent, or understand the needs of the electorate, or have ever demonstrated the slightest interest in politics."

"Well, it doesn't really matter what he's like," said Daniel, "because he's going to lose. Charles White has planned a terrific campaign."

"But a *Socialist*, winning West Derbyshire?" said Veronica dubiously.

"He's running as Independent Labour, and he's got Common Wealth backing him. There'll be dozens of trained campaigners canvassing voters, a press agent, a nine-point manifesto based on the Beveridge plan—the Conservatives won't know what's hit them. What have *they* got to offer, except more of the same? A rich, old family that thinks it ought to rule simply because it always *has* ruled? Why are we fighting against dictatorships on the Continent when there are people like the Duke of Devonshire trying to do the same thing here?"

"You ought to go up there yourself and help with the campaign," said Veronica.

"I will, if I can get any time off work," said Daniel. "This by-election is going to be a turning point for Britain. The people are sick of war, and they want to know that the new world will be a better, fairer place. They don't want yet another duke's son lording it over them."

Poor Billy. He's only running for Parliament because his father made him—which does imply a rather weak character, I must admit. And if he can't say no about *this*, then how likely is it that he'll defy his father to marry Kick? Oh dear, why can't *everyone* be as happy in love as I am?

17th January 1944

IT IS TOBY! It really *is* him, after more than a year and a half! Michael spoke with him when he arrived in Spain, and he's all right, not injured or sick or anything, and now he's in Gibraltar, waiting for a ship to bring him home, and Veronica has just gone to telephone Aunt Charlotte and Barnes!

I am too excited to write any more!

28th January 1944

I have so much to say, but don't even know where to start. My emotions have been lurching about so violently over the past fortnight that I'm not sure whether I'm up or down right now. I keep saying to myself, "At least he's alive. That's the main thing. Toby's alive and he's in England. He's home now—"

But then I get stuck, because I'm not sure he feels he *is* home. He isn't the same. I don't know who he is, and I don't think *he* knows, either. Everything is such a mess—although that's partly the result of our great expectations. We were so happy to hear that he was all right, so thrilled that he'd soon be back with us. It is just *too* cruel, to have this happen when we all believed our worries were over . . . But I ought to start at the very beginning. Write it all down, in the hope that it will make some sort of sense.

Well, Toby made it across the border into Spain. However, he and the four Americans with him were picked up almost at once by the Guardia Civil. The Basque guides managed to escape, thank heavens, but the airmen were all marched to Irún, a little border town, and were locked up in the prison there. Fortunately, they arrived at the same time as a Red Cross official who was conducting his weekly prison visit. He sent word to the British Consulate, and within hours, Michael had turned up, interviewed Toby, and driven him to San Sebastián, having already organized for the American consul to collect the other airmen. The next day, Toby was taken to Madrid, and from there to Gibraltar, where he was questioned by British military intelligence to confirm his identity and make sure he wasn't some Nazi double agent. After that, it was simply a matter of completing his paperwork and waiting for a ship to bring him to England. Apparently Allied servicemen are often transported back by plane, but there were a lot of Americans waiting in Gibraltar by that stage, and it seemed more efficient to move them all by sea. Michael had sent a message to Veronica from San Sebastián about all this, and then he telephoned her when Toby arrived in Gibraltar. Everything seemed to be going smoothly.

But in wartime, nothing ever goes to plan, and the Atlantic Ocean is as deadly a place as any in Europe, especially at night. Less than half an hour after setting sail, Toby's ship was torpedoed by a German U-boat. It was lucky, the authorities said afterwards, that the ship was so close to land. Lucky that many of the men were still on deck, close to the lifeboats. Lucky that they were hit just off the coast of Spain rather than in the middle of the icy North Sea. Lucky the weather was calm; lucky the survivors were picked up so quickly.

Nothing about it seems lucky to me. And we still don't know exactly what happened to Toby.

It seems he was thrown straight into the water by an explosion. Was this when the torpedo hit, or later, as the ship's fuel tanks went up in a ball of fire? How did he manage to swim, with his terrible injuries? How long was he in the water before he was dragged into a lifeboat? What sort of medical treatment did he receive in Gibraltar before he was flown to England with the worst of the wounded? No one seems to know.

We didn't realize any of this until it was all over. We were waiting in London—not even *worrying*, just impatient to see him—when Veronica received a message at work, saying there'd been an "incident" on board the ship and that Toby was in hospital in London. There followed a frantic few hours of telephone calls, of trying to find out where he was, how badly he'd been hurt, whether he was out of surgery, if he was permitted visitors. Thank heavens for Julia and her comprehensive knowledge of London hospitals. She came round in a taxi and whisked me off to the correct hospital, where she waylaid a doctor who'd just finished his ward rounds and then charmed a nurse into allowing me a brief, unofficial visit.

I think I was still in shock when I sat down at his bedside. It seemed incredible that Toby was *here*, in London. But then to have just been told—in a fairly offhand manner, by an overworked doctor who no doubt saw far worse injuries every day—that my brother had been badly burned, that they weren't sure if he'd lose his sight, that part of his leg had had to be amputated . . . I sat there, staring at the unconscious figure lying on the bed, and felt nothing at all. I wasn't even certain it *was* him. His head was shaved, his face was wrapped in bandages, the rest of him was covered in a sheet—it could have been anyone. It could have been a waxwork dummy or some grotesque, life-sized doll. When Veronica came home from work, she bombarded me with questions that I found impossible to answer. I just kept shaking my head, until Julia put her arm round me and said, very calmly, "Look, no one knows much at this stage. He's in a stable condition, they said. He didn't have any head injuries or internal bleeding, and that's the most important thing. I expect he'll need some skin grafts for the burns on his face and arm, but they have specialist hospitals for that now, and the staff in those places are very good. They've had so much practice at it these past few years, you see."

Her level voice went on, oddly reassuring despite—or because of—its frankness.

"As for his leg—well, I know it seems awful, but I think it's actually much better this way. I know someone whose leg was horribly injured by shrapnel, and he's had a dozen agonizing operations to try and fix it. It took months and months, and at one stage, he got an infection and nearly died, and he still needs a stick to get around. An amputation below the knee really isn't so bad. As soon as it's healed, they'll give him an artificial leg, and most people learn to manage them fairly quickly. It's just a matter of finding the right rehabilitation hospital. Daphne's cousin's a physiotherapist—I'll ask her. Or my boss at the station might know about it."

And then she made us eat some sandwiches, and rang Barnes to give her an update, and promised to track down Rupert the next morning to tell him, and was altogether an absolute angel.

A few days later, we received word that Toby was sitting up and talking, so I went to see him again. It was better and worse this time. Better, because I could recognize him as Toby; worse, for the same reason. His eyes were still bandaged, his throat was raw, and the medicine he'd been given for the pain had him drifting in and out of coherence. I held his hand and tried to converse in Julia's calm, reassuring manner, but it didn't work very well. Too much of my concentration was taken up with trying to hide from him how upset I was. I did tell him how pleased we all were that he was back, and how much we'd missed him, and (less truthfully) that we'd never given up hope that he'd return. But was that any comfort to him? Perhaps it only reminded him of the terrible time he'd had before he'd reached Spain— and who knows *what* had gone on during all those months?

So it was with some relief that I heard Veronica's raised voice in the corridor. I'd left a message at her work, but hadn't been sure she'd be able to get away. Then we heard the Sister in charge say, very loudly, "Only *immediate* family are permitted to visit patients on this ward!"

"Fine!" came Veronica's exasperated reply. "I'm his fiancée!"

Toby gave a little huff of amusement. "Julia tried that

one," he rasped. "God knows what the nurses will think of me now."

But Veronica was already marching in. She caught sight of us and I watched the emotions battle across her face as she took it all in—the bandages, the rubber drainage tubes, the frame holding the blankets up off his poor mutilated leg. It was over in less than a second—her step barely faltered—and then she was pulling up a chair and leaning over to kiss an unbandaged bit on the top of his head.

"What a dictator that woman is!" Veronica said. "*Immediate family*, indeed. I should have told her we were twins—that would have thrown her."

And somehow the conversation went on much better after that. There was one dreadful moment, though, when Toby said, "Where's Henry? Why isn't she here?"

And Veronica and I stared at each other, stricken, unable to say a word. Toby couldn't see our expressions, thank heavens, but he picked up on the silence. "Expelled again, I suppose," he said, then started to cough. At that point, the horrible Sister bustled in and announced, with apparent satisfaction, that we'd exhausted the patient and would be held responsible for any subsequent problems with his recovery, whereupon she threw Veronica and me out of the ward.

We made it down the corridor and around the corner before turning and clinging to each other. A minute later, a porter came whistling by and told us we were in the way.

"Sorry," said Veronica, brushing her eyes and leading me

over to a bench along the wall. We sat down. "Sorry," she said again, but to me this time. "Now I understand why you couldn't tell me anything about him before. It's a shock, isn't it? Seeing him like that."

I nodded, frowning fiercely to stop myself bursting into tears.

"Don't worry," she said. "I'll tell him about Henry."

"No, I will," I said. "Only . . . not right now."

"No," she sighed. "No, not now."

Then she said she had to get back to work, and I returned to the flat to telephone Aunt Charlotte. I'd decided to try to dissuade her from coming up to London until at least the following week—I thought it might be easier for her once some of those tubes and bandages had been removed. But in fact, *she* was the one who came up with a lot of reasons she should stay in Milford. She was coming down with another cold, she said, and didn't want to pass it on. Also, one of the stable girls had just run off with Mr. Wilkin's son-in-law, so things were very unsettled and busy. Besides, Aunt Charlotte really felt she ought to attend that district WVS meeting on Tuesday. She also asked me twice whether I was certain it *was* Toby. The whole story seemed so *unlikely*, she said. It simply didn't *sound* like him.

And all of this was before he went berserk and attacked an officer.

Not that I blame Toby one bit for that—it was entirely the fault of the hospital and the military authorities. What on earth were they *thinking*? Yes, I *know* it's routine for British servicemen who've escaped the Nazis to attend a debriefing session when they arrive back in England. I can see it would be useful, especially now the Allied invasion of the Continent is imminent and they need all the information they can get about Nazi operations in France. But surely they could have waited a few weeks longer? At least until Toby had recovered his voice completely, and wasn't needing constant injections for the pain? But no, a hospital orderly simply wheeled him off to some deserted office and dumped him there without a word of explanation, and of course, he couldn't see a thing with his eyes bandaged. Meanwhile, the man from military "intelligence" got lost in the hospital corridors, and when he finally arrived, one of his first questions was why it had taken Toby so long to get back to England.

Not surprisingly, Toby had worked himself into a towering rage by then. He refused to answer a single question—wouldn't even say his name—and demanded to be taken back to his bed. I'm not exactly sure what happened next, but it ended with Toby grabbing a telephone off the desk and hurling it at his interrogator. I suppose it's a good thing it missed, because otherwise Toby would be up on a charge, but honestly! If *these* are the people running the war, how on earth are we ever going to win it?

Anyway, they eventually got Toby back to his bed, but he was being so belligerent and uncooperative that the staff couldn't even change his dressings. Fortunately, Julia heard the whole story a few hours later from a nurse she knows, and in a remarkably short time, it was arranged that he be transferred to the burns unit of a hospital in Sussex.

"I hope I'm not being too interfering," Julia said when she telephoned. "But I can take him down there myself this evening, and I really think his burns ought to be assessed by the specialists there as soon as possible."

"Julia, of *course* I don't mind!" I said. "I'm so glad you found out what happened, and so grateful for everything you've done! But should he be moved, with his leg still—?"

"Well, the stump's actually healing very nicely, the doctor said. At the moment, it just needs the dressings changed regularly, and some massage and exercises, and they can do that in any hospital. I honestly think he'd be better off *anywhere* other than where he is now. That Sister's taken against him so badly that—oh, I have to go! I'm at the station, you see. I'll ring you again later."

And she was gone before I had a chance to ask whether he was in really terrible trouble with the military. I suppose that's the least of our worries, but he *is* still an RAF officer and under military discipline—

Oh, bother, the warning siren's started up. Another reason Toby's better off out of London, now that the Luftwaffe is trying to bomb the city to bits again.

21st February 1944

Today I took the train down to East Grinstead to meet Rupert, and we went to visit Toby together. I'd been longing to see Rupert because I hadn't spent any time at all with him since Milford, but I was also feeling rather anxious about it. Not about Rupert and me, of course—he writes such wonderful, loving letters and I feel entirely secure and happy whenever I think of him, which is quite often. No, I was worried about how rude Toby was going to be to him. I could just see Toby being consumed with bitter envy at the sight of an unscarred young man strolling in without the aid of crutches, and then Toby being as nasty to Rupert as he's been to all his other visitors. Possibly he'd be *worse*, out of resentment that Rupert hadn't visited earlier—even though poor Rupert is frantically busy with his work right now and only managed a visit this afternoon because he had some meetings in the area. And he *has* been sending kind, supportive messages via me, all this time—not that Toby's said anything much when I've relayed them.

I don't even know how Toby feels about Rupert and me being together, although I *have* told him. I'm not sure he was paying attention at the time—or perhaps he thought the information inconsequential, given all his other concerns. He didn't even say anything when I told him that *Simon* had written. I'd become enraged at Simon's long silence and sent him a furious letter, berating him for not caring at all about Henry or Toby. But apparently, Simon had been moved to another place and he hadn't received any of our letters for months. I'm still not sure whether to believe that, but he did send his condolences about Henry and said he'd write directly to Toby. It's anyone's guess whether he *has*, but if he hasn't—or if he's written to announce he's engaged to some local nobleman's daughter—then I suppose that might be contributing to Toby's black mood.

Anyway, when Rupert picked me up at the station, he saw at once that I was worried, and asked if something had happened. He was already aware of Toby's medical condition from my letters, of course—and really, it's mostly been *encouraging* news since Toby was transferred to the Queen Victoria Hospital. The doctors took the bandages off Toby's eyes straightaway and replaced them with saline compresses, and said that when the swelling went down, he should be able to see as well as ever. He wouldn't even need to have new eyelids constructed, the way so many of the patients in his ward did. Then, last week, he had an operation on his neck to allow him to move it more freely, and had his first set of skin grafts done, and the surgeon said everything had gone very well.

"Of course, it must hurt terribly," I said to Rupert. "Not just his neck, but also where they took the skin graft, inside his good arm. Being in constant pain would make anyone fractious. And his other arm is burnt, so he can't use crutches at all. He's not even allowed to move his neck. If he wants to go anywhere, he has to ask someone to help him into a wheelchair, except mostly he refuses to talk to anyone. And when he *does* speak, it's generally to say something rude."

"Is he rude to you?" asked Rupert, frowning.

"Not actually *rude,* just sort of . . . cold and dismissive. But I know he's angry at me. I had to tell him about Henry, you see, and he blames me."

"That wasn't your fault," said Rupert. "It wasn't anyone's fault—except the Nazis'."

"I know, but you can understand why he's upset. And then he had the most enormous row with Veronica yesterday. He snapped at one of the nurses, and Veronica told him to apologize, and he wouldn't. He said he was sick of being treated like a child, and she said that was because he was *acting* like one and . . . Oh, you can probably imagine the rest."

Rupert sighed. "Your aunt hasn't been up to see him yet, has she?"

"No, which is probably a good thing, because she's not the most tactful person in the world. But *he* thinks she doesn't want to see him because he's all . . . because of the way he looks now. Which is true, I think. I mean, it *is* distressing to see him this way, and she still half-believes he's some kind of impostor. So you see what a mess it is. Anyway, I thought I should warn you that he might be in a horrible temper."

"Well, if he *is*," Rupert said calmly, "it won't be the first time we've had a row, and I'm sure it won't be the last."

He parked near the main entrance to the hospital, and I led him down the now very familiar path, through the foyer, and down the corridor to Toby's ward. I could tell from the doorway that Toby was having a bad day, because he was still in bed, rather than sitting in the chair by the window. He wasn't even reading—just glaring across the aisle at a patient who was surrounded by noisy relatives. Then Toby caught sight of us walking towards him, and all the unscarred bits of his face tightened.

"Hello," I said. "I've brought you a visitor."

"So you have," he said flatly.

"Hello, Toby," said Rupert, smiling at him. "It's very good to see you."

"Is it?" said Toby.

"Yes, it is," said Rupert, pulling up a chair. "Sophie, won't you sit down?"

"Actually, I think I'll leave you two to have a chat by yourselves," I said. "I'll just put your clean pajamas here in your locker, Toby. I brought two shirts as well, and a couple of books. Oh, and some chocolates."

I'd queued for half an hour and spent a small fortune on those chocolates, but he barely glanced at them.

"Well, then!" I said. "I'll be outside if you need me." Then I went back the way I'd come, stopping briefly at the nurses' station.

"He's in a right mood today," observed Sister Connor.

"I noticed," I said glumly. "His best friend from school has come to see him, but one would think I'd brought along his mortal enemy from the looks he was shooting both of us."

"Ah well," she said comfortably, "if I hear any explosions, I'll go in and toss a bucket of water over him."

I smiled at her. "Thanks. Oh, and I brought you and Sister Patrick something." I handed over my second paper bag.

"Chocolate! Goodness me, we *are* spoiled!"

But I thought they deserved a lot more than chocolate for putting up with my brother's behavior, let alone having to deal with the dressings and bedpans and everything else. I bet they don't even get paid very much.

It was too cold and blustery to go for a walk outside, so I sat in the waiting room and read the newspaper I'd bought. Poor Billy Hartington had lost his by-election by five thousand votes. "A landslide victory for the common man and the Welfare State," the newspaper trumpeted. Then I turned the page and read about the United States embargo on oil exports to Spain. Apparently, the Americans had finally got sick of selling petrol to Spain only to have Spain ship it straight to France, whereupon the Nazis would use it to fuel the planes that shot down American bombers. Even the British Ambassador to Spain had made a formal protest to Franco last month, Veronica had told me. That was why she'd been so busy at work lately.

At that point, Rupert walked in and slumped down beside me.

"Are you all right?" I asked anxiously. "What happened?"

"Oh . . . you know," he said. He tilted his head back against the wall and closed his eyes. It had just occurred to me that an apparently healthy young man in civilian clothes might not be very welcome in a ward full of badly injured servicemen, but when I asked, he said no, there hadn't been any rude remarks about shirkers or conchies. In fact, it seemed the other men had been quite sympathetic because Rupert had shown such forbearance with Toby. Rupert gave me a brief account of their conversation (it was pretty much as I'd feared), but then he smiled.

"Do you know what I was reminded of?" he said. "Years ago, a cat of ours got caught up in a bale of wire. It was the barn cat, and he was more wild than tame. It took me half an hour to free him, because he kept thrashing about and getting even more tangled up. He had a few cuts—nothing major, but they must have hurt—and the poor thing was terrified, especially when I had to get out the wire cutters. They must have sounded so frightening. Anyway, I eventually cut him loose, set him down on the ground, and stood back. It took a few seconds for him to realize he *was* free. He looked at me, looked around the barn, took a few steps away—then he leapt up at me and clawed three long gouges down my arm before dashing off."

"Oh, Rupert!" I said. "Poor you!"

"They were only scratches. But the thing is, when animals are hurt and frightened, they lash out at whoever's closest."

"Toby isn't an animal, though," I said. "He's a human being."

"Well, we're all animals, really—just with a veneer of civilization. And who knows what barbaric experiences Toby's had over the past few years? Any one of them might have been enough to strip off the veneer." Rupert frowned at the floor a moment, then said, "Has he talked about any of that yet?"

I shook my head. "Not a word," I said, "and it's only because he's just had surgery that military intelligence aren't pressing him harder on that issue. Although it *did* help that the Colonel personally vouched for him. And it must be pretty obvious by now that Toby isn't a Nazi agent. If he *is*, he's doing a pretty bad job of it, drawing all this attention to himself by refusing to cooperate."

"Yes, I think they'll soon give up on trying to question him. But it'd be good for Toby to talk about it, and not simply because it's better to talk about traumatic experiences than suppress them. I know this sounds silly, but . . . well, he's acting as though he feels *guilty* about something. It might help if he could confess."

I stared at Rupert. "What on earth would he feel *guilty* about? Crashing his plane? Not finding his way back sooner?"

"I don't know," said Rupert unhappily. "I just know that he's acting the way he used to act at school when he'd done something he was ashamed of."

I thought about this for a moment. I could see what Rupert meant. "But we can't make him talk when he doesn't want to."

"No, not now. But with a bit of time, with someone he trusts . . ."

"He does get on all right with Julia," I said. "Mostly."

"I was thinking of you," said Rupert. "You're the one he's always confided in." Then he looked at his watch. "Oh. I'm really sorry, Sophie, but I'll need to leave soon."

I went to say goodbye to Toby, who was pretending to be asleep, then Rupert drove me to the railway station. He told me he'd probably be in London next week, and that he'd telephone as soon as he knew for certain.

"I wish we could see more of each other," he said after we'd kissed goodbye. "I wish I could be in London with you all the time. But work is just so hectic."

"Will it become quieter after the Second Front starts?"

"Busier, actually, at least for a month or two," he said. "After that . . . well, who knows? Perhaps the war will be over by then."

"Let's hope so." I leaned through the car window to give him another kiss, then reluctantly pulled away. "Go on. You'll be late for your meeting."

"I do love you," he said, with his sweet smile, and then he drove off.

He loves me! It still makes my heart leap when he says that. Somehow it makes all the horrible things going on so much easier to bear.

2nd March 1944

Toby's stump has now healed enough that the doctors think he can be fitted for his artificial leg. There was some talk of moving him to Queen Mary's Hospital at Roehampton, because that's where most amputees go and they have an artificial limb factory on site. But Queen Mary's has just been bombed again, so another hospital needed to be found, somewhere that had staff with the appropriate skills *and* was out of range of the Luftwaffe bombers. Of course, this search took a while. It wasn't till yesterday morning that Veronica and I received the official notification of his transfer from the Queen Victoria Hospital. We stared at the name of the new hospital, looked at each other, then said as one, "*Julia.*"

Bless her, she'd used all her contacts and influence to ensure he'd be sent to the Milford Park Rehabilitation Hospital. I hadn't even *realized* it specialized in helping servicemen who'd lost limbs, although I probably ought to have, given all the figures I'd glimpsed on crutches or being wheeled along the terrace over the years. Anyway, Veronica and I decided that I'd travel down to Milford this morning, and then, if it looked as though Toby was going to be there awhile, Veronica would try to arrange some time off work so she could join us.

I caught the early train, and Mr. Wilkin met me at the railway station, as he'd brought a load of pigs into town to sell. (Not Estella, of course, because everyone has a soft spot for her. Mr. Wilkin reported she was still going strong, bossing everyone about at the Home Farm and periodically producing enormous litters of piglets.) By ten o'clock, he'd dropped me off at the gatehouse, where I found Aunt Charlotte in an agitated state, pacing about the sitting room.

"I saw an ambulance arrive yesterday as I was walking back from the stables," she said. "I don't suppose one of *those* men could have been Tobias? The matron did telephone here early this morning—Barnes took the call—to say he'd arrived. But one wouldn't be expected to visit *immediately*, would one? He'd need time to settle in, wouldn't he?"

"Well, why don't we walk over now and see?" I suggested.

"Now?" Aunt Charlotte said uneasily. "Oh, but surely they have official visiting hours and so forth? One wouldn't want to disturb their . . . their therapies and so on."

"I'll just go and ask, shall I?" I said. "You can stay here."

"No, no, I ought to accompany you," she said. "Yes. I'll go with you. Barnes, where's my coat? No, not *that* one. My good coat!"

The mink looked rather odd worn over her battered old

jersey, jodhpurs, and riding boots, but I didn't mention this. There were more important things to discuss—specifically, Toby's current condition. To me, his improvement over the past six weeks had been miraculous, but I quite understood that his appearance (and probable mood) would be a shock to her, and I tried to explain this as best I could. However, I was also thinking of one of Rupert's recent letters, in which he'd pointed out that I wasn't responsible for the feelings of other people. Aunt Charlotte (or Toby) might feel sad or angry or frightened, but there wasn't much *I* could do to stop them feeling that— however difficult it might be for me to observe it.

But Aunt Charlotte didn't pay attention to anything I said, anyway. I might as well have saved my breath for trying to keep up with her as she strode along the driveway. Having finally made the decision to visit Toby, she was determined that it should happen at once, if not sooner. She bounded up the front steps of the hospital and flung open the doors—whereupon she came to a horrified halt. I suppose she hadn't been inside her own house since the hospital had moved in, and it can't have been pleasant to see dented metal filing cabinets and WHAT TO DO IN CASE OF FIRE posters taking the place of her beautiful marble statues and gilt-framed Rembrandts.

"Dreadful," she muttered, staring about the hall. "This is absolutely *dreadful*." She shook her head, then drew herself up. "Wait here, Sophia," she ordered. "I'm going to find the doctor in charge!"

And before I could stop her, she'd marched off. I just hoped she'd remember why we were *there*. I wandered past the empty reception area, then peered down a corridor towards what had once been the Velvet Drawing Room, wondering where Toby's ward might be.

"Well, well," said a voice behind me. "If it isn't the Angel Thief."

I whirled about. "What?" I said. "Oh—it's *you*." It was the man I'd seen on my last—my only—visit to the hospital, the patient who'd caught me sneaking out with our Christmas tree decoration.

"Me again," he agreed.

"You're looking well," I said, quite sincerely. His scars weren't anywhere near as livid as they had been, he'd acquired a very realistic glass eye, and his mouth was turned up in a smile that looked almost normal. If I'd passed him on the street, I'd hardly have blinked—although perhaps that was just because I'd become accustomed to seeing men with far *worse* disfigurements. "But why are you still here, after all this time?" I asked. It must have been at least three years since I'd seen him, and he was still on crutches.

"Oh, I only arrived yesterday," he said. "I've been working in London, pushing papers at the War Office. But it wasn't enough for the Nazis to shoot my Spit down in flames, with me in it. Oh, no—they had to come back and drop a bloody great bomb on my house last week. Smashed my leg to bits. I suppose I ought to be grateful it was the fake leg I'd taken off for the night and not the real one. Anyway, I'm here to get a replacement fitted."

"Oh, right," I said. "Well, you might have arrived with my brother. He's here for the same thing—I mean, a new leg. Have you seen him? Squadron Leader Toby FitzOsborne?"

"Hmm. Haven't met anyone of that name, but a couple of men turned up a few hours after I got here. He might be one of them. They're in the ward beside the—"

"Sophia!" came an imperious cry behind me. "Sophia, have you—" Aunt Charlotte rounded the corner, then stopped and stared at my companion. "Is that . . . *That* isn't your brother?"

"No, no," I said quickly, because she'd gone so pale. "This is, um . . ."

"Pilot Officer Sam Jones." He began the effortful task of shifting one crutch so he could hold out his hand to shake, but she'd already stepped back.

"Yes, how do you do?" she said coldly. Then she turned to me and said, "Sophia, don't stand about *chatting*. Come along, I want you to see what they've done to my house. There is a *bathtub* sitting in the middle of my *dining room*!" And she stalked off in a swirl of mothball-scented mink.

I began to apologize to the pilot, but he just shook his head.

"Don't worry about it," he said. "My grandma went just as dotty in her old age. Used to think the postman was her long-dead brother, kept insisting there was a cat trapped inside her teapot, that sort of thing."

"No, you see—" Then I decided an explanation would take too much time. "Sorry, I'd better go and find her before she offends anyone else. Where did you say that ward was?"

Toby, when we eventually tracked him down, was almost too tired to talk, let alone snap at anyone. He'd spent most of the past six weeks in bed or propped up in chairs, so his first session with the physiotherapist had been exhausting and painful. He did tell us it would take two weeks before his new leg was ready, and that he'd need to practice using it after that, so he supposed he'd be at Milford till the end of the month. Then a nurse arrived to change his dressings and we left.

Poor Aunt Charlotte was terribly shaken. She'd said almost nothing to Toby—she'd found it difficult even to meet his eye. After we were outside again, walking past the fountain littered with cigarette butts and sweets wrappers, she stopped and looked back at the hospital.

"Oh, Sophia," she said. "What has *become* of us?"

She sounded so sad and bewildered that I wasn't sure whether she was thinking of Toby, or the house, or the world in general, but I tucked my arm in hers and after a while, I led her slowly back down the driveway, home to Barnes.

Toby has returned to the Queen Victoria Hospital for his next operation, so I've moved back to London for a few weeks. I can easily get down to visit him by train, and I'm taking the opportunity to give our flat a spring clean and cook Veronica some proper meals. She's become far too thin—I think she subsists on tea and toast when I'm not around. Anyway, I was scrubbing some potatoes early this evening when Kick burst in.

"Is Veronica home?" she asked.

"Not yet," I said, wiping my hands. "Why?"

"I need to ask her whether she thinks England will turn Socialist after the war."

I couldn't help laughing, despite (or possibly, due to) Kick's earnest expression. "What on earth—?" I said.

"Well," she sighed, pulling out a chair, "Billy says Socialism is inevitable now. He says there'll be massive taxes, and the government will take over all the industries, and families like his will have to give up their estates."

"Ah," I said, the fog lifting. "So, if the Devonshire dynasty is going to become redundant anyway—"

"Then we can bring up our children as Catholics," she said, nodding. "But if there's any chance he'll be the next Duke, he says our children will have to be Protestants." She propped her chin on her hand and sent me a despairing look. "You know how I wrote to Daddy? Asking if he could organize a special dispensation from the Church so I could marry Billy? Well, the archbishop said *no!* Can you believe it?"

The Kennedys think they can buy anything—and with their money, they generally can. Just not this time.

"Oh, I just don't know what to *do*, Sophie!" wailed Kick. "I *love* Billy. I want to spend the rest of my life with him! And his mother's being *so* sweet to me. But *my* mother would never forgive me if I left the Catholic Church. She keeps telling me I'd be living in mortal sin."

Mrs. Kennedy has a distinctly flexible attitude towards reality. Kick's brother Joe is currently having an affair with a woman whose husband's off fighting overseas—*and* she was divorced before this marriage, *and* she's a Protestant. And Jack's just as bad as Joe, chasing after anything in a skirt. But does Mrs. Kennedy ever say a word about *their* immortal souls, let alone that of her philandering husband?

"Of course," Kick went on, "there *was* that one priest who

said it *wouldn't* be mortal sin, because I wouldn't be marrying Billy out of selfishness, I'd be doing it for love."

"Well, he's right," I said. "I'm glad someone in your Church is showing a bit of compassion and good sense."

"And Billy could get shipped out any day now, couldn't he?" she said. Poor Billy had been so stung by the accusations of cowardice leveled at him during the election campaign that he'd gone straight back into his regiment after the results were announced. "He'll be off fighting in France soon, and—oh, how *could* I be so selfish as to refuse him anything?"

She jumped up, determination written all over her freckled face.

"Thanks, Sophie, you've been a great help," she said. She gave me a hug, rushed towards the door, then came to a sudden halt. "Oh," she cried, "but I haven't even *asked* how Toby's doing!"

"He's making progress, thanks," I said. "Much less frustrated now that he can walk about and do things for himself. I'm sure he'll feel even more positive once this next set of skin grafts is done."

"Well, I've been saying a novena for him," Kick said, "to the Little Flower." Then she bounced off.

I stared after her, astounded—and a little awed—at how deeply embedded her faith was. No wonder the poor girl has been feeling torn in two over Billy. But even *more* astounding was our next visitor, who turned up five minutes after Veronica arrived home from work.

"Sorry, I know this is a bad time to drop in," Julia said, "but I've just come from the hospital."

"Is Toby all right?" Veronica asked sharply, letting a plate clatter onto the table.

"Oh, yes! Yes, he's fine. But I needed to talk to you about . . . well, about him, really."

"Sit down," I said. "Dinner won't be long."

"No, I can't stay," she said, but she obediently took a seat. "You see, I'd been thinking about where Toby could go after his operation. Did you know there's been another strepto-coccus outbreak in that awful Ward Three? Imagine if he got an infection—it would set him back *months*. I don't think he should stay in that hospital a minute longer than is absolutely necessary, once he's out of surgery."

"Yes, Sister Connor mentioned an RAF convalescent home that's not far away," I said. "But Toby didn't sound very keen on the idea."

"Well, he's sick of living with dozens of men. Never any peace and quiet, no privacy. I don't blame him. So I talked to a friend of mine who owns a cottage near East Grinstead. The tenants have just left and he said we could have it. It's tiny, but there aren't any stairs for Toby to have to manage and there's a lovely little garden. It's right on the bus route, too."

"I suppose *I* could go down and look after him," I said slowly. "At least, I could cook and clean and so on. I wouldn't be much good at changing his dressings, though. I know it's

449

weak-minded of me, but I still feel a bit faint whenever I see blood. And I'm not trained in first aid—I'd be so afraid of doing the wrong thing and hurting him."

"We could hire a nurse—" Veronica began, but Julia interrupted.

"Oh, no, I meant *I* could move in with him. I could do all the dressings and help with his exercises, and then I'd just have to take him in to the hospital when he has his doctor's appointments."

"But what about your job?" I said. "You can't take that much leave from the ambulance station."

"Well . . . I've handed in my notice," she said, avoiding our gaze and twisting the rings on her fingers in a very uncharacteristic display of nervousness.

"You've *resigned?*" Veronica said. "But Julia, if you leave the ambulance station, you'll get called up!"

"No, I won't," she said. "Not if I get married."

We stared at her.

"Oh dear!" she said, with a shaky laugh. "I feel like a young gentleman asking his sweetheart's father for her hand in marriage. But I did want to make sure you were all right with it and . . . well, there's your aunt to consider."

"Toby?" said Veronica. "You can't be serious. *He* can't be serious! How can he *possibly* have asked you to—"

"Actually, *I* did the asking. This time." She shot me a look, too quickly for Veronica to catch. "But he agreed with me. He always *did* plan to get married, eventually. And it makes sense to do it now—otherwise people will fuss about us living to-gether at the cottage—and it'll be easier for me to look after him properly if I'm his wife."

Veronica turned to me in mute consternation.

"Julia," I said, picking my words with care. "That all sounds very . . . sensible. But *marriage* is . . . I mean, what about love?"

"But I *do* love him," she cried, "and he loves *me*, in his own way. We're friends, really dear friends, we have been for years and years. And I'm tired of being alone all the time and, and . . . he *needs* me!"

Then the tears sparkling in her eyes spilled over, and I rushed over to put my arms round her.

"Sorry," she said after a minute, wiping her eyes. "I really am happy about it. I wish you could be, too."

"Well, we are," I said uncertainly, with a glance at Veron-ica. "We're just a bit surprised, that's all. Didn't you say you wanted children, after the war is over?"

"I do," she said at once, "and there's no reason why we can't have them! It's not as though he's had some terrible spinal in-jury. He wants children, too, he told me. And I thought *that* might make your aunt feel a bit happier about it. I know she dislikes me, but . . . do you think she'll try to stop us going ahead with it?"

"I don't see how she could. You're both of age, and you're both of sound mind," said Veronica (although her tone sug-gested she had some doubts about the latter).

"She *could* make things difficult, though," sighed Julia,

"with money and so on. And Toby doesn't need any more difficulties in his life right now."

"I honestly don't think she *will* object," I said. "She might grumble a bit at first, but I imagine she'll be very pleased he's getting married at all. That's part of why she's been so upset about him—she thought the family name was going to die out."

What she'd actually said to me at Milford last month was, "Oh, Sophia, *why* didn't he take my advice and get married before the war? When he was handsome and charming and *whole*? What girl will want to marry him now that he's so changed—now that he looks so *frightful*?" But, of course, I wasn't going to repeat that remark to Julia, or to anyone else.

"Besides, Aunt Charlotte *doesn't* dislike you," I told Julia firmly. "She's very fond of your family. You have a title and money, so she can't *help* but approve of you. And you've been so kind to Toby—to all of us—for so long. She ought to be *glad* to have you as part of the family."

"Oh, thank you, Sophie!" Julia said, smiling for the first time that evening. She looked astonishingly pretty—and very young. I tried to remember how old she actually *was*. About twenty-eight, I calculated, a few years older than Toby and Rupert. "You really *have* put my mind at ease," Julia went on. "Toby will be relieved, too. But you mustn't take *my* word for all of this—you ought to go and talk to him tomorrow." Then she chattered on for a few minutes about how long it might take to organize a registry office wedding and whether she'd be able to persuade her London housekeeper to come down to the cottage a couple of days a week. Then she had to dash off to have dinner with her father, who'd come into town to see his solicitor. "Wish me luck!" she said.

I rescued my slightly burnt shepherd's pie from the oven, and Veronica and I sat down to dinner.

"Well," said Veronica, after we'd silently pushed food around our plates for a while, "it's really only been *recently* that marriage has been connected with romance. Historically, it was all about alliances between families—everything to do with mutual advantage, and nothing at all with love."

"I just hope Julia isn't being all self-sacrificial because she wants to atone for Anthony in some way," I said. "Although . . . no, I really believe she cares for Toby. And they *do* get on awfully well with each other. And oh, I nearly forgot! She'll be a *queen* now, won't she?"

"For what that's worth," said Veronica, starting to laugh, "when Britain is overrun by Socialists."

"It's amazing, isn't it?" I said, shaking my head. "First Kick and Billy, and now these two."

"An epidemic of engagements," said Veronica. "I know *I'm* impervious to the disease—but I'm not certain about *you*." And she gave me a mock-stern look.

"Oh, I think I'm safe for a *little* while," I said, with a smile. "At least until the war's over."

A tale of two weddings. First was Toby and Julia's at Chelsea Town Hall. Toby looked very distinguished in his RAF dress uniform with all his medals, and Julia looked lovely in pale blue silk. A friend in the Air Transport Auxiliary had given her a torn parachute, and she'd dyed it and had it made up by a dressmaker to copy one of her old Paris frocks. She also wore a pillbox hat with spotted veil, white gloves, silk stockings, and indigo shoes (Veronica and I had given her all our clothing coupons as a wedding present), and she carried a posy of violets that her mother brought up from Astley. The formalities, presided over by a lugubrious clerk with an eye patch, were over in ten minutes, and then we all went to Claridge's for a five-shilling luncheon. Neither Rupert nor Daphne had been able to get time off work, so the wedding guests were just Julia's parents, Aunt Charlotte, Veronica, and me.

It was a rather strained meal. Lord Astley was his usual gruff self, Lady Astley seemed sad and subdued, and Aunt Charlotte was still feeling affronted by the shabbiness of the registry office and the "insolence" of the clerk (he'd referred to her at one stage as "Mrs. FitzOsborne"). Toby responded politely whenever anyone spoke to him, but was otherwise silent. He'd insisted on leaving his walking stick in the car, and I suspected his leg was starting to hurt. He also seemed uncomfortable being surrounded by so many people. He'd spent most of the past four months in hospital, with only an occasional visit to East Grinstead (where, of course, everybody is quite accustomed to seeing men with severe burns). Here in London, strangers stared, or averted their gaze, or muttered behind their hands to their companions. One woman regarded him with undisguised revulsion, then hustled away her small child. I wanted to run after her and slap her stupid face. How *dare* she! For all *she* knew, Toby had shot down a Luftwaffe bomber aiming for her house! If it weren't for him and hundreds of men like him, we could all be living under Nazi rule by now! I don't think Toby saw that particular woman, but he couldn't have missed all the others. For most of the meal, he looked as though he were trying to shrink back inside his skin, like a snail whose shell had been wrenched off, and he gave Julia a grateful smile when she said, "Darling, we really ought to be getting back now. You've an appointment with the physiotherapist at three."

"That," said Aunt Charlotte after we'd waved off Julia and Toby, and then Lord and Lady Astley, "was the most dismal wedding I've ever attended. I still don't understand why they couldn't at least have had it in a *church*."

"It would have taken longer to organize," I said, "and it's not as though either of them is religious."

"Religion has nothing to do with it," Aunt Charlotte said. "It's about respect for tradition. Julia did it all properly for her *first* wedding."

"At least no one got shot at this one," said Veronica.

"Yes, yes," said Aunt Charlotte distractedly. "It's all been so *sudden*, that's the problem. If only they'd had a longer engagement, then perhaps one might have been able to—oh!" She glanced about, then lowered her voice till it was nearly inaudible. "Julia isn't . . . That is, she's not in a *delicate condition*, is she?"

Veronica gave Aunt Charlotte an incredulous look, then said she had to be getting back to work.

"Well, I wouldn't mind if Julia *were*," Aunt Charlotte said to me later. "I'm sure they'll have very attractive children. After all, Tobias *used* to be a very handsome young man."

Then, just as I was about to snap at her, she added, "Oh, but Sophia, how I *wish* your dear sister could have been here to see this! She was always so fond of Julia. She would have been delighted by the entire thing—even that horrible little man at the town hall."

So I couldn't feel cross at Aunt Charlotte then.

The following week was Kick and Billy's equally sudden wedding, held only two days after their engagement notice appeared in *The Times*. They'd hoped to avoid publicity, but no such luck. All the newspapers, here and in America, went wild—and that was nothing compared to the reaction of Kick's parents after she told them of her decision. They'd bombarded her with letters and telephone calls and telegrams, alternately cajoling and threatening—but Kick refused to budge. I didn't go to the actual wedding (another registry office affair), but Veronica and I attended the reception in Eaton Square. Kick looked radiant in pink and kept exclaiming, "I couldn't be happier!" Billy seemed pleased, but rather overwhelmed by the hordes—Kick had invited all the Red Cross girls and GIs from her club, plus apparently everyone she'd ever met in England. However, the only member of her family in attendance was her brother Joe. I've never really liked him, but I have to admit he's been absolutely wonderful these past few months. He assured Kick that he'd stand by her, whatever she decided, and he did. When we saw him at the reception, he told us he'd grinned like mad at the newspaper photographers outside the town hall, "because they were going to snap away no matter what, so I figured I might as well look like I was having fun. My name's ruined in Boston now, anyway!" He was very funny about it. Then he went and fetched us a piece of wedding cake, and it was *real chocolate cake*. I hadn't tasted anything like it for years. There was champagne as well, and some beautiful speeches, and then Kick came over and showed me what Billy had had inscribed on her wedding ring: *I love you more than anything in the world.*

Oh, I nearly cried! Even though weddings are such happy occasions, they can be a bit sad, too, for the people not getting married. When I arrived home, I felt quite flat. Veronica had gone off to the Foreign Office to catch up with some work, which made me feel even more useless. What was I *doing* here in London? I didn't have a paid job anymore, and I wasn't really needed to help Toby. Julia had found someone to come in four days a week for the housework, and said that she was teaching herself to cook out of *Mrs. Beeton*. She also told me I was welcome to stay with them whenever I liked, but their cottage is tiny—only two bedrooms, each about the size of a shoe box—and it's even more crowded now that Aunt Charlotte's sent over all Toby's books and gramophone records and so on from Milford. I know Julia and Toby aren't exactly typical newlyweds, but I'd still feel in the way. I really ought to go back to Milford to help Barnes and Aunt Charlotte, but I confess, I keep putting it off. It's mostly because if I were there, I'd never see Rupert at all. He spends most of his time traveling up and down the coast, but has the occasional meeting at Whitehall, and on those days, he can sometimes get away for an hour or two, after a bit of complicated rearranging of his schedule.

That's what happened today. We had luncheon at a little restaurant near Piccadilly, and then he came back to the flat. I dragged him onto the sofa (somehow, the sitting room seemed more respectable than my bedroom, even though we were what Aunt Charlotte would have called "completely unchaperoned") and there was kissing. If truth be told, there was quite a bit *more* than kissing, although no actual clothes were shed. It's a good thing Rupert's such a gentleman, because there were moments when I felt really bold and reckless. At one stage, Rupert grabbed my hand, which had wandered a fair way, and gasped, "Have you done this before?" And I snatched my hand back and turned scarlet and mumbled, "Sort of." I felt absolutely *mortified*, but he just said, "Oh, thank God one of us knows what to do," and put my hand back where it'd been. Soon after that, though, he had to leave, because he needed to be in Portsmouth by four o'clock. Which I suppose was all for the best—for the sake of his virtue, and whatever's left of mine.

Oh, I am so *lucky* to have found him! It's true that things are a bit complicated because we hardly ever have any time together at the moment. But then, *life* is complicated—and at least being in love with Rupert is an *enjoyable* complication.

16th May 1944

Julia caught the train up to London yesterday morning to have her hair cut and make sure her house hadn't been demolished by bombs in her absence. Then she came over to the flat so I could show her how to make a Spanish omelet out of dried eggs.

"Hmm, I see," she said, studying my every move as though I were a Cordon Bleu chef demonstrating how to debone a quail. "Yes—I believe I've got it now."

"The most important thing is to remember to hold your breath when you open the tin of eggs, because they smell absolutely disgusting," I said. "But they don't taste too bad, as long as you mix them properly. Next time, I'll show you how to do scrambled eggs."

"That would be lovely," she said as we sat down to our luncheon of Spanish omelet and salad. "One would think that reading the recipes ought to be enough, but the problem is, they're written for people who already *know* how to cook. Still, it keeps Toby amused, watching me floundering about the kitchen. And then he gets to guess what his dinner is supposed to *be*, which is even more entertaining."

"I'm sure you're not that bad," I said, "and he's perfectly capable of making a sandwich if he doesn't like it."

"Oh, he never *complains*," she said. "And you know, he's much tidier than I am, and awfully good at washing up and things like that. And then dear old Mrs. Bunn comes in to help with the cleaning and do the laundry, so there really isn't all that much I have to do except cook . . . well, *learn* to cook. Toby's far busier than I am, actually—appointments at the hospital at least twice a week, and exercises to do at home, and he tries to go for a walk each day. He was even talking about digging up the garden beds and planting some vegetables, although there's not much point unless we're going to be there to pick them."

"Won't you be?"

"Well, the doctors say he'll probably only need one more set of skin grafts on his arm. Once they've decided they've done as much as they can, he'll get his medical discharge from the RAF. Then we can come back to London. Or go to Milford, or Astley, or wherever he wants—I don't mind."

"Has he talked about that? About his plans for the future?"

"Oh . . . not exactly. I mean, it's hard for anyone to plan *anything*, really, when this ghastly war just keeps going on and on. I know the Second Front is supposed to start any minute now, but who knows how long the fighting will go on after that."

"Does he talk at *all*?"

"Oh, yes! Yes, we chat about the books we're reading, and what's in the newspapers, and Mrs. Bunn always has some scandalous bit of village gossip to tell us . . ." Julia trailed off, then glanced over at me. "Actually, I wanted to discuss that with you."

She put down her fork.

"He *does* talk, but not about anything important—not about how he feels or about what happened to him. And I can understand why he wouldn't want to think about that, but Sophie, it's *festering* inside him. He has the most awful nightmares—talks in his sleep, wakes up screaming, the lot. I'm afraid he's going to start sleepwalking and really hurt himself. It's not as bad when he takes sleeping pills, but it can't be healthy to take as many as he does. I really believe he needs to have a good long talk to someone. Not me, it's obvious he won't talk to *me*. He sometimes gets these notions that he's a burden—which is utterly ridiculous, I keep telling him that—so I think he'd feel reluctant to off load anything *else* upon me. But he's always trusted *you*, Sophie. And he could tell *you* things, even horrible things, because you aren't living with him all the time. You wouldn't be constantly around afterwards to . . . to *judge* him, or whatever it is that he's worried about."

I was reminded of Rupert saying Toby needed to "confess."

"Of course I'd be willing to listen to him," I said. "But I don't think he *wants* to talk to me—or anyone else, for that matter. And we can't force him to speak."

"Ah, but I've got a plan!" said Julia eagerly. "You come

down and tell him the Colonel desperately needs an account of what happened. Make up some reason—the Colonel's trying to prove a certain group in Belgium is working for the Resistance or something. Tell Toby you'll write everything down in that secret code of yours, and no one but you and the Colonel will ever know who said it."

"You want me to *lie?*" I said. "To my own brother?"

"It won't be a lie if you *do* send it to the Colonel! He'll back you up, you know he will. And you don't have to tell me or anyone else any of the details. You can burn your notes afterwards if you want—although you'd be the only person who could possibly read them. The important thing is that Toby gets an excuse to talk about the whole thing."

"I don't know," I said uneasily. Apart from the dubious morality of lying to someone for their own good, I wasn't certain it *would* make Toby feel better. "I mean, even if he *were* to confide in me . . . I don't think he's ever going to revert to the cheerful, carefree boy we used to know."

"Oh, I'm not expecting the old Toby to return," she said. "I'm not even sure I want that person back—" She caught my look. "And no, it's *not* because I like having him all helpless and dependent on me. What I meant was that he used to be a beautiful, funny, self-centered *child*—well, I wasn't much different—and now he's grown up. I keep catching glimpses of how he might have turned out if he hadn't been tangled up in this horrible war. He still has a sense of humor, and he's far more perceptive and considerate than he might have been otherwise.

He has the potential to be such an interesting, compassionate man. But he's been so terribly wounded, inside and out, and it's only his outside scars that anyone's tried to fix. Not that he'd *ever* consent to seeing a psychiatrist or someone like that—"

"No, he wouldn't," I agreed.

"But he might speak to you," said Julia. "Please just think about it, Sophie. Even if all it might do is give him a decent night's sleep, it's worth trying."

She left that piteous note to reverberate around the kitchen for a minute, then changed the subject. Of course, after she left, I could think of nothing else but Toby. Still, I wasn't at all sure I could persuade him to cooperate. He'd seemed so angry at me for so long, and if he found out I'd deceived him in this, he might never forgive me.

On the other hand, was there really any danger of being discovered? Julia would never tell. And I *did* have a reputation within the family (not entirely deserved) for being scrupulously honest in all the little things in life, which made it easier for me to get away with the occasional whopping lie. And of course, I'd do anything to help Toby . . .

So this morning, I came down here to the cottage and told my carefully planned story to Toby—and he believed me. The weather has been lovely, so we sat out in the garden, I with my shorthand notebook, he in a wicker armchair, under a flowering cherry that kept shaking its incongruous pink confetti across my pages. I'd deliberately made the Colonel's "request" vague, telling Toby to say anything he could remember, no matter how trivial, in any sequence he liked. But he seemed to find it easiest to start at the very beginning and go on in chronological order from there—in fact, after the first few halting sentences, the words began to pour out and he seemed to forget all about the Colonel. Apart from occasionally asking him to slow down, I didn't interrupt, so the following is entirely Toby's story, in his own words.

Toby's Account of Events from May 1942 to January 1944; transcribed 16th May 1944

I don't suppose the Colonel needs to know much about the plane? There wasn't anything wrong with my Spit. It was just me. I was too slow. We were over Belgium, nearing the Channel, when a couple of Messerschmitts caught up with us. There was a tremendous bang and suddenly I was covered in glycol—that's what they use to cool the engine. All I could think about was getting out before the whole thing blew up. I shoved back the cockpit hood, rolled the plane over, and fell out. I'd never bailed out of a plane before, but I knew I wasn't meant to pull the rip cord of the parachute straightaway. I had to get clear of the planes—also, the longer I waited, the faster my drop would be, which would give me more time to hide on the ground before the German patrols arrived. I might have waited a bit *too* long, though. The chute opened with a horrible jolt, and what seemed like a few seconds later, I looked down and there were green fields looming up at me and then I hit the ground with an almighty thud.

I think I was knocked out for a minute or so. When I came to and rolled onto my hands and knees, I could see a boy running towards me across a field. I unhooked my parachute and started gathering it up, and he dashed around, helping me. He was about ten, a little freckled towhead—he reminded me of Henry. He kept saying "Deutscher" and pointing over at the road, and I heard dogs barking in the distance. The Germans were looking for me—for *us*, I suppose, because I knew at least one other plane in my squadron had been shot down. We hid the parachute under a hedge, and the boy tugged me away from the road, towards some houses on the other side of the field. But as soon as I put some weight on my right leg, I realized I'd done something to my ankle. Just sprained, I hoped, rather than broken—anyway, I found a stick and limped after the boy as fast as I could. We finally reached a little shed behind a farmhouse, and I sat down and took off my boot and my scarf and bandaged my ankle as tightly as I could. The boy ran off and came back with his older sister, who said the Germans were doing a house-to-house search, so I had to move. There was a ditch running alongside the shed, half full of stagnant water, and she told me to get into it and follow it till I reached the barn on the other side of the field, then hide in there. She thought that might throw the dogs off the scent.

So I climbed down into the ditch and crawled all the way to the barn, and buried myself in a pile of hay in there. My ankle wasn't looking too good by then and it hurt like hell, but then I remembered my brandy flask—you know, the one Henry gave me for my birthday. I'd been saving that brandy for an emergency, but I figured this qualified, so I drank the lot. Felt much better then. Just before it started to get dark, the boy arrived with an old shirt and some trousers, which was wonderful, because all my gear was wet through and reeked of ditchwater. He also said he'd found an RAF pilot lying dead outside the village, and showed me a silver charm and a letter he'd retrieved from the man's pocket. Well, I didn't need to read the letter—I recognized that four-leaf clover at once. God, poor old Alfie! He'd just got engaged, you know . . .

Anyway, the boy said the Germans had driven off with the body, and that someone from the Resistance would come and collect me soon, to take me to a safe house. He was such a brave little boy—and it was a stroke of luck his family spoke French. The next morning, I was picked up by a farmer in a pony cart. I'd landed somewhere near Zeebrugge, but I'm not sure which direction we traveled that day. I was starting to feel rather queasy. At the time, I thought it was all that brandy on an empty stomach, but it turned out I was coming down with something. Perhaps I'd swallowed some of the water in that ditch, or maybe it was sitting about for hours in wet clothes, I don't know. The pony cart took a long, meandering route to avoid the main roads, and by the time we got to the safe house, I was shivering too hard to talk. Which didn't exactly endear me to the poor people who lived there—they might have wanted to resist the Nazi occupation, but that didn't mean they were willing to nurse some stranger through a bout of typhoid, or whatever I might turn out to have. They had a noisy argument about it in Flemish, while I sat in the attic, throwing up into a bucket. In the end, they decided to move me on.

I don't even know how we got to the next house, but I woke up in a cellar. I had a fever and couldn't keep any food down. At one stage, a nurse came and gave me some medicine and strapped up my ankle. I think I was there a week, and then I was moved again. By then I could eat, and sit up, and must have been showing some signs of intelligent life. A man from the Belgian Resistance came and asked me some questions— who I was, which squadron I was from, that sort of thing. He said they'd have to wait till I could walk properly before moving me along their escape line to France. I gave him my watch to sell, because I was feeling pretty bad about these people having to look after me for so long. That was the only thing I had left. I'd given my silver flask to the boy who'd found me, and of course, my uniform had been taken away and destroyed. I remember thinking I'd be in real trouble if I got picked up by the Nazis. They're supposed to treat any Allied servicemen they find as prisoners of war, but they just shoot any locals they don't like . . .

Well. I'd lost track of the date—it was June by then, I think—but I got moved again, to a farm outside Bruges. The stables had a hiding place under the floorboards, just big enough for a man to lie down in, but mostly I stayed in one of the stalls. The Germans had taken away all the horses. I practiced walking up and down with a stick and I started to think I'd be on my way home soon. The Resistance people didn't tell me any details of their plans and I never knew anyone's real name— thank God—but I guessed this family was an important part of the escape line. There was a middle-aged man who'd been wounded in the last war, and two young women who I think were his daughters—one of them had a baby—and a nice old grandmother who brought me my food each morning.

I don't know how it happened. Perhaps some neighbor had a grudge against them and turned informer. Anyway, the Germans came. One morning I heard some cars drive up, so I grabbed my water bottle and my empty plate and dived into the hiding place. I'd just pulled the cover over myself when someone ran into the stables. I could hear scuffling noises, as though they were kicking straw over the floorboards on top of me. Then they ran out, and there was a horrible long silence. I had no idea what was going on. After a while, I heard shouting—German, I thought, although it does sound a lot like Flemish—and a few minutes later, there were all these people stampeding overhead. I could hear a girl pleading and crying, and I thought, *I should give myself up. I'll climb out, say that these people didn't know anything, tell them I'd discovered this hiding place all by myself—then the Germans will leave them alone.* But how likely was it that the soldiers would believe that? Maybe they had only vague suspicions that this family was part of the Resistance; maybe if I revealed myself now, I'd simply be signing the family's death warrants. So I just lay there, paralyzed with indecision, soaked in sweat, with all this crashing going on above my head. They were pulling the stables apart, it sounded like. Then, all at once, it was over. They stomped away and not long afterwards, I heard the cars start up and drive off.

Well, I wasn't stupid. I didn't know how many cars there'd been. They could have left a soldier guarding the doorway, for all I knew. So I stayed where I was, for hours and hours. It was like being buried alive in a very narrow coffin—totally black, except for a thin line of light down one side of the lid, and that grew dimmer and dimmer. A couple of times I fell asleep, then woke with a jolt, not certain if I was awake or asleep, dead or alive . . .

I still have nightmares about that.

It was early the next morning, just as it was starting to get light again, that I heard footsteps, then someone prizing up the cover of my hiding place. I was so stiff by that stage that I couldn't have run away or fought them off if it had been the soldiers. But it was a man in those black robes that priests wear. He helped me out, then told me the Nazis had taken away the entire family, except the baby. No one knew where they'd gone or what was going to happen to them—whether they'd be shot or hanged, or imprisoned in Belgium, or sent off to a concentration camp in Germany. The Nazis never told anyone—friends or family or the Red Cross—what they did to the Resistance workers they caught. The poor people simply vanished.

I felt sick. So ashamed, so *guilty*. I realized I should have sat in that field with my parachute and waited for the German patrols to find me. When I thought of all the people who'd helped me so far . . . that little boy I'd put in danger . . . Well, I told the priest that he had to leave me alone now, and I'd walk as far as I could get from the farm and then turn myself in to the authorities.

He hit the roof. I didn't know a priest *could* swear like that. He said they were all doing their duty as patriotic Belgians, and that *my* duty was to get back to England so I could rejoin my squadron and bomb the hell out of the Nazis. Then he dragged me outside to his battered little car and shoved me into the front seat, and we'd driven off before I knew what was happening. I never did find out if he was a real priest, but he was certainly a saint. He drove me to the outskirts of Brussels and then I was bundled into the back of a van that looked like some sort of official city vehicle. We drove straight past the German sentries, right into the middle of the city, and I was left with an elderly lady, who took me up to her apartment. I stayed there a couple of days because they were waiting for two more Allied airmen. In the meantime, the Resistance people took my photograph and organized false identification papers for all of us. When everything was ready, we caught a train to Tournai and then walked into the countryside, and over the border into France.

Oh—I forgot to say that there was a new set of guides for each stage of the journey, and it took a whole day and half a night to travel the thirty miles from Brussels to the border. I was starting to think half the Belgian population was working for the Resistance, and they were all so dedicated and diligent—

but, of course, terribly anxious. And little things were always going wrong. For instance, we ended up leaving Brussels later than planned because one set of documents didn't look convincing enough. We had to keep changing trains, then getting out and walking for hours to avoid the German patrols. But eventually we got across the border in the middle of the night and were handed over to a young man waiting for us in the woods.

Of course, there was another snag then. There were supposed to be *two* people to take us to Lille, and then accompany us on the train to Paris. The new man—Jacques, he told us to call him—had an argument with the Belgian people. I couldn't follow all of it, but I think Jacques was meant to collect three more evaders when we got to Lille, and the Belgians thought that was too many for one man to handle. They said we were bound to attract attention, but Jacques insisted it wouldn't be a problem; he could do it. Then the Belgians said something about a difficulty with our French documents, but Jacques said, "No, no, *I* have them!" And he took away our Belgian papers and handed us French identity cards, work permits, and train tickets. "There won't be any problem," he kept saying. "When have I ever been stopped?" Then he said we had to leave right then or we'd miss our train. So off we went to Lille.

The train to Paris was packed, but Jacques kept a close eye on all six of us airmen. I tried not to look at him, but whenever I glanced in his direction, he'd nod, as if to say everything was fine. And the more he did this, the more uneasy I felt, but I just told myself that things must be different in France. Perhaps the French Resistance didn't *need* to worry as much as the Belgians. Jacques had obviously done this many times before—he looked very confident.

The trip took a few hours and when we reached Paris, we climbed down onto the platform and I realized we were at Gare du Nord. Well, *that* sent an icy shiver down my spine, I can tell you. I couldn't help remembering the last time I'd seen it—when you, me, Veronica, and Simon were on our way to Geneva with that German officer chasing us—and now the platform was crawling with uniformed Nazis, and probably a whole lot more of them in plain clothes. As we walked through the station, there was a sudden commotion to one side and I saw a Nazi soldier with a baton beating up a little Frenchman. Everyone else was stepping round them, as if it were a routine occurrence. It probably *was*. I was certain that at any second, it would all be up for us, but no, we walked straight out into the street and kept going. That seemed odd to me, too, because I was used to having a new guide for each stage of our journey. But Jacques whispered, "Follow me and keep close, but don't worry, everything is all right. We are going to the safe house."

We walked and walked until we came to a residential area, with narrow streets and rows of apartment buildings. We were in a loose line, spread out so as not to look too suspicious, and I was at the end. Then I saw Jacques stop outside a building and light a cigarette, and one by one, the others drifted through the front door. I was just about to follow when I glanced further along the street and saw a car parked around the corner, a big black Mercedes. I could only see the front of it, but the man in the passenger seat was tall and blond, sitting up all stiff and straight.

And then I heard a voice say, very distinctly, *Gebhardt*.

Well. I still don't know if it was *real*, whether someone in the car spoke out loud, or . . . or maybe I was just spooked from seeing Gare du Nord full of Nazis and that's why I remembered *you* saying that, Sophie, the way you did when you caught sight of him at Calais all those years ago. I don't even know if it *was* him. I barely got a glimpse of him that time in Calais. But the men in the car were Nazi officers, obviously—who else would be driving a fancy car in Paris? The question was: had they just happened to park near this safe house, or were they waiting for us? Jacques was giving me impatient looks by then, so I stepped into the foyer of the building—with him following close behind—but all the hairs on the back of my neck were standing on end. It simply didn't feel right. He was *too* confident. I tried to catch the eye of one of the other airmen, but they were already filing into the elevator after Jacques. So I edged backwards till they started to pull the gate across, then dashed off down the corridor, looking for the stairs. If I was wrong, no matter—I'd just say I got confused. But as I was closing the stairwell door behind me, I heard new voices in the foyer—*German* voices—and I peeked out and there were three Nazis, led by that tall blond one, walking in through the front door. So I ran down half a flight of stairs and out another door, into a little courtyard hung with damp laundry. I scrambled over the brick wall into the next yard and then over a gate into a side alley. I was still standing there, pressed against the wall in the shadows, catching my breath, wondering if I'd just made a complete idiot of myself for nothing, when I heard someone shouting in German. And then, at the far end of the alley, I saw two of the airmen being led off in handcuffs down the street.

That bloody Jacques was a double agent. No *wonder* he never had any problems getting official documents! I thought for one wild moment about trying to rescue those airmen, but I knew it was absolutely hopeless. So I sneaked off down the alley in the opposite direction, and once I was round the corner, I strode off as though I knew exactly where I was going. Of course, I had no *idea* what to do next. I might have been able to find my way back to Gare du Nord, but it was full of Nazis and I didn't have any money to buy a train ticket, and where could I have gone, anyway? I knew no one in France, and even if I'd had some way of contacting the Resistance, they might well think that *I'd* been the double agent.

So I kept walking, feeling more and more panic-stricken and lost, until I was nearly bowled over by a barrel of cider. A man had been unloading them from the back of his lorry and one had escaped. So I grabbed it and rolled it back up the hill, and helped the man with the rest of the barrels, which he was delivering to the back of a shop. He was cursing away, about how his useless brother-in-law was supposed to have come along to help him, and why couldn't that shopkeeper get up off his lazy backside and give him a hand, and so on. After we finished, we sat down to mop our faces and he said he couldn't wait to get out of this stinking hot city, where everyone—present company excepted—was so rude and unhelpful. All he wanted was to get back home to Beauvais, even though it was fifty miles and that stupid *gazogène* he'd installed on his lorry to burn charcoal for fuel would probably conk out halfway there.

So I said, "Ah, Beauvais! What a coincidence, I'm heading that way, too!"

And he snorted, because he'd obviously picked up my accent and knew I wasn't French, and said, "Oh, yes? What do you do there?"

I explained that I was a farmhand—which was what my fake work permit said—and that although I wasn't familiar with the locality, I'd been told I might find work there.

And he nodded slowly, looking me up and down, and said, "You might. Lots of market gardens and dairy farms. Best to stay out of the town itself, though, unless you know someone there—and you'd need work papers." So I showed him my documents and he suddenly jumped up and said, "Right, let's get going. But if we get stopped, I just picked you up on the side of the road, understand?"

He wasn't part of the Resistance—he just hated bureaucracy, whether it was the German or the French variety. He pretty much spent the entire journey complaining about rationing and regulations and red tape, and how the government was practically *forcing* him to sell his goods on the black market. He dropped me off just outside Beauvais, pointed out the best way to go, and warned me to avoid Compiègne in the east, because the Nazis had set up an internment camp there.

So there I was, somewhere in Picardy, starving, homeless, the sun starting to set—but at least I wasn't being interrogated by the Gestapo. So I began walking along the path, thankful it was summer and not the middle of winter. I passed some farms, but every time I steeled myself to approach someone, I'd lose my nerve at the last moment. I felt I'd already used up all my good luck that day. I spent the night in a barn, pinched some carrots out of someone's garden, drank from their well. The next day I kept walking. I had this mad plan I'd walk all the way to Spain, then get in touch with the British Embassy there. But I was already lost—I had no map, no compass—and my ankle was starting to hurt again. There was no way I'd make it all the way south without help. Still, the longer I wandered about like a tramp, the less likely it was that anyone would *want* to help me. I must have looked pretty disreputable even then, in my grubby old farmer's clothes.

So I decided I'd stop at the next farm and ask if I could work for them in exchange for room and board. The first farmer gave me some bread and cheese, but said I couldn't stay. The second just shook his head. The third set his dogs onto me, but I ran off and climbed a tree, and they lost interest pretty quickly. I climbed down and kept on walking, avoiding the main roads, and as it started to get dark, I came to this falling-down cottage. A woman was staggering across the yard with some buckets of milk, and she plonked them down in the dust and gaped at me while I delivered my little speech. She didn't say anything after I finished—I was beginning to wonder if she was a bit slow—so I just smiled and shrugged and was about to leave. But then I thought I might as well offer to help the poor woman carry the buckets into the house, because no one else seemed to be around, and she nodded. It wasn't a very big farm—one outbuilding, a few cows standing about a field, a vegetable garden. We went through the back door of the cottage and set the buckets on the floor, and she gave me a long look, then said, "Sit down, I'll bring you food."

While I was eating, she told me her husband and his brother were prisoners of war and had been sent to a labor camp in Germany. Her mother-in-law had lived with her, but had died a few months ago. The woman—Marie—kept two cows and a few chickens. She made cheese, and lived off the vegetables she could grow in her garden. I felt so sorry for her. She was twenty-three, but looked forty. I said, "Why don't I stay for a while? I could fix your roof and help with the gardening. If you grew more vegetables, you could trade them—maybe for a piglet or some ducklings." She frowned and nodded at everything I said, and I saw she wasn't actually *slow*—it was just that she'd always relied on others telling her what to do, and now she felt terribly lost and lonely.

So I stayed. At first I was very careful not to be seen in daylight, but there were never any visitors. The farm was too small and too far off the main road for the Germans to bother raiding it. The nearest neighbors had had some sort of feud with Marie's husband, so they mostly ignored her. She didn't seem to have any relatives of her own. She only saw other people when she walked into the village, about four miles away, to sell her cheese. She never received any letters from her husband, or anyone else. I felt depressed just *hearing* about her life, but she'd never known anything better. She was so pathetically grateful anytime I smiled at her, or paid her any compliments, or even *listened* to her that I figured her husband must have been a complete bastard. She didn't seem to miss him much, except as someone to run the farm. And after a while . . . well, she started to become fond of me.

And I didn't discourage her. Of all the awful things I did to save my skin during all that time, I think that was the worst—taking advantage of how simple and unworldly and lonely she was. I pretended I returned her feelings because that way, she wouldn't hand me in to the authorities. I *did* care about her—I felt awfully sorry for her—but I wasn't in love with her. She thought I was, but only because I *wanted* her to think that.

Anyway, it backfired on me. She didn't want me to leave. I hadn't told her much about myself, but she knew I wanted to get back to England. I'd said I'd stay till the end of summer. I figured that would give me enough time to make contact with the local Resistance people, or at least find a map and work out a plan to travel south. But she didn't seem to know anyone or anything. The furthest she'd ever traveled was to Beauvais. She didn't have any money, and there didn't seem any safe way I could earn some, so it would be impossible to buy train tickets—not that I'd get very far with my fake documents, especially if Jacques had told the authorities to look out for me. So I stayed on through autumn, still trying to figure out some scheme that might work. Then it was winter, too cold to travel. When spring arrived, we were so busy with the garden, then one of the cows got sick and . . . Oh, I don't know. I'd sort of lost track of who I was, what I was supposed to be doing. It was so isolated there. Marie didn't own a wireless or buy any newspapers—the news would have been censored by the Nazis anyway—so I had no idea what was going on with the war. I was just living from day to day, the way she always had.

Then one morning, late in spring, I was carrying the milk across the yard when a plane went overhead, one of ours. It shook me out of my trance. I marched into the kitchen and said to Marie, "This can't go on. You have to go into the village more often, go to church, talk to people. You have to find out who the local Resistance people are."

She stared at me, then threw down her dishcloth and shouted, "No! I won't! Because if I do, you'll end up leaving me!" And we argued about it for weeks. I'd say, "If you loved me, you'd want to help me!" and she'd say, "If you loved me, you wouldn't abandon me like this!" And I *did* feel awful for her, but I couldn't stay there forever. I didn't feel I could push it too hard, though, because if she got mad at me, she might just decide to hand me over to the police.

Finally, towards the end of July, she went off to the village with a basket of cheese to sell on market day. When she came back in the afternoon, she told me the name and address of a Resistance man in Beauvais, and then burst into tears. The horrible thing was that I didn't trust her anymore. I didn't know whether she was crying because I'd be leaving, or because she knew I'd be picked up by the Gestapo as soon as I knocked on that door. Maybe they were already on their way to the cottage. Even if she herself hadn't engineered it, I didn't know who'd given her that name, or how trustworthy that person might be. I managed to calm her down and said, "Look, don't worry about it now. We'll talk about it tomorrow."

Then, as soon as I was sure she was asleep that night, I sneaked out of the house. I didn't leave a note. I didn't want to leave behind anything that might get her into trouble if the Germans searched the place—or if her husband ever came back. It was a cloudless night, so I could see well enough and I knew how to get to Beauvais without going along any main roads. I stopped halfway there and slept for a few hours under a hedge, then reached the town in the middle of the day. I knew the street was somewhere near the cathedral, and *that* was easy enough to find, and then I wandered round for an hour or two till I spotted the house. I kept an eye on it for a while, but I didn't see anything out of the ordinary. I don't know what would have been a suspicious sign, anyway, other than Nazis marching in and out. Eventually, I thought, *Well, there's nowhere else for me to go. I don't have any other options.*

So I went round the back and knocked on the door, and

thank God, it turned out all right. The woman there asked me a few questions, then some boys arrived in a pony cart and took me off to a place in the country. I was there for weeks. Most of the leaders of that particular escape line had just been arrested by the Gestapo, so everything had ground to a halt. They suspected a traitor in their ranks—well, *I* could have told them that. I did, actually, I told them everything I could remember about Jacques. Then another man arrived to interrogate me. They were a lot tougher, a lot more systematic, than the Belgians had been the year before. They'd devised this questionnaire for British airmen, asking all sorts of things that only we'd know about how the RAF worked, but also trick questions about life in England—what was the cigarette ration, that sort of thing. When they were satisfied I wasn't a double agent, they moved me to a safe house in Rouen and organized a new identity card and work permit for me. It was more complicated this time, because anyone traveling in the border zone around Spain needed a special certificate of residence. That would take time to arrange, and it was already September. Then I was moved on a few more times. The Gestapo were really putting pressure on the Resistance, and meanwhile, lots of American aircrew were crashing in the occupied territories, so all the safe houses were stretched to their limits.

Finally, in November, five of us Allied airmen, plus some guides, started to move south—first to Paris, then we took a series of local trains to Bordeaux, then on to Dax, which is close to the Spanish border. They had bicycles waiting for us there at the railway station, and we cycled to Saint-Jean-de-Luz, the Americans whining all the way about how tired they were. I suppose you know the rest—the Basques who ran the hotel there knew Captain Zuleta, and he came down to meet me, to confirm that I was who I said I was. It was so bizarre seeing him—not just because I'd thought he was dead, but because he was from a place so far away, so far back in my past. A lifetime ago—*more* than one lifetime ago, it seemed. And then, as you know, there were all those delays before we could set off over the Pyrenees into Spain.

Well, that was an experience. Clouds blocking out any moonlight, icy sleet, ridiculously steep paths—I think those Basque guides must have had goat hooves instead of feet—mud and brambles and slippery rock for hours and hours. Then towards the end, when we were at our most exhausted, we had to wade across the river in which two people had drowned not long before. We eventually clambered up the bank on the other side and were picked up almost at once by Spanish soldiers. Thank God the guides escaped. If *they'd* been caught . . . I don't think I could have lived with any more guilt.

Luckily, that friend of Veronica's turned up at the prison not long after we arrived. I thought it would be all right then. I honestly thought I'd made it home. So when our ship got hit, I was *furious*. I remember the explosion, remember being tossed up into the air and smacking into the sea, except *it* was on fire, too—there was a slick of oil on top of the water and it seemed the whole world was ablaze—and the only thing in my mind was, *How dare you!* I don't know whether I meant the crew of that bloody U-boat that torpedoed us, or Hitler, or God, but I was as mad as hell. I just *refused* to die in such a pointless, stupid way after all those people in Belgium and France had risked their lives to save me. So I ducked down and dived as far as I could, until I ran out of breath. When I popped up, I smashed my head on a broken door floating past, but at least I was out of range of the flames, so I grabbed the door with one arm and hung on grimly. I could hardly see, my leg felt like it was broken, the burns were agony in the salt water, but when I heard voices, I screamed back and kept on screaming, and eventually, I got hauled into a lifeboat . . .

Well. You know what happened after that.

Those goddamned Nazis. I hope they get wiped off the face of the earth when this Second Front starts.

I stayed overnight at the cottage on Tuesday, because it was dusk by the time Toby finally fell silent. Julia, who'd been flitting about anxiously indoors all afternoon, darted out at the sound of our footsteps, ushered us into the kitchen, and tried to feed us some dinner. Neither Toby nor I ate much. Toby looked pale and haggard, as though I'd spent the afternoon draining him of blood instead of words. I, on the other hand, felt weighed down with emotion, far too full of sorrow and anger and pity to be able to take in anything else. Presently, Toby swallowed some of his sleeping pills and collapsed into bed. Julia spent some time arranging blankets and pillows on the sofa for me, then retired herself, biting her lip. I lay awake for hours, staring into the darkness, forced to watch and re-watch a horrifying newsreel playing on the ceiling. Before my eyes, men hurtled out of the sky and smashed into pieces on the ground; mothers were dragged away from their babies and shot dead; the sea caught fire; people with open, smiling faces reached out helping hands, then suddenly turned into grinning skeletons wearing Nazi uniforms.

When I left the next morning, Julia gave me an extra-long hug and whispered, "I'm *sure* it was the right thing to do." Which only increased my disquiet, but she telephoned the following day, sounding almost like her old cheerful self, and said she'd had a long chat with Toby and that he seemed to be feeling much more at ease.

I wasn't, though. I felt awful. I hadn't told Veronica about Julia's plan, of course, but I suspected she'd figured some of it out. However, all she'd said when I arrived back from East Grinstead was, "Well, I'm certain it did Toby good, having you visit." Once upon a time, she would have pressed me for details—she would have interrogated me ruthlessly until she'd captured all the facts. Now, though, she seemed prepared to leave them in my sole possession. It was gratifying to have her trust me so deeply, but after yet another sleepless night, I started to wish I could unburden myself, if only in part, to *someone* else. Then I thought of the Colonel, who was the logical choice. At the very least, telling him would relieve me of some of the guilt I'd felt about lying to Toby.

I managed to arrange a short meeting with the Colonel in Kensington Gardens this morning.

"I *would* have invited you to luncheon," he said when we met at the Palace Gate, "except it's such a bore, having to conduct security checks on all the waiters beforehand, and search all the saltcellars for hidden microphones."

I wasn't *entirely* certain he was joking, but he seemed pleased to see me, so I didn't feel quite as bad about taking up his valuable time this way. (After all, I didn't *really* believe there was anything in Toby's story that might be of professional interest to the Colonel. There had been that traitor, Jacques—but Toby had already told the Resistance people in France about him.) I provided the Colonel with a potted version of events as we strolled through the park, and he listened with his customary careful attention. Then we reached the Round Pond, and we paused to gaze across its unruffled waters. The Colonel sighed.

"Amazing," he said. "That Toby survived all that, I mean."

"He was very lucky." I realized now just *how* lucky Toby had been.

"But it wasn't just luck," said the Colonel. "It also took skill, and charm, and nerve, and sheer determination. Another man might not have made it through that first week. Still, I ought to have learned by now never to underestimate you Fitz-Osbornes." He smiled at me. "Oh, and well done, Sophie, on getting Toby to open up a bit. It must have taken a great deal of strength to listen to all that."

And suddenly I felt much lighter.

"Speaking of FitzOsbornes," I said, after we'd turned back towards the palace, "I don't suppose you know anything about Simon? Where he is, or what he's doing? He did write to Toby, but he couldn't say anything much about himself, and I know Toby's concerned about him."

"Well," said the Colonel, "of course, that's all highly

classified information. However, I *can* say that Simon has a posting of vital importance to the war effort, that he's doing his job extremely well, and that he's eating a lot of spaghetti."

"He's in *Italy* now?" I said, trying to remember how the fighting was going there. The Allies still hadn't captured Rome, as far as I knew. "Oh. But he won't be sent to France, will he, when the Second Front starts?"

"The Second Front?" said the Colonel. "What's that? Haven't a clue what you're talking about. But no, probably not. And anyway, you're distracting me from the *real* reason I wanted to see you, which was to find out how my favorite nephew is. I haven't seen him for months."

"Oh, he's wonderful," I said, brightening at the very thought of Rupert. "He's terribly busy with his work—whatever that might be—but he's lovely."

"Oh, good," said the Colonel. "Although, I must say, you *did* take your time about it. His mother and I have been trying to throw you two together for years."

"My relationship with Rupert developed quite naturally out of our mutual interests, and had nothing whatsoever to do with any of your scheming," I said.

"That's what *you* think," said the Colonel smugly. "My scheming is not only consistently successful, but also completely undetectable."

2nd June 1944

Toby had a meeting at the War Office today, an official briefing for all the "Leaders of the Allied Nations Whose Headquarters Are in Britain." Well, the second or third tier of the exiled leaders, at least—I assume General de Gaulle already knows exactly how and when the Allied forces are going to invade France. I went round to Julia's Belgravia house beforehand to wish Toby luck. He was wearing a neatly pressed uniform and all his medals, but I was horrified to see him on crutches, with one trouser leg pinned up.

"What happened to your leg?" I said.

"The doctors chopped it off," he said. "Too mangled to save."

"Toby! Where's your *wooden* one?"

"It's upstairs. I thought Churchill might pay more attention to me if I limped in, looking like a true war veteran. I'm worried Montmaray has been left out of their invasion plans, you see, and I don't want them ignoring us."

"Darling, you look like that one-eared cat that used to follow Rupert around Oxford," said Julia. "Battered, but defiant."

"I was actually aiming for 'pathetic and pitiable' to attract some sympathy," Toby said, "but 'defiant' might be just as effective. Oh, here's the taxi."

"Are you sure you don't want us to come with you?" Julia asked.

"Better not. I don't think you're supposed to know anything about it," he said. "It's all so terribly high level and hush-hush, you see."

"Well, good luck," I said, kissing his cheek.

"Yes, darling, very best of luck," said Julia. "I know 'break a leg' is the traditional phrase before a big performance, but—"

"Best not to tempt fate," he agreed. "Right, see you in a few hours."

Then he clambered into the taxi and it puttered off. Julia closed the front door and led me back to the sitting room. "Oh, he's up and down," she said, in answer to my unspoken question. "More up than down these days, thank heavens. I really do think you were a big part of that, Sophie, allowing him to get all that off his chest. All those horrific experiences . . . and I know I only heard an edited version of it from him. Anyway, he seems *much* better. Although I suppose it *could* just be that now we're in London, he doesn't have to eat my awful cooking anymore. It's certainly improved *my* mood, being back in the capable hands of Mrs. Timms." Julia sank down into a sofa with a satisfied sigh. "Oh, but I *am* glad about this meeting, Sophie! Toby needed a reminder of how important he is."

"I just wish Veronica could have attended," I said, "but they wouldn't give her permission. Heads of state only. Still, perhaps it's all for the best, if Churchill's going to be there."

"You mean, after that speech he gave in Parliament, praising Franco to the skies?" said Julia. "Yes, sickening, wasn't it? But perhaps he just needed to butter up the Spaniards so they wouldn't interfere with the invasion plans?"

"Well, Veronica says the Fascist propagandists in Madrid have gone wild with it, and all the Basques and Republicans are devastated. She's absolutely furious at Churchill."

But that was nothing compared to how furious *Toby* was when he arrived back at the house two hours later.

"That bloody Churchill!" he said, stomping round the sitting room (he'd put his leg back on so he could stomp more effectively). "It wasn't *just* that he hadn't planned to liberate Montmaray—I knew it wouldn't be an immediate priority during the invasion. I'd always figured he'd need a reminder about us. But he not only ignored *everything* I had to say about Montmaray, he isn't even interested in the *Channel* Islands! And they're British territory! All those thousands and thousands of people who've been living under the Nazi jackboot since 1940, and he doesn't give a damn about them! I couldn't believe it!

"I said to him, 'If this invasion of France works, you realize the German troops stationed in the Channel Islands will be cut off from all their supplies? That means no food and no fuel. So, are you going to airdrop supplies to the civilian population?' And he said, 'Of course not, the Germans would take it all. Let 'em starve. Anyway, what have the Channel Islanders ever done to resist the occupation? Nothing! What a weak-livered lot of quislings!' He doesn't have a bloody *clue* what it's like living under Nazi occupation! The way the Nazis punish whole families, whole *villages*, if they catch one single person resisting them . . . And these people live on tiny islands, for God's sake—they don't have anywhere to hide. How can he *possibly* compare them to the Resistance in France?"

"I know, darling, it's awful," said Julia soothingly. "But we just have to wait and see how this invasion of France goes first. And even then, I'm not sure you'll be able to do very much about it—"

"Oh, *won't* I?" Toby said, narrowing his eyes. "We'll see about *that*."

I'd never seen Julia lose her temper before today, although I can't say I blame her in the slightest. Toby, it turns out, has torn up the paperwork for his impending discharge from the RAF, and is trying to get the doctors to certify him as medically fit.

"This whole thing is ridiculous!" Julia cried. "Toby, you've already done *enough*. If you absolutely *must* stay in the air force, then go and work at Fighter Command HQ or something. But it's *insane* to think of going back to flying!"

"Why?" said Toby. "Plenty of pilots have returned to duty after much worse injuries than mine."

"Who?" she demanded. "Richard Hillary? And look at what happened to him! Crashed his plane during retraining! Killed himself *and* some other poor airman!"

"Hillary's hands were so badly burnt, he could barely use a knife and fork. My hands are fine."

"Oh? And what about your *legs*?"

"Douglas Bader had two artificial legs, and he still managed to shoot down a couple of dozen German planes."

"And then he got shot down himself and now he's moldering away in some filthy Nazi prison camp! And that could just as well happen to *you* if you go ahead with this stupid idea!"

"Well," said Toby, "it's *my* decision to make, not yours."

"No, it isn't!" snapped Julia. "You shouldn't have married me if you thought you could do whatever you damn well please, with no consideration for anyone else!"

Poor Julia. Naturally, she's upset—she's already lost one husband in a horrible plane crash. And of course, everyone's on edge these days anyway. For one thing, we're all desperate to know how things are going in France, now that the invasion's finally under way. It began two weeks ago, just as I was starting to think it would never happen. There was a brief mention of "paratroopers in northern France" on the BBC news early that morning, and Veronica and I dropped our toast and stared at each other and said, "Is this it? Has it started?" She had to go off to work then, but I stayed glued to the wireless and at about ten o'clock, General Eisenhower made the official announcement that the Allied forces had landed in Normandy.

I cried. I thought of those tens of thousands of soldiers struggling up the beaches, battling their way through land mines and machine-gun fire and who knows what else the Nazis were hurling at them. I thought of poor Kick, frantic about Billy, and all the other families anxiously waiting to hear if their men had survived the landings. I couldn't just sit at home doing nothing, so I went out and walked about until I saw a church with its doors open. I wanted to go in and pray for the soldiers, but the vicar stopped me in the foyer and said no woman was allowed in *his* church without a hat. So I marched straight out again—I could pray just as well without his stupid church—and eventually made my way back to Kensington, where I spotted a lady carrying a bundle of secondhand clothes into the local Women's Voluntary Service office. So I followed her inside and signed up to help, and it's a good thing I *did,* given the pressing need for volunteers in London now.

Because that's the other thing making everyone sick with worry—these ghastly bombing raids, which seem so much worse than any we've experienced before. I don't know if that's because we're all sick and tired of the war and have reached the limits of our endurance, or because there are so *many* bombs, at all hours of the day and night, or because the very notion of "pilotless planes" is so creepy. This is the "secret weapon" that Hitler's been threatening for years to unleash upon us—little robot planes launched from France, designed to fly by themselves to London, where they run out of fuel and plummet to the ground and explode. Actually, I just heard another one go over, about five minutes ago. It's such a sinister sound—a sort of humming, like a motorbike engine, that gets louder and louder as it approaches. I sit there thinking, *Keep going! Keep going!* Because if the engine noise stops above one's head . . . well, one's had it. It's all over. (Of course, when I say, *Keep going,* I mean,

Keep going until you reach a nice empty stretch of land with no one around, and then explode in that.) The worst of it is that hundreds of people have been killed already, in just one week, and there doesn't seem to be anything that can *stop* the bombs. They can't be shot down over London, because they'll just explode wherever they land. And there are so many of them that the warning sirens are useless. If one wants to stay (relatively) safe, the only choices are to spend all day and night in a very deep underground shelter or else leave London. That's what I've mostly been doing with the WVS, helping organize the evacuation of women, children, and the elderly to the country—

Oh, Veronica wants the light out now in the cellar. I need some sleep, anyway. Will try to write more tomorrow, and meanwhile, I must keep reminding myself how incredibly lucky I am that Rupert and Simon aren't fighting in Normandy, and that Toby is—for the moment—out of action.

28th August 1944

Wonderful and horrible news, all mixed up. Paris has just been liberated and vast swathes of France are now free of the hateful Nazis, who are gradually being driven back towards Germany. But thousands of our men have already sacrificed their lives, and poor Joe Kennedy Junior was one of them. I felt so desperately sorry for Kick—for all of her family, really, but especially her. She telephoned me with the news and kept choking on tears and then *apologizing* for it, because she said Kennedys were brought up never to cry. Oh, it's so sad! Joe was the only one of her family who'd supported her when she got married—the only one who was kind and understanding when she most needed it—and she is devastated by this. She's flown back to the United States to be with her family, and the one good thing that might result from this awful tragedy is that her mother *might* now start to unbend a little about Kick's marriage. Thank heavens Billy has made it through all the fighting in Normandy—he's even been promoted to Major. Hopefully the

Allies will soon have defeated the Germans and then he can come home.

I must admit, I've been too busy to pay more than fleeting attention to the news from France. I work twelve hours a day at a community hall, where I give out clothes to people who've been bombed and then try to find emergency accommodation for them, which is basically impossible because half the houses in London are uninhabitable now—including ours. Last month, a flying bomb landed in our garden, blasted an enormous hole in the wall of Montmaray House, and tore the roof off our flat. It's lucky Veronica and I were at work at the time. We did manage to salvage quite a lot of our things, thanks to our wonderful ARP warden chasing off the looters, and now we're staying with Julia. She's working at the ambulance station again and Toby's based at an aerodrome in Sussex. He's learning how to fly some new sort of plane, but I have a horrible suspicion it's one of the planes the RAF uses to shoot down the flying bombs over coastal areas, before the bombs reach London. Of course, Toby may have already *finished* his training and been posted back to an operational squadron. He is very sneaky, and he knows Julia would throw a fit if she found out he was involved in anything so dangerous.

I also suspect that Toby is plotting something with the Colonel—I overheard a snippet of a telephone conversation between them. However, I haven't yet had the time or opportunity to investigate further . . .

17th September 1944

It does seem unfair, that I should be so blissfully happy when so many others are suffering. Oh, *poor* Kick—first Joe, and now this. She only had five weeks with Billy before he was sent off to France, and now he's lying dead in some muddy field in Belgium, and they didn't even have a chance to set up a *home* together. I haven't spoken with her yet—Lady Bosworth told me the news about Billy this morning—but I think Kick will be coming back to England as soon as she can arrange it. Billy's family is very fond of her and would probably be much more sympathetic company for her than her own family. Oh, but it's such a dreadful, dreadful thing for *all* of them.

And of course, there must be thousands of women being widowed every day, on both sides of the conflict. Why don't the Germans do the decent thing and *surrender*? Of course, if they were decent people, they'd never have invaded all those other countries to begin with, but the Allied forces are streaming into Germany now, so it's simply a matter of time before we win the war. Perhaps it won't be over by Christmas, after all . . . but please let it end very, *very* soon. It isn't simply that I want all the death and destruction to end, although I do. I must confess, it's mostly for my own, selfish reasons . . .

No, I *refuse* to feel guilty about being happy! I deserve, just as much as anyone, and certainly far more than people like Hitler, to have nice things happen in my life. And this is by far the nicest, most exciting thing ever to happen to me! Oh, how I wish I could gush about it with absolutely everyone I know! But Veronica's still in Spain, and Anne has moved to Edinburgh. And how could I possibly expect Kick to feel happy about it now—about the news that I am to be *married*?

How strange it seems, to be writing that in my journal for the first time! And yet, not really, because it also feels like the most natural, inevitable thing in the world. But let me set it all down in order, the way it happened.

I hadn't seen Rupert since the invasion of France started, which was more than three whole months of missing him. I kept writing him long letters, but had nowhere to send them, as he was constantly moving. He wrote me notes when he could, but each time he came to London, I was busy with my WVS duties, so we didn't ever manage to meet. It was awfully frustrating, but I knew how hard he was working and that his job must be very important. Finally, he telephoned Julia one morning and left a message asking if I could attend some official work function with him. Of course, I didn't have anything nice to wear, half my wardrobe having been shredded when our flat got bombed, but I borrowed a dress from Julia, and organized a few hours off work, and was waiting for him when he pulled up outside the house. Oh, just watching him climb out of the car made me feel so warm and happy! (How could I *ever* have wondered if I was in love with Simon, when I was nearly always flustered and anxious around him—and that was when I wasn't feeling absolutely *furious* at him for one reason or another?) And Rupert looked just as glad to see *me*. After quite a bit of kissing, he handed me into the car and we drove off.

"So," I said to him, "at last, I get to find out what it is you do!"

"I suppose so," he said, with his lovely smile. "It's not really a secret anymore—not this part of my job, at least. I think the newspaper reporters will be there this morning."

"Really? Where are we going, anyway?"

"Oh, didn't Julia tell you? It's a medal presentation ceremony."

"Rupert! Are you being awarded a *medal*?"

"No, no, not me. I just made the official recommendations. They were so brave and clever—well, you'll see. Here we are."

And we walked into a very grand room full of RAF officers and newspaper reporters, as well as a couple of men setting up one of those big cameras they use to film newsreels. Rupert found me a place to sit, then was swallowed up almost at once by a crowd of people wanting to speak with him. The gentleman sitting next to me leaned over.

"I trained him, you know," he said, with evident pride.

"Oh," I said. "Well done. Er . . . you mean, Rupert?"

"No, Gustav," said the man. "Isn't the other one named Paddy?"

"Um . . . ," I said. A stout lady in a fur coat was now being ushered past me.

"Mrs. Alexander, wife of the First Lord of the Admiralty," said the man, nodding his approval. "They do things properly, don't they? Ah, they must be starting."

For the people gathered at the front of the room had moved towards their seats, revealing a long table—upon which sat two cages.

Pigeons. I should have guessed.

A gentleman introduced as "Wing Commander Rayner, Head of the Air Ministry Pigeon Service" then stood up and spoke about each of the two pigeons in turn. Gustav had delivered the first message from a ship off the Normandy beaches, just after the Allied troops landed on the sixth of June. Paddy had been the fastest pigeon of the whole Normandy Operation, traveling 230 miles in under five hours in his job as an RAF messenger. Each pigeon received a medal and a kiss from Mrs. Alexander, to much applause and cheering. When the cameras had finished rolling, Rupert took me to meet all his colleagues, human and avian. Paddy was a bit shy, but Gustav looked rather proud of himself, puffing out his grizzled chest so I could read his little bronze medallion, which said: *For Gallantry.* WE ALSO SERVE.

"I've been working with pigeons since the start of the

war," Rupert explained afterwards. "At first, my job was to liaise between the pigeon breeders who donated birds, and the civil servants at the War Office, and all the various military people—smoothing ruffled feathers, so to speak. But then I moved to working mostly with the RAF. All their bombers and reconnaissance aircraft have pigeons on board so that if they crash in occupied territory, they can send a message back with the plane's coordinates. A lot of airmen have been rescued that way. I was in charge of the practical details—making sure the birds had comfortable lofts at the air bases, organizing corn rations, even arranging for farmers along the coast to shoot down birds of prey, which was awful, but we had to make sure our pigeons wouldn't get eaten. Then, when the planning started for the Second Front, things became even busier. The generals knew that once troops started moving over the Channel, they wouldn't be able to send any radio messages; otherwise, the Germans would realize the invasion had started and be able to pick up Allied troop positions. So pigeons would be an ideal means of communication, but that meant training a whole lot of soldiers and sailors to use them. And then, once the invasion began, I had to make sure there weren't any problems as the pigeons started coming in."

"Goodness, what an important job," I said as we walked towards his car. "No wonder you've been so busy this year! Will your work become a bit less frantic now?"

"Somewhat," he said. "But there are thousands of pigeons still in service, so I'll be needed until the war's over."

"And then?"

"Well . . . I did want to talk with you about that. Do you need to get back to work straightaway?"

I did, but we sat down for a minute on a piece of broken wall, overlooking a bomb crater.

"The thing is," Rupert said, "I don't know what I'll do when the war ends. Go back to Oxford and finish my degree, or apply to a veterinary school, or else find a job somewhere . . . and I'm not sure what's going to happen with my family, whether Charlie will ever come home, or what my father plans to do with the estate. It all depends. You see, I was thinking that whatever I do . . . well, I want to do it alongside you, Sophie. I simply can't imagine the rest of my life without you in it."

"Oh, Rupert! I feel exactly the same way about *you*," I said, beaming at him. "Perhaps we ought to get married, then."

"I think that's an excellent idea," said Rupert, leaning over to kiss me. "Very clever of you to think of it," he added, after we'd finally come up for air.

"Wait a minute, did you just get *me* to propose to you?" I said, both of us starting to laugh.

"I think so. I could get down on one knee and do it properly, if you like?"

We looked at the muddy, rubble-strewn patch of ground beneath us.

"Perhaps not," I said. "Oh, Rupert, I'm so glad about this! *When*, do you think?"

"Well, tomorrow, if it were up to me, but it might be more

sensible to wait till this job of mine is finished. I'm still not stationed at any one place. So that means when the war's over."

"And I really would *love* to have a peacetime wedding," I said. "In the church at Milford, with no one having to wear a uniform. Is that all right? Or would you prefer Astley? Or London?"

"Anything you want," he said. "Oh—but I ought to have warned you before that I haven't got much money."

"I know," I said. "I don't mind. I don't have any either, except for my allowance from Aunt Charlotte."

"And I don't have a house," he said, "or anywhere to live."

"That's all right," I said, looking at the bomb crater. "Hardly anyone does, these days." Then I rested my head on his shoulder, brimming over with happiness, knowing I was the most fortunate girl in the world.

29th October 1944

Well. We have *finally* discovered what Toby's been plotting. This afternoon, he convened a meeting of all the Montmaravian Privy Councilors currently in London—that is, Veronica and me.

"And you too," he said to Julia. "After all, you're the Queen of Montmaray."

"Oh, all right, darling," she said, handing me the plate of scones. "Just let me finish pouring the tea."

"Better turn the wireless on, too," he said. "In case of hidden listening devices. And Sophie, could you draw the curtains?"

He'd *definitely* been spending too much time with the Colonel. Veronica raised an eyebrow at me as she reached for the wireless.

"Right," Toby said, after the security arrangements had been judged satisfactory and we each had a cup of tea. "As you know, Churchill has shown absolutely no interest in ousting the Nazis from Montmaray—even though we've all dedicated ourselves to the war effort for years and years, and Henry sacrificed her *life* for this stupid, ungrateful country. Sorry, Julia, but it is. Anyway, as the Allied commanders are pretending we don't exist, I've decided we must liberate Montmaray ourselves. I have therefore devised a brilliant plan, which I am now going to explain to you in—"

"Why?" Veronica asked. "I mean, why do we need to do anything if Germany's on the verge of defeat and unconditional surrender? Why can't we just wait for that?"

"Because firstly, they're *not* on the verge of defeat," said Toby. "They're still sinking Allied ships, they're still putting up a ferocious fight in Italy and the Netherlands—and just wait till the main battle moves to their homeland. If that assassination attempt against Hitler had actually succeeded, it might be over now. But unfortunately, he's still around, so the Nazis could go on fighting for months and months. And secondly, I don't *want* to wait. I don't see why we should sit around doing nothing when everyone else is fighting. Look at the Spanish Republicans, rising up against Franco now! After all they've been through, forced into exile in France for all those years— and *they* haven't given up! *They're* not sitting about waiting for the Americans to rescue them!"

Veronica opened her mouth, no doubt to point out that the Republicans were currently being forced back across the Pyrenees by Franco's army. But Toby cut her off before she could speak.

"Besides," he said, "I want to go home."

Veronica closed her mouth.

"Now, here's my plan," said Toby. He produced a large manila envelope and shook some photographs out onto the table. We leaned in.

"Is that—?" I said, and he nodded.

"Aerial photographs of Montmaray, taken a few weeks ago," he said. "I needed up-to-date information. You can see they've rebuilt most of the castle—that's where the soldiers seem to be quartered. The village looks much the same, except for a new wharf, but there aren't any ships around at the moment, and there's only one plane on the airstrip. In fact, it all looks pretty quiet. I don't think they've ever had more than a dozen servicemen stationed on the island at any one time, and there's probably far fewer than that now. It won't be too difficult to land a plane there and overwhelm them."

"What's that?" said Veronica, pointing to a silver blob on the main part of the island, not far from the reconstructed drawbridge.

"Oh, probably some sort of ground-based radar."

"What's 'radar'?" I asked.

"A way of detecting distant objects. It sends radio waves into the air and if they bounce back, it means a plane's out there. It can tell where the plane is, how fast it's traveling, whether it's friend or foe. That's one of the main reasons the RAF was able to fight off the Luftwaffe so successfully from the start, because we could tell when they were coming. And of course, radar's the *only* reason we pilots ever managed to shoot down anything at night."

"You mean," I said indignantly, "that all those reports about that night fighter pilot, Cat's Eyes Cunningham, eating lots of carrots—they weren't *true*? He actually shot down all those bombers in the dark because he used this radar thing?"

"Imagine, the government lying to its own people," said Toby. "Shocking."

"If this radar is so effective," said Veronica, frowning at the photographs, "then surely the Nazis will detect any British planes approaching Montmaray. The soldiers there will have plenty of warning, and plenty of time to prepare themselves for a fight."

"Oh, but that's the brilliant part of my plan," said Toby. "You see, it won't *be* a British plane. The RAF has quite a few Luftwaffe aircraft in its possession by now. You know, from aircrew who've surrendered. And then there are planes that have crash-landed, that the RAF mechanics have fixed up to see how they work. They're the planes that I've been learning to fly these past few months."

"And I suppose in that time you've also managed to become fluent in German," Veronica said, sarcasm dripping from her voice, "so that if they challenge you over their radio system, you'll be able to reassure them. Oh, and when you land, you'll no doubt be wearing a Nazi officer's uniform, so they'll do whatever you say and you'll be able to talk them into surrendering!"

"You must be using your super-mind-reading powers," said

Toby, "because you're entirely correct, except for one small detail. It won't be me speaking German—"

But he was interrupted by Julia, who'd been studying the writing along the border of the photographs. "Who took these photographs?" she demanded.

"I did," Toby said. "I went down to Cornwall and borrowed a reconnaissance plane from Coastal Command."

"Toby! You *said* you weren't going to be flying any operations!"

"I said I wasn't going to be flying *in combat.* And I didn't. I just took a quick trip to Montmaray and back, and no harm done. They didn't even fire their anti-aircraft guns at me."

"Oh, excellent, they've got an anti-aircraft battery there as well!" said Veronica. "This is sounding better and better!"

"They didn't fire it because they're either slow and stupid, or they've run out of ammunition," said Toby patiently. "Their supplies must be getting pretty low, now that the Nazis have been kicked out of France and the Spanish have finally stopped helping them. It's an ideal time to launch our attack. Anyway, they definitely won't be shooting at one of their *own* planes, so we needn't worry about that. Obviously, there are still a few little details to work out, but overall, what do you think of my plan?"

"I think it's unnecessary, extremely risky, and altogether one of the stupidest ideas you've ever had," said Veronica.

"I can't believe they let you work in the Diplomatic Services," said Toby. "Soph, what do you think?"

"I'm already imagining a dozen things that could go disastrously wrong," I said.

"Oh, good," he said. "Well, write them all down, then we can figure out a solution for each problem."

"And what did you mean," I continued, "when you said that *you* won't be speaking German? Who will?"

Toby hesitated for the first time. "Um . . . well, there's someone who's volunteered to help. Perfect for the job."

"A German?" I asked.

"No, no. He just speaks German, knows a lot about Wehrmacht officer behavior . . ." Toby began to falter under Veronica's stare. "And he's . . . er, familiar with the terrain—"

Veronica jumped up, setting all the teacups rattling. "Absolutely *not*! You are *not* involving Daniel in this ridiculous scheme!"

"Well, that's up to him to decide, isn't it?" said Toby. "I just happened to mention the idea to him, and he said he wanted to help."

"When was this? When you *just happened* to be visiting Bletchley? And I suppose you *just happened* to have arranged with the Colonel for Daniel to be released from his duties there?"

"Mmm," said Toby, suddenly very busy shuffling his photographs into a pile.

"Right! That's it! I'm going to telephone him this instant!" she shouted, and stormed off.

And that was the end of our meeting.

After dinner, I tackled Julia, the only person who might possibly be able to talk Toby out of this.

"Oh, I *know*, Sophie," she said at once. "I know exactly how you feel! I wish Toby would just wait till Germany surrenders. But I'm not sure anyone can stop him, he's so determined to go ahead with it. Even though it seems terribly dangerous . . ."

"I think Toby *wants* it to be dangerous," I said. "I think he wants a chance to have his revenge on the Nazis. To pay them back for what they did to him, and to Henry."

"Yes, you're right, I think he does," she sighed. "Still, I must admit, he's brightened up a lot since he started planning this thing. I had a vague idea of what it might be, of course . . . And you know, the Colonel wouldn't have agreed to help unless *he* felt it was a feasible scheme. That's the only thing making me feel slightly better about it. Oh, you *will* help Toby, won't you? You and Veronica? Because you're both so clever and you know Montmaray. He needs you to make this work."

Toby walked into the kitchen just then with his notebook. "Simon," he announced to both of us. "Soph, do you know where exactly in Italy he *is* now? We'd better get him back. We might need a spare pilot."

Julia and I looked at each other after he'd gone back upstairs.

"Well," I said, giving up. "Just as long as he doesn't try to draft *Rupert* into this."

We spent most of today ensconced in what Toby insists on calling "HQ"—a large second-floor bedroom he's converted into
his study, the wallpaper of which has now disappeared under
dozens of maps, diagrams, photographs, meteorological charts,
and scrawled lists, as well as a dartboard featuring Hitler's face.
It turned out Churchill was quite enthusiastic about the idea
of a commando raid on Montmaray when the Colonel told
him our plans, but his generals all said they didn't have any
ships, planes, or men to spare for such a "strategically insignificant" mission. The most they could promise was some help
afterwards, collecting prisoners of war, and clearing up any land
mines or unexploded bombs. Upon hearing that, Toby put in a
request for Jimmy Smith's bomb disposal company, because the
poor boy's been abroad for months and Alice is going out of her
mind with worry over him. Of course, there won't be any need
of their bomb-disposal services until we've got rid of the Nazis,

which depends on us coming up with a foolproof plan—and sometimes I'm not sure we're *ever* going to manage that.

This afternoon, Daniel joined us for one of our interminable meetings. We still didn't come to any firm decisions, but he did prove quite effective at mediating between Toby and Veronica, who keep having the same argument over and over again.

"Even if there *are* only six soldiers stationed there—and I must say, the evidence for that isn't very convincing—it still means *three* of them for each of you," said Veronica. "That's why I ought to come with you."

"Well, you can't," said Toby. "And it's got nothing to *do* with you being a girl, so don't even start on that. The plane only seats two. Therefore, unless you can learn to fly a plane or speak fluent German in the next fortnight, you'll just have to be in charge of the support crew in Cornwall."

"Anyway," said Daniel, putting his arm round her, "there won't *be* any physical combat, so it doesn't matter how many of them there are. We're going to *talk* them into surrendering."

"Yes, how's the script going?" Toby asked me.

"Well, I've written three scenarios so far," I said, frowning at my notebook, "but none of them sound all that plausible to *me*. I mean, Nazi soldiers aren't *really* going to believe that Hitler's committed suicide and the war is over, are they?"

"Well, what if Daniel tells them that all the Nazi generals have banded together behind Hitler's back?" said Toby.

"Because they want to negotiate a peace treaty, in order to save the Fatherland from annihilation?"

"But would a high-ranking Nazi officer bother flying to some remote island outpost to inform the soldiers there?" I said. "Especially if there *are* only six of them?"

"What about if I've come to tell them they're being posted back to Germany, because that's where all the fighting is going on now?" said Daniel.

"Yes, I wrote one about that," I said. "But there's still the question of why you'd want to disarm them before they left the island."

"And surely we'd bring a bigger plane if we were meaning to transport troops," pointed out Toby. "The problem is, we've only got access to a two-seater. Well, there *is* another plane available, but I'm not sure I could land it safely on that tiny airstrip."

"I think *this* scenario's the best," said Veronica, who'd been reading my notebook. "Daniel accuses them of treason—says one of them was picked up on a listening device, overheard making jokes about Hitler's sanity, so they're all being taken back to Berlin to stand trial."

"But do Nazis *have* trials?" Toby said. "They just shoot traitors on the spot, don't they?"

"Either way, it provides a plausible excuse to handcuff and disarm them," said Veronica. "Or some of them, at least."

"And they're bound to have said *something* bad about Hitler at some stage," I said, scribbling down notes, "so they'll all be feeling a bit guilty and be more likely to go along with it. I'll add some bits about Daniel being sympathetic to them. You know, 'I hate to do this to you, I can just imagine what it's like being stuck out here in the middle of nowhere, but just cooperate with me, and we'll get it all sorted out as soon as possible, and then you can have some leave in Germany.'"

"Sounds good," said Toby. "Show it to Daniel when you're done. Now, what's next on the list? Oh, yes, communications. I'm not sure yet how we're going to contact the authorities after we've recaptured the island. We obviously can't use the German radio system—"

At that point, Julia came in with her tape measure, to check Daniel's size for the Nazi uniform she's sewing him. And then it was time for tea. So we still haven't figured out even *half* of what we need to do . . . but we're getting there.

30th November 1944

I seem to have spent a significant proportion of this war feeling either very bored or very anxious, and at the moment, I'm managing to experience both at once. So I have taken out my journal, in the hope that writing down a detailed description of events thus far might provide some distraction from our nerve-racking wait. We've been sitting here, in this wooden hut on the edge of a wind-blasted Cornish heath, for more than six hours now. Well, *I* am sitting—Veronica is wearing a groove in the floorboards with her pacing, and Simon keeps leaping up to peer out the window in the direction of the airfield. I don't know what he expects to see there. The message we're anticipating is far more likely to arrive from the other direction— along that bridle path that leads to the farmhouse pigeon loft where Rupert is stationed. Meanwhile, Julia remains in London by the telephone, ready to alert the Colonel if anything goes wrong—not that there's very much he'll be able to do if it *does* . . .

Oh, but I'm meant to be distracting myself. Very well—I'll write about Simon. It was rather disconcerting at first, to have him back with us again. He looked so unchanged—perhaps a little older, and rather more tanned than the last time I'd seen him, but just as handsome. Yet how *could* he be the same, when I felt so differently about him? For I realized at once that my complex, intense emotions of several years ago had been smoothed flat by the weight of subsequent experiences, so that all that remained was a mild affection. Any resentment or anger had been brushed aside long ago. Veronica initially seemed far less inclined to forgive him for his Great Disappearing Act (I'd always *wondered* how much she'd known about Simon and me). But then the two of them had a noisy argument about what time he'd said he'd be arriving, and now they seem to have settled back into their usual, comfortable level of squabbling. As for *Toby*—he looked so pleased to see Simon again that I couldn't help thinking that my brother's feelings, at least, were exactly the same as they'd ever been. And Simon did such an excellent job of disguising any shock he felt at Toby's altered appearance that I felt a rush of gratitude towards my cousin, and was suddenly very happy that he'd returned . . .

Except he's just left again—gone out to talk to the RAF pilots sauntering down towards our hut. They were all madly curious about Toby's Luftwaffe plane when he landed it here yesterday afternoon. Then Daniel arrived with his suitcase of Nazi uniforms, which was even *more* entertaining for them. Fortunately, most of the pilots at the air base were either asleep or on duty when Toby and Daniel were preparing to leave this morning, so we didn't have a crowd gawping at us. It was quite bizarre enough as it *was*. Veronica bidding a passionate farewell to a Nazi general (and I must say, for someone who once professed a lack of interest in physical love, she seemed remarkably proficient at kissing, and Daniel didn't appear at all lacking in expertise, either). And there was Toby in his Luftwaffe uniform, going through a third meticulous check of the plane and firing a lot of intelligent-sounding questions at the RAF mechanic. Then Rupert and his farmer friend arrived with their baskets of pigeons.

"Wanted to wait till the last minute," Mr. Briggs explained, still puffing from his rapid walk. "You see, I put each cock pigeon in a cage with his favorite hen, then take him out again after five minutes, before they have a chance to . . . well, consummate their marriage, you might say. Makes them extra keen to fly back to their nest, as quick as they can."

"Oh, the poor things," I said. "It sounds so cruel."

"It is," agreed Rupert. "I can just imagine how they feel." Then he climbed into the plane to fasten the pigeon baskets into place.

"Right!" said Toby, striding over and rubbing his hands. "The plane's ready. The pigeons are being strapped in. We've had the traditional phone call from Aunt C forbidding us from going ahead with our plans, which we're ignoring, as per usual. Someone pry Daniel away from Veronica, then we can be off. Oh wait, where's Simon?"

Meanwhile, I could hear Veronica saying to Daniel, "It's not too late, you know. You can still change your mind."

"We'll be fine," Daniel told her. "We've gone through every possible problem that might come up. We couldn't possibly be more prepared. Anyway, don't forget—I've got a gun now, and I've been trained how to use it." And he patted the pistol in his holster.

"That is not reassuring in the least," she said, but she let go of him and stood back to watch him scramble into the plane.

"Yes, let's hope Daniel's excellent communication skills carry the day," Toby murmured to me, "because he's a bloody awful shot."

"That's not *his* fault. It's just that his eyesight's not very good," I said. "Anyway, you said there wouldn't *be* any fighting."

"That's right, there won't be," said Toby emphatically. "Absolutely not. Oh, there you are, Simon. Did you get that weather update?"

Simon handed it over, then stared past Toby at Rupert, who'd just jumped down from the plane.

"Rupert!" said Simon, stepping forward and holding out his hand. "Good to see you again. I believe congratulations are in order. You're a lucky man."

"Oh, thank you, Simon," said Rupert. "Yes, I certainly am." They shook hands, looking each other straight in the eye. For some reason, I'd always pictured Simon as the taller of them, but if anything, he was a fraction shorter. Perhaps he'd shrunk. Then Simon turned away, back to Toby.

"There's a storm brewing," he said, nodding at the piece of paper Toby held. "Coming in from the west."

"It's the Bay of Biscay in late November," said Toby. "Of course there's a storm brewing. But it won't reach Montmaray until at least noon—probably a couple of hours later. You know what it's like at this time of year."

"You could postpone this, you know."

"The weather will be just the same tomorrow, if not worse," said Toby. "Right, let's get going! *Au revoir*, everyone." He embraced first me, then Rupert.

"Take care," Rupert said. "Don't take any risks, just turn straight back if it looks bad."

"Oh, *you're* just worried about those birds," teased Toby. "Bye, Veronica. Yes, yes, I'll look after your *boyfriend*. Or is he your fiancé now? No? Oh, Aunt C *will* be relieved. There's still hope for you and that Elchester nephew, then."

He climbed into his seat, still tossing quips over his shoulder. I think I was the only one who'd overheard what he'd said quietly to Simon as he'd hugged him goodbye: "If anything happens, you'll look after Julia, won't you?"

The RAF mechanic bustled about, checking latches and gauges, exchanging signals with Toby through the windscreen. Then we all stood back—were forced back, really, by the roar of the engines. The plane rumbled down the tarmac, gathering speed and power, and then exploded off the end of the runway in a furious blast of noise. Within seconds, it was streaking across the sea, the early-morning rays catching one side and turning it, for a moment, into a brilliant flash of white. Then it was gone.

"I wish Henry could have been here to see this," I said, into the sudden silence.

"If Henry had been here," Veronica said, "she'd have stowed away on board the plane."

I sighed.

"But perhaps she *is* here," said Veronica, tucking her arm into mine. "Or at least, with Toby. I think she'd find this sort of thing hard to stay away from, don't you?"

It was a kind thing to say, because I know she doesn't believe in any sort of afterlife. I squeezed her arm gratefully, and then we walked slowly to the hut with Simon, while Rupert and Mr. Briggs followed the path back to the farmhouse.

And that was . . . let's see, nearly seven hours ago. Simon has returned from his chat with the pilots and has just squashed the stub of his third cigarette into the ashtray beside the telephone. I can tell it's annoying Veronica, but so far she's refrained from snapping at him. Now Simon's fiddling with his lighter.

"How long have you been keeping those journals, anyway?" he says abruptly, looking at my book.

"Um . . . eight years," I say, after a short calculation.

"Eight *years!*" he says, eyes widening in either mock or actual horror. "Oh God, and you're writing down *this* conversation, too, aren't you? Is there *any* aspect of our lives that's managed to escape your scrutiny?"

Veronica laughs. "In a hundred years' time, there'll be copies of Sophie's journals kept in libraries," she says. "People will study them to try and understand our quaint, old-fashioned ways."

"All I can think is, thank God they're written in code," says Simon. "My secrets are safe."

"Oh, they'll probably have invented decoding machines by then," says Veronica airily. "I mean, if we can have robot bombs now, then surely they'll have invented robots that do *helpful* things in a hundred years' time."

"Perhaps they'll have abolished war by then," I say.

"One would certainly hope so," says Veronica, rubbing her arms. "Heavens, it's *freezing* in here, isn't it? Or is it just because I've stopped pacing up and down? I'm going to walk across to the car to get a blanket. And to get some *fresh air*." She gives the ashtray a meaningful look, then walks out . . .

As soon as Veronica was out of earshot, Simon leaned over the table towards me.

"Sophie," he said, "I want to apologize to you."

"What for?"

"For leaving," he said. "For not even telling you I was leaving. And for not being here when you . . . Well, I don't know if you ever really *needed* me. But I should have stayed—or at least stayed in touch—and I didn't. I behaved very badly."

"Yes, you did," I said. "But *you* were having a pretty awful time, too, as I remember it."

"I just felt I had to get as far away as possible," he said. "Not from *you*, particularly, but from everything here. I hated my job, and I felt so guilty about Toby. And in a way, it *did* help, going abroad . . ." He trailed off, apparently lost in unhappy memories.

"Was it very dangerous, what you were doing there?" I asked, after a moment.

"Yes," he said. "Dangerous enough that I had to stop thinking about the past, because the present was so overwhelming. And dangerous enough that I realized I wanted to live. That if I died, it still wouldn't bring Toby back. I honestly did believe he was dead, you know, so when I heard the news . . ." He glanced at me. "It seemed like a miracle. As though I'd been given another chance. I still haven't quite taken it in, and of course, he's so changed . . . But Sophie, the thing is—and I don't mean this as an excuse, although it sounds that way—I always figured you'd be all right. I knew you were stronger than me, and that you'd . . . endure. Despite everything."

"You're right," I said. "That *does* sound like an excuse." Then, as his face fell, I couldn't help smiling. "Oh, *Simon*. It was all such a long time ago. I was angry at you, but I got over it."

"And now you're . . . happy?"

"With Rupert? Oh, yes! I didn't think I *could* be this happy. Although it's difficult when he's away all the time, but that's just for a bit longer. When the war's over . . . well, we'll all be happier then, won't we?"

"Will we?" he said.

Poor Simon! I'm not stupid enough to think that everybody in the world wants or needs the same things in life, but I can't help wishing he could have a person of his own to love, and to love him back, the way I found Rupert. Although perhaps that would be too simple for Simon. He is a rather complex person. Perhaps he'd need *two* people of his own.

"Are you going to be staying in England now?" I asked him.

"I suppose so," he said. "Depends on what happens with *this*." He looked at the clock. "Oh God, it's been nearly seven-and-a-half hours. That should have been more than enough time for them to—"

The telephone rang, and we both jumped. Simon recovered first and snatched up the receiver.

"Chester speaking," he said. "Yes. What? Really? Are you *sure?*"

"Is that Rupert?"

"Shh!" Simon said, grabbing a pencil. "Yes," he said into the telephone, "yes, I *know* you're familiar with his hand-writing, but they could have forced him to write it. Did he use the code? If it's a genuine message, it should contain the word *Benedict* . . ."

Veronica came pounding in.

"Is that Rupert?" she cried.

"Shh!" I said, pointing at the message Simon was scrib-bling down.

"Right," said Simon. "Yes . . . Oh, is there? I'll wait." He moved the receiver from his mouth and said, "A second pigeon's just arrived." He started scribbling again. "Yes, got that. See you soon."

Simon hung up the telephone. Then he looked at us, an enormous smile spreading across his face.

"They did it," he said, and he started laughing.

And as we whooped and threw our arms around each other, a piece of paper fluttered to the floor and was crumpled underfoot. I retrieved it later, though, and this is what it said:

Safe arrival at 1030, found 6 soldiers, all surrendered weapons & were handcuffed. One extra Nazi turned up when searching Great Hall. Lucky for me, Benedict in customary place & still sharp. No life-threatening wounds inflicted on Nazi, but pls arrange immediate collection of 7 German POWs. Also, bring champagne. Airstrip cleared for use; recommend easterly approach. Swastika torn down, Montmaray flag now flying over castle. Currently cloudy, gusty NW winds, predict late-afternoon rain, but it is a GLORIOUS MORNING AT MONTMARAY.

King Toby

Four Years Later

21st August 1948

My eyes have been fixed upon my work for the past hour, but I
just now glanced up from my desk to find the mist rolled away
and the window awash with blue—the clear, pale blue of the
sky, floating above the pure, deep indigo sea. Why *is* the sea
here such an intense color? Why is it so powerfully evocative?
During our years in exile, I'd sometimes catch sight of a silk
dress or a piece of glass of a similar hue, and feel an unexpected
pang of sorrow and happiness and longing, before realizing why.
It's funny how that works. When Rupert gave me my engagement ring, he said he'd chosen it because the sapphire was the
blue of my eyes. To me, it was the color of home, of Montmaray.
Although perhaps they're all the same thing—perhaps that's
how my eyes turned out this way, from all that childhood gazing
out of castle windows at the sea. The view is still so utterly mes-
merizing that I'm compelled now to push my typewriter aside,
in order to stare out the window . . .

No, that's not true, not entirely. (And if I can't be honest with myself, here in the privacy of my own journal, what hope is there for my work?) The truth is, I've stopped typing because I can't quite bring myself to translate the next few pages of my old wartime journal, not just yet. Simply reading the first sentence brought back such a rush of emotions that I had to close the book and fumble for my handkerchief. Admittedly, I *have* been rather weepy lately. Pretty much anything can set me off—I burst into tears the last time Rupert brought home another of those starving, flea-infested kittens that lurk about London's alleyways, waiting to ambush him. ("THE POOR THING NEVER EVEN KNEW ITS MOTHER!" I wailed to Rupert, sobbing into his shoulder as he tried to make up a bottle for it in the kitchen.)

But my memories of that first trip back to Montmaray after its liberation are even more heart-rending than orphaned kittens. Oh, how tiny the island looked from the air! How pathetic, really. That poor little rock, struggling to keep its chin above water in the midst of all that heaving ocean. Even after we'd landed, it seemed so much smaller than I remembered. And then there was the starkness of the landscape—such a contrast after those gentle verdant hills of Dorset. Montmaray was jagged black rock sparsely covered with shrubs, stiff grass beaten flat by the wind, and no trees at all. The Americans who flew us there seemed quite baffled by our interest in the place.

"Ma'am, you *sure* you don't want to come back with us?" one of them asked Veronica after the prisoners had been loaded into the plane. "That castle seems awful cold. And bare."

"No, thank you, Sergeant," she said brightly. "We have enough supplies for a week, and now that you've set up the radio system, we can contact the authorities if we need anything. We'll be absolutely fine."

"Yes, ma'am," he said dubiously, with a glance at my tear-smeared face and Simon's grim expression. And we hadn't even seen the *worst* of it then. After the plane departed, we walked back up to the castle, where Toby was kicking the last of the swastika banners into the bonfire he'd kindled in the courtyard. I had a moment of wishing I could set the whole *castle* on fire—not to destroy it, but to purify it. Of course, the soldiers had already done a fairly thorough job of burning its contents. They'd long ago run out of fuel, so they'd chopped up anything that would ignite—the family portraits that lined the walls of the Great Hall, our grand piano, the kitchen chairs, the wardrobes upstairs, and our sandalwood chest full of heirlooms. Anything of value had been stolen, of course, carted off to Germany even before the war began.

The only thing they'd left untouched was Bartholomew's longsword, Benedict, which remained hanging over the chimneypiece in its scabbard, and it was several months before we understood the reason for this. When Daniel interrogated the soldiers at their prisoner-of-war camp, one of them reported that he'd read about the sword before the war. Apparently, our old friend Otto Rahn had gone back to Berlin and published an article about Montmaray, and it included a garbled version of the legend about Benedict protecting the FitzOsbornes for eternity.

It seems that this was interpreted to mean that a curse would fall upon anyone outside the family who touched the sword. Veronica said this was further evidence that Nazis were complete idiots in thrall to a lot of superstitious nonsense, but Toby said there must be something in the legend, because he really *had* needed the sword to disarm that last, unexpected Nazi soldier, and things could have got very dicey indeed if Benedict hadn't been in its regular place and still razor-sharp. The other thing we discovered was that a couple of the soldiers believed the upstairs rooms were haunted, and refused to sleep up there. I like to think that was the Blue Room ghost doing her bit for the war effort.

But all of that came later. Our first hours at Montmaray were spent wandering about in a daze, gaping at the destruction. The chapel, with all its windows blown out and seagulls nesting in the rafters. The library tower, reduced to a pile of broken stone. What had taken minutes to destroy would take years, perhaps decades, to rebuild. Still, the Germans had already made a start on repairs, if only to make their lives easier. There was a sturdy bridge across the Chasm; the curtain walls and gatehouse had been reconstructed in solid concrete; and the castle sported a new roof, complete with guttering and a large water tank. But just as I was feeling a little more friendly towards the soldiers, I noticed Veronica and Daniel having an urgent-sounding conversation in the courtyard.

"No, don't," said Daniel, grabbing her arm. "Veronica, please, you don't need to see it now! Leave it to the military investigators."

Which was how I found out about the slave laborers, the men the Nazi soldiers had brought to the island to build the concrete fortifications and the gun emplacement at South Head, to enlarge the airstrip and keep it in good repair, to tend the castle's vegetable gardens. These men were left to house themselves in the ruined cottages in the village and to try to feed themselves with whatever fish or rabbits or seabirds they could catch after their long days of backbreaking labor. They starved, of course, some of them to death, and the bodies were piled up to rot in one of the cottages. The survivors were collected at the beginning of 1944 and taken to a German concentration camp, where they were forced to make the rocket bombs that later devastated London. It turned out nearly all of the men were Spanish Republicans who'd escaped to France after the Civil War and then were interned after the Nazi invasion in 1940. None of them lived to see the end of the war.

That was the hardest thing of all to bear—the knowledge of how those men had suffered at Montmaray. It turned the destruction of our property, even our years in exile, into something almost inconsequential. And there seemed nothing we could *do* to make it any better. But the Nazis kept meticulous records of all their prisoners, and so Veronica, with the aid of her Foreign Office colleagues, managed to trace many of the men's families. At least we could tell them the truth, if they wanted to hear it. And they did, for the most part. Some of the families even came out here last year, to watch the new commemorative stained-glass window in the chapel being unveiled.

Julia commissioned one of her artist friends to design it, and I'd worried it might be a bit *too* modern and abstract, but it's absolutely beautiful, especially when the light streams through it. All the men's names are in it, so no one can ever forget them . . .

And now I think I might as *well* have translated those journal pages, after all, given how long I've dwelled on all that heartbreaking tragedy. Goodness, I'd really better write something more cheerful next. What has been my happiest experience since the war ended? Well, our wedding, I suppose—yes, that was lovely. Walking out of the church at Milford into the dazzling sunlight that morning, arm in arm with Rupert, knowing we'd be spending the rest of our lives together. Veronica had pointed out that a civil wedding in London would be quicker and easier to organize, but I had my heart set on wearing a white dress, with the Reverend Mr. Herbert officiating, and the Colonel giving me away, and Veronica as my bridesmaid. So that's what we had, even though the occasion wasn't *quite* as grand as Aunt Charlotte had always dreamed. Rationing was still in force, so my dress was one of Julia's old debutante gowns with lace sleeves added, and the cake didn't have any icing, and we couldn't manage to buy any camera film, so there weren't any photographs. And Barnes wept all the way through the ceremony, although she assured me afterwards that that didn't mean she disapproved of it. And we missed Henry dreadfully, of course (I could just imagine her refusing to wear a bridesmaid's frock, and insisting on Estella being appointed a flower sow, or page pig, or something). Dear old Carlos had passed away in his sleep by then, but his two sons made their presence known at the church hall reception by stealing all the sausage rolls. Still, it was a *wonderful* wedding. I suggested to Veronica and Daniel that *they* might like to have one, too, but they remain firmly attached both to each other and their anti-wedding principles.

Anyway, if Veronica got married, she'd have to resign from her job—and she'd never do that, especially as she was one of those who helped convince the Gowers Committee that women should be allowed to take up permanent positions in the Foreign Office. Of course, women are still restricted to only ten percent of its annual intake and have to remain single. Overturning that ruling is the aim of Veronica's *current* campaign, although I don't know when she ever finds the time to work on it, between her job, and doing evening courses at the London School of Economics, and helping Daniel with—

I was just interrupted by Davey, who toddled through my open door with an armful of blanket.

"I making a nest," he announced.

"Are you, darling?" I said. We make concerted efforts not to spoil him, but he has such a sweet, serious nature and is so utterly adorable (those big dark eyes of Simon's in Julia's heart-shaped face, that mop of chestnut curls) that it's rather an uphill battle for us.

"Yes, I making a nest," said Davey, nodding emphatically. "For you."

Davey thinks the recent appearance of four kittens in that dark cupboard under our kitchen sink is the most fascinating thing ever—certainly more interesting than the arrival of his own little sister six months ago. We have explained to him that humans, unlike Sooty the cat, tend to give birth in hospitals, or at least bedrooms, and that my baby isn't due for several months. I reminded him of this, and he listened with his usual solemn courtesy. Then he said again, very patiently, "I making a nest for you," and dragged his blanket over to the cramped space between the wardrobe and the dressing table. I decided to let him get on with it. (He seems to have inherited more than his fair share of the FitzOsborne stubbornness, although I suppose that *could* just be how two-and-a-half-year-olds *are*.) He was busy adding some cushions he'd taken from the window seat when Toby poked his head around the doorframe.

"Have you seen—?"

I tilted my head at the wardrobe.

"Ah," said Toby. He raised his voice. "Well, I'm looking for someone small. Someone light on their feet."

"Not me, then," I said.

"Someone who can tiptoe into the henhouse and pick up the eggs with careful little hands—"

"*I* doing it, Daddy!" said Davey, scrambling out of his blankets and dashing over to Toby. "I doing it!"

"Oh, *there* you are," said Toby, scooping him up. "I wondered where you'd got to."

"I making a nest," Davey explained, pointing.

"Yes, you did mention your plans for that. Lucky Auntie Sophie, getting such a nice nest! I'm not sure she needs your sister's teddy, though, so we'll take that back. What's this? Oh, a book. Well, yes, Auntie Sophie *does* love books."

I'm not sure Rupert's copy of *Advanced Canine Surgery* would provide much distraction during labor, but it was a kind thought of Davey's.

"Right," Toby said. "Now, shall we go downstairs? See if the hens have left us some eggs?"

"Yes! *I* doing it. *I* finding the eggs."

"What would I do without my helpful boy?"

Davey shook his head. "I dunno," he said.

I don't know, either. It was only when Davey was born that Toby gave up drinking, more or less. For a long time before that, Simon and Julia had been quite worried about him. He was elated by Montmaray's liberation, and even proposed leading some commando raids on the Channel Islands. But in the end, all he could manage was to get Churchill to agree to the Red Cross delivering food boxes to the Channel Islanders. And then the war kept dragging on, for months and months, and Toby sank back down into despondency. It wasn't helped by the continuing raids on London, the robot bombs having been replaced by enormous V-2 rockets that traveled faster than sound and blasted open craters big enough to swallow a couple of houses.

It was one of those rockets that killed Aunt Charlotte. She and Barnes had come up to London for a WVS meeting and were doing some shopping beforehand when a rocket landed next to the building Barnes had just entered. Aunt Charlotte, waiting across the road in a tea shop, ran straight outside and shoved past an ARP warden who tried to stop her entering the tottering ruins. As she was searching through the rubble, a brick wall collapsed on top of her, killing her instantly. Poor Barnes was carried out ten minutes later with a broken arm and terrible cuts and bruises, but it was the loss of Aunt Charlotte that caused her the greatest agony. They'd been each other's closest companion for more than thirty years. I still worry sometimes about Barnes feeling lonely. We did ask if she'd like to move to London to live with us, as Rupert and I have plenty of room in our flat, but she said she prefers country life. I think she's happier having all those familiar people around her in Milford, and her friend Harkness, our former butler, runs a gentleman's outfitter's in Salisbury, not far away. Aunt Charlotte left Barnes a lifetime lease on the Milford Park gatehouse and a generous pension, so she's quite comfortable, and we visit her whenever we drive down to Astley.

The main house at Milford Park has been leased to a girls' school now. It was too much bother to try to convert it back into a house, and it wasn't as though any of us were planning to live there in the near future. Aunt Charlotte bequeathed most of her fortune—which was even larger than I'd realized—to Veronica, Toby, and me, with an insultingly small allowance to be paid to Simon, on the condition he continue to manage her estate. None of us felt that was fair, so Veronica arranged for everything to be transferred to a family trust, with the four of us as equal beneficiaries. As it's turned out, Simon does most of the work involved with managing it, anyway. Aunt Charlotte cannily bought up a lot of bomb-damaged properties during the war, and we are gradually fixing them up and selling them, or tearing them down and rebuilding. Our first project was Montmaray House, which we converted into four big apartments. (Rupert and I live in the top one, and if I peer out our kitchen window, I can just about see where our poor old garage flat used to be.)

It's turned into quite a business, restoring all these properties. I take care of most of the paperwork and show potential buyers around the new places. That's the best part—talking to the couples who come in, often with a baby or toddler in tow. They exclaim over the fresh paint and the shiny white stove and the large windows, and immediately start planning where their furniture will go. They tell me their stories, too—how they lost everything in the Blitz and have been staying with her parents ever since and never have a moment's privacy, or about the outrageous rent they're paying for a basement bedsit with nowhere for the children to play—so I always feel as though I'm doing a really worthwhile, helpful job. Not that I'm doing it single-handedly, of course. Simon arranges all the council permits and deals with the builders, Julia liaises with the architects and designs the interiors, and Toby provides a sympathetic ear when we've had a hard day and looks after the children. Our office is in Julia's Belgravia house, where Toby, Simon, and Julia live together very harmoniously—although Toby prefers Montmaray to London, and periodically tries to talk us all into moving here.

"Oh, darling, I adore our island summers," Julia said yesterday, "but what would we *do* here for the rest of the year?"

"Turn the castle into a hotel," Toby said promptly. "We could set up a diving resort, get that Cousteau chap involved. Think of all those exciting shipwrecks off South Head!"

"Darling, there's a *reason* all those shipwrecks are there. Those waters are far too treacherous for divers. Anyway, don't divers prefer nice, warm tropical reefs?"

"Well, then, we can make Montmaray a very exclusive retreat for rich people who want to get far away from everything."

"*I* think this island ought to be a puffin sanctuary," said Rupert. "I don't think you realize how unique this habitat is."

"It can be a special haven for puffins *and* rich Americans," said Toby. "We'll get Daphne to send us all the rich Americans she knows."

Julia continued to look doubtful.

"Perhaps later," she said, "but we're far too busy at the moment with this new project in Bethnal Green. I don't think Daniel realizes how *difficult* it is, designing low-cost houses that are nice to live in."

"I still don't understand how he managed to talk Simon into that," said Toby.

"Oh, Simon realized that if he didn't agree, Veronica would

start in on him next," Julia said. "Anyway, Daniel can be awfully convincing. I suppose that's how he got into Parliament."

Daniel was elected as Member of Parliament for Whitechapel a few years ago, during that general election that saw Labour sweep into power. Churchill may have been a stirring leader at the height of battle, but he didn't have much interest in building a new England, so it's no wonder he got tossed out. I'm quite fond of Mr. Attlee, the new Prime Minister. He looks like a bank clerk and doesn't talk very much, but what he *does* say always seems sensible and fair. Britain was—still is—in such a mess after the war, but Mr. Attlee's brought in a lot of good reforms to do with education and health and welfare. I also approve of him nationalizing the coal mines and railways, because I think that's more efficient and better for the workers—although I'm careful not to say that aloud in Lord Astley's presence.

Rupert's father hates absolutely everything about the new government, of course, but especially the taxes. If he died tomorrow, the death duties on his estate would be so high that Astley Manor would probably have to be sold. He *could* avoid that by signing over the manor to Rupert now, but I can't see that happening. Lord Astley does approve of me (especially now, with a baby on the way), but he wasn't too pleased about Rupert ignoring his advice and enrolling at the Royal Veterinary College, and he's utterly scathing about the animal hospital that Rupert and his friends have set up in Stepney. They only charge those who can afford to pay, and subsist largely on donations, so I doubt Rupert will ever make a living wage from it. I told him it was lucky he'd married an heiress, and he said, "You mean, I'm lucky to have married a beautiful, clever, kindhearted heiress," and I said, "Yes, exactly," and gave him a kiss, because really, I'm the lucky one, to have such a lovely husband. It's also fortunate that Rupert has become quite good at disregarding his father's outbursts—which, oddly enough, seems to have earned him some grudging respect from Lord Astley. Anyway, they will have to make peace sooner or later, because Rupert will probably be the next Lord Astley. Charlie survived the war, but wants nothing to do with his father or the estate, and sailed back to Canada as soon as he was released from hospital. He was in a dreadful condition when the Allied troops freed him from his prison camp. The Nazis had kept all the Allied prisoners of war chained up and hadn't fed them properly, and then forced them to march from Poland to Germany as the Russians moved closer.

And Charlie's suffering, as awful as it was, was nowhere *near* as terrible as what happened to all those millions of people in the Nazi concentration camps. We were all stunned by those first horrific photographs of Belsen and Buchenwald, and it just got worse and worse as more facts emerged. It didn't even help much when the Nazi leaders were tried at Nuremberg. It's true that I felt a moment of grim satisfaction when Ribbentrop and Gebhardt and the others were sentenced to death. At least they'd been given a trial, forced to account for their actions in front of the judges and the world. Some of the Nazis even showed signs of remorse. But it would have been better if those acts had never taken place, better if those Nazi leaders had never been *born*. And what about the tens of thousands of lower-ranked Nazis who will never be prosecuted, the ones who worked in the concentration camps and enforced Hitler's terrible laws throughout the occupied territories? What about the Soviet soldiers who massacred all those Polish prisoners at Katyn? What about the British and the Americans—who knows what any of *them* might have done? The very notion of "war crimes" seems absurd—as though war can ever be conducted *without* killing and stealing and destroying! War itself is a crime, by the standards of normal, civilized society.

That such evil exists—that so many of the men on trial at Nuremberg looked so *ordinary*, like teachers or doctors, that some of them actually *were* doctors—well, it's terrifying, when one thinks about it. That's why I kept putting off having a baby. I told Rupert it would be better for us to wait till he'd finished his vet training, but really, I didn't feel it was right to bring a helpless child into a world full of war criminals and atomic bombs.

So, having this baby will be the bravest thing I've ever done—or the most foolhardy, although I suppose it's a bit late to worry about that now. But it's heartening, really, how optimistic most people are—that so many of them are picking up the threads of their lives and knitting them together as best they can. And then there are the really bold ones, those embracing entirely new futures—daphne, for example, moving to New York, and Rebecca, joining the convent. I keep wondering how Henry would have fared in this tumultuous new world. I think she would have *loved* it. I miss her all the time, especially here at Montmaray, but I'm consoled now, a little, when I remember she died doing what she loved, that she didn't suffer, probably didn't even have time to realize what was happening. Like poor dear Kick, killed with her boyfriend in that plane crash a few months ago, on their way to a romantic weekend in Cannes. Perhaps that would be the best way to die. I can't even contemplate life without Rupert, and he feels the same about me, so it would be very sensible of us to die together, quite suddenly—but in about fifty years or so, when our children are completely grown and capable of getting along without us.

Well, regardless of when we shuffle off this mortal coil, at least my own daughter won't have the same experience I had, of being faced with her mother's frustratingly indecipherable diary. I've only translated my old journals up to 1944, but I still (hopefully) have a few more months to work on them before the baby arrives, and at least all of my recent journals are in English. (I haven't the same need for secrecy these days.) Of course, it is quite complicated, figuring out what to include in my translations. Apart from trying to edit out the boring bits, there are facts that I promised not to reveal—about Anthony's death, for example—as well as secrets that never truly belonged to me. It's all very well to order myself to tell the simple truth, but everyone's version of the truth is different, and mine is no doubt even more peculiar, protracted, and personal than most . . .

Oh, Rupert has arrived to escort me to luncheon. Actually, he offered to bring a tray up to me, but Davey is tugging insistently on my hem, urging me downstairs so I can admire the new chicken that's unexpectedly hatched. So, in a minute or two, I will rise and make my way out of the solar, which Toby insisted Rupert and I have as our room this time, and along the gallery, spotlit with those clever skylights that Julia devised. I will inch down the tower steps, each bump and hollow of the stones as familiar to me as my own hands, and into the bright, clean kitchen, where something delicious will be simmering on Vulcan's burnished stove top. Then, after luncheon, I might—no, I *will*—walk through the Great Hall (magnificent now the clutter has been cleared away) and sit in the chapel for a while. It's a very calm, peaceful space, bathed in jewel-colored light, and I often go in there for a bit of a think. And later, when the sun begins to sink and the infinite sky is streaked with red and gold, I'll stroll out into the courtyard—perhaps even climb the steps to the gatehouse. And I'll gaze across the Chasm to the other side of the island, where I can still sometimes catch sight of a curly-haired urchin running joyously through the tall purple grass, her faithful dog at her heels.

Author's Note

This novel is a blend of historical fact and imaginative fiction. Real peo-
ple, groups, and organizations mentioned include Neville Chamberlain;
Adolf Hitler; Joseph Stalin; Joachim von Ribbentrop; the League of Nations; the Women's Voluntary Service (WVS); Air Raid Precautions
(ARP); the Women's Institute; the Royal Air Force (RAF); the Auxiliary
Territorial Service (ATS); the Auxiliary Air Force (AAF); the Women's
Royal Naval Service, also known as the Wrens; the Women's Auxiliary
Air Force (WAAF); the Air Transport Auxiliary; the Mechanised Transport Corps; the Red Cross; the Foreign Office; the Ministry of Food,
headed by William Morrison and then Lord Woolton; the Kennedy
family; Billy Hartington and the Duke and Duchess of Devonshire; the
Duke and Duchess of Windsor; Unity and Deborah Mitford; Oswald
and Diana Mosley; the British Union, the Right Club, the Nordic League,
the Anglo-German Fellowship, and The Link; Tyler Kent, Anna Wolkoff,
and Archibald Maule Ramsay; Oliver Cromwell; Winston Churchill and
his daughters, Sarah, Diana, and Mary; King George VI and Princess
Margaret; Clement Attlee; King Leopold of the Belgians; the Local
Defence Volunteers (LDV), later known as the Home Guard; Lord
Beaverbrook; Francisco Franco, the Falangists, and the Guardia Civil;
President Franklin D. Roosevelt; Sally Norton; Cecil Beaton; General

de Gaulle, Queen Wilhelmina of the Netherlands, the Grand Duchess of Luxembourg, Dr. Beneš of Czechoslovakia, and General Sikorski of Poland; Rudolf Hess; Douglas Bader; Michael Creswell at the British Embassy in Madrid; Leslie Hore-Belisha; Samuel Hoare, the British Ambassador to Spain; the Ladies of Llangollen; Lady Astor; Charles White; Richard Hillary; General Eisenhower; Lea Rayner, head of the Air Ministry Pigeon Service; Mrs. A. V. Alexander, wife of the First Lord of the Admiralty; John "Cat's Eyes" Cunningham; and Jacques Cousteau. Where real, historical people appear in the novel, I have used their biographies, their own writings, and other evidence to try to make their actions and words as true to their known lives as possible. However, the FitzOsbornes, Stanley-Rosses, Bosworths, Elchesters, Blooms, and other characters are figments of my imagination.

While Montmaray does not exist, most of the world events described in the novel actually occurred. These include the Molotov-Ribbentrop Pact between the Soviet Union and Nazi Germany; Germany's invasion of Poland and the subsequent declaration of war by Britain; the evacuation of city children to the British countryside and to North America; the sinking of the SS *Athenia*; Britain's internment of enemy aliens, including Jewish refugees from Germany; food, clothing, and petrol rationing; the conscription of British men and women during the Second World War; the requisition of British property and businesses by the War Office; the "Phony War"; the Soviet Union's invasion of Finland; Germany's invasion of Norway, Luxembourg, Belgium, the Netherlands, France, and the Channel Islands; the evacuation of Allied troops from Dunkirk; the spy scandal at the American Embassy in London; the imprisonment of Oswald and Diana Mosley; Italy's declaration of war; the attempted kidnapping of the Duke and Duchess of Windsor by German agents; the British bombing of the French Navy at Mers-el-Kébir; the Battle for Britain; the Blitz; the sinking of the *City of Benares* passenger liner while it was evacuating children to Canada; Hitler's meeting with Franco at Hendaye; the Battle of Barking Creek; the People's Convention; the North African and Middle East campaigns; Germany's invasion of the Soviet Union; Japan's bombing of Pearl Harbor and the subsequent declaration of war by the United States; Japan's invasion of China, Burma, Malaya, Hong Kong, Singapore, the Dutch East Indies; and the Philippines; the interrogation of German prisoners of war at the "London Cage" in Kensington Palace Gardens and the imprisonment of captured German generals at Trent Park; the failed Dieppe raid; the Beveridge Report; the Katyn massacre; the death of General Sikorski; the Allied invasion of Normandy; the Belgian and French escape lines for Allied servicemen and the imprisonment, torture, and execution of French and Belgian Resistance workers by the Nazis; the U-boat campaign in the Atlantic; and the V-1 "flying bomb" and V-2 rocket raids on England. The island of Montmaray, Montmaray House, Milford Park, the village of Milford, and Astley Manor are fictional, but most of the other places mentioned in the novel are real.

Information about home life in England during the Second World War came from *Wartime: Britain 1939–1945,* by Juliet Gardiner; *Keep Smiling Through: The Home Front 1939–45,* by Susan Briggs; *Voices from the Home Front: Personal Experiences of Wartime Britain 1939–45,* by Felicity Goodall; and *The Home Front: The British and the Second World War,* by Arthur Marwick. *Debs at War: 1939–1945, How Wartime*

Changed Their Lives, by Anne de Courcy, and *The Call of the Sea: Britain's Maritime Past 1900–1960,* by Steve Humphries, contained helpful descriptions of women's experiences during the war, while *Finest Years: Churchill as Warlord 1940–45,* by Max Hastings, and *Human Smoke: The Beginnings of World War II, the End of Civilization,* by Nicholson Baker, provided useful political and military context. The story of Bamse came from *Sea Dog Bamse: World War II Canine Hero,* by Angus Whitson and Andrew Orr.

Fighter Boys: Saving Britain 1940, by Patrick Bishop, provided invaluable information about the experiences of fighter pilots in the RAF, as did *First Light,* by Geoffrey Wellum; *The Last Enemy,* by Richard Hillary; and *Never Surrender: Lost Voices of a Generation at War,* by Robert Kershaw. Most of the information about Toby's escape from Belgium came from *The Freedom Line: The Brave Men and Women Who Rescued Allied Airmen from the Nazis During World War II,* by Peter Eisner, and *Wingless Victory: The Story of Sir Basil Embry's Escape from Occupied France,* by Anthony Richardson.

Information about Spain came from *Ambassador on Special Mission,* by Samuel Hoare, Viscount Templewood; *They Shall Not Pass: The Spanish People at War 1936–9,* by Richard Kisch; and *Chief of Intelligence,* by Ian Colvin, while *The Duchess of Windsor,* by Michael Bloch, and *King of Fools,* by John Parker, provided descriptions of the Nazi plan to abduct the Duke of Windsor. "Petticoat Diplomacy: The Admission of Women to the British Foreign Service, c. 1919–1946", by Helen McCarthy [*Twentieth-Century British History (2009) 20 (3): 285–321*], was an invaluable resource when I was writing about Veronica's experiences at the Foreign Office.

Most of the information about the Kennedys and Billy Hartington came from *Kathleen Kennedy: The Untold Story of Jack's Favourite Sister*, by Lynne McTaggart, and *Black Diamonds: The Rise and Fall of an English Dynasty*, by Catherine Bailey. I also consulted John F. Kennedy's *Why England Slept* and Rose Fitzgerald Kennedy's memoir, *Times to Remember*. Stephen Dorril's *Blackshirt: Sir Oswald Mosley & British Fascism* and Anne de Courcy's *Diana Mosley* provided details of the Mosleys' imprisonment and the activities of Fascists in Britain during the war.

Quotes from the following poems and novels were used:

"Ode on Melancholy," by John Keats (page 69)

"Ode on a Grecian Urn," by John Keats (page 252)

Jubilate Agno, by Christopher Smart (page 350)

Pride and Prejudice, by Jane Austen (page 398)

Toby also misquotes from "The Charge of the Light Brigade," by Alfred, Lord Tennyson, on page 287.

The quote from *Picture Post* (page 72) was cited in "Imperial War Museum's Ministry of Food: Terry Charman Explores Food Rationing," by Terry Charman, *Culture24*, 15 February 2010. The quotes from *If the Invader Comes* (page 136), a booklet published by the British Government in 1940, were cited in Juliet Gardiner's *Wartime: Britain 1939–1945*, and the letter about "the old school tie," quoted on page 263, was cited in Arthur Marwick's *The Home Front: The British and the Second World War*.

There are also several quotes from, or references to, speeches by British politicians, which were delivered either in the House of Commons or as broadcasts on the BBC. These include Chamberlain's declaration of war (page 4) and his "Missed the bus" (page 111) and Norway (page 119) speeches, as well as Churchill's "Blood, toil, tears and sweat" (page 121), "We shall defend our island" (page 135), "Never in the field of human endeavour" (page 181) and Soviet Union (page 280) speeches. Leo Amery delivered the "You have sat too long" speech (page 120) in 1940. Churchill's "Let 'em starve" comments about the Channel Islands (page 493) were noted on the minutes of a Cabinet meeting in September 1944, and his description of the Channel Islanders as "weak-livered . . . quislings" came from a conversation with Lord Louis Mountbatten (both quotes are featured in the *Captive Islands* exhibition in the Jersey War Tunnels).

Thank you to Zoe Walton and Nancy Siscoe, for their patience, encouragement, and invaluable editorial advice throughout the process of writing this series; the hardworking teams at Random House Australia and Random House Children's Books (U.S.); and Rick Raftos and Catherine Drayton.

The FitzOsbornes of Montmaray

1850–1955

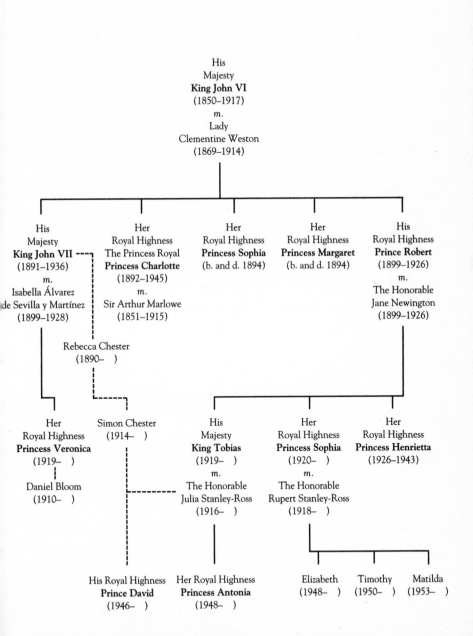

His
Majesty
King John VI
(1850–1917)
m.
Lady
Clementine Weston
(1869–1914)

His
Majesty
King John VII
(1891–1936)
m.
Isabella Álvarez
de Sevilla y Martínez
(1899–1928)

Her
Royal Highness
The Princess Royal
Princess Charlotte
(1892–1945)
m.
Sir Arthur Marlowe
(1851–1915)

Her
Royal Highness
Princess Sophia
(b. and d. 1894)

Her
Royal Highness
Princess Margaret
(b. and d. 1894)

His
Royal Highness
Prince Robert
(1899–1926)
m.
The Honorable
Jane Newington
(1899–1926)

Rebecca Chester
(1890–)

Her
Royal Highness
Princess Veronica
(1919–)

Daniel Bloom
(1910–)

Simon Chester
(1914–)

His
Majesty
King Tobias
(1919–)
m.
The Honorable
Julia Stanley-Ross
(1916–)

Her
Royal Highness
Princess Sophia
(1920–)
m.
The Honorable
Rupert Stanley-Ross
(1918–)

Her
Royal Highness
Princess Henrietta
(1926–1943)

His Royal Highness
Prince David
(1946–)

Her Royal Highness
Princess Antonia
(1948–)

Elizabeth
(1948–)

Timothy
(1950–)

Matilda
(1953–)